TO CAPTURE WHAT WE CANNOT KEEP

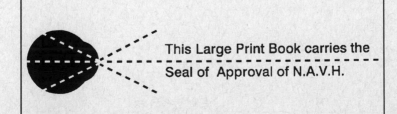

TO CAPTURE WHAT WE CANNOT KEEP

BEATRICE COLIN

THORNDIKE PRESS

A part of Gale, Cengage Learning

GALE
CENGAGE Learning·

Farmington Hills, Mich • San Francisco • New York • Waterville, Maine
Meriden, Conn • Mason, Ohio • Chicago

LIBRARY OF CONGRESS CATALOGING-IN-PUBLICATION DATA

Names: Colin, Beatrice, author.
Title: To capture what we cannot keep / by Beatrice Colin.
Description: Large print edition. | Waterville, Maine : Thorndike Press, 2017. |
    Series: Thorndike Press large print basic
Identifiers: LCCN 2016048502| ISBN 9781410497741 (hardcover) | ISBN 1410497747
    (hardcover)
Subjects: LCSH: Large type books. | GSAFD: Love stories.
Classification: LCC PR6103.O443 T6 2017 | DDC 823/.92—dc23
LC record available at https://lccn.loc.gov/2016048502

Published in 2017 by arrangement with St. Martin's Press, LLC

Printed in Mexico
1 2 3 4 5 6 7 21 20 19 18 17

To Paul, with love

Before they meet at such an impressive height, the uprights appear to spring out of the ground, molded in a way by the action of the wind itself.

— GUSTAVE EIFFEL, 1885

■ ■ ■ ■

I

■ ■ ■ ■

1

February 1886

The sand on the Champ de Mars was powdered with snow. A huge blue-and-white-striped hot-air balloon swooned on its ropes in front of the École Militaire, the gondola tethered to a small wooden platform strung out with grubby yellow bunting. Three figures, two women and a man, hurried from a hired landau on the avenue de Suffren across the parade ground toward the balloon.

"Attendez," called out Caitriona Wallace. *"Nous arrivons!"*

As she paused on the steps to wait for the other two, Cait's vision spun with tiny points of light in a darkening fog. She had laced tight that morning, pulling until the eyeholes in her corset almost met, and now her chest rose and fell in shallow gasps as she tried to catch her breath — in, out, in and out.

"We made it," said Jamie Arrol as he reached her. "That was a close thing."

"Here are the tickets," she told him. "You get on board. Your sister is just coming."

In the wicker gondola twenty people waited impatiently, the men in bell-curve beaver hats, and the women — there were only two — in fur-lined traveling coats. But the balloon attraction wasn't full, not on a cold winter morning with a sky so leaden it looked as if it might descend any moment, not at eleven o'clock in the morning on a Monday.

The ropes strained in the wind that blew up from the Seine, a wind that whipped the sand and the snow into a milky haze. The showground smelled of new rope and hot tar, of smoke blown from the charcoal brazier of the balloon, and underneath it all a note of something alcoholic. A flask, Cait thought, was being passed among the male passengers above. She could do with a little sip of something herself. Once on board, however, all would be well. She would not let herself imagine anything untoward, she would not visualize the gondola rising upward until it burst into flames or hurtling down until it smashed into pieces on the ground or floating away over the rooftops like Gambetta in 1871. No, she wouldn't let her fear get the better of her. She had read the promotional leaflet thoroughly. They would be tethered to the platform by a long chain. It was quite safe. And when they had made their ascent and reached a height of three hundred meters, she would look out and see the whole world clearly.

"Come on!" she cried out to her charge. "They're all waiting!"

As Alice Arrol finally approached the steps, her pace became little more than leisurely. A small group of Parisian ladies were standing at the base of the platform, their parasols raised to stop the wind blowing their hats away. After throwing the ladies a glance, Alice's face stiffened into an expression that suggested nonchalance.

"Actually," she said as she adjusted her gloves and stared up into the overcast sky, "I think I'll stay here."

Not five minutes earlier Alice had been almost ecstatic with excitement. Cait found it hard to hide her dismay.

"Are you sure? Wasn't the balloon excursion your idea?"

Alice's eyes widened in warning and her mouth curled into a small smile.

"Don't be ridiculous." She laughed. "I wouldn't dream of setting foot in such an undignified contraption!"

13

Alice's cheeks were flushed and her ring-lets had turned into a golden frizz around her face. She had kept her hair color, the blond not turning dark. It made her look younger than she really was; her skin, nursery-pink and chalk-white with a touch of blue around the eyes. She was nineteen but often taken for much younger. Cait felt a rush of affection toward her. She still wore her newly acquired adulthood badly, like an oversize coat that she hoped to grow into.

The balloon operators started to untie the ropes. Cait glanced up at the lip of the basket. There was no sign of Jamie. She would have to tell him of the change of plan. She turned back to Alice.

"Will you wait here?"

"Are you going to go without me?" Alice asked.

At that point, the idea hadn't even oc-curred to Cait. Of course she should stay behind; she was a companion, paid to ac-company and supervise Alice and her brother, Jamie Arrol. Also, at thirty-one, she was far too old to be spontaneous. Worst of all, heights, steep ascents, and theater seats in the upper circle all terrified her. And yet, as she had told herself in the carriage on the drive to the showground, she would get the chance only once in her lifetime and so she must take advantage.

"Maybe I should," she said. "Would you mind?"

"No, don't remain on my account."

"And you'd be safe? You wouldn't move an inch from this spot."

"I won't be seduced, I promise. Just go, Mrs. Wallace."

"The tickets are already paid for," Cait called as she climbed toward the outstretched hand of the balloon handler. "It would be a terrible waste if we didn't use them. Your uncle would be outraged! Mortified! Can you imagine?"

She looked back just as Alice laughed out loud, then quickly covered her mouth with her hand. Ironically, for a girl who spent so long perfecting her expressions in the mirror, she was prettiest like that, when she forgot herself.

When the last few sandbags had been tossed over the side and the ropes coiled, the pilot leaned on a lever, air rushed into the brazier, the fire roared, and the balloon began to rise with the upward momentum of an air bubble through water. Cait shut her eyes and held tight to the wicker edge of the basket as the balloon ascended. Despite everything, it was just glorious.

Eight years earlier Cait had had no idea

that she would end up here, rising into the sky above Paris, practically weightless, impossibly high. She had been married, settled, grounded. Her husband, Saul Wallace, was handsome and debonair, their home in Glasgow was large and comfortable; their shared future stretched out in front of them like the red roll of a carpet. There would be children, holidays, anniversaries.

Saul was just thirty-two when his train left one side of the River Tay and failed to reach the other. It was three days after Christmas, December 1879. As Cait sat beside the fire and opened a novel, she had not known — how could she — that at that moment their life together was ending, that the Tay Bridge had collapsed and Saul Angus Wallace was drowning in black-water currents beneath several tons of hissing iron.

The hot-air balloon had reached the end of its chain and came to a sudden, jolting halt. She opened her eyes. The brazier roared, the balloon still floated in the air, the world was as she had left it; Paris below and the sky above. For a moment she focused on breathing. She wouldn't let herself think about the empty space beneath the gondola. She wouldn't imagine the altitude they had reached. The other pas-

16

sengers rushed from one side to the other, clearly unconcerned that they were suspended by nothing more than hot air. No one else was fearful, no one else stood, as she did, several feet from the basket's rim in the grip of a private terror.

"What a view!" Jamie Arrol was peering over the edge, almost hysterical with happiness. "Come and look."

"I will," she said. "In a minute."

He turned and noticed that she was alone.

"Miss Arrol changed her mind," Cait explained.

"She missed out." He shrugged. "There's the Panthéon . . . the Arc de Triomphe . . . and over there . . . I think that must be Notre-Dame! Look!"

Cait steeled her resolve, then cautiously, tentatively, hesitantly peered over the edge. And there, far below, were Baron Haussmann's wide boulevards that followed the line of the old walls of the city, the green blot of the Bois de Boulogne, the pump of black smoke from the factories in the south, the star spokes radiating from the Place de l'Étoile, and, closer, the Place du Trocadéro. And there were lines of carriages as tiny as black beetles, people as minute as ants, the city as small and regular as a set of children's stone building blocks placed on a painted sheet.

"Well?" said Jamie.

The image blurred, her head began to pound; it was too much. She stepped back.

"You're shaking!" Jamie laughed. "Wait until I tell my sister."

"I'm fine," she told him. "At least, I'll be fine in a minute. Go, go and make the most of it."

Despite the heat from the brazier, the air was far colder up here than on the showground. Her hands were indeed trembling, but it wasn't just the chill. What scared her most was not the thought that she might fall out of the gondola, but the sense that she might be seized at any moment by an overwhelming compulsion to jump. Since her husband's death she had often felt this panic, as if she existed in a liminal space, half in and half out of the world.

In the quiver of the heat coming from the fire, she tried to focus on something, anything. She heard a small click and turned. A man was standing behind a small wooden box on the other side of the basket, his face absorbed in thought. He wore a softly knotted bow tie and, unlike the rest of the passengers, wasn't wearing a hat. As if he felt her gaze, he blinked and looked around. For no more than a fraction of a second, their

18

eyes met. Cait's heart accelerated, a rapid knocking against a solid wall of whalebone and wool. She swallowed and glanced away. What on earth did she think she was doing? What kind of a lady returned a man's gaze? She turned and sought other, safer distractions. Next to her a party of Americans were discussing restaurants.

"Five francs for an apple on a plate," one of the men was saying. "It was daylight robbery."

"But the wine was very reasonable," his companion pointed out.

"That may well be, but they saw me coming. I aim to avoid dining at our hotel for the remainder of my trip. The French have a nose for gullibility, so I hear."

She was suddenly aware that the man without the hat had come to her side of the balloon and was looking out across the river toward the north of the city. She concentrated wholeheartedly on listening to the Americans' accounts of terrible food and horrendous hotel experiences. But she was conscious of him, of his proximity, of the wooden box he was carrying, of his hair swept back from his forehead falling in loose, dark curls over his collar, of the rise of his frozen breath mingling with her own.

"Fleas!" one voice rang out. "Fleas every-where!"

"I had bedbugs," another agreed. "They even got into my toothbrush."

The man took another, smaller wooden box out of the first box and carefully attached it to three metal legs. It looked like some sort of photographic device. Photography was the new craze in Paris, and she had seen dozens of men carrying those mahogany and brass boxes, strolling up and down the Quais or setting up in the Luxembourg Gardens.

She could see now that he was slightly older than he had first appeared, maybe around forty. His dark hair was flecked with gray, his coat was finely cut and his shoes polished; he looked cared for. And yet there was something in the way he moved, in the slant of his shoulders and the way he took up space in the world that she recognized. He was a man who was, or had been, lonely.

As she watched, he opened the box and extended a small concertina shape from the front. And then he stepped to the side of the gondola and leaned over. Cait felt a surge, the momentum of falling, headlong, into nothingness. Of its own accord, her hand reached out and grabbed his arm. He turned.

"Madame?" he said.

"Excuse me," she blurted out in French. "But you looked as if you were about to —"

Cait opened her mouth but couldn't say the word.

"Throw myself over the edge?" he asked in French.

She blinked at him.

"I was going to say 'fall.' "

"Not today, but thank you for your concern," he said.

He glanced down to where her hand still gripped his sleeve. It was her left hand, bare now of the wedding band she used to wear.

"I'm so sorry," she said as she let him go.

"Not at all. Are you all right?"

"I have a fear of heights," she explained.

How ridiculous that must sound, she thought suddenly, how lame, how patently untrue, in a hot-air balloon of all places. His eyes, however, were on her face, his gaze unwavering. He wasn't laughing.

"I spend a lot of time in the air," he said.

"Really? What are you, an aerialist?"

He laughed and his face lifted. It was not, she decided, an unpleasant face.

"Close," he said. "Are you enjoying it?"

"It certainly is an experience," she replied. "I've never been in a hot-air balloon before. I'm not sure I would again."

21

"I rather like it. The sensation that one is attached to the Earth only by a chain. And now, if you will excuse me for one moment, I must take another picture."

He moved his camera toward the edge, looked through a tiny hole in the back, and adjusted the concertina in front. Once he was satisfied, he turned a dial, reached into his case, found a flat black box, and attached it to the camera's back.

"You're English?" he said as he pulled a thin metal plate from inside the box.

"Scottish," she replied.

He smiled, then consulted his pocket watch.

"I'm exposing the plate," he explained. "It must be kept very still for twenty seconds exactly."

She held her breath as he counted out the seconds.

"Voilà!" he said as he wound the shutter closed again. "Just in time."

She looked up and noticed that a thin mist had begun to descend, enveloping the balloon in white.

"We'll have to imagine the view instead," she suggested.

He turned and gave her his full attention again.

"Then imagine a tower," he said. "The

22

tallest tower in the world. It will be built right here on the Champ de Mars for the World's Fair, to celebrate the hundredth anniversary of the French Revolution. You won't have to come up in a balloon anymore."

"That!" she said. "But everyone says it's going to be awful, just a glorified pylon."

He laughed and began to put away his camera.

"Or a truly tragic lamppost," he said.

There was a sudden tug and the balloon dropped a couple of feet. The passengers let out a cry of alarm, followed quickly by a show of amusement. Maybe they weren't all quite as fearless as they appeared.

"That was short," said Jamie, appearing suddenly at her elbow. "And you can't see anything now. Not sure it was worth the price of the ticket."

"You should take the steamboat, a *bateau-mouche*," the Frenchman suggested. "The route from Charenton to Auteuil is the best and only costs twenty centimes. It takes you through the whole city by the river."

The two men began to chat, as men do, about professions and prospects. Cait felt a spike of disappointment; she wished that Jamie hadn't come looking for her.

"You're an engineer," said Jamie. "What a

coincidence! You might have heard of my uncle, William Arrol. Our company is working on the Forth Bridge near Edinburgh. And we've almost finished one across the Tay, to replace the one that collapsed."

He glanced briefly in Cait's direction. The balloon was yanked down another couple of feet. Something within her plummeted in tandem. She had forgotten herself. She was thirty-one years old; she'd had her chance.

"What are your current projects?" Jamie asked the engineer.

"A tower made of iron," he said, and smiled at Cait.

"Not Eiffel's tower?" said Jamie. "The one they're going to build somewhere around here?"

"I designed it," he replied. "Together with my colleague, Maurice Koechlin. We work for Gustave Eiffel."

Cait covered her mouth with her hand. Beneath her fingertips her cheeks burned.

"You should have told me," she said. "There I was, calling it a truly tragic lamp-post."

Jamie glanced at her. Clearly she had spoken out of turn. The Frenchman, however, didn't seem offended, but amused.

"I called it that, not you. Today I was trying to take some photographs of the site for

24

our archive," he explained. "We start digging the foundations next week."

"Really! And how long do you expect construction to take?" Jamie asked.

"It must be ready for the Great Exhibition, so two years at the most. And once she stands, you will be able to see her from all over the city."

"Impressive! You know, I'm training to be an engineer myself."

Cait was surprised to hear Jamie say it. His uncle had paid for school, for university, and when he had dropped out, he had given him an apprenticeship in his company. A directorship was promised, but first Jamie would have to prove himself, working his way up, like his uncle had, from the shop floor. He had learned the basics of civil engineering by drawing endless plans and drilling rivet holes, but he had not shone, coming in late and going home after lunch. After several strained conversations with his uncle, it was agreed that he would take a sabbatical to think things over. While traveling for the last six months around Europe, he had considered careers such as wine merchant or chocolate importer.

"I'm afraid I didn't catch your name?" Jamie asked.

"Émile Nouguier," the Frenchman replied.

"So if you designed it, why isn't the tower named after you?" Cait asked.

"Eiffel bought the patent from us," he replied. "And now as well as building it, he is paying for most of it."

"I heard it was going to cost him millions of francs," said Jamie. "Is that true?"

"It is. Although he hopes he will recoup most of it through ticket sales."

The gondola landed with a thump on the sand of the parade ground. The American passengers gave a spontaneous round of applause.

"It's been a pleasure, Monsieur Nouguier," Jamie said. "Is your wife on board?"

"Alas, there is no one that fits that description."

"We're in the same boat, then," Jamie said. "You must meet my sister."

Émile Nouguier bowed in Cait's direction.

"No, I'm just a family friend," she said. "Caitriona Wallace."

"Forgive me," he said softly in French. "Caitriona."

A small jolt raced through her. He had addressed her by her first name. It was better, she decided, to ignore it. It was better to appear oblivious to his overfamiliarity.

"Well," she said, "good luck with your tower."

"Thank you," he replied.

Almost all the passengers had disembarked. The crew were coiling ropes and piling sandbags. Water was thrown over the basket of hot coals.

"Mrs. Wallace!" said Jamie, standing on the platform steps, waiting to help her down. "Can't wait all day!"

Alice was standing at the bottom, her face doll-blank. The ladies with the parasols had gone.

"How was it?" she asked.

"You should have come," Cait replied.

"There's someone I want you to meet," Jamie called out from behind.

Alice looked at Cait in horror. *Who on earth,* her face seemed to say, *could be worth meeting on a hot-air balloon attraction?*

"May I present my sister," Jamie said once the engineer had reached the bottom of the steps, "Miss Alice Arrol. This is Monsieur Nouguier, the highly esteemed engineer."

Jamie was hardly subtle; the young unmarried sister, the blatant advertising of her availability, the implication that Nouguier might be of the right social standing to take an interest. But if the engineer was aware of any of this, his face didn't reveal it.

"Mademoiselle," he said with a small bow.

"Enchantée," Alice replied.

There was a small, expectant silence.

"How long are you staying in Paris?" he asked Jamie.

"Just until the weekend. We're on a Grand Tour, of sorts. After meandering through the Low Countries, we spent too long in Rome. We had to miss Venice entirely. But our stay in Paris has been thoroughly worthwhile now we've met you."

Cait was painfully aware, as she had been many times in Paris, of their poor mastery of social etiquette, of how clear it was that they had come from a less sophisticated place. Their manners were parochial, so parochial that they didn't even realize it.

"If you have time before you leave, I would be happy to receive your call." Nouguier handed Jamie his card. "As an engineer you might be interested in seeing the workshop in Levallois-Perret."

"I would indeed," said Jamie. "Thank you."

Once Émile had taken his leave, Alice rolled her eyes.

"Please," she said, "don't drag us to a workshop."

"Do you know who that was?" Jamie whispered. "He works with Gustave Eiffel, *the* Gustave Eiffel. And he's unattached!"

"Jamie!" she said. "Before you start your matchmaking, I'd like to point out that he wasn't even wearing a hat!"

"Shh," said her brother. "He might hear you."

But Émile Nouguier was already halfway across the parade grounds, heading toward the Seine, his figure a dark stroke against the sand. As Cait watched, it started to snow, and within a minute he began to disappear, fading from black to gray to nothing at all.

2

And all was white. Émile looked up into the space where the tower would stand, into the slow swirl of snow as it gracefully descended. Ice flowers, as snowflakes were sometimes known. He caught one in his hand and watched as it melted into a drop of water. Were beautiful things more beautiful when you couldn't keep them? The tower wouldn't stand for long: twenty years. Compared to other structures of its size, it was a blink of the eye, a single heartbeat, an ice flower.

He pictured Gabrielle lying on his bed that morning, her dark hair undone and her clothes unlaced. How much longer would their affair continue? A week? A month? Surely not much more? He suddenly longed for simplicity, for honesty, for a lack of artifice and an open-eyed gaze like that of the woman he'd just met in the balloon. But this was Paris and nothing was simple.

Relationships always came with caveats.

Gabrielle thought him lucky to have her. She moved in the kind of circles in which he was not welcome; she modeled for artists and had been intimate with most of them, or so she led him to believe, name-dropping Degas, Renoir, and Monet, and the boat parties they had thrown for her at Maison Fournaise. She made it no secret either that she was married to a lesser-known painter who didn't mind what she did. Once she'd mentioned a daughter, a girl of about eight, whom they farmed out to grandparents.

The affair had begun three months earlier when she and Émile had hailed the same cab outside a theater on the Place du Châtelet. It was raining hard, and both had insisted the other take it until a gentleman in a top hat jumped in front and took it himself. To quell their mutual outrage, a cognac or two in the theater bar had seemed like a good idea. Later, Émile hailed another cab and this time they both climbed inside.

Of course, he knew that the relationship was unsustainable, untenable, indefensible, but it suited them both, for the moment. He gifted her with nice clothes and jewelry and she returned the favor in other ways. If he ever felt guilty, he paid a visit to her favorite shop, Boucheron, on the Place

Vendôme.

"Are you coming to the opening?" Gabrielle had asked him that morning. She stood in front of a small mirror, adjusting her hat and fixing it with pins.

"Will your husband be there?" he had asked.

"He is exhibiting twelve paintings. So yes, I expect he will."

"Then no."

He turned, lay flat on his back, and stared up at the ceiling.

"He is still upset that he wasn't chosen for the Impressionist show in New York," she went on, oblivious.

"And are there any paintings of you?" he asked.

She stopped what she was doing and looked over at him.

"A few," she replied. "Why?"

"No reason."

He climbed out of bed and began to dress. And as he fastened his collar and buttoned his braces, he remembered the rush of his heart beneath the palm of her hand, the capitulation of his body beneath her fingertips. Possession in the beat of the blood but not in the heart. So why did the idea of her being with another man rile him?

Gabrielle was watching him in the mirror.

Finally she turned.

"Émile," she said, "you're in a temper, aren't you?"

"No! I must go to work, that's all. I'm going to be late."

"But it's not even eight."

She took off her hat and cast it aside. She undid his collar, she kissed his neck, his ear, his mouth; then once more she took his hands and drew him toward the bed.

"I'd like to paint you," he had whispered after.

"But what on earth would I look like?" She laughed. "A steel girder for a face, perhaps, with two rivets for eyes?"

This was what she really thought of him; he was an engineer, not an artist. And yet there was art in his work, in the soar of a structure and the arch of a bridge, in every framework of light and air and iron.

"You might think differently of me when you see our tower," he said.

"How can metal bolted to metal be art?" Gabrielle replied.

"Wait and see. Wait until you stand at the top and look out at the whole city below."

"But why would I want to do that?" she insisted.

"Why wouldn't you?" he replied. "Because you can!"

She looked at him, her chin raised and her eyes narrowed. "I'll believe it when I see it," she said, and rolled away from him.

His father had had several mistresses over the years. They came to the glass factory after hours, when the furnaces were cooling and the glass blowers had gone home for the day. Émile remembered them all clearly, Isabelle with the red hair; Chantelle, the wife of the baker; Miriam, who had a beautiful singing voice. His mother must have known — everyone else did — but dealt with it stoically. Cedric Nouguier was a factory owner, an important man in the small town of La Villette on the outskirts of Paris. As long as he avoided scandal, he could do what he liked.

At his age, however, Émile needed a wife, not a mistress. But what could he offer her? Although he had inherited an apartment in Paris in the fifth arrondissement, he rarely used it. He traveled for work — Portugal, America, Hungary, Russia — and lived for months on end in hotels. The tower construction would be one of his first jobs in Paris, and he sometimes wondered if he saw the city, the world, his life, like a visitor might — fleetingly, as if he were just passing through. A blink or two and it would be gone. And yet he must marry and have

34

children soon — a rich woman, preferably, with money to invest in his family's factory. He was reminded of these facts weekly when he visited his mother, who lived in the hope that she could one day die peacefully, safe in the knowledge that the Nouguier family with all its elderly dependents and antiquated business was still a going concern.

The snow hadn't settled, and it melted into the cobbles as soon as it landed. Émile walked along the Seine past lines of barges heading into the city. They were moving so slowly that they left nothing more than gentle ripples on the surface. Most of their weight was below the waterline. He looked down and saw himself in the black water, reflected, fragmented, pulled apart and put back together again over and over until the water smoothed, dark as glass.

3

Even this far out of the city, the river was full of paddle steamers and river barges, light yawls and chain tugs, with great wheels heaving up dripping lengths from the riverbed. Several *bateaux-mouches* were tied up at the pontoon when they arrived, but only one, a stream of smoke coming from its chimney, looked ready to depart.

"Quand partez-vous?" asked Cait.

"In two minutes," the captain replied in English.

According to a timetable pinned inside a wooden frame, it would take about an hour and a half to reach Auteuil on the other side of Paris, and a little less to return. While Jamie arranged a time with the carriage driver to pick them up, Cait looked out across the water. It was a breathless day, the winter light the color of green tea. A string of small rowing boats bobbed in the swell. A little farther down were a floating restaurant, a bathing house, and a wash house. Several women were lathering sheets in the freezing water from a wooden platform. As she watched, a shaft of sun broke through the early-morning haze.

"We could sit outside?" suggested Cait once they had bought their tickets and had them stamped.

"Too cold," said Alice.

And so they found a bench inside the cabin next to a steamed-up window. The boat wasn't busy; several elderly couples who sat staring straight ahead in silence, a woman with three small children, and a nun. The air was thick with the smell of mildew and tar and engine oil and, underneath it all, the faint, fetid stink of the river.

"It doesn't look like much at all," Alice said as she wiped the window and stared out. "Where are we again?"

"A town called Charenton," Cait replied.

"I know that. But is there anything here apart from the river?"

Cait opened the guidebook and looked in the index.

" 'Situated between the Bois, the Marne, and the Seine,' " she read out, " 'a place chiefly known for its lunatic asylum.' "

She looked up at Alice and they both started to laugh.

"So much for the quest to find the chic," said Jamie, "the elegant, the *je ne sais quoi.*"

"I told you we should have gone shopping," said Alice.

"Give it a chance," said Jamie. "We haven't even left the dock yet. And I'm determined to see as much of Paris as I can in the time we have left, not just the insides of department stores or hansom cabs."

Cait stared down at a map of Paris's canals and rivers, blue snakes on brick red. In two days they would be heading back to Dover, crossing the Channel, and taking the train from London back to Glasgow. And she was filled with apprehension, with dread, with an almost unfathomable melancholy.

She had left her tenement flat in Glasgow in the autumn of the previous year, covering all the furniture with dust sheets and canceling all the deliveries. On the day of their departure it had been raining heavily and the gutters were filled with fallen leaves and the black swirl of city dirt. She sent her small case ahead and made her way from Pollokshields into the city on foot, following the route of the railway line. As she waited for Alice and Jamie at the station, it was only the rain and the thought of getting wetter than she already was that prevented her from walking home again. Why, she asked herself, had she accepted the role of lady's companion, of chaperone to Alice Arrol? But she knew why; it was the type of job taken by women who have no other option.

The villa had been sold, along with the wedding silver, years earlier. After being badly advised, however, Cait's financial investments had dwindled to almost nothing. She lived in a modest one-bedroom apartment on the second floor of a building that looked across the railway. Once she realized that her savings wouldn't cover the bills for much longer, she had answered an advertisement in the *Glasgow Herald.*

"What luck," William Arrol had said at the interview. "I have been looking for a woman of exactly your quality."

He went on to tell her that he'd discounted a dozen women already for reasons he would not go into. But then he leaned forward and began to laugh.

"Between you and me, one of them was so old," he said, "that she needed a companion of her own just to get up the stairs. Another, too young. She looked as if she was out to snatch any eligible man for herself. But you, you're a mature woman. You dress well. You're educated, refined, and you have a reliable manner. Mrs. Wallace, you're the perfect lady's chaperone."

He sat back, pleased with his appraisal. Cait did her best to hide the effect of his words.

"Before I agree to anything," she said, "I'd need to know what the job involves."

"I'm so sorry," said Arrol. "I'm jumping ahead of myself. You'd be a lady's chaperone to my niece and, to a lesser extent, my nephew, for six months. They're going on the Grand Tour, as I believe it's known, to absorb the culture of the Continent and complete their education. I would pay all expenses and offer a generous stipend. If that sounds acceptable, then the position's yours."

Alice and Jamie Arrol arrived at the station fifteen minutes late, in a fluster of umbrellas and excuses, accompanied by four men carrying two huge trunks. Most of their friends had come along to see them off. As the porter installed them in their carriage, the guard gave all three a good talking-to. He wouldn't wait, not even for the likes of them. Then, as the train finally pulled out of the station, Alice had opened the window, waved goodbye to the crowd, and cried a little.

"I'll find her a rich husband," Jamie called

out. "A German baron or an Italian prince."

"What you need is a wife," someone called out. "To take you in hand."

Even as the train began to gather speed, Cait still thought there was time to change her mind. She stared out of the window as they sped south and, just for a fraction of a second, caught a glance of her flat, its windows black and empty. It was then she realized there was absolutely nothing to go home for.

The London train was busy, but as they sat in the first-class restaurant, she was the only one who steamed gently as her clothes dried. In Dover, waiting for the boat, the sun came out. She hadn't packed a parasol and so she let the autumn sun warm her face. Behind her were eight years of rain.

The steamboat was about to depart, the gangplank raised and ropes stowed. A carriage drew to a stop on the road and three young men and three young women clambered out. A couple of them ran down to the pontoon and begged the captain to wait for them.

"Why can't they catch the next one?" Alice said.

"Maybe they're trying to escape from the asylum?" Jamie whispered.

The captain waited; the boat wasn't full. The gangplank was lowered again and the group came aboard lugging baskets and bottles, blankets and pillows. The men wore colored shirts and bright silk waistcoats under their coats. One of them carried a small wooden guitar. The women wore tea gowns in pale blue, dusty pink, and deep red velvet. One carried a bouquet of flowers.

"I don't think they're lunatics," Alice whispered. "They look like artists."

"Isn't that the same thing?" asked Jamie.

"I think it's a wedding party," said Cait.

Alice peered through the window and watched as they set everything down on the benches outside. And then she sat back and looked disappointed.

"Why aren't we sitting outside?" she said.

"Because you didn't want to," Jamie replied. "Remember?"

"Why did you listen to me? You never usually listen to me!"

Jamie caught Cait's eye and sighed. His sister, his face seemed to say, was impossible.

They had been in Paris for a month, staying in a small suite in the Hôtel Meurice on the rue de Rivoli. If it had been up to their uncle, they would have found cheaper lodgings. He wouldn't discover until later, however, when he received the bill in the post. But what would William Arrol know? Alice had insisted that they had to mix with the right sort of people, and he was clearly the wrong sort.

The son of a spinner, William Arrol had started work at nine and studied mechanics and hydraulics at night school. By the time he was thirty, he was running a successful engineering business, the Dalmarnock Iron Works. The firm had won contracts for dozens of projects, including the Bothwell Viaduct and the Caledonian Railway Bridge, and made him a small fortune. When his own wife, Elizabeth, failed to produce any heirs, he turned all his attention to his widower brother's children, Alice and Jamie. His nephew, he hoped, would eventually take over the business, while his niece, with his financial support, would make a decent marriage. His money was new, but his values were resolutely conservative.

With the steam up, the paddles spinning, and the funnel puffing smoke, the boat moved out into the middle of the river and began to head downstream. They chugged under bridges, along the edge of open fields, and past the dripping brick walls of factories. Sometimes they stopped to let more

43

passengers on and others off, but never for more than a few moments. As they approached the center of Paris the river's edge became built up with warehouses. The city relied on its waterways, and the barges they passed carried everything from flowers to cattle, fresh fish to coal.

The Seine divided around the Île de la Cité, and the narrow channels became congested as they passed Notre-Dame. At the Hôtel de Ville, half a dozen barges were unloading and the air was sweet and tart with the smell of apples. On the deck one of the artists picked up his guitar and started to pluck it. The woman in red velvet, the bride, Cait guessed, laid her head in the lap of a young man with a pale beard and stared up at the stone spans of the Pont Neuf. Another man poured a bottle of red wine into six glasses and broke a baguette.

"À votre santé!" he called out to his friends, to the other passengers, to the people who peered down at them from the bridge above. *"Bonne chance!"*

A little farther on, they passed the Louvre in silence. Alice had refused to go inside; she had balked at the suggestion of any more Grand Masters or ancient Egyptians. Surely, she had insisted, the Uffizi in Florence had been enough art. The steamboat moved on, stopping at the Jardin des Tuileries and then, on other side, the lavish Hôtel des Invalides.

"It looks bigger from the river," said Alice. "What's inside it again?"

"The tomb of Napoleon," said Jamie. "I think we should visit it."

"Haven't we seen plenty of dead people already?" Alice asked. "How long did we spend in Père-Lachaise Cemetery? Hours and hours."

"Not long enough," said Jamie. "It's only out of consideration to you that we're not visiting the catacombs."

"What on earth is interesting about a pile of bones?"

"If you would take a look, maybe you'd find out," he replied.

Jamie glared at his sister. He had become increasingly less diplomatic as the trip progressed. Alice, no matter how sweet, had never been reasonable.

At the Champ de Mars, piles of earth were heaped along the quayside. Several horses and carts were carrying away loads of rubble. A dozen men were digging with spades. The sound of hammering echoed across the water.

"What have they done?" Alice lamented.

"It's the tower," said Jamie. "They've

started on the foundations."

At the far side of the site, Cait could make out a couple of men taking notes. She wondered if one of them was Émile Nouguier.

"I'm going out," said Alice. "For a breath of air. Alone, if you don't mind."

She glanced around to see if either Jamie or Cait would challenge her.

"Go on, then," said Jamie. "Nobody's stopping you."

Cait suddenly felt sorry for him, stuck with two women in one of the most exciting cities in the world.

"You don't have to stay with us all the time," she said. "Why don't you get off at the next stop? We could meet you for dinner at the hotel later."

Jamie stood up, the tension in his face immediately lifting.

"Now, there's an idea," he said. "I would rather like to see the Titians in the Louvre before we leave. And do you think I should call on my engineering friend? He might consider me rather remiss if I don't. Now, where's the card he gave me?"

He pulled it out of his waistcoat pocket.

" 'Émile Nouguier,' " he read out, his accent poor.

Cait felt a flush of heat in her face as she

46

corrected his pronunciation.

"You'll have to send a note first," she said. "You can't just turn up unexpectedly."

Jamie turned and stared at her. "You think I should just forget it, don't you?"

The boat bobbed on the swell; they were simply passing through the city, tourists ticking off the sights one by one, nothing else. She should stop wanting more, stop craving the unattainable, especially with her history. But then again, what did it matter? They were going home in a couple of days. There was nothing at stake, nothing at risk.

"On the contrary. I'm sure Alice would like to go too," she said. "If you arranged it."

"Alice?" Jamie repeated with a frown. And then he smiled. "I'm sure she could feign an interest in engineering for a little while at least. Good thinking! I'll ask him if he can receive all three of us."

The boat was pulling in to moor at the Trocadéro.

"Go on, then," she said. "If you're going."

"Thank you, Mrs. Wallace," he said as he placed his hat back on his head. "And would you tell my sister that I'll see her at dinner?"

"In due course. Right now I think she is somewhat occupied."

They both looked out the window. Alice was clutching the boat's railing. But her eyes weren't on the view. Instead she watched, with a mixture of horror and delight, as one of the women, still with a glass of red wine in one hand, pulled up her skirts to reveal purple bloomers and danced alone on the deck.

4

"That's Georges Seurat," Gabrielle whispered to Émile. A tall, thin man with a high forehead and pointed beard stood in the corner. "And those are his paintings."

They were landscapes, mostly, hung from floor to ceiling among hundreds of other canvases. The one nearest was called *Le Pont de Courbevoie.* Émile stepped a little closer. It was made up of tiny dots of paint; what looked like purple from a distance was in fact bright red beside pale blue. Elsewhere, Seurat had used light beside dark and warm colors beside cold.

"I know where this is," he said. "It's the north side of the island, La Grande Jatte. Didn't he paint the island before? What's the work called?"

"*A Sunday Afternoon on the Island of La Grande Jatte?*" said Gabrielle. "You've seen it? Isn't it terrible? The people look like dolls. Did you hear about what happened

49

when he exhibited it in Brussels last month? There was an outrage!"

She was whispering; the gallery was crowded. Everyone wanted to see what the fuss was about and now they peered at Seurat's work, some blinking rapidly, as if the bright colors and the vibrant tones were too much for their eyes.

"I doubt he'll ever sell the thing," Gabrielle went on. "It's huge too. Such a waste of time!" She looked up and Seurat caught her eye. She gave him a small bow of her head.

"That's him, you say?" said Émile.

"Please don't speak to him. You'll be stuck for hours while he goes on and on about science and harmony and all these theories he's dreamed up with his friend Paul Signac, who, incidentally, is even worse."

"Maybe I should buy it?"

Gabrielle looked genuinely shocked.

"*La Grande Jatte*? Have you lost your mind? It would be a criminal waste of money, money you'd never get back. Besides, what would you do with it?"

"I'd hang it in my apartment," he said.

"But Émile! You'd never get it through the door!"

She laughed, her head tossed back to reveal her throat. It wasn't just for his benefit. As well as the general public, the gallery was full of artists and dealers — the former in clothes of unusual colors, with large mustaches or the brown-weathered skin of a long stay somewhere hot; the latter in sober, expensive suits with pocket watches. This was the opening of the third exhibition of the Société des Artistes Indépendants. Unlike the official salon, the Société had no rigid selection policy or jury and was open to any artist as long as he or she paid a small fee. By coming to the opening of the exhibition, everyone wanted to be noticed, to be acknowledged, to be appreciated. And yet, to what end?

"Nobody's selling anything anymore," Gabrielle whispered a little later. "It's not like the old days. And those hideous paintings by Seurat. I'm sure they put people off."

The show was being held in the cavernous Pavillon de la Ville de Paris on the Champs-Élysées. Two stories high with a ceiling of glass, the Pavillon had been built for the World's Fair in 1879. Now the colonnaded foyer was used for exhibiting sculpture while thousands of paintings had been hung in the galleries. The private view wasn't particularly busy, and yet still hundreds of people swarmed up the stairs and along the balconies to cram into the galleries, most of them looking for artists they'd read about in the newspaper.

"Look at that," said a young woman in English. "If I half close my eyes —"

For an instant, Émile thought the voice sounded familiar and turned. It was a girl and her elderly mother, a pair he didn't recognize, who started when he looked at them as if he had just asked for spare change.

"Pardon," he said in French.

That morning he'd received a letter from the young man he had met in the balloon, requesting a tour of the workshop. It wasn't unthinkable, he told himself, that they would come to the private view. They might even be here, in another gallery, at this very moment. And he suddenly remembered the chill of the air, a hand on his sleeve, the taste of smoke on his lips.

"Who on earth gave her a ticket?" Gabrielle said.

A large woman had appeared at the door of the gallery, unaccompanied and a little out of breath. She wore a pink ruffled evening gown with a huge bustle, in a style that was long out of fashion. A velvet ribbon was tied around her neck and her ample cleavage was decorated with artificial flowers. Even in the pale light that filtered through the blinds that covered every window, it was impossible not to notice the splatter of something dark across the hem of her skirt — wine perhaps, or mud. Émile felt a pang of sympathy for her. He wondered if she'd noticed. She would most likely notice later, when it was too late, and would feel the slow seep of shame spread across her body like the stain.

"The Folies-Bergère is on the rue Richer," someone whispered, loud enough for everyone to hear.

The woman jutted out her well-padded chin. She had no time for these people, her face seemed to say; she had other business to attend to. Her eyes ran over the crowd several times before they fell on Seurat. And then she adjusted her bodice, pulled back her shoulders, walked right over, and kissed him full on the lips. The room inhaled as one, a mass suction of indignation and barely disguised horror.

"His mistress," Gabrielle mouthed. "Aren't they both perfectly awful? Let's go."

Gabrielle took his arm and they wandered on through other rooms, rooms hung with hundreds and hundreds of paintings.

"So much mediocrity," she said. "Everyone thinks they can be an artist now. And the thing is, they can't."

53

"And where are you?" he asked. "I'd like to see the paintings of you."

Gabrielle turned and gazed up at him. In the half-light, her skin was pale, her bottom lip a deep, dark red.

"In the next room," she said, her large eyes blinking with concern. "But please? Don't —"

"Don't?"

She didn't reply. Instead she glanced away toward a door that opened onto the balcony above the main foyer. And then with a handful of skirt in her hand, she turned and sailed toward it. *Don't.* The word echoed in his head. Don't make a scene? Don't fall in love with her? He wasn't sure he could even if he wanted to.

That evening, Gabrielle wore an off-the-shoulder dress. Her hair was pulled into a swirl on the top of her head. Her shoulders were narrow, her waist even more so. Earlier, he had wanted to reach out and place both hands on those slender hips, their line drawn by thin bones of steel inside her corset, and pull her to him. As if she could feel his eyes on her, Gabrielle had turned. But instead of catching his eye, she had looked beyond. He glanced around. An elderly well-dressed gentleman with a monocle was staring in her direction. Gabrielle's mouth was slightly open and a tiny smile had formed on her lips.

"Monsieur Nouguier," called a voice. "Thank you for coming. My wife assured me you would."

A man was limping toward him with his hand outstretched. Émile felt a wash of guilt; so this was Gabrielle's husband.

"Wouldn't miss it for the world," Émile replied.

"Come," the painter said, "come and see my new work. It is the best, I think, the best I have ever done."

Gabrielle's husband was nothing like he had imagined. Although his accent was middle-class, the painter looked unkempt, poor, ill. He smelled of raw garlic and pigskin leather, of stale wine and smoke. As Émile followed him through the crowd, he noticed that one of his legs was wasted. His collar was frayed and the heels of his boots worn down. What misfortunes had befallen the artist aside from polio? And how could he bear to share his beautiful wife with anyone?

"The light is better in this room," the painter said. "It faces north."

Émile purposely waited until he was right in the center of the gallery before he looked at the work. A woman reading a book; a

55

woman gazing at herself in the mirror; a woman asleep in bed, her face turned away; a woman naked, her hair filled with flowers, her face caught in a smile.

"You like them?" the painter asked.

It wasn't Gabrielle; the limbs were too clumsy, the line wasn't fluid, the turn of the chin was not graceful enough. And yet, it was.

"I do," he said. "Very much."

Later, Émile stood at the window of the cloakroom and watched a line of carriages roll through the rain on the Champs-Élysées. A man with one arm stepped out from beneath a tree. He unbuttoned his filthy shirt and splashed water around his neck and chest. And then he rubbed his beard, his face, his body, his stump. But this was city rain, the kind of rain that left streaks of black down polished windows and smuts on clean washing. Émile suspected that the man would soon be even dirtier than he was before the rain began.

Had the man been in Paris in May 1871, he wondered, the "bloody week" when the streets of the city had been piled with the corpses of insurrectionists and the air thick with smoke as Paris burned? Was that where he had lost his arm? Émile had missed the siege, had been away working in the Austro-

Hungarian Empire on a bridge over the Tisza River. He had not suffered.

Once, when she had drunk too much, Gabrielle described the sound of the wind in the eaves mixed with the distant stutter of gunfire. She told him that she had spent that week in their rooms in the upper reaches of Belleville with her younger sisters, half-starved by the Prussian siege, waiting for her father, a member of the Paris Commune, to come home and bring them some bread. He didn't return that night or the following day. It wasn't unusual. He often disappeared for days after he had administered one of his beatings. But this time he didn't come home at all. Her mother had eventually been called to identify his body in a pile beside a wall in the Père-Lachaise Cemetery. As the eldest daughter, she went too. Here they learned that her father, after being pursued past the last resting place of Balzac and the poet Delavigne, had been caught, tied up, placed against one of the perimeter walls, and executed by a firing squad.

"When I saw him, all I felt was anger," she told Émile. "His pockets were empty. He didn't have any bread. All he left us were bruises."

Although it was the Prussian Army who

surrounded the city, who cut it off and forced the inhabitants to eat anything they could find to survive, to slaughter the animals in the zoo and harvest rats, the killing of the Communards was done by the government troops once a treaty had been signed and the enemy had withdrawn. Gabrielle rarely talked about her childhood, and maybe it was no wonder: an abusive father, a mother who had died of syphilis, two sisters who succumbed to consumption, a spell herself of scarlet fever, which had weakened her heart . . . a catalogue of ill health and violence, of poverty and bitterness.

And yet, unlike others from the slums, people whose cheekbones had been sharpened by a hunger that never left them, none of the past showed in Gabrielle's face. In fact, her looks had quickly taken her out of Belleville. At twelve, she had been spotted by a painter and hired to model. For the next fifteen years, she had moved from one artist to another, from filthy garret to drafty attic. Aside from acquiring a husband along the way, her upward trajectory was slow but steady. She gradually grew more elegant, gathered admirers, and built social currency. She no longer was paid by the hour; she was above that. Her lovers, her artists, her friends reimbursed her in other ways, in paintings or dresses, jewelry or outings to the opera. Soon it was almost impossible to tell where she was from. Her neck was long and aristocratic, her voice low and cultured. Émile had thought her melodramatic when she had told him that she carried nothing with her from her girlhood but her soul. As he got to know her, and her soul, a little better, he realized it was true. But sometimes he still saw the girl in her, the girl who starved and sobbed for bread.

The racks of coats and hats smelled of wet wool and camphor. But at least the cloakroom was empty; at least it was quiet. Émile sat down on a divan and ran his fingers through the tugs in his hair. He looked down at his hands, hands that were growing old. It was time to move on, to disengage, to take responsibility. What was he doing with his life?

With a twist of the handle, the door opened.

"Here you are!" said Gabrielle, standing in the doorway. "I've been looking for you everywhere. In fact, I was just about to give up."

There was the catch of blame in her voice, as if it were his fault that he had made himself so hard to find.

"It's too crowded," he explained. "I needed some air."

Gabrielle closed the door behind her. She took a deep breath and sighed it out again. And then she smiled.

"Anyway," she said, "you'll never guess what!"

He shook his head.

"He sold them," she said. "He sold them all."

Suddenly he saw that her eyes were shiny and her cheeks were flushed.

"I knew it," she went on. "I knew it would happen eventually. We're all going out to celebrate!"

And then she paused. "I'd love it if you came too," she said, "if you'd like to, that is, but of course I would understand if you'd rather not. I mean, don't feel obliged."

She invited him and uninvited him in the same breath. That was the way she was.

"Actually," he said, "I have to work."

Gabrielle nodded. That's what he did. Work. Slaving away in some faceless office. She'd once asked him to explain his profession but stopped him after a couple of minutes.

"It's as if you're talking Russian," she had said. "I don't understand a word!"

Outside, a man let out a shout of a laugh.

A woman called to another and asked her to wait. There was a shift in the air — people were starting to leave. Gabrielle swept back a strand of hair, then leaned down to kiss him.

"Well, at least you're here," she said. "Thank you so much for coming."

"Incidentally," he asked, "who bought them?"

She paused, her mouth still a few inches from his, as if the idea had never occurred to her before.

"Some dealer or other, I expect," she said, standing upright again. "No one else — I mean, no one who matters — has sold more than a study or two."

"Not even Seurat?"

"Certainly not Seurat."

For a moment she was still. And then her eyes fell on Émile again and she blinked twice.

"It wasn't that bad, was it?" she said.

He buried his face deep in the folds of her blue silk dress, the dress he had helped choose and pay for, the dress that she had yet to thank him for, and inhaled.

"Did you like the paintings?"

"Not as much as I like the sitter. Let's lock the door and do it now," he whispered. "Among the coats."

She laughed. "Don't you ever think of anything else?"

"No," he said. "Never."

And then she seemed to freeze.

"What?" he asked. "What is it?"

"It's nothing," she replied, looking away.

"Gabrielle?"

"All right," she said. "I hate to ask, but can I borrow twenty francs?"

He pulled away from her, took a note from his wallet, and handed it over.

"It's a loan," she said.

"Of course it is," he said.

"You're sweet," she said, and kissed him on the top of the head. "What do you think? Of the dress?"

"Exquisite," he replied.

She spun around, and Émile circled her waist. Hanging beneath her overskirt was a small, soft leather bag with something hard inside.

"What's this?" he asked, and drew it out.

"It's nothing," she said, and tried to snatch it from him.

"It doesn't feel like nothing," he said, holding it just out of her reach. As he opened it, a small object fell out and rolled across the floor. He picked it up before her corset would allow her to bend down and fetch it herself. Her smile had gone.

"Give it to me," she said, her eyes dark with a hostility he had never seen before.

He placed a small, silver-plated syringe in her open palm. She closed her hand, dropped it in her bag again, and without another word, she left.

5

It was early and the city was still veiled with mist, the high reaches of apartment buildings softened, smudged, as if run over once with a piece of artist's putty. Eiffel's workshop in Levallois-Perret was a short cab ride away from the city center, in the seventeenth arrondissement just to the north of the Bois de Boulogne.

"I hope you appreciate how incredibly exciting this is going to be," Jamie said. "We're going to meet Gustave Eiffel. The man's a genius!"

"The Committee of Three Hundred don't seem to think so," Alice said. "What did they call his tower? Useless. Monstrous."

"Who told you that?" he asked.

"You did," she replied. "It was in the newspaper, don't you remember? You read it out to me."

Jamie wiped the condensation from the window and stared out toward Fort Mont-

64

Valérien in the distance. "What do they know?" He shrugged.

"Quite a lot, I'd imagine," Alice countered.

"It will be the tallest tower in the world, Alice," he said, turning back to her. "Three hundred meters high. And what's more, it will be made of iron, nothing else but iron, like a bridge. Mrs. Wallace, what do you think?"

"Hard to say. It could, in fact, be wonderful," she replied.

Alice sighed out loud and then turned on her brother. "It will be a building without a skin, not wonderful at all but utterly grotesque. I can't believe you've changed your mind, Jamie."

He leaned back and smiled. It was unlike him not to say something inflammatory in return, to make a pointed remark. But there was a buoyancy, a new lightness, about his manner. Only a few days before he had seemed to be suffering from claustrophobia, his movements tense, his sighs provocative, as if he were straining at the leash, desperate to escape from the confinement of their company. And suddenly it seemed as if a door had opened somewhere and he was already halfway through it. He was relaxed, resigned, beyond them somehow.

A change of subject was clearly what was needed. Alice rose to the challenge.

"Did you hear?" she said. "Miriam Morrison, the daughter of your Latin master, is in the family way."

"Who told you that?" Jamie said.

"I had a letter from Tiffie yesterday. The family tried to keep it secret, to send her off to some place in Dumfries for unmarried mothers, but word got out."

"The poor girl," said Cait.

"Haven't seen her for years," said Jamie, and stared out the window.

"Where were you last night?" Alice asked. "I knocked on your door and there was no answer."

"Not with Miriam Morrison anyway." He laughed.

"James!" Alice said. "It's not a joke."

He paused before answering, as if working out which lie to tell.

"It was too hot in my room," he said. "I just popped out for a breath of air."

"Why didn't you just open a window?" Alice asked.

Cait, sensing another argument was about to develop, stepped in and agreed that yes, the hotel overheated the bedrooms, but if you opened the window the noise from the street was bad.

"I had to open the window in the water closet," she admitted.

Alice and Jamie both stifled a snigger. This was how she appeared to them most of the time; eccentric, contrary, and she encouraged it.

"Just be careful," Cait said.

"We don't want to find your body floating in the Seine," said Alice.

Out of the center of Paris, the streets were narrower, the buildings taller, the walls hung with strings of damp washing or painted with advertisements for absinthe or cointreau. Children threw rocks into dirty brown puddles while girls only a few years older, with strings of imitation pearls around their necks and jewels of rain in their hair, waited in doorways for customers. It had shocked Cait at first, the poverty, the brazenness with which young women sold themselves, the casual attitude toward destitution and morality.

And yet Paris, Cait realized, put on a good face. With its grandiose new layout, vast open spaces, great monuments, and a brand-new sewer network six hundred kilometers long, the city had been constructed for one class at the expense of another. There were thousands of sumptuous apartment blocks and there were enough fabulously wealthy, titled, fashionable, and rich people to live in them. But they were virtually invisible, cosseted away in carriages and behind ornate metal gates; they ate behind heavy curtains in restaurants like Paillard's on the rue de Rivoli, and spent the summers at Cabourg or Deauville, Biarritz or Baden-Baden.

The previous residents of the center of Paris, however, the ones who had once lived in shacks beside the Louvre or in the narrow streets of the Île de la Cité, the ones whose great-grandfathers and -grandmothers mothers had stormed the Bastille, proclaimed France a republic, and dropped the guillotine on the necks of the monarchy and their supporters almost a hundred years earlier, had been pushed to new, poorer housing in the outer arrondissements. But they came back, to Les Halles, to the rue de Rivoli, and to the Bois, bringing with them all the noise and commotion they had always brought. And then there were the hungry, the homeless, the lost, the insane, and the terminally sick, who stared out at you from the polished steps of the Opéra Garnier, or from beneath the neatly trimmed trees on the avenue des Gobelins or boulevard Saint-Michel, because they had nowhere else to go, because although

Haussmann would have liked to suggest otherwise, it was still their city as much as anyone else's.

Although it was now a capital laced with balconies and verdant parks, with public squares and lavish theaters, there was also something about Paris that could not be bricked over, that could not be rationalized with straight lines and regulated facades. No matter how it looked, the city would always be much more than just its architecture. There was a friction in the air; it was in the churn of the river and the taste of resin from the vast forests that spread out almost all the way to Beauvais in the north and Orléans in the south. The medieval and the modern age mingled beneath the bridges of the Seine, while above the city the white, white dust from the construction site at Sacré-Coeur mixed with black soot and stink that rose from the slums of the Marais or the dilapidated streets that lined the railway in Montparnasse, to create a fog that in the right light looked almost silver.

Levallois-Perret had once been a small village on the outskirts of Paris. Haussmann's arrondissements had pushed most of the industry to the edge of the city, and the village had become an industrial zone where warehouses and factories sat beside small abandoned gardens. Eiffel's factory was surrounded by a high wall but was easily identified by the constant stream of heavily laden horse-drawn wagons heading out of its wooden gates and the stink of sulfur and burning charcoal. As the carriage approached the main gate, Jamie inhaled deeply.

"Doesn't that remind you of home?" he asked. "Of the Dalmarnock works?"

He looked across at his sister but she was silent, her mouth clenched shut.

"Why are you like this, Alice?" Jamie snapped.

"Like what?"

"Don't you want to make something of yourself?"

"I want to make a good marriage, if that's what you mean. What else would you suggest?"

"You mean you want to go back to Scotland and molder."

"It's where we happen to come from," she replied. "And I don't intend to molder anywhere for a second."

"Both of you," Cait said, "just stop."

"Wouldn't you rather stay here," he continued, "if you could? I mean, what is there in Glasgow for any of us?"

"I don't know what you have planned, but

the answer's no," Alice said. "And you can't make me. For one thing, I don't even know him."

It took a moment for Jamie to work out what she was talking about.

"You mean the French engineer? The dashing Monsieur Nouguier?"

"Is that what his name is?" Alice said, and stared out the window.

"Isn't this all a little premature?" said Cait. "As Alice said, she met him once, in passing."

"Has that ever been a prerequisite for marriage?" said Jamie. "I hardly think so."

"And besides," said Alice, "I am expecting a proposal."

"If you mean from Pig-nose . . . could you set your sights any lower?"

"Enough," Cait warned.

"His name," Alice said pointedly, "is Hogg. Mr. Arthur Hogg."

"Whatever you want to call him, he has money but he has no sense of humor. The perfect husband!"

Alice's face had turned scarlet. She looked close to tears.

"Don't listen to him," said Cait. "Jamie, I think you should apologize to your sister."

"For what? For stating the obvious? She thinks it too. Don't you, Alice?"

71

Alice opened her mouth. Nothing came out.

"See!" said Jamie.

The carriage pulled to a halt.

"Just don't call him Pig-nose," said Alice.

A side door opened onto the covered stockyard. Twice the size of Arrol's Dalmarnock works, it was piled high with short lengths of iron and wooden barrels filled with metal bolts. On the main floor dozens of workers were carrying girders or lifting sacks, stoking fires or bolting lengths of metal together; at one side was a line of huge radial drills, on the other, a series of pulleys and hooks that hung from the ceiling. The atmosphere was opaque with dust and the smell of hot metal, with the dull thud of the hammer on the anvil and the high-pitched whistle and whine of the drill.

"Impressive," said Jamie.

"Filthy," said Alice. "So where now?"

"Nouguier instructed that we should go straight to the main office."

Instead of leading them inside, however, where draftsmen sat hunched over their desks, Jamie took them through the yard. Alice was wearing a white dress, a fur stole, and a new hat decorated with peacock feathers. She hadn't wanted to let her brother have his own way when they had so little time left in Paris. But finally she had agreed to visit Eiffel's workshop and had risen to the occasion and made an effort, wearing a brand-new outfit only just back from the dressmaker's. Everything in the stockyard, however, was covered in a film of black grease, the kind that rings fingernails and seeps into the lines of the palm.

"Be careful not to touch anything," Cait told Alice.

But it was too late. Alice's fingertips had already left five small black spots on the bodice of her dress.

"Oh!" she cried, and looked at Jamie.

"We told you not to touch anything," he retorted.

"That's easier said than done," she replied.

"Cover it with your fur," Cait suggested. "You won't be able to see it."

Alice tugged her fur stole tighter. She examined her hands and wiped the streaks of grease away with her handkerchief.

"And why," she whispered, "why are they looking at us like that?"

A dozen workers had stopped what they were doing and were staring across. One of them lifted his cap. His face was dark with soot, but the skin around his eyes was splayed with tiny white creases.

"They're just curious," Cait said. "Are you

sure that this is convenient?"

"Why wouldn't it be?" said Jamie.

Émile Nouguier was waiting for them outside the office at the top of a metal stairwell. In the light that fell in long dusty beams through the glass above, she saw immediately that his smile was genuine.

"Welcome," he said.

Cait had chosen her most somber dress — gray-and-black-checked wool. Alice in her white dress with her fair ringlets and her new hat shone brightly beside her.

"Thank you," said Jamie. "Sorry we're late. You remember my sister?"

The engineer bowed to Alice, then turned to Cait.

"And Madame Wallace?" Jamie continued.

"Of course," he said.

She offered her hand. It was the way a married woman should greet a man, that was all, but Cait was suddenly breathless, suddenly uncomfortable, suddenly self-conscious, as he took it and gave it a small press.

"But you should have used the visitor's entrance," he continued. "You came through the yard."

Alice looked at Jamie pointedly but didn't comment.

"We wanted to see the stockyard and the

workshop firsthand," Jamie said. "An impressive setup."

"Everything you see is for the tower," Nouguier replied. "Every piece will be drilled or shaped here and then transported to the site."

"That sounds like quite an undertaking," Jamie said.

"It certainly is. According to our calculations we need eighteen thousand different pieces and more than two million rivets."

"Goodness," said Alice.

"And how will you assemble it?" asked Jamie.

"We shall start with the foundations and work up," he replied. "Once each piece has been fashioned, it will be transported to the site and riveted into place by hand."

"And will that work?" asked Alice.

After a pause so short that it was barely noticeable, the engineer laughed.

"One hopes so. Let's begin," he said as he ushered them along the corridor.

"As well as dozens of metalworkers, we employ a whole floor of draftsmen."

"When can we meet the great man himself?" Jamie asked.

"Monsieur Eiffel is very busy," he said. "But I'll certainly see if he can spare a few moments."

He paused at a window that overlooked the yard. "As you can see, we're working on the piles that will be inserted into the concrete slabs of the foundations."

Huge lengths of iron glowed red hot as they were hammered and shaped. Here, the noise of the drill was earsplitting. Nouguier had to shout to make himself heard.

"To make sure the tower is absolutely level," he went on, "we're going to use compressed-air caissons . . ."

Alice yawned. The drilling stopped.

"Maybe you would you like to take a look instead?" Nouguier suggested. "It sounds very dull if I explain."

Alice blinked several times in quick succession, then gave a tiny shake of her head.

"Perhaps," Cait suggested in French, "maybe we could wait somewhere —"

"Isn't the girl interested at all?" he replied in French.

Cait smiled but didn't answer.

"What about you?" he continued. "Why don't you come without her?"

"What's he saying?" Alice whispered.

Cait tried to deflect the directness of the comment.

"Is there anywhere we can wait?" she asked.

The men strode off along the corridor

together while Cait and Alice sat down on a hard wooden bench. For a moment they were silent. Cait closed her eyes and suddenly remembered the low gray horizons of Fife underlined by the distant ocean, and the way the sun glanced across the land like the brushing of a careless hand. When had she been there last? Had it been with Saul shortly before they were married? Or was it as a child on a holiday to St. Andrews? And why would she remember it now? Maybe it was the last time she had felt that happiness was a given? And then Alice's voice cut through, bringing her back to the engineer's workshop in Paris.

"He is rather dashing," she was saying. "And I wouldn't have to come here, would I, not often, at least?"

Cait opened her eyes. Alice's face was creased with concentration.

"I mean, you didn't, did you? When you were married? Go to your husband's office?"

Although the sun was still bright, a shadow descended. Cait tried to tell herself that it was a long time ago. But time was not linear. The shock of what had happened had not lessened, it was just buried deeper, and sometimes the blinding awfulness, the sheer indignity, the intolerable shame of it opened inside her like a night bloom.

When Cait didn't answer, Alice turned and examined her face. "I'm so sorry," she said. "I'm an idiot for mentioning it."

"No, don't worry," Cait replied, and gave her a half smile.

Convinced that the awkward moment had passed, Alice picked up her train of thought and continued.

"You see, half of me doesn't want to get too old to marry and end up on the shelf. And the other half wants to run away."

"You won't end up on the shelf, Alice."

"I know. There's always Pig-nose."

"Mr. Hogg sounds like he has many fine qualities. You mustn't listen to Jamie."

Alice turned and looked at Cait.

"What do you think of him?" she whispered. "The engineer? Do you think he could be a good match for me? Uncle William would be over the moon. But he's so old!"

"Is he old?"

"He must be at least forty."

"That's not old. Not for a husband."

But Alice was barely listening anymore. Instead she was caught up in her own train of thought.

"I'd have to learn French," she went on. "Maybe you could teach me? And then once we were married we could move into a nice little house near the Bois and have lots of French children called Pierre or Mathilde."

"Alice, maybe you should take it one step at a time."

"But my uncle's been so good to us. I don't want to disappoint him."

A door slammed on the floor below. Jamie's laughter, a short burst, was followed by the scuff of feet ascending the stairs. They were coming back.

"How do I look?" Alice asked. She blinked her large eyes at Cait.

"Lovely," Cait replied. It was true. She did.

"But what about the dress?"

"He doesn't care about the dress, Alice."

Émile, Jamie, and a smaller man of about fifty with a sweep of white hair appeared at the top of the stairwell. As soon as he saw them he approached Cait and bowed.

"Mademoiselle Arrol?" he said. "Gustave Eiffel."

There was a slightly awkward moment as Alice stepped forward.

"Actually, I'm Mademoiselle Arrol, Monsieur Eiffel," said Alice. "I think you are acquainted with our uncle?"

He looked from Cait to Alice and bowed once more.

"Please excuse me," he said. "Indeed I am. He is a wonderful engineer and extremely engaging company. I am a huge admirer."

Alice seemed to relax. She smiled and pulled her fur stole a little tighter around her body.

"He's hard at work on another bridge," she said, and glanced at Émile. "Across the River Forth, near Edinburgh."

"Ah yes," Eiffel replied. "We all intend to make a special trip to Scotland to see it when it is finished."

Alice beamed with pride as if it were her bridge, her river. Jamie had been watching them all closely. Finally he saw his moment.

"I'm sure that our uncle would agree that we would like stronger ties," he said. "To find a way to link up Paris with Scotland. In fact, I have a proposal."

Alice inhaled sharply. Her blue eyes were wide with horror.

"Don't look so shocked." Jamie laughed. "I have a few ideas of my own. Ideas that involve me and me alone. Monsieur Eiffel? I'd like to come back and work as an apprentice on the tower. Would that be possible?"

He looked expectantly at the engineer.

"I have no objection in principle," Eiffel replied. "Monsieur Nouguier?"

But Émile Nouguier was distracted; a clerk was running along the corridor toward them. Monsieur Eiffel was wanted at once in the workshop.

"Monsieur Nouguier?" Jamie prompted once Eiffel had wished them good day and set off along the corridor. Nouguier blinked rapidly, rubbed his eyes, then apologized.

"I was up at five," he explained. "I'm sorry."

"We should go," said Cait. "We've taken too much of your time already."

Alice's eyes darted from Jamie to Nouguier and then back again.

"But the tower!" she said, and added a short laugh. "Aren't there plans or something that we could look at? Quickly, I mean."

Alice waited with her head cocked.

"I would be happy to show you the original drawings," Émile was compelled to reply.

A look of relief spread slowly across Alice's face.

"Oh yes," she said. "I would be interested. Very interested indeed, as a matter of fact."

Cait raised her hand to cover her eyes. She blinked, but there was something wrong with her sight, a darkening blur right at the center of her vision. They always started like this, her headaches. First the blindness, followed by crinkles of flashing light, and then the thump of pain on one side of her face. She sat back down on the wooden bench.

"I'm sorry," she said. "I think I'll stay here. It's my head."

"Mrs. Wallace has these turns," Alice explained. "But she'll be right as rain in a moment."

"You go," she told them all. "I'll be fine."

She was suddenly aware, however, of a presence close by.

"Would you like anything?" Émile Nouguier asked.

She could tell that he was crouching down in front of her. She just couldn't see him.

"A glass of water. If it's not too much trouble."

By the time he returned, the blinding throb had shifted from the center of her vision and was pulsating in a small rainbow to the left. She could see again. She stood up as he approached and took the glass.

"Thank you," she said. "Where are the Arrols?"

"With one of my colleagues. How are you?"

"Much better now," she said brightly. "It's nothing serious. The doctor said it was neurasthenia, nervous exhaustion that manifests itself in what he called a migraine."

"Ah yes, my mother suffers from those too. Did he give you something?"

"Indian hemp. It certainly lessens the severity of the pain. But then again, they use Indian hemp for everything — for coughs and for cholera even!"

Nouguier laughed. "For insanity and Graves' disease."

"For epilepsy and opium addiction," she continued.

"If only it worked," he said softly.

He seemed momentarily lost. She adjusted her hat.

"It was kind of you to take time out of your day," she said.

"Not at all," he said.

His gaze shifted from her eyes to her mouth and back again.

"When do you leave Paris?" he asked.

"In two days' time," she replied.

"Will you come back?" he asked. "To Paris, I mean?"

"I shouldn't think so."

There was a pause, a tiny interlude, when she was aware only of his eyes and the rise and fall of his breath.

"Anyway," she said, handing him back the glass, "I'm sure you need to get back to work. Could you tell the others that I'll wait for them in the carriage?"

"Of course," he said. *"Au revoir."*

Not "goodbye," but "until we meet again." They would never meet again. She'd had her chance. But even so, her neck prickled as she imagined his eyes running down the length of her, her shoulders, her waist, her hips, her narrow bustle. At the bottom of the stairs, she hesitated, then turned and looked back. And there he was, still standing at the top, the empty glass in his hand, watching her leave.

6

It was March, and Paris was approaching the end of the *petite saison.* Émile knew there would be a flurry of balls and dances, dinners and salons. After Easter, the *grande saison* would begin with the Concours Hippiques, a horse show on the Champs-Élysées. Then more balls and horse races and exhibitions parties, until the middle and upper classes left Paris for summer, heading north to the Côte Fleurie, or south to the Côte d'Azur on the Blue Train.

For the rest of the city, the seasons were not simply a backdrop for the fashion conscious. The heat, the cold, the wet, and the dry had to be borne with the addition of a scarf or two or the removal of a layer of undergarments. This year he had noticed the weather was unseasonably warm. On the rivers, the numerous *guinguettes,* or open-air dance halls, that lined the banks had opened earlier than usual. And in

Montmartre, the outdoor cafés that looked over the whole city tentatively unlocked their terraces while washerwomen toiled up the hill — or La Butte, as it was known — with baskets of wet sheets to hang out on the wasteland next to the windmills at the top.

Émile paused to light a cigarette at the doorway of the artist's atelier. As he inhaled, he felt someone's eyes upon him. He turned and looked over his shoulder, back along the length of the street down toward the boulevard de Clichy, but saw no one. The narrow streets below smelled of sour wine and stale air, of last night's tobacco and this morning's piss. The *maisons closes,* or brothels, the circuses and cabarets, had been shut for only a few short hours, but by midmorning some were already opening for business, their doors pushed ajar to give the illusion of being aired.

"Looking for a model?" A thin woman of about thirty stepped out of the doorway opposite so suddenly that Émile dropped his cigarette. She was dressed as a shepherdess, with a wooden crook, bare feet, and a brown dress over a grubby white chemise. While her outfit suggested an Arcadian simplicity, her eyes projected something altogether more knowing.

"I don't think so," he replied, and pulled out his cigarette case to extract another. "Not today."

The woman adjusted her bodice and took a couple of steps toward him.

"I've been painted by all the masters," she said. "By Poussin, even."

"I very much doubt that you were painted by Poussin," Émile said. "He's been dead for two hundred years."

"Not him," she said with a shake of her head. "This man was very much alive. Said he was studying at the École des Beaux Arts. Respectable too. Why wouldn't I believe everything he told me?"

She smiled up at him and there was something in her face that he recognized, the certainty that he had what she wanted and that she had the wherewithal to get it.

"I'll model for you for fifty sous a day," she said. "Far less than what you'll pay in there. I'll do it nude for a franc."

The slight swell of her breasts was visible beneath her chemise. Her breath was sweet with tooth decay. He turned away.

"Madam," he said, "I am afraid what little talent I have would never do you justice. And now, if you'll excuse me, I am late for class."

He bowed, turned, then made his way

through the courtyard and up the narrow steps to the artist's studio.

"You'll come back," she called after him. "My name, for next time, is Jeanne."

A small number of men were waiting at the top of the steps outside the wooden door. The door was locked, but several of them still tried the handle once or twice, just in case. The artist's studio was an attic room with glass panes in the roof. Although the light streamed in all day, it was too hot in summer and too cold in winter. The tutor, a former member of the Académie, an old man with a whiskered face and broken spectacles, seemed to pay no attention to the temperature. He opened up the studio, without heat or fan, and provided instruction to aspiring artists for a monthly fee of ten francs. There was a waiting list. But despite, or maybe because of, the demand, he was late. He was always late, and the men, as usual, were impatient. Many had arrived hours earlier to secure a good spot and had turned sour and morose with boredom. Émile took his place at the end of the queue and finished his cigarette.

"Poussin," he said to himself again.

The majority of Paris's artists, the students at the École des Beaux Arts or at Suisse, the independent atelier, all lived here, in

Montmartre. It was little more than a village, part of Paris and yet not, not with the creak and rush of the windmills and the buzz of bees drifting down from the Abbesses's vegetable gardens. Beneath the stink of the city and the smell of turned earth, you could taste turpentine and oil paint almost as soon as you reached the lower slopes of La Butte. At the bottom of the hill were the successful painters; Renoir and Degas lived and worked near the boulevard de Clichy. Farther up, where the streets were steeper and the rooms were cheap and cramped but had a view to compensate, were all the rest — the men who dreamed of exhibiting in the official Salon or the Salon des Indépendants and who spent all their money, and probably their parents' money too, on lessons and paint from Maison Edouard, on Côte du Rhone, and on whores. No wonder so many of them got sick and caught the pox; no wonder so many of them were found lying on the street, just a crumpled heap of clothes beneath an open window high above. The ones who survived seemed to exist on air and ego, on sex and soup.

Finally the tutor appeared, shuffling through the courtyard below with a stick in one hand and a bundle of bones wrapped in cloth in the other. He unlocked the door to the studio and stood back as the students rushed in to claim a space. A classical sculpture had been placed at the front of the class, a study of an athlete in marble. As they set up their easels and sharpened their pencils, a young man stepped into the studio and, without a word from the tutor, began to undress. This week's class, the tutor announced, was in human anatomy.

"Look," he said once he had the students' attention. "Look at the way the bones are connected, at the way they move beneath the skin." He picked up the model's arm and bent it. "Consider the skin tone, the illumination from within. This can be achieved by building up layers of pigment like Delacroix, Rembrandt, and Dürer. But to paint well is not just a matter of technique. An artist has to understand the human body both inside and out. It is not just a matter of capturing the fleeting surface."

There was a mutter of acknowledgment, of agreement. They all knew that he was referring to the work of the Impressionists.

"Here is a pelvis," he said, holding up the bones. "And the femur, the tibia and fibula of the left leg. When you draw today I want to see that you understand the bones beneath the skin."

Slowly he maneuvered the model into position: sitting down, with one knee raised and one arm outstretched.

"Well?" he asked. "Who is this? You?"

He pointed at Émile. The pose looked familiar, but Émile had no idea. He shook his head. The old man seemed to find this amusing.

"Have you ever set foot in the Louvre?" he asked.

"Many times," conceded Émile, his face blanching.

"Well?" he asked the rest of the class.

"It's *The Creation of Adam,*" they chorused. "By Michelangelo."

Émile shrank a little into his shoes. Of course. He should have known that. Although the original was in the Sistine Chapel, there were numerous studies in pencil in the Louvre.

He could almost hear Gabrielle's laugh, the tickle of her amusement tainted with scorn. But she had no idea that he had tried to keep up his art, studying painting or drawing whenever time would allow. After he spent days calculating exact measurements and gradients, using rulers, a sector, a compass, and a pair of dividers, it was a relief to work with just a pencil and paper and draw what was in front of him. His style

91

was the exact opposite of his technical work; his line was loose, economical, free. And he wanted to capture what he couldn't keep, the fleeting, the transient.

Since the night of the show, he had barely seen Gabrielle. Finally they had arranged to meet in a small café in Montparnasse that he had chosen because they were unlikely to meet anyone he knew there. As she approached his table — late, of course — he saw immediately that the sales of the pictures still elevated her mood. She walked with her head held a little higher, her smile pulled a little wider, her eyes filled with a kind of brightness that seemed focused on an entirely different beyond from everybody else's.

After she had pressed her cheek to his, twice, and coffee had been ordered, she seemed finally to notice him.

"How are you, anyway?" he had asked.

"Better for seeing you," she had replied, then reached for his hand and held it. Something within him seemed to plummet. Their affair was like a horse and carriage without a driver, careering forward toward a catastrophe all of their own making.

After a moment, he withdrew his hand and pretended to wipe the perspiration from his brow.

"It's hot in here," he said.

"You work too hard," she replied.

She blinked and he saw that her pupils were huge and black. What had she been taking? Laudanum? Opium? Morphine? He knew that it was pointless asking; she would vehemently deny it. They had both fallen silent. Once you removed lovemaking from the equation, he realized that they had little to say to each other. Émile drank his coffee quickly, draining his cup right down to the sugar granules at the bottom. Gabrielle started to play with her spoon, spinning it on its end with the tip of her finger.

"What was America like?" she asked suddenly.

The previous year, Émile had spent a month in New York helping Eiffel install the metal framework for the Statue of Liberty. He remembered the ripple of the Narrows, the uncompromising glare of the sunlight on the water and the taste of the slums in his mouth. He remembered the wide streets of the grid and the lush green space of Central Park. And he remembered the first time he had seen a huddle of "street Arabs," as they were called, six or seven homeless children, some as young as five or six, sleeping barefoot in a doorway outside a hotel on West Twenty-Third Street. One of them had thrust a small, filthy foot onto the pavement, or sidewalk, as it was known. As he watched, a middle-aged lady all dressed up in silk and pearls had climbed out of a carriage and then simply stepped over the foot as if it were nothing but a length of broken stick or an old umbrella handle before heading into the paneled interior of the lobby toward the restaurant to dine on oysters, he supposed, and fine wine.

"It's wonderful if you have money," he replied.

"And why shouldn't we?" she said. "If we were to go, that is. I mean, what is there to keep us here?"

He turned to her, but he could tell by her face that she was elsewhere again, caught up in the drift of an imaginary future. Although he did not like himself for it, he had been unable to stop himself from asking the question.

"Did you find out?" he said. "Do you know who bought the paintings?"

His words were like cold water in her face. She blinked rapidly.

"No," she said. "He wouldn't tell me. Why? Do you know?"

He shook his head. He would never tell her. And neither, he knew, would her husband. He sat back and closed his eyes. What was he doing? What was he becoming? He should break it off now, quickly, before any more damage was done. And yet he had become unwittingly addicted.

"Gabrielle?" he had said, reaching for her. "Come back to my apartment? Is there time?"

But once she had visited the water closet and fixed her face, there was only time to leave.

The students at the artist's atelier were of two types. The thin ones with the pigment in their hair and deeply engraved frown lines on their foreheads were the serious ones, the ones who had given everything for their art. The rest were men like Émile, men whose smart dress, well-filled bellies, and clean hands gave them away as men with jobs, as amateurs.

As Émile tried to draw the model, the studio was silent but for the flutter of pigeons on the glass high above and the scratch of pencil on paper. He tried to capture the bones beneath the skin, but he could not help noticing that the model's skin was not made of cool white marble; it sweated, it twitched, the muscles were not firm but slightly wasted. There were scars and the marks left by badly fitting shoes and the fastenings of clothes, and the model's face had the ruddy complexion of a heavy drinker. When, finally, the model was allowed to relax, he had to unfold himself out of his position, as every joint and every muscle ached with the effort of staying still. It was not an easy pose to hold.

The tutor passed among the students, making comments and using his own pencil to correct a line or emphasize a contour. When he reached Émile, however, he stood and stared at his drawing for a moment in silence and then moved on. It was then that Émile realized that the other drawings in the room bore no real resemblance to the model in front of them; the artists had all drawn Adam.

At lunchtime, some of the students had packed up their easels and either headed back down the hill — they sat in the shade of cafés like Le Chat Noir — or climbed higher to the café beneath Le Moulin de la Galette. The tutor wiped his nose on his sleeve and then began to sketch the model's upper body, each muscle, every bone, picked out in light and shade.

"I learned to draw from drawing corpses," he told the ones who remained. "At the Académie. They do not get cramps or tire easily. Oh yes, the dead are indeed a joy to draw."

Without any warning, an image entered Émile's head: Gabrielle, her body naked, her eyes open, and her skin the smooth flawless white of a corpse. He was gripped with a sense that something awful would happen to her and it would be his fault. It suddenly seemed as if he was going to suffocate; he struggled to inhale enough air. He loosened his tie, then gathered up his jacket and rolled up his sketch. Once outside, he tried to calm down, to breathe normally. He put his hand against the cold stone of the courtyard wall and let its rough surface chafe his skin. There were other women, women whose lives were not shot through with tragedy and addiction, women who were not already married. He would write her a letter; he would end it tomorrow.

7

With a hiss of brakes and the long, low sigh of the train's whistle, the London train came to a stop on the tracks just outside St. Enoch Station in Glasgow. They were on the bridge high above the Clyde. It was dark, but Cait could still make out the paddle steamers tied up along the Broomielaw, the loom of dredgers, the black spindles of the steam cranes unloading cargoes of coal and, in the distance, the lights of the Govan ferry. Nothing had changed since they had left for Europe; the air was still hazy with coal smoke, the skies still threatened rain, and there was a thick, damp fog rolling in from the Kilpatrick hills. Even the smell was the same — rust and soot, collieries and roasting hops from the brewery. The train finally jerked twice and began to roll into the station. Cait sank a little farther into the seat; after six months of traveling, they were finally home.

"I wonder if anyone will be here to meet us," said Alice.

"I shouldn't think so," Jamie replied. "Out of sight, out of mind, as they say."

"Did you send that telegram in London?" she asked.

Jamie clapped his hand to his mouth. "I knew there was something I was supposed to do!"

Alice looked momentarily horrified.

"He's teasing," Cait said.

"I knew that," she replied with more emphasis than was necessary.

As soon as they had come to a standstill in the vaulted glass and iron cavern of the station, the second- and third-class passengers hurried off the train and streamed in one huge mass toward the omnibus stop and the taxi rank. The first-class passengers, however, took their time. They climbed down and congregated on the platform as dozens of porters swarmed into the carriages to unload their cases and trunks, traveling bags and paper parcels onto a flotilla of wooden trolleys. And then, once their baggage had been checked and checked again, some waved to their drivers while others headed off toward the main entrance to wait for their carriages.

Of course, there was a welcoming party

for Jamie and Alice. After a suitable pause, they stepped off the train to a round of applause.

"At last!" squealed three young girls as they rushed to embrace Alice. "Did you see everything?"

"Everything!" Alice replied. "And it was wonderful!"

Cait smiled as she pushed her hair into her hat and fastened her traveling cloak. Not the Panthéon, *too busy;* not the great cathedral at Chartres, *too dark;* and not the Duomo in Siena, *too boring.* But it was true that she had seen a great many stations and grand hotels and shopping arcades.

As she waited for the porter to lift her case off the train, Cait noticed a man waiting on the fringes of the crowd with a bunch of red roses in his hand. Alice must have noticed him too but was pretending she hadn't. After a moment, however, it seemed as if he considered he had waited long enough.

"Look here, Miss Arrol," he announced so loudly that everyone turned. "I was informed that you would be arriving today. I was here for the nine thirty-eight. Unfortunately my informant was mistaken that you had taken that train, since you had in fact boarded the ten forty-three. Did you receive my letters?"

The welcoming party parted to allow him access to its heart, to Alice. A rush of panic crossed her face.

"Mr. Hogg, what a surprise," she said. "And roses. How generous!"

She had indeed received his letters. She had just never gotten around to replying to them.

"Well, did you?" he asked again.

"No!" Alice lied. "I'm afraid not, Mr. Hogg. On the Continent the post is very unreliable. But never mind. How nice to see you again."

Mr. Hogg, who had suffered some kind of unfortunate skin condition as a boy, had a face as pitted and coarse as the skin of a Seville orange. And yet his eyes were of a vivid blue. His skin, however disfigured, now glowed with expectation, with pleasure, while his upper lip glistened with a thin film of sweat.

"You're looking —" began Mr. Hogg. But he had no adjectives or metaphors at his disposal. He was not, he often announced, an expressive kind of man. And so he left the sentence hanging unfinished and then cleared his throat.

Alice blinked and smoothed down her dress. And then she fixed her face into an expression that sought to hide her disappointment.

"Mr. Hogg is in the butchering trade," Alice explained to her friend.

"Pies," said Mr. Hogg succinctly.

Someone stifled a giggle. From another platform a whistle blew, and with a great sigh of steam and smoke, a train prepared to leave.

"Well," said Alice. "We must —"

"Indeed," said Mr. Hogg with several nods of his head. And then Alice let out a squeal.

"It's Tiffie!" she said as a girl in a huge white hat approached. Behind her a man in his late thirties, her husband of a year, glanced at his watch. As the welcoming party shifted to admit Alice's friend, Mr. Hogg and the husband were both excluded.

In all the furor, Cait had climbed down from the carriage without anyone noticing. Alice did at one point glance over her shoulder as if she had forgotten something, and Jamie caught her eye and gave a small private wave, but then they were both swiftly swept away by nephews and cousins and school friends and long-lost acquaintances. Cait watched as the Arrols and their entourage made their way through the station, their voices shrill, their laughter filling the empty concourse. Four porters hurried behind them, each pulling trolleys piled high with luggage. Mr. Hogg trailed in their wake, the roses still in his hand, unsure if he was invited to wherever they were going.

Now there was only one case left on the platform and it was hers. A porter looked around to see if there was anyone else, a man, to tell him what to do. When she was first married, it used to amuse her, the way drivers and porters were deaf to her voice and only seemed to hear her husband's. Did she have to speak louder, or lower, to be heard?

"Madam," the porter asked, "does this belong to you?"

They both looked down at the suitcase, shabby from six months' use. It did not look like much, considering.

"Yes," she said. "It's mine."

"You're not being met by anyone?" he asked.

She shook her head no.

"Where to, then?" he asked as he picked up the case.

"The rank," she told him. "I'll take a hansom."

It was as they were walking through the station, she a little behind the porter, that she noticed William Arrol standing beneath the clock, tapping the tip of his huge umbrella on the ground impatiently. Now that the London train had disembarked, the station was almost deserted. As soon as he saw her, he raised a finger and marched across.

"Mrs. Wallace, what a pleasure to see you back home safe," he said. "Did you have an interesting time?"

"Very," she replied.

His eyes darted over her shoulder.

"I'm afraid you missed them," she said. "By about ten minutes."

He looked disconcerted. "I got held up at the office."

Outside, it started to rain, a sudden downpour that thundered onto the glass of the station roof. He paused and glanced up.

"We ordered it in especially," he said. "To welcome you home."

For a second she wasn't sure how to respond. And then she realized he was joking.

"Why, thank you." She smiled. "And how is business?"

"The construction of the Forth Rail Bridge is going well," he said. "I'm just back from Queensferry. And the new Tay Bridge will open to traffic in July."

"Will there be a ceremony?" she asked.

"Not this time," he said softly. "Out of respect."

He paused. "How are you getting home,

incidentally? Is anyone meeting you?"

"I'm going to take a cab," she said brightly.

It took a moment for her words to register. And when they did, he seemed shocked.

"I'm so sorry. My nephew should have sorted this out."

"No, really," she said. "It's fine."

"My coachman will take you," he said. "I insist. It's the least I could do to thank you for bringing them both back in one piece."

"You haven't seen them yet," she replied.

He frowned at her for an instant and then let out a short blast of a laugh.

"Aye, right," he said.

William Arrol was a large man with hands as wide and short as trowels. As if to make up for the hands, his lack of education, and his impoverished background, he was always beautifully dressed, his white hair combed, his muttonchops trimmed, his collar freshly laundered. And yet, although he may have been unaware of it, he betrayed himself in a multitude of tiny ways; he wore too much cologne, his sleeves were cut a little too short, he mispronounced words, such as *premise* and *expertise* and *emphasis*. Once you got to know him, however, he revealed the kind of intelligence that could not be learned from a book.

"I appreciated your letters," he said as

they walked through the station. "Your regular updates. Always cheered up my breakfast. Thank you for taking the time."

"It was the least I could do," she said. "And how is Mrs. Arrol?"

Only the tiniest twitch in his eye suggested how difficult he found the question to answer. It was rumored, rather unkindly, that Arrol's wife was "soft in the brain." She rarely went out and was always said to be suffering from some ailment or other. He was building a house in Ayr for her with a vast conservatory and a view of the Firth of Clyde.

"Better," he replied. "Thank you for asking."

As she climbed into his carriage, he stood on the curb holding the umbrella high above her head to shelter her from the rain.

"What about you?" she called out. "How will you get home?"

"I'll walk," he said. "I like a stroll in the evening."

"But the rain?" she began.

"I'm made of stronger stuff than rain," he replied. "I promise you I won't rust. And Mrs. Wallace, I'm sure we'll see each other again soon, but in the meantime if I can do anything for you, just ask."

And with a bang of his hand on the roof,

he signaled for the driver to move off.

Apart from the pile of unopened mail that lay on the floor, her apartment was exactly as it had been when she had left it. The main door still creaked and needed oil, her old straw hat still hung on the hat stand in the hallway, the bed was made up without a crease in the counterpane. And yet, everything felt cold to the touch, every surface was covered in a layer of dust. The window in the kitchen had been left open a crack and it had let in six months of damp and dirty Glasgow air. Outside, a train let off a low exclamation as it hurtled south toward Crossmyloof. She could hear the murmur of conversation in the flat below, the short judder of a man's laugh and the higher pitch of a woman's voice.

She lit the lamp and walked through the rooms, seeing them now as a stranger might. The ceilings were high but the rooms meanly proportioned. The furniture, all chosen for a different house on a larger scale, seemed crammed into the space, leaving little room to move around. In the pantry, the cupboards were filled with stacks of bone-china plates and soup tureens, the drawers with boxes of cutlery and fish slices, and in her bedroom, the linen press was stacked with Indian cotton sheets and embroidered tablecloths for dinner parties and family parties and christenings that never happened. She saw now it was a repository for expectations that had been scaled down, a museum to a life not lived.

The morning they had left Paris the sky had been a fathomless blue, the air so clear and clement that everything they were about to leave behind — the streets, the people, the smell of roasted coffee and chestnuts — seemed sharper, the colors deeper and more saturated, the verticals and perpendiculars of the city engraved rather than drawn. And in the distance, so faint that it might have been imagined rather than heard, the regular rhythm of hammer on iron.

Cait had been adamant that they arrive at Gare du Nord at least an hour before departure. As she hurried Alice and Jamie into the station and organized their luggage, she had rushed and fussed and scolded and tipped. Reservations, connecting trains, newspapers and refreshments, porters, ticket officers, conductors, and fellow passengers were all she would let herself think about. On their trip around Europe, she had been the one who had smoothed the way, persuading museum attendants to let them in at closing time, reserving the best seats in theaters or trains; organizing what Jamie labeled her "little miracles."

That morning, however, if she had paused for just one moment, if she had let herself dwell on the fact that they were leaving Paris, France, the Continent, that they were going back to Scotland, she knew that her eyes would begin to fill and the pea-sized lump in her throat would swell. Cait wasn't friendless; she wasn't alone. Although her parents had passed away, there was her sister and her young family to visit. Anne was married to Saul's younger sibling, George Wallace. He was like Saul and yet he was very different; he had none of his elder brother's restless energy. But more significant, he didn't have Saul's temper. For that Cait was glad.

She had bought the family small gifts, tiny glass animals from Rome and wooden string puppets from Germany. And yet she couldn't face them right now, she couldn't face their sympathy and concern, no matter how well-meaning; she couldn't face that moment when she would find herself standing outside their house, just before she was about to ring the bell, when she knew she would soon be bathed in the warmth of the light and the sound of the children's laughter from inside. It was a lacking, a wanting; she would rather be alone than feel bereft.

Here, in her cold drawing room with its view over the railway line, she sat in her traveling cloak and watched the flickers from the spluttering lamp dance across the floorboards. How could she stay here? How could she possibly leave? She closed her eyes and let her head sink to her knees.

Cait dreamed of the spike of Eiffel's tower, blackened iron that would puncture the clouds above. She dreamed of a man behind a camera watching her through a tiny lens. She dreamed that Émile Nouguier was asking her a question but she had no idea what he was saying. She woke with a start with a crick in her neck and pins and needles in her arm. The damask of the divan had left its pattern on her skin. The clock on the mantel read half past six. It was still dark. Outside, however, the road was already busy with coal merchants and milk carts and bakers' vans trundling over the railway line to Strathbungo.

She stood up and stretched, then went through to the bathroom and washed her face. She would make a list; she would organize her day. There were clothes to be sent to the laundry and groceries to order, letters to answer and financial affairs to attend to. And then, once she had recovered from the journey, she would go and see the church minister and offer her services as before. She had enough money now to keep her going, if she was frugal, for a couple of years at least. And then what? Well, she would just have to cross that bridge when she came to it, as her grandmother used to say. There would be plenty to occupy her for the time being; visiting the sick, decorating the church for holy days, and raising money for orphans in Africa. It was what widows of a certain class did. They gave a helping hand; their time was consumed with projects of a charitable nature often in distant lands. She saw now it was not entirely selfless — it kept their minds from dwelling on the aching emptiness of their daily lives.

Cait took off her traveling clothes, laid them on the bed, and opened the wardrobe. Here were the clothes she had left behind, the gray walking dresses and mourning gowns in black and lilac. They had hung untouched for months, the ghost of her arm inside the sleeves and the faint scent of her perfume along the neckline. She touched the crepe, the bombazine, the Melrose, and the Henrietta, the fabric stiff beneath her fingertips. A moth fluttered out from between the drapes and folds and she watched it flap around blindly in the pale morning light.

A week later, she stood in the dressmaker's with a couple of swatches of cloth in her hand.

"In this red?" the dressmaker said.

"And one in the blue paisley," Cait confirmed.

"With the smaller bustle?"

"That's right. In Paris everyone is wearing them smaller now."

"I'll get to them right away," the dressmaker said.

There was a note of doubt in her voice, however, that Cait felt obliged to address.

"I'm not romantically involved with a Frenchman, if that's what you're thinking. But it does you a world of good — travel, I mean. Even a day out to Troon is a tonic. Do you know Troon?"

"No," the dressmaker said.

Cait ran her fingers along the bales of fabric, the satins and velvets, the voiles and cottons in every color from the palest mustard to the darkest purple. The dressmaker, a thin woman in her fifties who wore lavender-colored crepe, had been recommended by Alice.

"Should be ready in a fortnight," she said with a closed smile once she had tallied up

112

the price. "Good day, Mrs. Wallace."

As Cait walked along Buchanan Street toward the train station, she looked up. The sun was setting and the sky had turned a deep rose. The sandstone of the tenement blocks on the street across the road glowed crimson. It was the first day it hadn't rained since she had returned.

As she turned onto Gordon Street, she was suddenly filled with doubt. Earlier that week she had deposited William Arrol's check in the bank. In one day, however, she had spent far more than she intended. New dresses made out of decent cloth were expensive, especially if they were made by Alice Arrol's dressmaker. What had she done? How could she have been so extravagant? Why on earth had she spent so much money? What was the point when no one was looking, when there was no one to notice what she wore? It was only the prospect of the dressmaker's scorn that prevented her from turning around, going back, and canceling her order.

A continuous stream of traffic, horses and carts, trams and hansom cabs, headed down Jamaica Street in the direction of the river. The station entrance was on the other side of the road. As she waited for a gap, she could smell the smoke and steam of the

113

locomotives inside the station; she could hear the loudspeaker calling out the names of the stations: *Whifflet, Ardrossan Harbour,* and *Cathcart Circle.* The traffic was relentless; she would miss her train at this rate. Eventually the traffic thinned a little and she started to cross. And then a voice called out from behind.

"Mrs. Wallace! Hold on a minute!"

It was Jamie Arrol. Beside him was an elderly man she didn't recognize.

"I knew it was you," Jamie said. "Only a lady with real class would step with such confidence out into the middle of a busy Glasgow thoroughfare."

"I'm not sure if that is a compliment or not," she said with a smile. "How have you been keeping?"

"Well, thank you. Missed me?"

"I've missed you and Miss Arrol, yes."

"I thought you'd be glad to be shot of us both." He laughed.

"Not at all."

"The French call ladies of Mrs. Wallace's caliber *formidable,*" Jamie explained to his companion.

"I see," he replied. "It does indeed sound like a compliment, although I am not familiar with the French language."

In response, Jamie thumped the old man

on the back as if he had cracked a joke.

"Anyways. My sister mentioned that you had an appointment with her dressmaker this afternoon," Jamie resumed. "I thought I might bump into you. And here you are! It is my great pleasure to introduce a dear friend. This is Mr. Sinclair."

"Delighted to make your acquaintance," said Mr. Sinclair, holding out his hand. "I've heard a lot about you."

"Really," she said as she shook his hand and looked with some alarm at Jamie.

"Our adventures in the Continent are the talk of the town," he bluffed. "And you, my dear Mrs. Wallace, have a starring role."

A crowded omnibus was approaching, the clatter of its wheels on the cobbles so loud that for a moment they couldn't talk.

"Don't worry," Jamie clarified once it had passed. "You always come out well."

Mr. Sinclair smiled and the two points of his ample white mustache wiggled ever so slightly. Apart from the mustache, he was completely bald, with just a wisp of hair flying loose behind his left ear.

"I'd say rather more than well," he added.

He shifted his weight from one leg to the other and smiled down at her. But he was so tall, and his eyes so magnified behind the glass of his wire-rimmed spectacles, that she could not meet his gaze.

"How is life at the ironworks?" she asked Jamie.

"Can't complain," he replied. "But I won't be there for long, I hope. I have plans, as you know."

He gave her the hint of a smile. She had learned to be wary of Jamie's plans. After being discussed at length, after books had been bought and expert opinions sought, they were always, without exception, unceremoniously dropped. Most of Jamie's passions didn't last long, a couple of weeks at the most. It was the same with women. Jamie could turn from smitten to totally uninterested in the course of a couple of hours. The women whom he had courted and then cast aside so rapidly were sometimes heartbroken but often angry. The lucky ones retained some form of compensation, jewelry or scent that he had bought them in a fit of amorous generosity. The rest would wonder what they had done or said or worn to make him cool so quickly. It was not Cait's place to reassure them that it was unlikely to have been their fault. It was not her place to say anything. But she felt for them, for those poor young women who would learn to harden themselves against men, against hurt, against risk, and whose lives would be poorer because of it.

"What kind of plans?" she asked tentatively.

"Right now I'm not at liberty to say," he replied. "But I'm sure you can guess."

The conversation lulled. Neither man, however, seemed in any rush to go. She heard a whistle and visualized her train letting off a blast of steam on the platform. She would endeavor to bring the exchange to a close as quickly as possible.

"Are you in the city on business, Mr. Sinclair?" she asked. "Or pleasure?"

His right hand gravitated immediately to his left wrist. With a glance, she noticed that he was wearing a mourning bracelet — no, not one but two, each one woven out of human hair, one dark and one fair.

"I had an appointment with a solicitor," he said. "My dear wife passed on a few months ago and there were affairs to sort out."

"I'm so sorry. May I offer my condolences?"

"Many thanks," he said. "It was expected."

This was a conversation that clearly could not be rushed. Mr. Sinclair took off his spectacles and polished them with his pocket handkerchief. And then he gave a brief summation of his life and losses so far.

"They're together at last," he said with a small smile. "In God's arms."

"Mr. Sinclair is an old family friend," Jamie explained after a respectful pause. "I was at school with his nephew. What line are you in again?"

"Ironmongery," he replied as he replaced his spectacles.

"Gourock, isn't it?" Jamie asked.

"Greenock," he corrected. "The shop is on Market Street. We live on the Esplanade. You know the Esplanade, Mrs. Wallace?"

"I'm afraid not, Mr. Sinclair," she replied.

"By we, I mean my sister, Miss Amelia Sinclair, and I," he felt compelled to explain. "The house is now rather too big for the two of us, but it's hard to give up such wonderful vistas across the River Clyde."

Once again, they stood in silence and Cait contemplated the grim scenario of a dead wife and child, a spinster sister, and a beautiful view.

"Well, this has been an unexpected pleasure," she said once the interlude had stretched to an acceptable length. "I'm afraid I have a train to catch."

Jamie's elbow gave his friend a sharp, short jab in the side. Mr. Sinclair's face suddenly reddened.

"Church," he bellowed.

Cait stared at him. His mustache had started to quiver.

"I was wondering," he went on, "if you'd do me the pleasure, Mrs. Wallace, the pleasure of allowing me to accompany you to church?"

He rubbed his nose. His hands, she noticed, were shaking too. Jamie was watching her expectantly.

"Well, I . . ." she began. "I'm flattered, but . . ."

"Go on," said Jamie. "I've been singing your praises to my dear friend here all afternoon. I've been telling him about your charm, your beauty, your sophistication. And then, what serendipity, here you are!"

A young man, just passing, overheard and looked over at her appraisingly. This time it was Cait's face that flushed.

"Would you?" Mr. Sinclair asked hesitantly.

Maybe it was this softness, the crack in his voice and the glaze in his eye, that made her change her mind. But in truth, how could she refuse and not appear rude?

"Very well." She nodded.

Mr. Sinclair sighed, but then he looked slightly puzzled.

"When I'm in Glasgow I usually attend St. Andrews in the Square," he said. "Would that be acceptable? And then we could go for a stroll through the Green. If the rain holds off."

She momentarily stiffened. She had married Saul in that church. But how could he have known?

"That would be fine."

"Shall I send a carriage?"

"No. I'll meet you outside. At quarter to eleven."

"Splendid," he replied.

Jamaica Street was suddenly empty, no buses or hansom cabs, apart from a solitary rag-and-bone man and his cart. After she had said goodbye, she ducked behind it, ran up the steps, and caught the train with only seconds to spare. All the way back to Pollokshields West, however, she stared out at the factories and tenements, their windows bright rectangles of light, and wondered what on earth she had agreed to.

"I think about him," she told her sister.

Anne blinked. Her mind was on the baby who lay in her lap and who had finally fallen asleep after an hour of grizzling, the baby who was almost impossible to lift and place in the crib without waking up.

"The thing is," Cait went on, "I don't even know him. I only met him twice. And there is no possibility . . ."

Cait stopped. For a moment they were both silent. What else was there to say on the matter? After raising her finger to her lips, Anne rose as smoothly as she could and placed the baby, her fourth, in the cot. He woke, cried a little, then settled again.

"At last," she whispered. "He's teething, I think. Now. Where were we? Oh yes, Mr. Sinclair? Well, what do you think of him? He's rather elderly, but he certainly is eligible!"

"Have you been listening to anything I've been saying?"

"Of course I have!"

Her sister blinked several times. Cait had to quell the desire to scream, to rage at her sister's blithe acceptance of so much good fortune: healthy children, a charming husband, a lovely home that was always warm and comfortable. Instead she sipped her cup of tepid tea.

"No, you haven't."

"Does Mr. Sinclair have children?"

Cait shook her head. "He had one, but she died of diphtheria as a baby."

"Oh," Anne said. She reached across and laid a hand on her own child as if she could ward off the disease with a touch. "How sad. But in some ways better. For you, I mean."

Cait gazed out the window at the bare winter tangle of trees in the garden. "Maybe," she said.

"In my opinion, for what it's worth," Anne said, "you just have to take what comes along."

"Anne," she interjected.

"After all, you have no idea how long it could be before the next one appears. If at all."

Cait looked at her sister. She spoke without irony, without guile; she had no idea about life, at least not her life.

"And about the Frenchman," Anne went on, "that engineer. Even if you do find yourself thinking about him, you have to make yourself stop."

For a moment they were silent. Although what Anne was suggesting sounded mercenary, she was probably right. She should just take what came along.

"And, I mean," Anne said with as much tact as she could muster, "nothing actually transpired with the engineer? He made no formal approach?"

Cait shook her head no.

"Actually, there was talk of matching him up with Alice," she said.

Anne looked relieved.

"But anyway, he's bound to have someone already," Cait went on. "There's bound to be a woman somewhere."

"He's French. He probably has two!" Anne paused. "Cait?"

Finally she looked up and met her sister's eye.

"I'd say possibly three," Cait replied. "Or maybe even more?"

"Not four?" whispered Anne.

And they started to laugh until they couldn't stop except to wipe their eyes, and the baby woke and let out an indignant wail at all the noise.

8

At Levallois-Perret, Émile worked seven days a week. While Maurice Koechlin and his team of draftsmen produced page after page of technical drawings, Émile oversaw the fabrication of every single individual part of the tower. Each piece had to have the rivet holes drilled in precisely the right place; on-site, everything had to be an exact fit.

After work, he usually stopped for a glass of claret at a bar beside the Parc de la Planchette. He hadn't heard from Gabrielle in more than a month. It was the best way, the clean break. Maybe she had left Paris. He imagined that she might be in New York or Boston, living the kind of life she wanted. He hoped she was happy. Although she would never know it, he had done everything in his power to make it so.

As he was searching for a few coins to pay the waiter, he noticed a newspaper lying on the bar. It was Wednesday, and on Wednesday evenings, if he was in Paris, he had dinner with his mother. According to his pocket watch he was already an hour late. He left some money on the counter, hurried out onto the street, and hailed a cab.

Madame Nouguier lived alone in an apartment in the sixteenth arrondissement that was far too large for one person. Most of the rooms had been closed since the death of Émile's father, the furniture swathed in cotton sheets to keep the dust at bay, and the blinds drawn across the windows. Now his mother spent most of her time in a small room at the back of the house that was conveniently placed near the kitchen and the bathroom. She had various afflictions that she alluded to but never fully explained and was regularly called upon by a young doctor whose patience seemed infinite. Émile sometimes suspected that she invented her symptoms just to keep the doctor coming. If that were so, did he know it and humor her? He was sure to overcharge her, and yet who, he wondered, was taking advantage of whom?

Although a housekeeper came in every day to cook, clean, and sometimes accompany his mother on a short drive in her carriage or a stroll to the lake in the Parc Monceau and back, he knew she must be lonely. He decided then and there that he would visit more often; he would drive her out of the city, maybe even take her on holiday.

"Maman!" Émile called as he let himself in.

His mother rose to her feet behind a small cluttered table to greet him. It held everything that she might need for the day: her cologne, her pen and ink, her medicines, her writing paper, her face powder, and boxes of her jewelry. She was almost seventy and although everything about her had softened — her clothes, the food she ate, even the light that filtered in from the window through the permanently drawn blinds — her mind was still as sharp as it had ever been.

"Émile," she said, and held out her hand. Even inside, even alone, she wore white gloves. He raised her hand to his mouth, as he always did, and kissed the stiff fabric.

"At last!" she said. "I was beginning to give up hope!"

"I'm so sorry. I was held up at work."

"Well," she said with a sigh of disappointment, "you're here now. I have a few things for you to sign. But you can do that after dinner."

As usual, her housekeeper had left two

plates of cold food on the counter. This time there was roast beef, tomato farcie, asparagus tart, and a basket of sliced bread, now stale. Once Émile had poured some wine into a couple of dusty crystal glasses, he carried the food to his mother's little table and sat down opposite her.

"Is this enough?" she asked. "Is the food to your taste?"

Although the smell of what she kept on her table infused the food and wine, and made everything taste of eau de toilette and syrup of figs, he assured her that it was perfect.

"And how have you been?" she asked once they had sat down.

"Not bad," he replied. "You?"

"Where do I begin?" she said.

First she recounted family news, babies born and people passing on, bouts of ill health and bad luck, all of which, since she was not immediately involved, she conveyed with unabashed relish. Most of the stories she had told him before, but he feigned surprise and amusement at the right moments as required. Finally a silence fell.

"You look tired," she said suddenly.

"I am, a little," he replied.

"Are you eating well?"

"Well enough."

"And your work?"

She said the word "work" with some disdain. After school, Émile had refused to go straight into the family business and help run the factory and instead had studied engineering and architecture at university. It had caused a small scandal at the time. Maison Soucht had been in the family since the sixteenth century and produced glass and lead crystal: wine decanters, enameled lamps, and Christmas tree baubles — all beautifully handcrafted. When Émile had joined Eiffel's company and begun to design and construct bridges, his parents had believed it was only a phase. The Nouguiers were not employees and never had been. Almost twenty years later, however, she was still waiting for him to grow out of it.

It hadn't been an issue until the sudden death of his elder brother, Bertrand, eighteen months earlier. Now, as the only son and sole heir, the factory and everything connected with it belonged to Émile. So far, however, he'd had as little to do with it as possible. Once a week, after dinner at his mother's, he signed checks, he went over accounts, he tried to foster an interest in the business. Without Bertrand, however, the factory had begun to lose money. Émile blamed the recession, but he knew his mother blamed him.

"The tower is going well," he told her. "You must come and visit the site."

Louise Nouguier sliced her tomato in two and loaded a small amount of food onto her fork, but didn't agree to anything.

"That's not what they are saying in the newspaper," she said.

"Good news doesn't sell papers," he said.

His mother was an avid newspaper reader. But rather than argue with him, she let it drop.

"So?" she said, and looked up at Émile expectantly.

The food stuck in his throat as he swallowed. How could so small a word become so loaded?

"Mother," he warned, "if I had any news of that nature I would have told you."

She sighed, put down her cutlery, and glanced down at the Persian carpet.

"I must get this carpet cleaned," she said vaguely. "Before I pass it on to you."

Her tone was reproachful. Was this part of the bargain: she passed on the carpet and in return, he did what she wanted? It was a high price to pay for a carpet. Didn't she realize that he had no strong attachment to the things that she so diligently retained for him?

"Aren't you going to eat?" he asked.

She shook her head.

"I ate a little before you arrived," she said. "And I find Fauchon too rich sometimes."

He finished his food with her eyes on him.

"Dessert?" she asked. "There is crème caramel on the counter. It will only go to waste if you don't want it."

"Aren't you having any?" he asked.

She waved away the idea with her hand.

"At my age you want very little," she said.

But he knew what she desperately did want: for him to take responsibility for Maison Soucht, to provide her with a well-bred daughter-in-law, to produce some grandchildren who would to keep the Nouguier lineage going and confirm that her life had not been an exercise in loss but added up, like the arithmetic she had never been at liberty to study.

Her marriage to Émile's father, like most of the marriages in her social circle, had been arranged by their parents. She barely knew Cedric Nouguier when she walked down the aisle and yet the future of both families depended on a successful union. The factory needed to modernize, and it was her dowry that had financed the purchase of a new coal-fired furnace. Her younger sisters remained unmarried —

there was no more money for their dowries — and they both still lived modestly on allowances provided by the business. Louise Nouguier seemed to think that her son was unaware of what was at stake, of how much self-sacrifice and good faith had been invested over the decades, of how this unspoken arrangement was a cornerstone of everything she believed in. Women were facilitators, supporting structures, like the wooden scaffolding they were using to construct the tower. And he suddenly felt sorry for her, a life lived out by proxy. Even now she was watching him as he ate, savoring each mouthful as if she could experience the dessert by osmosis.

"Was it good?" she asked once the sweet custard and dark syrup was gone. He replied that it was excellent, but in truth he had barely tasted it.

After she had made him a coffee — small, black, strong — she produced a pile of checks, each one already made out to one of the dependents.

"Your aunt needed a little more this month," his mother told him. "She has been unwell. Would that be all right?"

"You know you don't have to ask," he replied.

"Bertrand always wanted to know," she

said, "if the figures changed. And your father never signed anything until he'd checked the books."

"I'm sure it's all in order," he said, then signed them one by one with a flourish.

Saying good night was always difficult. His mother's parting embrace seemed perfunctory enough, but he knew how hard it was for her. He hated to leave her alone in the huge apartment that had once been full of life, and yet he couldn't wait to escape; the atmosphere was as thick and viscous as burnt caramel.

"Try not to be late next week," his mother gently chided.

"I'll do my very best," he replied.

"And a little good news," she said, "would do me the power of good."

Outside he inhaled deeply, desperate for a rush of fresh air to fill his lungs. If only Bertrand had not died. If only his older brother had married and had had a son or two then he wouldn't be in this position. Rather than hail a cab, Émile decided to walk, to clear his head. As he made for home he gradually calmed down; he tried to see the situation objectively. He was only forty-one; he had plenty of time to find a girl, marry her, and have children. Or a woman, a woman like the Scottish one. At the thought of her, however, he felt a chime of regret; he would never see that one again.

The *allumeurs de réverbères* lit the gas lamps along the great boulevards and avenues with their long poles. The lights glowed like golden orbs compared to the brilliance of the spluttering electric-arc illuminations on the Place de l'Opéra. But the rest of Paris was dark at night, the city spread out beyond the bright streets like a bolt of the blackest cloth. Walking home had seemed like a good idea at the time, when the sky in the west was still ablaze with the setting sun. But night had fallen faster than a theatrical curtain, he had lost his bearings, and he had ended up in the narrow pitch-black streets of the Marais. He started to walk more quickly than before, each footstep taken with a heavy, deliberate stride to deter any potential robber or murderer or thief who could be lurking in a doorway. Even though his mind urged him to run, he kept a steady pace and cleared his throat or coughed at regular intervals, just to give an impression — untrue — that he was unafraid. At one point, a door opened suddenly — a luminous rectangle of yellow light — and made him jump. A man appeared in silhouette and was pushed out by a large woman, who yelled that he was never to come back. The door slammed, and for a moment both he and the man were left in total darkness. And then the door opened again, the woman moaned, and the man was pulled back through the door into her ample embrace.

Émile hurried on: left, then right, then left until, to his profound relief, he stumbled upon the gray stone facade of the Louvre. He managed to reorient himself; it was not far, he realized as he crossed Pont des Arts and strode along the Quai de Conti, not far at all. Finally, there was his own street, there was his building, and there at last, the door to his apartment.

There was a lamp lit in his bedroom. Although he couldn't remember leaving it on, he was glad of its illumination as he slipped his key in to the lock. He glanced quickly behind him to check he wasn't being followed, then opened the door and stepped into the internal courtyard as quietly as he could so he wouldn't wake the concierge, a bad-tempered man from Avignon.

He took the stairs rather than wait for the elevator. On the landing below his own he could hear the sound of someone singing softly. It was coming from his apartment. Although he'd never heard her sing before, he recognized Gabrielle's voice. The concierge must have let her in. His head swam with a mixture of the claret he had drunk and his own unease as he unlocked the door.

Gabrielle lay on his bed, her eyes closed, her hair loose, and her dress pushed up around her thighs. Around the walls, every single one facing the wall, were the paintings he had bought at the Société des Artistes Indépendants exhibition. They had been stacked in the hallway, the canvases parceled up and unopened since they had been delivered. And now the floor was covered in torn paper and pieces of string, testimony to how frantically the wrappings had been ripped off.

For a moment he didn't move. He waited for her to sense his presence. But it was soon clear that she was oblivious, she was distracted, delirious. As he watched, she sat up, pulled a metal syringe from her bag and slowly rolled down the top of her stocking. Émile seized her wrist before she could push the plunger. Her head fell back as she turned and tried to focus on him, her eyes half-closed and her mouth ajar.

"You!" she said. "I thought it was just me and the dark muse." She glanced down. The white of her thigh bloomed blue and purple where the needle had already entered.

"What have you done?" he whispered.

"My dear Émile," she replied, "I could ask the same question of you?"

And now he saw that each of the paintings around the walls had been ripped, the canvas torn from top to bottom. A kitchen knife lay on the ground below the window.

"You could have told me," she went on. "Why did you buy them, you of all people? And I thought, I thought at last that all this meant something —"

"Gabrielle," he butted in.

"Don't speak. You're only making it worse."

Émile crossed the room and picked up the kitchen knife. He ran his finger along the torn edge of one of the canvases, the surface now slack and curling, the paint cracked and peeling. As he cleaned the blade, he finally let the surge of indignity, of self-righteousness, race through him. Was it so bad, what he had done? Her husband hadn't seemed to think so; in fact, he had been very persuasive.

Gabrielle was still sitting motionless on the bed with the syringe in her lap. She looked small, vulnerable, pathetic. He wondered if a single centime of his money had gone to her child.

"*Chérie,*" he began, "if I did anything that hurt you, it wasn't intentional."

136

"You knew exactly what you were doing," she replied. "You wanted to humiliate me."

"I wanted to help —"

"Like hell you did."

He blinked as his eyes welled and his throat narrowed. What right did she have to speak to him like this?

"I'm sorry," he began, "but I never intended . . ."

"Stop!" she yelled.

She covered her face with her hands and started to sob, to cry in great heaving gasps. It was unbearable. He went to her; he knelt before her, cupping her bare shoulders with his hands.

"Gabrielle," he whispered.

"Don't touch me!" she yelled, pushing him away and rubbing the top of her arms as if his fingers had scalded her. *"Get out!"*

Her eyes were as hard and unyielding as enamel. And so he turned, let himself out of the room, and set down a chair facing the bedroom door. Early the next morning, just as the sky was lightening, the door opened. Gabrielle was dressed and made up. Without a word, she walked past him and let herself out the front door.

A week later his concierge sent him a message at work. He was to come at once. He found Gabrielle wrapped in a blanket in front of the fire. Her face was white, her lips bitten, and her eyes sunk deep into her head. He sent for his doctor, who came within the hour. After a brief examination, he recommended bed rest and Indian hemp. The next day, Émile sent a note to her husband explaining that she was safe. He received no answer.

"I have to go back to work," he told her. "And I must see my mother. But I will be back after that."

He went to the office, tried to catch up with everything he had missed, and then he spent a few hours with Madame Nouguier. After dinner he looked over the glassworks accounts and signed some checks before making his excuses and heading home. He needn't have rushed. The ashes in the fireplace were cold. Gabrielle had been gone for hours.

The trees were a haze of new green in the Bois de Boulogne. The air was filled with the rich smell of the damp earth, while up above flocks of starlings blotted and wheeled in a sky of the emptiest blue. The coachman dropped him off at the main gate of the park, at the Porte Dauphine, and Émile declined his offer of help to carry his large bundle. On foot, he crossed the path to the lakes and the other to the racecourse and set off to find a secluded spot somewhere near the river. Once he heard the crack of a musket fired nearby. It was a little late in the day for a duel, but still they came, the wronged husbands and the audacious lovers, the insulted and the abandoned, squabbling over women like gulls over a fish.

The pyre of paintings caught fire easily. The wood of the frames spat sparks as they split, and the canvas curled and shivered before it turned to ash. Émile watched the lick of flames as it crept along Gabrielle's pale skin, her face, her smile, turning them black before wiping them out forever with one gentle stroke.

9

Even at night, Glasgow seemed to glow. The great furnaces of the Caledonian Railway Locomotive Works in Springburn and the shipbuilding yards and rolling mills of Fairfield's in Govan roared all night, turning the low-lying clouds that blew in from the Campsies a dirty ochre. That evening, a new locomotive was being taken from St. Rollox to Stobcross Quay on a horse-drawn dray. There it would be loaded by crane onto a boat and shipped out to India or South Africa or China. Some of the men who had worked on the locomotive — the iron molders and the boilermakers, the smiths and the erectors — paraded behind it all the way to the docks. Others applauded from the pavements or waved from their windows as the huge steam train passed by at little more than walking pace, its vast boiler and chimney cap carried slowly along almost twelve feet above the cobblestones.

The tram that Cait was riding on stopped to let the steam train pass. Everyone strained in their seats or crowded forward to the driver's cab to get a better view.

"They must be making one of those a fortnight," the driver called out over his shoulder.

"Wherever there's a railway," said a man at his elbow, "you'll find the work of a Glaswegian."

The city lay beneath a fug of smog and smur. At William Arrol's ironworks in Dalmarnock, the yard was full of steel girders on their way to the Queensferry workshop for the new Forth Bridge. Arrol's office was on the first floor above the erecting shop. In his letter he'd asked if she could drop by sometime the following day to see him about a personal matter. Cait's timing was unfortunate, his secretary told her. Arrol had just been given the news that a twenty-year-old rigger had died in a fall from the Forth Bridge construction site.

"Shall I come back another time?" Cait asked.

"Mr. Arrol always keeps his appointments," she replied.

Cait knocked on his door and was commanded to enter. Inside the office the shutters were closed and the fire was lit. At first, although the room was stuffy with tobacco, it seemed as if no one was there. Then somewhere, glass clinked against glass. Whiskey, she could smell it, was poured.

"I keep telling them," William Arrol said, "that if they work high they must use the safety cages. Have you informed his family yet?"

She saw now that Arrol was sitting in an armchair facing the windows with a whiskey decanter in his hand.

"Mr. Arrol," she said. "It's me."

He turned and his face screwed up in the light from the door behind her. "Mrs. Wallace," he said. "Of course. My apologies."

He stood up, put the decanter of whiskey back on the tray, and turned on a lamp. On his desk a huge drawing was held flat at each end by two cabinet cards. With a glance she saw that both cards were photographic portraits of his wife, Elizabeth.

"I'm sorry to hear the bad news," she said.

"What can you do?" he said. "These young fellows, they are foolhardy, reckless. Actually, it's exactly this that I wanted to see you about. Tea?"

"Please."

"I hear that congratulations may be in order?"

"Excuse me?" she said.

"An engagement? At least, that's what the jungle drums are saying. Please, sit down, I won't be a moment."

Of course she had been expecting it, she had seen Sinclair's proposal coming — how could she not? It was in the deferential bow of his head and the flourish of his handwriting when he wrote out her name, it was in his light touch in the middle of her back and the way he examined her when he thought she wouldn't notice, like a horse that he was considering purchasing. After all, he had told her, it made perfect sense. Although he was older, they were united in the loss of a spouse. And yet the fingers of his right hand still rolled those hair bracelets around and around his wrist. Would he ever remove them? Couldn't he put them away in a drawer? And just the thought of the cold strands of his first wife's and daughter's hair touching her skin filled her with revulsion.

"May I think about it?" she had replied when he had finally asked her. They were standing in the doorway of her tenement block to shelter from a burst of torrential rain. Sinclair's face had turned rigid in response. This hadn't been the answer he had been expecting.

"Of course," he said with a small guffaw. "How long?"

"A week," she said.

"But no longer," he clarified.

She was just about to let herself into the building when she noticed that he had something else to say.

"You must miss it," he said, "the conjugal duty."

"I beg your pardon?" she said.

"You were a married woman. Don't look so shocked. Even older fillies like a bit of sport at the right time of the month. Especially one like you — I can tell."

His mustache wiggled. His eyes were hidden by the shadows reflected in the glass of his spectacles.

"I await your answer with bated breath." And he then turned and hobbled off toward the railway station.

This had been six days earlier, and in that time she had barely slept. It wasn't only the fact that she felt absolutely no desire for Roland Sinclair, nothing but a vague heaviness behind her face, like the early onset of a cold. It was the fact that she had no good reason not to accept his proposal, at least none that she could admit. She was thirty-one years old; she had no income of her own. Roland Sinclair was solvent, he was unattached, he was respectable; it was a foregone conclusion. She would marry him and become Mrs. R. Sinclair. They would live on the Esplanade with his sister. And he would come to her for what he referred to as "sport."

Arrol came back into his office with a tray loaded up with a china tea set, two cups and saucers, and a cake.

"Sugar?" he asked once he had poured the tea and added milk.

She shook her head.

"No?" he said as he handed her the tea-cup. "By the looks of you, a little sweetness might do the power of good."

"Does everyone know?" she asked.

He raised his eyebrows and nodded sagely. She drank some tea, then placed the cup back in its saucer.

"I must give him an answer by tomorrow," she said.

Arrol stared at the floor for an instant before he spoke. "You don't have to agree," he said.

"How can I refuse?" Cait said. "I have no grounds."

And then she placed one hand over her face and sobbed. Arrol pulled a clean handkerchief out of his pocket and handed it to her. Outside on Dunn Street the sound of men drifted up as they laughed and teased and swore.

"I'm so sorry to trouble you again when you have so much on your plate already," she said as she wiped her face.

"No trouble," he replied. "A woman like you needs to be careful. Once bitten, twice shy. Isn't that what they say? Especially after what happened last time."

She stared at him. What did he know about her marriage?

"Last time?" she repeated.

Arrol gave her a puzzled look.

"They said it was cross-bracing. And the workmanship was inferior. But it was all poor, in my opinion. The design, the construction, and the maintenance."

"Ah yes. Of course."

She suddenly felt foolish, hysterical, and so she focused on folding up the handkerchief.

"The new Tay Bridge is finished, so I hear," she offered.

"It will open in July. Do you know how we're building the new bridge across the Forth?"

"Of course," she said. "It's very exciting."

"It is the first bridge in the world to be built entirely out of steel — not iron, but steel," he clarified. "The structures will work on the balanced cantilever principle; each of the three spans will initially stand alone. And then we will build them out foot by foot and inch by inch across the river until, with any luck, they will meet."

"You mean they might not?"

"We must have faith." He smiled.

"In God?"

"In mathematics," he replied. "Once it is complete, it will be safer than any other bridge ever built. But still there will be that moment, that reaching out of one arm to another when nothing is certain, nothing is fixed."

For a moment they were silent.

"Mr. Arrol," said Cait, having regained her composure, "just exactly what was it that you wanted to see me about?"

"I'm worried about my nephew, Jamie," he replied. "I have the sense that his spans may never reach, so to speak."

"What has he done now?"

"He wants to go back to Paris."

"I think he mentioned it," said Cait. "When I saw him last."

"Says he has the chance of apprenticeship with someone at Gustave Eiffel's firm. Wants to work on the construction of his iron tower. Why, I asked him, when we're in

147

the middle of building the bridge across the Forth?"

"Have you tried talking to him?" she asked.

Arrol let out a short burst of indignant laughter, then picked up his whiskey glass and poured what was left of it into his tea.

"I was going to ask your opinion. About whether you thought it was a good idea. But now, now an idea has occurred to me that might offer a possible solution for all of us."

The factory whistle sounded from the other end of the yard, long and low with a dip in the middle. And in that brief lull, as the men below put down their tools and picked up their dinner pails, as their wives and daughters heard the whistle and stoked up the fire beneath a pot of potatoes or began to brew a pot of tea, she blinked. What Arrol suggested had been the very last thing she expected to hear. She opened her mouth as if to speak and then closed it again.

"Well?" Arrol said.

"Paris," she clarified.

"We're talking about Jamie. And Alice, who would marry a lamppost if it asked her."

Cait's heart was beating too fast, speeding

ahead of herself. She took as deep a breath as her corset would allow and then looked straight at William Arrol.

"Are you perfectly serious?"

He stared at her in the half-light. "It wouldn't all be plain sailing. You'd be the responsible adult to my two wayward charges again."

She picked up her teacup and took a sip. Her hand shook.

"And how long were you thinking?" she asked.

"As far as I'm aware, the tower has to be finished for 1889, for the Exposition Universelle, the World's Fair. If nothing else, it would provide you with a viable reason to put off your man Sinclair, at least for the foreseeable future."

Although she was aware of a rapid rising, a throwing off of weight, of ballast, this time there was no sense of vertigo, no grip of fear.

"I'll do you a favor and you'll do one for me," he continued. "You would be the metaphorical safety basket, to keep my reckless young niece and nephew safe. Yes, the more I think on it the more I like it. A perfect plan for all."

Arrol seemed to relax. He stretched out his legs and crossed them.

"All except the Sinclair fellow, of course," he added.

"Mr. Arrol," said Cait, "you have no idea how much this means to me."

"I can take a fair guess," he said, and laughed. "Cake?"

■ ■ ■ ■

II

■ ■ ■ ■

10

June 1887

The foundations of the tower were finished; four huge metal caissons, or shoes, as they were known, had been sunk into the ground, two near the river and two farther away from it. This was how the construction always began, Émile knew, with a subtraction rather than an addition; the workers had removed hundreds of kilos of earth and stone, shoveling it onto carts and into wagons to be taken away by train or barge. And now the site looked like an archaeological dig, an uncovering of the remnants of another civilization whose particulars were forgotten but whose scale was enormous, whose ambition was gargantuan, and who had left behind a geography of vast walls and massive girders.

They had to dig much deeper on the side of the river to make the foundations stable. The men had quarried down through damp clay and wet sand, through mud studded with broken crockery and shards of glass, with splinters of animal bone and flakes of flint, and now the air reeked of decayed things, of sulfur and rot. Cutting across everything, however, making your eyes water and the world intermittently gray and indistinct, were clouds of woodsmoke. The fires seemed to burn day and night, purifying and polluting in equal measure.

The smells reminded Émile of Auvergne, where they'd built the Garabit Viaduct, and Portugal, where they'd constructed the Maria Pia Bridge over the River Douro. In the center of Paris, however, just across the river from the lavish towers of the Trocadéro Palace and straddling the entrance to the Pont d'Iéna, the site seemed to smell worse than usual. Maybe it was the city; maybe it was depth of the hole? The excavation felt messy, vulgar, an unsightly tear in the city's flawless fabric. No wonder so many people came to gawk and stare, to point and peer.

Since the first day they had begun digging, a line of carriages had been pulling up at the curb on the Quai d'Orsay and letting out scores and scores of curious, indignant, or outraged onlookers. Men in bowler hats strolled slowly past, or paused at the perimeter to lean on their walking sticks and wait for something to happen. Ladies, their cloaks billowing out in the wind like the feathers on a crow's wing, scurried by, their faces covered with handkerchiefs against the dust and the smoke and the deep, damp, unsettling smell of the foundations. There wasn't a lot to see at first. All the site did was to confirm what people already thought: the construction would be a monstrosity, a truly tragic lamppost. And yet Émile knew that the tower would soon begin to rise; the works were on schedule. At this rate they'd reach the first platform before Christmas.

"Monsieur!" a voice cried out from the other side of the site. "Monsieur Nouguier?"

He turned and squinted across the rubble and the wagon tracks. Out of a billow of smoke came a figure, a man dressed in black coattails and a tall hat, as if about to go to the theater or the opera or the ballet. As they watched, he tripped over a rock, let out a curse, and then continued toward them.

"Who is this?" Émile asked the foreman.

The foreman shook his head. "I don't know who gave him permission to enter the site," he said. "As soon as I find out, they'll be reprimanded. We can't have members of the public stumbling around. Damned liability. I'll escort him out."

155

As the man came closer, however, something about him looked familiar.

"Hold on," Émile called to the foreman. "It's all right. I know him."

Jamie Arrol clasped Émile by the hand and shook it vigorously.

"They told me you'd be here," he said. "I went to Levallois-Perret first, you see. Bit of a wasted trip. Anyway, it's so good to see you again. And glad to see that you didn't start without me."

He turned and motioned his hand toward the site.

"Actually we started months ago," Émile said hesitantly.

"I'm joking," the man replied. "Obviously. Anyway, it's nice to see you again."

Émile stared at the Scotsman he had met five months earlier. What on earth was he doing here?

"It's Arrol," the man explained. "Jamie Arrol? Remember?"

"Monsieur Arrol, of course," he replied. "Having another holiday?"

After the tiniest pause, Jamie Arrol laughed. "Very amusing," he replied. "Look here, I have a letter for you."

From his inside pocket he pulled a white envelope sealed with wax, and handed it over.

"It's all there," Arrol said. "Permission to take up an apprenticeship on the project as was suggested. My uncle William Arrol is already acquainted with Gustave Eiffel, so he was quite happy about the arrangement. *Vive* the auld alliance!"

Émile stared down at the letter as he tried to formulate a response. Had he offered him an apprenticeship? He couldn't remember doing so.

"I do hope this is satisfactory," Jamie Arrol said, sensing his hesitancy. "Your colleague, Monsieur Eiffel, suggested it, remember?"

Émile didn't. If Eiffel had suggested it, then Eiffel could deal with him.

"But once I'd spoken to my uncle," Jamie went on, "we agreed it would be better if I could work with you. Gustave Eiffel must be very busy, and besides, your area is more my area of interest."

Émile folded the letter and put it in his pocket. He would speak to Gustave first thing in the morning. This was not acceptable.

"You'll be glad to know that we are already installed in Paris," the young man went on. "We have an apartment near the Champs-Élysées. In fact, I'm ready to start . . ."

A gust of smoke blew between them and

he began to cough.

"Damn this smoke," he said.

"We?" Émile queried when the fit had subsided. "Did you say 'we'?"

"I brought the clan!" he said. "Actually, only my sister, Alice. You met her! Made quite an impression."

Émile nodded, although in truth, he barely remembered the man's sister either. But the woman in the balloon — her hand on his sleeve, the look of concern in her wide gray eyes, the shape of her as she had walked down the stairway at Levallois-Perret — he remembered that.

"Just you two?" he asked.

Jamie Arrol squinted at him. "She didn't bring a husband, if that's what you mean. Not that she was short of offers."

Émile smiled but declined to comment. A Parisian would never talk about his sister like this, as if she could be bought and sold like a bag of apples. And he wondered how long Jamie Arrol would last. Paris was a city that could make and ruin you; it could raise you up and then drop you without warning. No wonder Parisians were so guarded, so reserved. The ones who gave themselves away willingly, or who revealed their innermost secrets after a bottle of wine, or who laughed too loudly at the Chat Noir and spent too much money at the casino, weren't Parisian.

A train was approaching from the Gare des Invalides along the riverside, and the roar of its engine and the clatter of its wheels made conversation impossible for a moment or two. Émile turned and began to walk back toward a huddle of temporary huts. Jamie fell in step beside him.

"I have an allowance from my uncle," he said once the train had passed. "Not hugely generous, it must be said, but what needs must. Eiffel wouldn't need to pay me a sou, of course. I am here to learn!"

Did he really think he could just start work on a project of this importance just like that? An apprenticeship was a serious and time-consuming undertaking. He had turned down at least half a dozen applications from highly suitable candidates already. As the young man took his hat off and wiped the sweat from his brow, Émile turned to him.

"You must understand," he began.

But Jamie Arrol's attention was elsewhere, his eye fixed on a carriage that was waiting next to the Pont d'Iéna.

"Monday," Jamie said as he took off across the quai. "I'd say around ten a.m.? I'll meet you here?"

"Wait," called Émile. But his voice was drowned out by the clatter of a passing cab. As he watched, Jamie Arrol gave the driver instructions, climbed into his carriage, and it sped along the river in the direction of Notre-Dame.

The office at Levallois-Perret was locked up, but the night watchman let Émile in. At the back of a drawer in his desk was a box of the photographs he had taken from the hot-air balloon of the tower site before its construction. He laid them out across his desk. Here was the Champ de Mars with the Trocadéro faintly visible in the distance. And another, looking in the other direction, was the École Militaire. Next were several views of Paris from high above, the radiating avenues around the Place de l'Étoile and the distant rise of Montmartre. Finally there was a plate that he had taken as a test shot. It showed the passengers inside the gondola. And yes, there among the crowd of men in high hats and women in fur, through the distorting heat of the brazier, clinging onto the wicker edge of the basket with her eyes closed, was the Scottish woman. He touched the photograph and left a print. If only he could remember her name.

11

Cait sat on the balcony and unwound her hair. No one could see her up here, only the starlings in the sky and the bees that flitted from one potted lavender to the next. Her room was on the top floor, the attic, of the house the Arrols had rented — a thin, tall house with pale blue shutters on the rue Cardinet. On the one hand, she would have preferred a room lower down, but on the other, she loved the view. Just as long as she didn't stand too close to the edge, she felt safe; her vertigo was manageable.

Below was a small, dark garden with a mossy marble statue beside an ornamental pond filled with carp. The trees, ash and lime, were spindly and sparse, and seemed to spend all their energy reaching skyward. If she had been a tree, she would have done the same; up here you could see for miles, an uneven vista of roofs and chimney stacks, garrets and church spires, of slate and lead, redbrick and green-hued copper. A gentle breeze brought the smell of warm limestone and fresh coffee, of baking bread and lilac from the neighbor's garden. Cait closed her eyes and felt the soft beat of sunlight on her eyelids and through the fine weave of her white cotton night shift onto her pale Scottish skin.

She had been waiting to suffer for almost a month now. She had been expecting to feel contrite the moment she had decided to tell Roland Sinclair that she would not marry him. But still nothing came. Her sister, Anne, had burst into tears when she had told her, and said that Cait would pay for it, that nothing good ever came out of a rash decision. Her brother-in-law, normally a taciturn man, had tried to make her change her mind and, when she wouldn't, suggested that she see a doctor. It was true that she did look different. Ever since her meeting with William Arrol, she couldn't sit still. To go to Paris for two years was beyond anything she'd ever wished for. And maybe, she told herself, she would come back. And maybe she wouldn't. No wonder she couldn't sleep, she couldn't concentrate, she'd lost her appetite. Although she tried to hide it, even a cup of tea had revealed the tremor in her hands.

"When are you going to break it to the poor man?" Anne had asked her. Cait had momentarily forgotten Roland Sinclair. He seemed to belong to a different life.

"This afternoon, all being well," she had said.

"All being well? How could it possibly be well, Caitriona? Word will get out, people will talk. I wish you'd listened to me. It will be quite awful. For all of us."

"I'm sorry, Anne," she said. "To be the cause of such distress. You do not warrant it."

Her sister waved away her explanation with a hand. "If only Saul had never climbed aboard that beastly train. If only you had persuaded him not to go to Dundee, then we'd never be in this situation in the first place."

Cait had blinked; her eyes smarted. How could Anne suggest that the train crash had been avoidable, that what had happened was her fault? If only she knew how much she had paid for it.

"Don't you think?" Anne added, defensive in case she'd said too much.

But then the baby had started to cry and the nanny was calling her and the conversation ended. Having a widow as a sister was clearly a social calamity for Anne. Cait was the thirteenth at table, the odd one out, the lost last piece of the jigsaw puzzle. And yet there was so much that her sister didn't know. There was so much that no one knew.

Roland Sinclair had sat in the shade of a banana tree in the Kibble Palace in the Botanic Gardens and fiddled with his mustache. After an initial silence, he'd taken the news equally badly.

"This is quite a setback," he had said. "A harsh and bitter blow of a sort I have never experienced before. And let me tell you, Mrs. Wallace, I have had more than my fair share of setbacks."

"It was never my intention to cause you hurt."

"Well, you have," he said, taking off his spectacles. "You most certainly have."

And he stared at her so she could not miss the reddening of his eyes. Although she was not indifferent, it seemed that he had not known her for long enough to warrant such sorrow. If he felt any love for her, and she doubted he did, he had never summoned up the courage to actually express it. She remembered his words *united in loss.* Their relationship would have been one constructed out of the end point of two other lives, not the best place to start a relationship in any regard.

Eventually, Roland Sinclair had cleared his throat, blown his nose, and collected himself.

"My sister will be extremely put out," he had said. "An announcement has already been sent to the *Glasgow Herald.*"

"You can always cancel it," she suggested.

He shook his head and stroked his hair bracelets.

"Amelia hates to cancel anything," he replied. "She feels as if it is tantamount to some sort of personal failure. Ridiculous, I know, but one gets into habits. I'm not sure how I'm going to break it to her."

"I hadn't actually," Cait said carefully, "accepted."

"But as my sister said, why would you decline?" he replied. "My offer was of the sort that does not come twice in one lifetime. Especially, and please don't take this the wrong way, Mrs. Wallace, especially not to a woman in your circumstances. Amelia said you would have to be mad not to jump at the chance."

Amelia Sinclair had given Cait one long stare when they first had been introduced, as if she could tell just by looking if she was trustworthy, if she was sincere, if her circumstances were reduced enough to make her acceptance of her brother's proposal a foregone conclusion. She seemed to think that they were.

"No children," Amelia had clarified.

"That's right," Roland had replied.

Tact clearly wasn't her forte. She was proud of saying what she meant and meaning what she said. Dinner had been long and awkward.

"Our guest speaks French," Roland had told Amelia.

"Not much use to her up here," she had replied. "So I hear that she's been married before?"

At this point Cait had begun to realize that Amelia was going to refer to her in the third person for the entire meal.

"I was," she said carefully. "Sadly, he died."

"In the Tay Bridge disaster," Amelia replied. "I heard."

For a moment they all sawed away at their brisket.

"Ask her if they found the body," she said to Roland.

"Please!" he replied. "Not while we're eating."

In the Kibble Palace, a boy of about six ran past them. And then another.

"It's not fair," the second one shouted. "You're not playing by the rules! No one likes a cheat!"

Cait and Mr. Sinclair sat staring into space, both still united in loss, him with wet eyes and her with dry.

"I should go," she said eventually. "Before the rain starts."

"The forecast is good," he replied. "But then again, the forecast could be wrong. Facts can be read in such a way as to provide the wrong impression."

"Mr. Sinclair," she began.

"You know," he interjected, "I really did like you, Caitriona."

"I liked," she began, "I mean, I like you too."

"Isn't that enough? A fondness. A friendship. A compatibility of sorts. Love may arrive at a later date."

He reached across and took her hand. His palm was as soft as tissue paper.

"Are you sure?" he asked. "Really sure? Paris is all very well, but you'd be nothing there — a chaperone. Surely you're more than that? And what will happen when you come back? You aren't getting any younger. There is always the possibility, and I hope you don't mind me saying this, but without a man to support you, there is the possibility that you end up destitute."

She inhaled, long and slow. Everything he

said was true. And she had seen those fallen gentlewomen at church, their mouths pinched with worry, their pockets full of stale crusts and sugar lumps. Mr. Sinclair was looking at her, his irises magnified, big and blue as children's marbles. Maybe he was right. She was being rash and impulsive and foolhardy. Hadn't she learned anything?

"Because, as my sister always says," he added, " 'A bird in the hand is worth two in the bush.' "

And then Cait knew that no matter what the circumstances, no matter the cost, no matter how foolhardy the alternative was, she could never be happy with a man who uttered inanities at a moment of crisis. Especially if they came from the mouth of his sister. He was still looking at her hopefully. She removed her hand from his and turned to face him.

"I have already given my word to the Arrols," she said. "I'm sorry."

He closed his eyes and sighed. Now he had his final answer. She glanced at her watch. He took it as a prompt to rise from the bench.

"I was going to catch the seventeen forty-three," he said. "But there's a chance I'll make the sixteen oh-seven. Would you mind?"

They paused at the gates of the gardens. She was going one way, he the other.

"Well," he said.

"You should catch your train," she replied. "If you hurry."

Only, Mr. Sinclair seemed to have lost his sense of urgency.

"Maybe I'll come out to Paris and pay you a visit?" he said.

"You'd be very welcome."

"I may do that." Roland Sinclair's mouth smiled, but his eyes remained unmoved. He would never come to Paris. They both knew it, but it seemed the right thing to say under the circumstances.

A woman strolled by in the direction of Byres Road, a woman with strands of gray in her hair and a black dress. Roland Sinclair's eyes followed the swish of her bustle. Despite what he had just told her, she was sure he would recover.

"Goodbye, Mr. Sinclair," she said, and shook his hand.

"Goodbye, Mrs. Wallace," he said, then turned and took his leave.

Within ten minutes, the sidewalks were dotted with spots of rain.

Every day since they had arrived in Paris, the sun had shone. Gradually, Cait felt the muscles in her shoulders, in her jaw, and in her back relax. Without being aware of it, her body had been coiled and sprung against the Scottish climate, where even in summer the air was cut with a chill wind or the edge of damp, the rain always just about to blow in from the west.

Although the sun blazed outside, everything inside the rented house was dark. It wasn't just the mahogany furniture, the sagging divans, the curtains, or even the ancient oil paintings on the walls; it was also the fact that the shutters were kept closed to keep out the sunlight. A long-serving housekeeper and a gardener had been retained to keep the place in order. After breakfast, Cait would walk through the rooms opening the windows to let fresh air circulate. The housekeeper would follow her around, after a suitable interval, closing them again.

That morning, she could hear the murmur of voices downstairs. Alice was learning conversational French with a tutor, an elderly man who gazed at her over his glasses as she mispronounced words with more patience than Cait could have mustered.

"At school we said *je suis,*" she could hear Alice saying. "With an *s* at the end."

"And in France," the tutor replied evenly,

"we don't say it. It is gone, dropped. Like *oui* or 'yes,' we said *suis*."

"Are you quite sure?" Alice asked.

"Oui," he replied.

"So it's settled?" Arrol had confirmed that day in his office in Dalmarnock several months before. "You'll chaperone them."

It wasn't a question but a statement. Long columns of pale Scottish sunlight fell across the room, illuminating the float of a thousand dust motes. Arrol rose out of his chair and offered her his hand.

"I know I can trust you," he had said. "A woman of your caliber."

How quickly, she thought at the time, everything changes. How fast a problem can metamorphose into a solution. And she felt a stretch inside, as if something within her reached out to something beyond, a soar of iron into thin air.

"One more thing," Arrol had suddenly added. "I hear that there is a man, one of Eiffel's engineers, no less, who has shown an interest in Alice. Could you help her a little, do a little social engineering? He sounds suitable and she is twenty now, a critical age for a young woman, as you know."

The sun passed behind a cloud, leaving

the room in darkness again.

"Rather him than that confounded butcher who keeps sniffing around," Arrol went on. "What was the Frenchman's name again? Émile something-or-other?"

Émile Nouguier. Why not? she asked herself later as she walked back toward the city along the London Road. Alice Arrol was young; she was pretty, she was well provided for. And maybe all that had passed between Émile Nouguier and her that day at the top of the stairs was the giddiness of half-remembered vertigo.

They had been in Paris for almost a month and still their paths had not crossed. Jamie had forbidden them from the tower site for the time being. He told them he wanted to establish himself with Nouguier before he started complicating things with his sister.

"He's not going anywhere, Alice," he said. "Be patient."

"Has it ever occurred to you," said Alice, "that I may want to visit the site because I'm interested?"

"In the tower?" he said. "No, I have to say it never did."

Jamie had a point. As soon as they had arrived, Alice had bought every fashion publication she could find. And then she had visited a dressmaker and a corsetière, a shoemaker and a milliner, and ordered underskirts and overskirts, bodices and petticoats, corsets, capes and trains, plus hats and boots and slippers. All she needed, she had complained to Jamie, were the occasions to wear them.

"We have months and months," he had told her. "There will be plenty of occasions."

On Cait's balcony, the wind seemed to pause, as if momentarily distracted. From the stables at the far end of the garden, a horse whinnied and another answered. In the east, the sky was a shade of slate, heavy with an approaching storm. The city air had turned thick and golden as syrup.

She rose and was just about to head back inside when she looked down and saw a black cat leap from the lilac tree to the wall and then down onto the flower beds. It was so graceful and surefooted it seemed to know exactly where it was going. At the fishpond, it sat and just observed, its head switching back and forth as it followed the bright dart of orange beneath the surface of the water. And then, with one swipe of its paw, it scooped.

By the time Cait had thrown on a nightgown and run down three flights of stairs, the cat was gone and the fish was lying motionless on the flagstones. It hadn't been mauled or bitten or even scratched; it was perfect. And yet the fish's eyes had already clouded over; it had drowned in the sweet garden air.

She was suddenly aware of a presence and turned. The housekeeper stood in the doorway staring at her in alarm. What was she doing, her face seemed to say, standing in the garden in her nightgown? Where was her sense of common decency?

"Mrs. Wallace," Alice's voice rang out from inside. "Come and see."

There had been a delivery from the dressmaker's. The French lesson forgotten, Alice was standing in the hallway, a brand-new evening gown in her arms.

"Isn't it divine?" she said.

But then she saw the expression on Cait's face. "You hate it!"

"No, not at all," Cait replied.

The dress was ruffled with a heavily beaded bodice. It was made of an amber silk brocade exactly the same color as the dead carp.

12

When he was in Paris, Gustave Eiffel lived in an apartment near l'Étoile. Although he'd lost his wife more than a decade earlier, he had never remarried. Instead he lodged near his daughter, Claire, and her husband, Adolphe, who worked with him at the firm. His other five children had mostly grown up or left home — the youngest was at boarding school. The Parisian apartment was cavernous, the furnishing tasteful, without any hint of the person who had chosen them. Like Émile, Eiffel was barely there. For the last few decades, he had spent most of his time traveling all over the world, to the Americas, Europe, and the Far East, visiting clients, proposing plans, or working on-site.

Ever since Émile had started working for him, he had been struck by Eiffel's single-mindedness. It wasn't just about the money — there was more than enough — but the absolute faith he had in his own convictions. It was evident in his use of materials and his approach to building bridges, his courage with regard to challenging everything from the established order to the elements. Émile remembered the day when a riveter had fallen into the water from the Garabit Viaduct. Eiffel hadn't hesitated before diving in to the River Garonne to rescue him.

Modesty, however, wasn't one of his attributes. At the time of its building, the Maria Pia Bridge over the Douro had the biggest span of any bridge ever constructed. But as Eiffel liked to point out, the lightness of its wrought-iron form meant that it wouldn't spoil the view. The bridge was not only strong enough to withstand a hurricane-force wind but undeniably elegant. Eiffel was also a canny businessman. He courted journalists and persuaded them to write favorable articles about him and his work. He gave lectures. He printed handbills and distributed them. His growing reputation was such that he was invited to work on projects as far afield as Chile, Budapest, and New York. And now for the tower, the centerpiece of the World's Fair, he had come home to France.

The drawings for the tower had been made by Nouguier and Maurice Koechlin years earlier. Stephen Sauvestre, the architect, had added a few finishing touches. Despite competition in the form of a proposal for a three-hundred-meter tower made of granite with a huge electric furnace on top, Eiffel's tower was chosen by the Exhibition Commission. The City of Paris would contribute one and a half million francs, Eiffel another five million, to cover projected costs, and in return, he would receive all income from the tower for the next twenty years. Koechlin, Nouguier, and Sauvestre would each receive a percentage of the profits, should there be any. It was a huge financial risk for Eiffel. It was quite possible that no one would be interested in the tower, let alone pay to ascend it.

From the lobby, Émile could hear the clatter and laughter of the scullery maids in the kitchen, the sound of a baby crying, and above it all, in a higher pitch, the chatter of a pair of songbirds in a cage. He found Gustave at the back of the house, working at a table on the terrace. Two of his daughters were with him, Claire and Valentine, each nursing inconsolable babies. The noise seemed to have little effect. Spread out in front of him were sheets and sheets of plans.

"Working on a Sunday?" Émile asked.

"Nothing major," he said, rising to greet

him. "Just an underwater bridge across the English Channel and a new Métro line."

This was also typical of Eiffel. He was often at work on half a dozen projects at once, each more technically challenging than the last. If it was too easy, he quickly lost interest.

"And I hear that I may be asked to submit a bid for the Panama Canal."

Émile frowned. "Are you sure we should get involved with that?" he asked.

"That's exactly what we said," his daughter Claire interjected.

The French Panama Canal Company had been beset with problems ever since it had begun construction six years earlier. Thousands of workers had died on-site, in accidents or from malaria or yellow fever. Conditions were said to be atrocious. The contractor, Ferdinand de Lesseps, the man who had built the Suez Canal, had already spent millions that he had raised from French investors.

"Lesseps has finally given up on his idea for building it all at sea level," he replied. "At last they seem to have come around to my way of thinking. The only way to build it successfully is to use a series of metal locks, just as I told him in the first place. With your skills and mine, Émile, we could make it work. Could you take a look over the drawings before I submit them?"

As Eiffel never stopped working, he expected the same from his employees. Like him, they put in twelve-hour shifts in summer and worked from sunrise until sunset in winter. Émile's ears were full of the sound of the drill and the hammer. He even heard them in his dreams. When Émile didn't answer, Eiffel put down his pencil.

"Claire?" he called out. "Valentine? Could you make yourself scarce for a moment?"

The two young women glanced at each other and then gathered up their babies and moved to a shady spot farther along the terrace.

"Is anything the matter?" Gustave asked.

For a moment Émile was silent.

"All right. I'm worried," he admitted. "About the construction of the tower."

Gustave raised his eyebrows. His pale blue eyes blinked once.

"As long as each rivet hole is accurate to one-tenth of a millimeter," he said, "then all will be well."

Émile took out his handkerchief and wiped his forehead with it. The air above the city hung low and heavy. There were 2.5 million rivets. It was his responsibility to make sure that every single hole was exactly placed. And what would happen if they weren't? On-site, iron girders of up to three tons apiece were maneuvered into place; if the rivet holes didn't match up, then the pieces wouldn't fit together. There would be no tower.

His eyes still stung from the black dust that filled the workshop. His hair, his clothes, and his skin smelled of scorching metal and burning coal that no amount of soap could completely remove. Sometimes it seemed that they had taken on an impossible task. To build outward, to span a valley, to build a bridge or viaduct, was one thing, but to build up, to construct something so high, higher than anything ever built before, seemed like trying to articulate a dream. Even though he had designed it, he found it almost impossible to visualize hundreds of meters of metal struts beneath his feet and a view glimpsed before only from the gondola of a hot-air balloon.

"Is it the Arrol boy?" Eiffel asked.

Émile let out a brief sigh of exasperation.

"That too! He's hopeless."

He had put the Scot in charge of a tiny area of production. Émile had checked the work on the third day. He had used the template he had been given, but upside down. Consequently all the holes had been drilled in the wrong place. Almost every single girder had to be discarded. Émile had tried not to show his annoyance, he had tried to bottle his frustration, but how many pieces had gotten through without him noticing? How many would cause problems further down the line? Jamie Arrol, however, didn't seem in the least contrite.

"In Scotland, we do most of the drilling on-site."

"That may well be," Émile had replied. "But for this project we have decided to drill at least sixty percent of the rivet holes in the factory. Not only will it be faster to assemble on-site, it is also safer and quicker. It is imperative that we finish on time."

Jamie Arrol had yawned and sat down on a workbench.

"Are you well?" Émile had asked.

"Just tired," he had replied. "Burning the candle at each end, as they say."

After that, Émile had asked the foreman to double-check all the work he had supervised and report back to him.

"Am I being demoted?" Jamie Arrol asked. "Is that it?"

It was certainly an idea, an idea that suddenly appealed to Émile.

"A sideways move," he had told him. "Come and see me tomorrow in my office on Monday. I have another role for you."

It was a lie. He had no idea what he would do with him.

"Fire him," suggested Eiffel, "if he's hopeless."

He nodded. It was the obvious solution.

One of Eiffel's grandchildren, a girl of about four, came running over and climbed onto Émile's lap.

"Did you bring me some chocolate, Monsieur Nouguier?" she asked.

"I did, Geneviève, but your grandfather ate it all!" he replied.

She stared at Gustave, who pretended to look guilty.

"But I brought you something else," Émile said.

"What?"

"Tickles," he replied, and started wiggling his fingers.

The child squealed with laughter as she clambered down from his lap again.

"Bring me some next time," she said, once she was out of his reach. "And don't let Grandpapa eat it."

"I won't," he replied. "I promise."

"Geneviève," called her mother, "what are you doing?"

"Nothing," she said.

"Come here and stop bothering the

grown-ups."

They both watched as the girl ran back to her mother.

"Children like you," Gustave said.

"The feeling's mutual," he replied.

But even the child couldn't alleviate his obvious unease.

"So as we were saying," Gustave continued, "you'll get rid of the hopeless Scot. Tomorrow."

"It's not that . . ."

"You have the authority," he said softly. "I give you the authority!"

Émile shook his head. "It's the tower — it's never been done before."

"But that doesn't mean that it will fall down," Gustave replied. "Paris has never seen wind speeds of one hundred fifty miles an hour, but we have calculated for them."

"Yes," he admitted, "we did."

"Because its real strength is in its voids," he continued. "The wind will have virtually nothing to hold on to. It will pass straight through. You know that."

"A building without a skin." Émile nodded.

"As light as a single apartment block."

"But what if we have neglected something we don't even know about?" Émile blurted out. "What then?"

A maid appeared with a jug of ice water and two glasses on a tray. Eiffel poured.

"So you love children. Then why not marry and have some of your own?" he asked as he handed Émile a glass.

"With respect, what has that got to do with anything?"

"Mistresses are all very well, but relationships without foundations . . . structurally speaking, they are unstable. Especially if the mistress in question is already married."

Émile had never spoken of his private life to Gustave. Was he referring to Gabrielle? And if so, how in the world had he found out about her?

"It took me five attempts," Eiffel went on. "I was turned down four times by four different women. My family wasn't of the right class, too nouveau riche. Finally I found Marie. I wooed her. I left nothing to chance. I calculated every single permutation, every risk factor. I had set my sights on her and I would not give up. Finally, she accepted my proposal."

Émile remembered Marie. She was always surrounded by children. Her death had been a shock to everyone. She was so young, so full of vitality.

"But then I learned something I had not expected," Gustave went on. "Once I was married, I learned that every day you move into a new dominion, none of it chartable, none of it able to be calculated in advance. Some are easy, some not. Who can know what it feels like to hold your own child? Who can imagine your son growing taller than you? Or for your daughter to weep and to know that there is nothing you can say that will make her feel better?"

What was he trying to tell him? That this wasn't about the tower at all. Émile was silent for a moment and then drained his glass.

"But I know bridges," Gustave continued. "And this is just a bridge of a different shape."

Émile closed his eyes and laughed. This was why he loved Gustave. He never knew what he was going to say next.

"Do you have any more illuminating advice?" he asked.

"I hear the Arrol girl is unmarried," Eiffel teased. "Her brother may be no good, but she may be a better fit. Rich too, by all accounts."

Émile placed his empty glass on the table.

"Well?" Gustave asked.

"You want me to fire him and marry her?"

"Might be an idea."

"I should get back to the factory."

"Don't leave it too late."

"The factory won't close until sundown," Émile replied.

"You know that's not what I mean."

Émile took a cab to the Place d'Anvers in Montmartre and walked up the hill. The narrow streets were full of noise and stale air and the smash of bottles on the cobblestones. Couples hunched in doorways or stumbled up staircases open to the elements. High, high above, through an open window, he heard the slap of a hand on skin followed by a gasp of pain, or possibly pleasure.

The shepherdess was still waiting in the doorway, almost as if she had never left it. She saw him and her mouth pulled into a small smile.

"You're a little late for class," she said.

He walked toward her and looked down into her face.

"I'm not here for class," he said.

She laughed a coquettish laugh, short and hollow.

"Why not come to my studio?" she said. "It's *en plein air.*"

"As long as you promise not to mention Poussin," he replied.

Against the cool stone of the abbey, the shepherdess lifted her skirts. She was naked beneath. He ran his hands down her thighs.

"Turn around," he said.

As the nuns sang and the lights of the city flickered in the dusk below, he suddenly remembered the Scottish woman's name.

"Caitriona," he whispered.

"It's Jeanne," the shepherdess whispered. "Go on, then. I'm waiting."

Émile blinked twice and the scene seemed to change before his eyes. The damp wall, the stink of a latrine, the dirt underfoot, and above it all the thin, lonely lament of the nuns. What was he doing? He pulled down the woman's dress and extracted a note from his wallet.

"Here," he said. "Is that enough?"

She turned around, then frowned at him. "I charge more," she said. "For this sort of art."

As she held her hand out for another note that she knew would come, the shape of her face rearranged itself into another face: Gabrielle's.

He stepped back.

"You need a doctor, not a model," the woman said as she slipped the money down the front of her chemise. "Now, Poussin, there was a real man."

13

It was the end of the season, the Fourteenth of July. The air was full of pale dust and horse chestnut pollen — a soft green haze that settled over everything, covering statues and park benches, headstones and café chairs. No one minded, no one cleaned; it was almost August, when Paris would close, paper blinds pulled down over every window to curl and bake in the heat of the mid-summer sun.

According to *Le Figaro,* the celebrations for Bastille Day would have a Venetian theme. There would be gondolas on the Seine, two open-air masked balls, one outside the Bourse and one in front of the Opéra. All the bridges would be decorated with ribbons and flags and flowers. Once it was dark, as well as thousands of extra lamps being hung between the Avenue de Champs-Élysées and the Place de la Con-corde, a vast fireworks display would take place at Trocadéro. Not everyone, however, would be celebrating the anniversary of the French Revolution. The Third Republic, the current government, was still called La Gueuse, or "the slut," by the monarchists. Traditionally, they closed their shutters and spent the whole of the Fourteenth of July in the dark, as far away from the festivities as possible.

Jamie had been given the day off and lay in bed until ten a.m. Over breakfast, they planned out what they would do; the parade, then possibly a ball.

"At last," Alice said. "An occasion! One hopes it will be better than the last one."

"You didn't object," replied Jamie. "And I thought you liked ballet."

"I don't think anyone was there for the dancing, Jamie," she replied. "Especially not you. Remember?"

Two weeks earlier they had gone to a show at the lavish Opéra Garnier. From the moment they had arrived at the theater, it was clear that the performance had begun long before the curtain rose. Young women in elaborate evening gowns cut to wear with the most rigid of corsets, and jewels that sparkled in the light from the huge candelabras that lit up the grand staircase, pretended to ignore the knots of young men who gathered at the doors to the stalls. The men, in contrast, pushed and shoved one another, laughed and joked. And yet there were many lingering glances and meaningful lowering of the eyes, half smiles, and raised eyebrows — a secret language of availability and flirtation, or of feigned disinterest and rejection.

Cait had paused on the steps to take in all the gold and marble, the silk and satin, to inhale the smell of lavender pomade and scent of Guerlain. Alice, whose new gown had been cut a little too tight, and whose shoes were of a style with a higher heel than she usually wore, looked strained as they ascended the marble staircase to their box in the dress circle. As they waited in line for the usher to show them to their box, she had gazed at the other young women enviously. They looked so relaxed, so comfortable, so effortlessly elegant.

The doors to the boxes were set into a curved wall and were opened with a special key. Once pulled shut from the inside, the doors were flush and no one could enter. The box was private and yet exposed. Although the stage was the central focus, once they had taken their seats they were displayed to the auditorium, Cait thought, like jewelry in a shop window.

"There's no one here," Alice had said a little too loudly as she surveyed the occupants of the other boxes and flapped her fan.

Below in the stalls, where the space between each row was too narrow to admit a lady's skirt, a few gentlemen turned and looked up at them. One of them called up in English.

"I'm here. Isn't that enough?"

At that moment, however, the house lights dimmed and the curtain began to rise noisily, drowning out a brief splutter of laughter from the other men and hiding Alice's embarrassment.

"Do we know him?" she whispered to Jamie.

"Of course we don't," Jamie said. "We don't know anyone."

As the orchestra began to play and the dancers took the stage, the man below glanced up more than once.

"He's staring," Alice whispered. "What shall I do?"

"Look away," Cait instructed.

"It's easy for you to say."

At the interval, Cait glanced down at the man in the stalls, at his wide, handsome face. Now that the house lights were up, there was no mistaking the expensive cut of his clothes and the attractive, arrogant tilt of his chin. As the scenery was changed and the jets in the gas lamps below the stage were opened wider, he glanced up at her and his eyes glinted in the light.

"See?" whispered Alice. "See!"

A bell rang and the audience returned to their seats. As the second half began, the man's attention focused back on the stage. He was not the only one. Even Jamie was transfixed as the prima ballerina, a small black-haired dancer in silver tulle, made her entrance. Alice looked from Jamie to the stage.

"Oh," she said. "So that's why we're here."

At the end of the ballet, Alice insisted they leave their box before the encores had ended. She hurried down the wide marble stairs of the theater to the foyer, glancing over her shoulder at the doorways to the stalls. Then she sent Jamie off to find their carriage. Many moments later, well after the rest of the audience had left, the man from the stalls strolled by.

"Don't look," whispered Cait.

But Alice looked.

"Mademoiselle?" the man said, and tipped his hat.

Alice met his gaze, her eyes running from his face to his feet, then back again.

"Good night," he said in English before heading out of the main entrance.

It was no use scolding her. It was doubtful they would meet the man again. But it meant something to Alice; she had finally made an impression.

Bastille Day was clear and bright and even early in the morning was punctuated by the distant pump and blast of brass. The air smelled of holidays — of starch and clean washing, of chocolate and warm leather. The housekeeper had prepared their breakfast, then left to spend the day with her sister in Fontainebleau. Without her, the atmosphere inside the house lifted. A breeze played in the curtain and a few petals fell from the flower arrangement on the hall table and were blown across the floor.

"I can see her now," said Jamie of the housekeeper. "Her and her sister, both wearing black from head to toe, shriveling in the heat, eating snails with a pin."

"You're so cruel," said Alice. "What has she ever done to you?"

"Nothing. I just don't like her! The way she looks at me. She hates us all, you know."

"Maybe 'hate' is too strong a word," suggested Cait.

"How about 'loathe'?" Jamie suggested.

"Or 'despise'?"

"She does what is expected of her, no more or less," Cait said. "That's what we pay her for."

"That's what Uncle pays her for," Jamie corrected.

For a moment they were all silent.

"Will he be there?" Alice asked. "At the Bois?"

"Will who be there?" Jamie replied.

"The engineer?"

Jamie sighed and picked up the newspaper.

"Well? Yes or no?"

"Yes!" he replied.

"How do you know? Did he tell you?"

"No, my dear sister," he replied. "He didn't, and in actual fact, I have no idea of his movements. But you demanded an answer and I gave you the one I thought you might prefer."

Jamie looked up from the paper and caught Cait's eye. She looked away.

"Has he even mentioned me?" Alice went on.

"Of course he has, my beautiful Alice. You are the main topic of our conversation."

"Jamie!" warned Cait.

"If I were you," he went on, "I wouldn't read this. It might put you off Frenchmen for life!"

The papers were full of the Pranzini trial. Henri Pranzini, the accused, as well as being smart, handsome, witty, and fluent in eight languages, was also a confidence trickster, a thief, a gambler and a womanizer. After killing his lover, her servant, and the servant's baby, and stealing bonds, jewelry, and money amounting to a thousand pounds, he intended, it was claimed, to flee to America with another young woman he had seduced using his murdered lover's fortune.

Alice glanced over the article that Jamie had handed her. "How on earth could one fall for a man like that?" she said. "Surely you would suspect? Mrs. Wallace, what do you think?"

"Maybe he was very charming."

"But still. You'd just know, wouldn't you?" said Alice.

Cait spooned a lump of sugar into her cup and then another, then a third, then a fourth. Alice and Jamie stared at her.

"Do you have something to tell us?" asked Jamie.

Cait stopped stirring her tea and stared at him. How did he know? No one knew.

"Four sugars in your tea!" said Jamie.

She swallowed. It was all right.

"But lumps are smaller, surely?" she replied.

Jamie and Alice exchanged a glance.

"Are you all right, Mrs. Wallace?" asked Alice.

"Yes, perfectly fine."

"It's just that usually you take your tea without sugar."

"A little sweetness," she replied, "never hurt anyone."

There was a small, loaded silence.

"It says she was a *'demimondaine,'*" Alice said. "What does that mean?"

"It means she was a lady of the night," Jamie told her. "A tart, a whore."

Alice took a sip of tea as if to wash away the taste of the words.

"And what will happen to him if he's found guilty?" Alice asked.

He made a slicing motion with his hand across his neck.

"Oh," said Alice. "That's horrible."

"It's what they do in France. Chop people's heads off and then celebrate for a hundred years."

Cait drained her cup and rose from the table.

"We better go," she said. "If we want to see anything. Are you ready, Alice?"

Alice, of course, was not.

They were so late that they couldn't get anywhere near the parade. By the time they reached the Bois it was busier than they'd ever seen it. Families had laid out blankets on the parched summer grass or sat on the benches in the dappled shade of the trees. A stream of landaus, fiacres, and victorias sped past, heading toward the racecourse while dozens of horsemen and -women cantered along the bridle paths.

At first they followed the crowds and strolled along gravel paths that ran alongside the Allée des Acacias and the Allée des Poteaux. After an hour, Alice started to complain about the heat and the crowds and her tight-fitting shoes and so Jamie offered to row them around one of the lakes.

"It'll be cooler out on the water," he suggested. "And less crowded."

The lakes, the Inferieur and the Superieur, were side by side. Only the former rented rowing boats. Alice reclined on a cushion in the bow of their skiff, closed her eyes, and let her hand drift in the water. Away from the main drags, the Bois was so calm, so peaceful. Even though they were only a mile or so from the center of Paris, apart from the splash of their oars, the intermittent chatter of birds, and the short bursts of high laughter that came from the nearby woods, it was almost silent. Cait sat under a parasol and watched the water boatmen as they skated across the surface. A black heron stood motionless in the shallows before spreading its huge wings, rising up, and wheeling away through the trees. A swan came up to the boat and peered at them, either curious or in search of bread.

"Jamie!" screeched Alice. "Row faster!"

"It won't hurt us," said Cait.

From nearby, a voice rang out, a falsetto imitation: *"Jamie, row faster!"* Another boat was approaching fast from the far bank, rowed by two young men and weighed down by another three. It passed by in silence, leaving such a swell that their own boat was set rocking back and forth in its wake. Jamie raised his hat but received no response. Once they were out of earshot, one of the men said something and the others all roared with laughter.

"Idiots!" said Jamie, then glanced at Alice. Her expression was fixed into one of great suffering.

At lunchtime, they decided to moor the boat at one of the islands. On the largest was a restaurant designed to look like a Swiss chalet, which could be reached from the shore by a flat-bottomed boat.

"It was a gift, apparently, to the empress

Eugénie from her husband, Napoleon III," Cait read from the guidebook. "She saw the chalet in Switzerland and was so taken with it that he had it dismantled and rebuilt here, in the Bois."

"I wish someone would do that for me," said Alice. "So shall we?"

"It looks expensive," warned Jamie.

"It looks perfect," said Alice.

After they had been shown to a table and been given menus, Alice pulled out her phrasebook, a "manual of conversation," from her wrist bag. Jamie snatched it from her, opened it at random, and began to read.

"Listen to this: 'I have had a slight attack of the gout, which has forced me to keep to my room for a fortnight!' "

"Give it back," said Alice softly.

"This is even better: 'I am very much inclined to be sick.' I hope we never need that one. Or this: 'I want a diamond that makes a great show and costs very little.' Don't we all?"

"Mrs. Wallace!" pleaded Alice. "Do something!"

"Jamie!" said Cait.

He pushed the book across the table at Alice.

"I hope you order tripe," he said as she tucked it back into her bag. "By mistake."

Alice's eyes suddenly widened.

"What?" Cait asked.

"It's him," she whispered. "The man from the ballet!"

At the next table, with a woman of considerable age and an elderly gentleman, was the young man who had sat in the stalls that night at the Opéra Garnier. He was working his way slowly through a plate of oysters.

"Are you finished yet, Clément?" the woman asked him in clipped French. "One forgets how intolerable the city is in July."

"No, Mother," he replied. "Not yet."

"Mother," Alice mouthed.

As he dislodged another oyster with a knife, doused it in lemon juice, raised it to his lips, threw back his head, and swallowed, the older man glanced around the restaurant with obvious distaste. Cait took in the couple's clothes, their shoes, their jewels. The cuffs were frayed and the old man's silk waistcoat spotted with grease stains. They were what she had come to recognize as *le gratin,* which meant, literally, the upper crust, the titled. Although their clothes were shabby and they were notoriously mean, many of them lived in huge mansions in the Faubourg Saint-Germain. She glanced away as the younger man swiveled around in his seat and raised a hand to summon the waiter.

"Garçon?" he called. "The bill."

The waiter rushed over immediately.

"Certainly, Count," he said.

"Count," whispered Alice.

The man from the ballet either hadn't seen them or pretended he hadn't. His father paid, placing a pair of spectacles on his nose and laying out the notes and coins in little piles. Then the count helped his mother with her cape, fetched her cane, and slowly they made their way to the door. A few seconds later, however, he was back again with a waiter, looking under his chair for a lost scarf. Almost casually, he stepped backward toward their table so the waiter could pull out all the chairs. He was turning something around in his fingers, something white, which he dropped into Alice's lap without anyone, except Cait, noticing. Alice's face blushed from pale pink to puce. It was a note.

"Is this it?" said the waiter, holding a white silk scarf that he had picked up from the floor.

"That's the one!" he said.

Once he had left the restaurant again, Alice began to unfold the note underneath the table.

"What are you doing?" Jamie asked.

201

"Nothing," she replied. But Jamie was too quick. He leaned across the table, snatched the note out of her hand, and quickly glanced at it. And then he held it above the candle on the table and burned it.

"Jamie!" Alice cried. "That was mine!"

"My dear sister," he said. "Surely even you know by now that men like that will ruin you as soon as look at you. Isn't that right, Mrs. Wallace?"

He looked to her to provide the appropriate response.

"It certainly was a little forward," she replied.

"He looked perfectly respectable," Alice said. "He's a count, for heaven's sake."

"Even more reason to stay away from him."

"But why on earth should I?"

Jamie leaned forward in his chair.

"Because, put quite simply, we're not his sort," he said. "Or hadn't you noticed?"

"And what sort are you talking about?"

Jamie shook his head and let out a snort of indignation. "Has it slipped your mind that we're from Glasgow? Glasgow, Scotland?"

"But we're not exactly poor, are we? Besides, I thought you wanted to marry me off to the first eligible man who turned up.

What's wrong with that one?"

"Everything," he replied.

Alice had barely touched her lunch. And now she rose and excused herself.

"She might be right," Cait said. "He might have had perfectly honorable intentions."

Jamie didn't respond as the waiter cleared their table.

"And he seemed pleasant enough," Cait went on.

The waiter, balancing their plates in one hand, swept the tablecloth of crumbs with the other.

"Would you say, Mrs. Wallace, that you're a good judge of men?" Jamie asked once the waiter had finished.

"That depends on the man. Some are easier to read than others."

"With respect, what exactly was wrong with Roland Sinclair?"

Despite the fact that the dining room was warm, Cait suddenly felt cold. She sat back in her chair.

"Nothing," she said. "He was perfectly nice."

The waiter returned with three small coffees, each one flavored with a twist of lemon.

"My uncle wouldn't support me to come here on my own," Jamie said. "And then he suggested that you come with me. And that we bring Alice."

"That's right," she replied. "It was the only way he'd let you come back to Paris."

Jamie picked up his coffee cup but didn't drink. "I suppose I should thank you for your act of self-sacrifice," he said.

"No need," she replied.

"Out of interest, would you have married him?"

"With respect, Jamie, I don't think it appropriate for you to ask that kind of question."

She gave him a half smile, a smile that suggested some kind of internal sensitivity, a rawness that still chafed.

"He seemed to like you. A great deal, in fact," Jamie went on. "Wasn't that enough for you?"

He wouldn't stop, would not let it go. She felt her face begin to flush.

"Marriage shouldn't be entered into lightly," she replied. "And simply being the object of a man's adoration is not, in my opinion at least, an adequate reason. And besides, there are other factors of which you have no knowledge."

He looked at her and raised his left eyebrow. For a moment they sat in silence. Her irritation began to ebb. Jamie Arrol was young. He had never felt the lurch that comes in the middle of the night with the realization that you have made an irreversible mistake.

"Well, I suppose it's always an option," Jamie said. "If things don't work out here, you could always pick things up again with Sinclair."

"Perhaps," she said.

"We'll just have to make sure we don't come a cropper," he said softly, "for all our sakes. Now, where has Alice got to?"

"I'm sure she'll only be a moment."

"She's a liability!"

"She's just naive."

"If we can just get her married off," Jamie said, "then all will be fine."

Cait picked up the teaspoon from her coffee cup and placed it in her mouth. The metal was cool and crusted with sugar. Suddenly Jamie sat forward and waved an index finger.

"I've got it," he said. "I know what we'll do." And then he paused for dramatic effect.

"What?" said Cait.

"We'll invite Monsieur Nouguier around for tea," he said. "A pot of Darjeeling, a plate of patisserie, and some toast and Gentleman's Relish, *chez* Arrol. Could you do the honors? He won't say no to you."

It was unlikely he would have time for tea. According to Jamie, Nouguier worked twelve-, thirteen-, fourteen-hour days.

"Well?" asked Jamie.

"I'm sorry," Cait said, replacing the spoon on her saucer. "But I'm not sure he would even remember who I am."

He let out a long, slow sigh. "Well, that's that, then," he said.

A group of people at the next table laughed uproariously at a joke.

"It doesn't seem fair," Jamie said once the noise had quieted down again. "I can put it off for another ten years, I'd say, take my time. But it's different for women. We don't want Alice to end up on the shelf. Or to marry a man who makes pies."

"They're not called pies in France," Alice said as she returned, seemingly fully recovered. "But tarts! Talking of which, has anyone ordered dessert? We need to sustain ourselves for tonight's ball."

14

Émile sat up in bed and threw his pillow on the floor. His room was airless. Even though the window was wide open, there was no breeze, nothing to cut through the viscosity of the summer heat. And the sheet was too crumpled, the mattress too soft; the wire springs of his bed had begun to corkscrew themselves up through the felt and horsehair and the cotton ticking into his ribs. He lay down again, his head flat, and tossed one way and then the other, trying to find a comfortable spot, an area of the bed that was still cool. The clock on the wall had just chimed two; he should be asleep. In four hours' time he had to get up for work. But the more tired he felt, the more his mind seemed to spark. And every time he closed his eyes, his head rang with half-remembered words, with the scrape of anxiety, with the suffocating rise of his heart in his chest.

The day before, on-site at the Champ de Mars, a beam was about to be lowered from a hoisting gin. The foreman shouted out a warning. Everyone had moved out of the way — everyone but Jamie Arrol, who was standing, waving at someone, completely oblivious to what was going on around him.

"Arrol," Émile had called out in English. "Watch out!"

But the Scot had not heard. Instead, he had taken off his hat and begun to smooth down his hair. A vision raced through Émile's mind: the boy lying on the ground, his body crushed by iron. The beam began to tip.

"Hey," Émile yelled again. "Get out of the way!"

Émile began to run, pushing people aside, skidding and sliding through mud and sand, across the broken earth of the showground. He wasn't going to make it.

"Arrol!" he screamed. "Move!"

Jamie heard his name, turned, his face suddenly creased with alarm, as from another direction, a young worker dived forward and pushed him to the ground. The metal beam fell with an almighty crash behind them, missing Jamie by a couple of inches but crushing the boy's foot.

Afterward, as the workers all rushed to

the boy's aid, trying to lift the beam to get
him out from under it, Émile had grabbed
the Scot by the collar and yelled at him in
French. He told him that he was a fool, that
he had no business being on the construction site if he couldn't look out for himself.
Arrol's eyes had widened in incomprehen-
sion and then — and this to Émile was
unforgivable — had glanced over his shoulder. Émile let him go and looked around.
At the perimeter of the site was a woman.
Tentatively, she waved. For an instant,
Émile imagined it was the woman in the
balloon and his heart leapt involuntarily.
But then he saw it was not: she was too
short; her body was too thin; she was too
stiff in her clothes.

"Is she yours?" he asked in English.

"I know her, if that's what you mean,"
Jamie had replied. "I don't know what she's
doing here, though."

Émile took a deep breath. He should not
lose his temper in front of the men. The
beam had been shifted and the boy was free
now, but his face was white and his eyes
elsewhere with pain and shock. Someone
wrapped him in a blanket. Someone else
was sent to fetch a doctor.

"When you are here," Émile told Jamie in
slow, faltering English, "you work. On your

day off, you play. Understand?"

Arrol shrugged nonchalantly, but his face reddened.

The doctor said the boy had been lucky; the mud and the sand had taken the brunt of the beam's impact. His left ankle was broken, but it would heal. Later, when Émile was queuing up at the cook tent for a bowl of soup, he overheard the men talking about Arrol's female friend.

"Isn't she one of the Chabanais girls?" said one of the engineers.

Le Chabanais was a *maison close.* It had a reputation as the most luxurious brothel in Paris, with gaming rooms on the ground floor and private rooms on the first.

"I doubt it," said another. "Madame doesn't let them out during the day."

"A bit like us, then," one quipped.

They laughed until one of them turned and saw Émile standing there.

"Sorry, boss," he said. "No disrespect intended."

Émile had placed his empty bowl back on the trestle table, his appetite lost.

After work, he had asked the foreman for the injured boy's address.

"I'll take you," said the foreman.

The boy lived in the thirteenth arrondissement, in an *appartement meublé,* a furnished building. Although the area had once been wealthy and the apartments generous, it was now overcrowded and squalid. They passed a tavern, the kind of establishment where the metal plates and cutlery used to serve food were chained to the tables. None of the buildings were connected to the sewer, and the odors of cesspits, of damp straw and rotting food that clogged up the drains were so strong that Émile had to cover his mouth with his handkerchief.

"This one," the foreman said, and stopped at a doorway.

In this building, the windows of the lower rooms were whitewashed in lieu of curtains. The landlord had divided up the drawing rooms and lavish bedrooms above, putting in platforms to make two floors instead of one. On the second floor Émile was shown to a small wooden ladder. At the top, a door opened onto a warren of rooms set around a huge chandelier, the lowest of its crystals falling only inches from the floor. It was impossible to stand upright; Émile had to stoop. The worker lay in bed in the back room, a filthy curtain drawn across the top half of what was once the drawing-room window. The smell was awful, of unwashed clothes and chamber pots. Was this the kind of apartment Gabrielle had once lived in? It certainly couldn't be any worse.

A young woman sat at the end of the bed with a string of rosary beads in her hand. She was not much more than fifteen but already heavily pregnant.

"How is he?" he asked her.

The girl nodded but didn't speak. The boy was sleeping, his foot raised on a stuffed sack. Émile pulled out a note and then another and gave them to her.

"Come on," said the foreman. "We don't want to wake him."

"You'll keep paying him, won't you?" he asked the foreman afterward.

The foreman didn't appear to hear his question; he certainly didn't reply.

And no wonder Émile couldn't sleep now. No wonder he couldn't dismiss what had happened as an unfortunate accident. He would send the boy a weekly sum out of his own pocket. He would make sure that the worker and his family were provided for. It was the least he could do; he couldn't take them out of the slums, but he would do what he could.

Outside the night was pitch-dark. He could hear the sound of two cats fornicating, all teeth and claws and agony. And then there was silence. But still that awful noise, the sound of ferocious need, remained in his head like an echo. And yet there was nothing to worry about. The construction was going well; the four legs of the tower were growing in size. Thirty meters at the last measurement; the bolts in the trusses were being taken out and replaced by heat-sunk rivets. In a week the hoisting gins would be taken down and in their place they would position pivoting cranes and then pyramidal wooden scaffolds. Soon they would reach the first platform. The construction had been straightforward and was still on schedule. What Jamie Arrol did in his own time was his business. And the boy would recover; the doctor said so. Yet why did Émile still feel so ill at ease?

The answer was so simple, so clear, he felt it like a sharp pinch on the skin. Arrol wouldn't be happy about it, but he could deal with that. Émile would tell him he'd made a mistake, that his lack of time made the relationship untenable, that he could maybe come back and work on a different project at a different time. Yes, he'd promise him anything just to get rid of him.

At last Émile felt at peace. It was the only answer. He listened to the approach of the street sweepers, their brooms sluicing water from the hydrants along the gutters. A horse-drawn tipcart would soon pick up the mounds of rubbish that were dumped on the streets every evening for collection. Gabrielle used to tell him he should never sleep with the window open in Paris. But he would not think of her. Not now. Finally he gave up on sleep. He climbed out of bed, brewed some coffee, lit a cigarette, and stared out at the eggshell blue of the slowly lightening sky.

August in Paris was a dead month. Most of the bakeries, the cafés, the florists, even some of the great halls of Les Halles were shuttered. Everyone who could afford to left the city. The ones who remained were the working poor, the tourists, and those who were building a tower. Or not, in Arrol's case.

As he was pulling on his jacket, Émile noticed a white envelope on the floor near the door. It was a letter, redirected from his office. How long, he wondered, had it been there? He ripped it open and unfolded a page of heavy white paper. The handwriting was dense, elegant copperplate. He was invited to tea with Mr. Jamie Arrol, Miss Alice Arrol, and the author of the letter, whose signature was undecipherable, on Sunday at five in the afternoon. He made an instant decision; he would reply with a regretful apology. Sunday was his only day off. And then he changed his mind; maybe this was an opportunity to speak candidly to Arrol, sooner rather than later.

On Sunday, just before five, Émile arrived at the front door of the house where the Arrols were staying and rang a large brass bell. A housekeeper answered the door almost immediately, which made him wonder if she had been hovering behind it. She didn't try to hide her opinion of the Scottish tenants as she took his coat and showed him into the parlor. It was clear in the rise of her chin, the arch of one eyebrow, and in the tiny draw of her lips over her teeth.

"You're welcome," she said, before turning and closing the door with greater force than was necessary. Although the word was in his mouth, he hadn't actually thanked her yet.

From the floor above he heard the whisper of voices and the faint creak of footsteps. He walked over to the window, took off his hat, and looked out over a small garden with a fishpond in the middle. Sunlight glanced off the surface of the water and a breeze in the trees above sent down a flurry of leaves. He'd been so busy working that he'd barely noticed. The year had turned. In a matter of weeks summer would be over and autumn would arrive.

He had gone over what he would say to Jamie Arrol several times. He would firmly but pleasantly inform him that his services were no longer required. The boy would be upset, for sure, but that couldn't be helped. And then it would be done.

"Monsieur Nouguier?" a voice rang out behind him. "We are so happy you could come."

He turned. A woman in a gray silk dress stood in the doorway. Her eyes gazed straight into his with a directness he immediately recognized.

"We have met," she began. "Before —"

"We have," he said.

"You seem surprised."

"I am!"

She opened her mouth but then paused.

"I also remember your name," he said. It was in his mouth, ringing in his ears like a minor chord, spoken out loud before he could hold on to it. "You are Caitriona."

She swallowed and gave him a tiny glance. He had used her Christian name, and with the informal pronoun.

"I am usually known as Mrs. Wallace," she replied.

"Please excuse me," he said, returning to

a formal tone.

He was suddenly aware that he had been staring. He gathered his face into a more acceptable expression.

"I have a photograph of you from the day in the balloon. It must have been months ago now."

"Really? I wasn't aware —"

"It was a test shot. I stumbled upon it just the other day. And now here you are."

She smoothed down her skirts even though they didn't need it.

"I would like to see it," she said. "One day."

"I would like you to have it," he said. "A gift."

She smiled but didn't reply. Someone else was approaching. A young woman dressed in an elaborate gown of pale-blue brocade made an entrance into the room and walked to the center. She turned her head a little to the left and then she seemed to compose herself, as if about to launch into a dance.

"Monsieur Nouguier," said Mrs. Wallace. "You remember Mademoiselle Arrol too, I expect?"

"Of course," he replied.

The young woman didn't look at him directly. She took in his shoes, his cuffs, his hair, and then seemed to fix her gaze on a point just above his head.

"Would you like to partake of a cup of coffee?" she asked in very poor French. "Or would you prefer tea? Assam or Darjeeling? We have both, you see," she added in English, "although I must admit I find it hard to tell them apart."

"Either," he replied.

The housekeeper arrived with a tray. Over a cup of Assam, Mademoiselle Arrol told him that she was learning French, and gave him another demonstration. And then she asked him about the tower.

"I heard it would fall down," she said. "That it wasn't safe."

Émile shook his head.

"I don't think it will fall down," he said.

"You mean you're not sure?" she replied with some alarm.

"Benjamin Franklin claimed that there are only two certainties in life," he said. "Death and taxes. But no, I'm sure it will be quite safe."

For a moment the only sound in the room was the small chink of his teaspoon in his china cup. This wasn't going well.

"So has Paris been kind to you?" he asked. "Did you attend a ball on Bastille Day?"

Alice's mouth twisted. "We couldn't get tickets," she said, and stared at the door.

"I'm sorry," he said. "They are hard to come by."

"Do you know people?" Alice asked suddenly.

"People?"

Finally she looked him in the eye, but only for a fraction of a second.

"Yes, you know, people in the arts, in society, with titles, those kind of people?"

It was as if the air had all been sucked from the room and up the chimney. He coughed and pulled out a handkerchief. To ask that kind of question confirmed that it was unlikely that she would ever know the right kind of people.

"There is cake," said Mrs. Wallace before he could compose a suitable answer. "And jam for the tea, if you'd prefer."

"Ah yes," he said, willingly changing the subject. "In Russia we drank tea with jam. It was rather nice, if I remember."

Miss Arrol was staring at him, a full-on stare that was not unlike a frown.

"Well, do you?" she asked again.

Émile stirred a spoonful of jam into his tea. She would not drop it. She hadn't taken the hint. This was worse, much worse, than he could have imagined. The girl was just as bad as her brother.

"Miss Arrol, I am an engineer," he said

with a shrug. "Not a socialite."

In response, her nostrils flared, just a little. He took one sip and then another. If he drained the cup, then maybe he could leave sooner.

"More tea?" the girl asked. "I prefer the tea we drink at home. It's not the same here. And so expensive!"

Alice Arrol smiled, and she suddenly looked younger, like a child dressed up in adult clothing. How old was she? Surely more than sixteen? No more than twenty?

"My brother calls it puddle water, doesn't he, Mrs. Wallace?"

He took this as a cue to glance across. Caitriona, Mrs. Wallace, was sitting with her hands folded in her lap. She smiled but did not look up.

"Where is he?" Alice asked. "No, don't get up, I'll go. Jamie!"

She hurried out of the room, her dress rustling like paper. There was a moment when the room was silent but for the regular, distant tap of Mademoiselle Arrol's footsteps on the stairs.

"We have all begun to drink coffee instead," Mrs. Wallace blurted suddenly. "I prefer it now, to tea."

"We are a nation of coffee drinkers with aspirations toward tea," he replied. "Listen," he went on, suddenly switching to French. "I had no idea . . ."

She gazed across at him, her eyes pale gray glass in the garden light.

"I had no idea," he continued, "that you were here, in Paris."

She sat back a little and her mouth parted. "I had no idea either," she said, "that we would return. But here we are."

She smiled, and a couple of strands of her hair blew across her face. She did not seem to notice and appeared, momentarily, to be elsewhere. The door, caught by a breeze, slammed shut and made her start. And then with what looked like a great effort, she sat forward, took another sip of her tea, and placed it back in the saucer decisively.

"Monsieur Nouguier," she said. "I like the idea of this tower. But tell me, what is its purpose? Is it for show? For spectacle?"

The moment seemed to slow down, impossibly, but unmistakably. She seemed to be querying more than logistical justification.

"It's lightness and air," he replied, "completely open to the elements."

"It's not serious, then? A huge toy, perhaps?"

He frowned. What was she suggesting?

"If you want to look at it like that," he

agreed. "But the fact is that it is not trying to be anything other than what it is. Nothing is hidden and the reverse is also true; nothing in the city can hide. From the top on a clear day, you will be able to see everything. It will all be gloriously transparent."

"It's what we want, isn't it?" she said. "Transparency. One so rarely finds it."

"Don't you?" he asked.

"No," she said.

What was she telling him? He pulled at his collar. The room was stuffy. Without another word, she rose and took three small paces to the window. As she struggled with the latch, he put down his cup and saucer and stood up. He wanted to assist, that was all, he told himself later, to help her open the window. But before he reached her, she turned around, her head and upper body in silhouette against the muted colors of the garden, like a photograph taken against the light.

"You should know, Monsieur Nouguier," she said in French, "that my employer, Mr. Arrol, has the greatest respect for you and your work."

"The feeling," he said, clearing his throat, "the feeling is mutual."

"And he would like stronger ties," she

went on.

His eyes ran over her face, back and forth as he tried to read it.

"I see," he said.

"And how is Jamie's work?"

Émile paused. What he could he say? He was about to let him go, to dispense with his services.

"Good," he lied.

"Good?"

"He needs supervision," he said. "But we're getting there."

She looked relieved, then turned and opened the window. A blackbird began to sing in a tree outside.

"Life has been difficult since my husband's death eight years ago. . . ." She paused and began again. "Mr. William Arrol has been very kind to me. I'll write and tell him today."

Émile had the feeling that, just as he had, she had given away more than she'd intended, not only in her words, but also in the way she said them.

"Please," she said in English. "Please sit down. Have some cake. Alice chose it."

The cake was made of macaroon and raspberries — a beautiful confection topped with spun sugar. Émile raised a forkful to his mouth but could not eat. His appetite was gone.

"He's out!" announced Miss Arrol when she returned. "And I told him you were coming! He must have forgotten. Now it's only me, I'm afraid."

Outside, the skies had clouded over and it had started to rain, a sudden summer downpour.

"Why are you both sitting in the dark? And who opened the window?" Alice continued. "There's a fearful draft!"

A lamp was lit and the window closed again. Émile talked to the Arrol girl, about the weather and about Paris, but his eyes were drawn back once and then once again to the woman he had met in the balloon.

"Have you heard of some artists called Impressionists?" Alice asked him.

"Of course," he replied.

"Are their paintings as shocking as everyone says they are?"

"I rather like some of them," Émile replied.

"You've seen them?"

"Anyone can see them. They have exhibitions."

"Where? When?"

"I know of one that will open in the autumn," he said. "It is not showing well-known painters such as Monet and Renoir but some of the lesser-known ones."

Miss Arrol turned to Mrs. Wallace, and then back to Émile.

"Really?" she said.

And then he realized that he had talked himself into a corner where the only way out was an invitation.

15

"Well, that was a waste of time," Alice said once the engineer was gone. "And he didn't eat any of his cake. Wasn't that rather rude?" And then she picked up her skirts and headed toward the parlor, closing the door behind her.

Cait stood and listened to the sounds of the house, to the bad-tempered clatter and slap from the kitchen, and the sound of the rain on the roof. To be standing alone in the hallway seemed suddenly fitting, a metaphor for who she was, stuck between floors, between rooms, between youth and old age, a person without status, without a husband, without a future. Was this living or merely waiting for the inevitable?

There was a small knock at the front door. The housekeeper was busy downstairs and so Cait opened it. Émile Nouguier stood on the steps, his face, his hair, and his shoulders wet through.

"I'm so sorry to disturb you again," he said. "But I think I left my hat."

The coat cupboard was next to the front door. It was lit by a pane of glass that let in borrowed light from the hallway. She told herself that it was just the chill in the air that made her hands shake as she looked through the pile of hats on the rack, the bowlers and boaters; she supposed it was the sound of the rain that made her shiver as she searched through the straw hats and the claques that the previous occupants had left behind.

"What kind of hat was it?" she asked. "Is this it?"

She held out a top hat. The engineer stepped into the closet behind her and examined it.

"Let me try it on," he said.

It was, however, too small.

"Maybe that one?" he said, pointing to another.

She lifted the hat off its hook and held it out to him. He reached out with both hands to take it. For a moment he was looking directly at her. In the hall they both heard the housekeeper's clogs on the stairs. And then the light in the hall was extinguished and they were left in the half dark.

"This one?" he said softly as he pulled the

hat, and her, toward him.

She was so close to him that she could smell his soap. She was so close she could feel his hot breath on her skin as his face traveled up and down the curve of her neck. If I can't see him, does it count? she asked herself. If he doesn't touch me, does it mean anything?

"Mrs. Wallace!" shouted Alice from the parlor. They heard her open the door into the hallway and come out. A shaft of light spilled through the glass above and into the closet. All around their heads the air danced with dust motes like tiny flakes of silver snow. Cait opened her mouth to answer. The engineer gave his head a tiny shake. Maybe he was right. What would she say? How could she explain if Alice found her here, alone in the closet with the engineer? Alice called out again and then, to her relief, she clattered up the stairs.

Once she had gone, Cait was aware that they were standing only inches apart, with only a hat between them, and that Émile Nouguier was looking straight at her. She knew the right thing to do was to pretend their conspiracy of silence had never happened; she knew she must let go. And yet still she let the moment stretch until it could stretch no further.

"This one?" she asked, and let go of the hat.

Émile swallowed, then placed it on his head.

"Nice," he whispered. "But unfortunately not mine either."

She started to survey the hooks, looking rapidly through coats and jackets and scarves and stoles, through all the garments the owners of the house had left behind, riffling through places where a top hat could not possibly be. But it was preferable to turning around.

"Well," she said, "I can't see any other."

The house was completely still as they stepped out of the closet. At the front door he bade her goodbye once more. She couldn't meet his eye.

"I'm so sorry about your hat," she said softly.

He leaned forward to whisper in her ear.

"I just remembered," he said. "I wasn't wearing one."

16

The carriage stopped outside a large mansion on the rue de Berri. From the street you could hear the chatter of people's voices and the soft chime of glass and crockery.

"We won't stay long," said Eiffel. "It's bound to be tedious."

"I'm surprised you agreed to come," said Émile.

"I'm surprised the baroness invited me," he replied.

"Monsieur Eiffel?" called out a woman's voice as they were handing their coats to the English butler. "Where have you been? You're late!"

The baroness stood on the stairs as if she had been waiting for them.

"My dear," he replied with a bow, "may I offer my sincerest apologies?"

"I should think so," she scolded as she came down the stairs to greet Eiffel. "You had better have a good excuse."

"Foolproof," he replied.

"I am sure it is." She laughed.

"First, may I present my most esteemed colleague, Monsieur Émile Nouguier?"

She turned as if noticing him for the first time. Then she raised her chin, smiled, and offered her hand in greeting. Following Gustave's example, Émile leaned down and gave her hand a small perfunctory peck. It was cold and dry and smelled of Pears soap.

"Everyone is dying to meet you!" the baroness said to Eiffel as she took him by the arm and led him up the stairs. "You're the star of tonight's little salon."

The baroness wore her wealth lightly. Judging by her mansion it was considerable. Like many of her social class, she rarely went out into the city, but instead could afford to bring the city to her. Invitations to her salons were highly prized. As well as wonderful food and excellent wine, it was a sign that you had been noticed, that you were of some cultural value.

The corridor she led them along was candlelit. On the walls, between the mirrors, hung a series of large portraits. Painted in the previous century, they depicted men and women whose poise and dress had been captured in oil as sheer as their own reflection.

"My husband's ancestors," she said with a wave of her hand toward the portraits. "Mine are all in the Louvre."

In the ballroom, three young women had arranged themselves decoratively on a divan, like a floral centerpiece on a table. They were vastly outnumbered by men, who perched on chairs or who stood awkwardly around the edge of the room. Some of them were expensively dressed, in silk waistcoats and wing collars, with canes and monocles, while others wore dusty suits and paint-splattered boots, stained morning coats and shoes without socks. The cumulative effect was of a group of strangers on a railway platform. All of them looked as if they were waiting for something to happen, for the evening to begin, for the small talk to finish, and for someone to say something interesting.

A long table down one side of the room was laid out with bowls of grapes, nuts, and figs. Canapés almost too beautiful to put in your mouth — curls of smoked salmon and jeweled tomatoes, shimmering beads of Black Sea caviar and quail eggs in aspic — had been arranged on huge porcelain platters.

"Please eat," the baroness commanded. But no one came forward. No one dared be the first.

"She is the great-granddaughter of Napoleon," Gustave whispered as he lifted two glasses of Champagne from a tray. "Her husband was a banker. She hated him and is said to be madly in love with her half brother, unrequited."

They both glanced across at the baroness. She wore a lilac satin dress, pearls in her ears and in strings around her neck and wrists. As if aware of their gaze, she turned and gave Gustave a smile. Her eyes, Émile noticed, were an unusual color, dark but closer to purple than brown.

"She seems very fond of you," Émile said.

"She collects people," Gustave explained. "Painters and musicians and architects."

"No," Émile continued, "I mean more than that."

Gustave shook his head.

"That will never happen," he said simply.

"What do you mean?" Émile asked. "Why not?"

"My dear boy," he replied as he sipped from his Champagne glass, "we may be able to span huge ravines with iron, but in France, men like us, professional men, no matter how wealthy, still cannot cross the social divide. We can marry young women of adequate means, however; in fact we must marry them young, start with a clean slate, so to speak."

"You make marriage sound like the purchase of stationery." Émile laughed.

"Not a bad analogy."

"Surely it's changing."

"Maybe," Gustave agreed, "but not fast enough for us. Or him, although he is too foolish to realize it."

Gustave's attention was drawn to the door. Émile turned to follow the line of his gaze. A young man strode in with a riding crop in one hand and a top hat in the other. The women stopped talking. At least two of them blushed. Without acknowledging anyone, he picked up a glass of Champagne, gulped it down in one swig, and then went straight to the food and began to help himself, gouging mounds of glittering jelly and heaping roe onto his plate.

"The brother?" asked Émile.

"That's the one," said Gustave.

"And the young women?"

"Suitable matches, I expect," he said. "Take a look. Any take your fancy?"

Émile smiled but did not look.

"I say!" said Gustave. "Do I take it that you have finally taken the plunge?"

Émile laughed. "There is someone," he replied. "But we'll see."

Gustave appraised him. "The harder the chase, the greater the prize, in my opinion."

"Clément!" the baroness called out. But her brother's mouth was so full that he could not return the greeting. Once he had swallowed, she kissed him on both cheeks and whispered something in his ear. He nodded, then turned back to help himself to more food.

"He has been out riding in the Bois," the baroness explained as she surveyed her ruined spread. "The fresh air gives one such an appetite."

Good looks in the family had obviously been distributed unfairly. While the baroness was handsome, rather than beautiful, her younger brother had the full mouth and large, long-lashed eyes of a girl.

"What does he do?" Émile asked.

Gustave stared at Émile and blinked twice. "Do? He's an aristocrat," he replied. "He gambles his parents' money. He fucks his way around Paris."

"I thought we had got rid of all of them."

Émile's last sentence was uttered in a whisper. The baroness and her brother were approaching.

"May I introduce —" she began.

"So you're the man who's ruining my view," the young man said without waiting for her to finish. He grinned widely, but it wasn't entirely clear he was joking.

"Maybe you will change your opinion once the tower is completed," Gustave said.

"I doubt it," he replied. "I hear it will soon be visible from all over Paris. A calamity, in my opinion."

"Is that so?" said Gustave.

"It is. If I had my way I'd pull it down tomorrow."

There was a small, tense silence. Everyone in the room had stopped talking and was listening to the conversation.

"Ignore him," said the baroness in an attempt to smooth away any awkwardness. "My little brother is a philistine. He doesn't like anything under a hundred years old."

"Apart from women, obviously," he said, and glanced across at the divan. "So what's it called, this tower? Something saintly, I expect."

Gustave put down his glass.

"Actually it's called the Eiffel Tower," he said softly.

"What or who on earth is Eiffel?"

"I am," he said. "I am Eiffel, Monsieur Gustave Eiffel."

The count stared at him. "Really," he said. "Is that allowed?"

"It is," he replied. "We live in a republic.

236

This, I'm sure everyone in this room will agree, is the age of man?"

It was the cue that the guests had been waiting for. As one, they turned to their neighbor to argue over Auguste Comte and Karl Marx. The baroness sighed with something approaching relief. The night had finally begun.

Later, much later, when what was left of the canapés had congealed and silver jugs of coffee were being poured instead of wine, Émile noticed a commotion coming from the front door. It was remarkable not only for its volume but also due to the fact that nobody else took any notice.

"I will not leave," a man was shouting. "I will not go until I have seen that man. Where is he if he's not here?"

But Clément, as everyone in the salon knew, had left hours earlier without saying either farewell or where he was going.

"How can such beauty be so intrinsically ugly?" Gustave remarked as they pulled on their coats to leave.

17

Cait walked through the Parc Monceau, past beds of flowers and exotic trees from the Orient, which would keep blooming until the first frost. She came to the park when Alice was busy with French lessons or dress fittings. There she would wander for hours along the gravel paths, past the lily pond and the Egyptian pyramid. Or she would linger beside the carousel to watch children on the painted wooden horses as they slowly revolved to the grind of the barrel organ.

The invitation from the engineer had just arrived. If they were available, his carriage would transport them to an exhibition opening the following week. Since he was working late he would meet them there.

Sunlight lit up the trees. Like daubs of paint, the leaves were cadmium yellow, maroon, and burnt umber. She inhaled the scene, breathing in the smell of roasting chestnuts from the hawker's stall and the sweet scent of the Percherons, the draft horses that pulled the double-decker omnibuses along the boulevard de Courcelles. Beneath it all, however, she could still taste the velvet darkness of the coat cupboard and sense the heady charge of the engineer's proximity.

She paused at a flower bed to admire a small bush covered with flowers. The petals were red and purple veined with blue, the colors of a bruise. Maybe Émile saw her only as a woman to be taken, used once and then discarded. How could she possibly risk her position with the Arrols for something so tenuous? She picked a flower, then crushed the petals to release the scent. Alice would make a good match for the engineer; she was young, she was rich, she was malleable. And yet they did not seem to like each other. Although Arrol wanted him as a husband for his niece, there was a limit to how much she could actually do.

She headed toward the double set of gates that led from the park to the street. Here the sidewalks were filled with people rushing home or to work or to meet their wives, their lovers, their children. She stepped aside for a nursemaid pushing a large perambulator, but the woman gave her a startled look, as if she had no right to be walking on that particular sidewalk at that particular time. Maybe she looked different, foreign? Maybe she always looked that way; maybe it was something in her blood, her background, her past?

Her father had been an army chaplain posted to India. Wives were expected to accompany their husbands for the duration. What did Cait remember of her parents now? The smell of mothballs and quinine, the softness of her mother's cashmere shawls between her fingertips, and strange, haunting sounds of their words, words she had never heard before, like *bandana* and *dharma*. Both had perished in the great cholera epidemic of 1863.

Cait and Anne had been brought up mostly by their grandparents. Her grandfather was a judge, a man who could speak Latin and Greek and often quoted Virgil to make a point at the dinner table. He had no time for dancing lessons or needlepoint but believed in education for both men and women. Since he didn't trust anyone else to provide it, he took it upon himself to teach both girls himself. While other young women their age were learning the polka and embroidering linen for their trousseaus, Cait and Anne, with varying levels of success, were studying French and philosophy, mathematics and the classics. It almost killed him, he joked, until he died quite suddenly of a heart attack while reading up for a lesson on Kant. On his gravestone were engraved an image of an open book and the words MEDICINE FOR THE SOUL, words that had been inscribed above the library in the ancient city of Thebes.

At nineteen, Cait had been restless, over-educated — sharpened, she saw now, like a new pencil. And while her looks attracted considerable attention, her tongue quickly diffused it. Although her cheekbones were high and her eyes large and long-lashed, there was an intensity about her that didn't translate well to small talk and pleasantries. But what was there for young women of their class aside from marriage?

Her sister, Anne, met George Wallace at a tea party hosted by her piano teacher. He was handsome, witty, and together with his brother, Saul, ran a legal practice in Park Circus. George wasn't a gifted pianist — neither was Anne — but they both shared a fondness for Bach, especially his easy pieces. He called on her the next evening and the one after that, and within a week, they were officially courting, with her grandmother as chaperone.

Cait was introduced to Saul a fortnight later. She kept quiet, as Anne had instructed. Saul, likewise, said very little but gave her a parting gift, a book of romantic poetry. He was, Cait admitted later to her sister, tall, silent, but utterly beguiling. Saul was twenty-eight, his brother thirty-two, both of an age to take a wife, but it was the former who took the lead. After a courtship so brief that there was barely time to proclaim the banns, Caitriona Rose McNeish married Saul Angus Wallace in St. Andrews on the Square. Cait swore that she would love, honor, and obey before God, twenty witnesses, and a small black dog that sat at the back and watched the entire ceremony until someone realized that it didn't belong to anyone there and shooed it out. Within three months of meeting, and two months before Anne and George, they acquired a full set of china, a chest of linen, enough cutlery to feed almost sixty guests, and a small villa in Pollokshields that had just been built. There was plenty of room to expand, space to grow.

Why did they marry so quickly? What was the rush? Were both bride and groom consumed with a terror that they would be unmasked, found out? Because neither was quite what they pretended to be. Once he had won her over, Saul seemed to lose interest. And contrary to her expectations, Cait discovered that marriage was not as easy to follow as the iambic pentameter of a sonnet. Love could not be wrought, like words, into a pleasing shape. The silences that had once seemed so mysterious began to grate. She tried to engage him in conversation, in discussions about the novels of Trollope or Dickens, or on the merits of Beethoven over Brahms. One day he admitted that he didn't care for music or art or even romantic poetry; in fact, her constant chatter exhausted him.

She wasn't, she knew, the perfect wife. She was bookish and argumentative and he told her so almost daily. In fact, he said, she drove him to distraction. She began to bite her tongue, to swallow her words, to stop asking difficult questions. For a while, at least, the marriage seemed to improve. Cait waited. She waited for him to notice her in the new outfits she'd had made, clothes that took no account of the temperature or the time of the year; she waited for him to come to her at night; she waited for him to love her. And he did, she was sure of it, for a short time at least. She remembered the glaze in his eye and the tenderness in the graze of his lips on the top of her head on their wedding day, she recalled the gentle brush of his hand and the firmness of the press of his body into hers, and she believed the fault must lie with her.

After a few months, however, it was clear that the physical side of their marriage would not play out the way she hoped it would. Unlike her younger sister, who conceived almost immediately, Cait failed to fall pregnant. And gradually, time passed and the numerous rooms in the villa remained empty while the slow drip of frustration and blame, of despair and despondency, corroded her heart like rust. Can one recover, she asked herself now, from the corrosion of the heart? And if so, how could one know it was sound again?

Alice insisted on wearing her gold taffeta ball gown to the exhibition opening. In her hair she wore a small matching hat and, to travel, a long black opera cloak.

"It's an exhibition," she explained. "People dress up. Even I know that!"

As they waited for the carriage, Cait was suddenly apprehensive. How would it be to see Émile again? Would he know just how often she had thought of him since the coat cupboard? Would she give herself away?

It began to rain around four, and by the

time the carriage arrived, the streets were beginning to flood.

"Where did he say it was being held?" said Alice as she peered out.

"He didn't," Cait replied.

As they drove north, the city became increasingly dark, the only light coming from candles placed in windows. Finally they drew up at the Restaurant du Chalet on the boulevard de Clichy, a place that blazed more brightly than any other establishment on the street.

"There must be some mistake," said Alice. "This isn't even a gallery."

The coachman, however, confirmed that they had indeed arrived. Even from inside the carriage they could hear raised voices and laughter, accordion music and singing, coming from the restaurant.

"I can't go in there," said Alice. "It doesn't look at all respectable."

"I'm sure it's perfectly respectable inside," Cait suggested. "It's an exhibition."

"A low-class exhibition."

The door to the restaurant flew open. A young man staggered out, leaned down, and was promptly sick in the gutter. Alice blinked and sat back.

"Need I say more?" she said.

"We can't come all this way and leave

again," said Cait. "Not after he sent a carriage. That would be very rude."

"I'm not stepping foot in there and that's final. You'll have to go. Make up some excuse. Tell him I took ill or something."

"But it was you whom he invited."

"Please?" said Alice. "And can you thank him for me?"

Cait pulled back the thick red velvet curtain at the door of the restaurant and stepped inside. Around a hundred people were gathered, gossiping and drinking glasses of wine, some well dressed, others not. In the far corner, Émile Nouguier was chatting to a man with a pointed beard. What was there about the configuration of his shoulder and the line of Émile's jaw that drew Cait's eyes straight to him? He turned, saw her, and smiled. And her face burned as if she had stepped out of the cold and into the heat of a blazing fire.

"Madame Wallace," he said. "You came. May I introduce you to Georges Seurat?"

"*Enchanté,*" Seurat said with a bow.

"I was just asking him what he is going to paint next," Émile explained.

"I'm going to paint your tower. If you ever finish it."

"Oh, we will," Émile replied. "We have to. What else will they use for the opening of the World's Fair? You should come and take a look at the site."

"I have! It's like two pairs of legs, women's legs, wide open."

Émile glanced quickly at Cait to see if she was offended. She pretended she hadn't heard. Seurat rocked on his heels, then spotted someone in the crowd he had to talk to and bade them both goodbye.

"I'm sorry about that," Émile said.

"No need," she said. "Is he well known?"

"No, not really," he said. "We met at an exhibition. I bought one of his paintings, a study really. Where is Miss Arrol?"

"Miss Arrol decided to wait in the carriage. I'm afraid she developed a headache on the journey."

"That's a shame. Maybe she could come back another day when she feels better?"

"I'll certainly suggest it."

The moment stalled. Cait was suddenly aware of his eyes on her.

"Well," Cait began, "thank you for the invitation. Alice and I are most appreciative, but I really should be getting back —"

"You're here now. Let me show you around."

"That's kind of you but —"

"It won't take long," he said. "I insist."

Émile directed her to the main salon and

steered her toward the first painting.

"The show was organized by a Dutch artist called Vincent van Gogh," he explained. "He formed a loose group he calls the Impressionists of the Petit Boulevard. They're younger than the well-known Impressionists. Maybe you've heard of them? Toulouse-Lautrec? Signac? Bernard?"

"I haven't," she admitted.

The paintings were depictions of bars and city streets, some painted in bright dots of color and others in fluid lines. They were unlike anything she'd seen before, like images of the world through the refraction of her headaches but without the pain.

"So?" he asked. "What do you think?"

"They seem to move before the eyes," she said. "They shimmer. The effect is rather beautiful."

"Exactly! I knew you'd like them!"

Cait glanced out of the window at the carriage outside. How long had she been? Five minutes? Ten?

"There are other ways of regarding the world," he continued. "The transient nature of light, the way the sun strikes when you're least expecting it, bringing parts of the world to life until they look like nothing you've ever seen before. They break all the rules."

"Is that allowed?"

He laughed. "Surely rules in life serve only one purpose?"

Émile's eyes were watching for her reaction, looking into her face as if he could guess what she was thinking. And then a volley of raised voices came from the other side of the room as an argument broke out. A bottle smashed, a woman screamed, a dog started to bark.

"I must go," she said. "Alice is waiting —"

"Let her," he replied softly.

A door slammed and the gallery fell quiet again. Someone started playing the piano in another room. Her heart was thumping, out of time. She could not meet his eye. Instead she focused on the curve of his collar and the fold of his necktie, the deep blue of a magpie's wing.

"Nouguier!" a voice shouted. "So this is where you got to! I hear you want to make a purchase?"

A gentleman — a dealer, she presumed — appeared at Émile's elbow with a notebook and pencil in his hands.

"Excuse me," the man said when he saw Cait. "I'll come back later."

"Actually, I was just leaving," she said.

Finally she let herself look Émile in the

eye. It was safe now; she was saved by formality.

"It has been a pleasure," she said.

"I'm glad," he replied. "May I show you to the carriage?"

Cait shook her head. "It's just outside," she said.

"Then please pass on my regards to Mademoiselle Arrol. May I wish her a quick recovery?"

For a moment she was puzzled. What on earth was he talking about?

"Her headache?" he prompted.

"Of course," she replied.

"You're all right!" Alice said as Cait climbed into the carriage. "I thought you'd been kidnapped! You were such a long time. Was it awful?"

"No, it was fine," she replied.

"It didn't sound fine."

"The paintings are worth seeing. We should go back another day."

But by the look on Alice's face, she knew that they never would. As they drove home along the boulevard de Clichy, Alice winkled off her shoes and rested her head on Cait's shoulder. And then, lulled by the motion of the wheels on the cobbles, she dozed. Their uncle had given Alice and Jamie everything, the best start in life. They were luckier than they knew. And now Arrol expected Alice to marry well. If only it worked that way. If only they were chess pieces on a board and not unpredictable, fallible, imperfect people.

Cait stared out at the empty streets as the rain lashed down. She suddenly wished she were outside, soaked to the skin, her clothes saturated, her face, her mouth, her eyes blurred with rain.

"I think I'm going to have to disappoint Uncle William," Alice said softly. She had not been sleeping after all. "I don't think I will ever be Madame Émile Nouguier, no matter how much he wishes it."

"I'm sure your uncle would like you to marry the man of your choice," she replied. "And not his."

"Surely you don't believe that?" Alice said.

The horses were slowing. The carriage stopped in front of their house. The coachman climbed down and opened the door, an umbrella held aloft. As he waited for Alice to pull her shoes back on, a man on a bicycle wobbled past, his wheels cleaving through the puddles, the brim of his hat tipping with water. He stopped abruptly a few feet away and dismounted. It was Jamie.

"My brother's bought a bicycle," said Alice. "What an idiot!"

"Good evening!" he cried out when he saw them. "Fancy coming for a ride sometime?"

"You must be joking!" said Alice.

"I don't know," said Cait. "They say that everyone will be riding one soon, both men and women. We should try it."

Alice found it hard to swallow her amusement. Clearly the idea of her chaperone on a bicycle was hilarious.

"Would you really?" she asked.

"Of course! In fact, let's make an afternoon of it."

"I know! You could ask Monsieur Nouguier," said Alice. "One last try for my uncle's sake?"

The coachman was waiting. Cait folded up the rug and smoothed down her skirts.

"I'm sure he'll be too busy," she replied as she rose.

"Dearest Cait," Alice said, taking her hand and holding it, "I'm so glad you're here, with us, in Paris. Why not ask him and see?"

18

The air smelled of burning leaves and wild mushrooms. As they sped through the forest, Émile caught a glimpse of groups of foragers searching the damp ground for girolles and cèpes. Jamie Arrol was farther ahead of them now, the wheels spinning as he pedaled as hard as he could. It wasn't a race, although he seemed to act as though it were. His sister let out the occasional scream when they hit a pothole or veered off the bridle path and onto the grass verge.

"Be careful!" she yelled. "Look where you're going."

Miss Arrol hadn't wanted to learn to ride a bicycle, so they had taken tandems. Now she was perched in front of her brother, while Cait Wallace sat in the seat in front of Émile, hands gripping the handlebars at either side of her. Her letter had arrived the day after the exhibition, two lines, one thanking him, the other wishing him well and suggesting they meet on a Sunday afternoon to go on an excursion by bicycle.

At first the two tandems had trundled along side by side before one shot ahead and the other fell behind, and vice versa, the girls laughing, the two men gasping with the effort of it. And then the road had narrowed and become a path and Jamie had taken the lead.

"Is this too fast?" Émile called out.

Cait shook her head no.

Émile had to admit that cycling was indeed wonderful; the wind in his hair, his speeding heart, the rush of danger. Cycles had improved dramatically over the last twenty years. Now there was what was known as the "safety bicycle." The wheels were both the same size, the seat was lower, and there was a chain-driven back wheel. For the first time, he was considering buying one. But it was undeniably hard work; the tires were thin and every single shard of stone beneath the wheels sent a judder up the frame. No wonder they were once called bone shakers.

The back of Cait's neck was visible to him despite the height of her collar. She wore a dark blue serge outfit — sober, elegant, a perfect contrast to the luminosity of her pale skin. As he caught his breath, he thought he detected the faintest trace of perfume from her hair, all tucked and looped into her straw hat. And he had to stop himself from leaning forward to inhale.

The study he had bought from Seurat was still wrapped in brown paper on his hall table. It was a small painting of a model, captured from behind. Her head was bowed forward a little, and from her shoulders to her bottom the skin was so perfectly rendered that he had the sense that were he to touch the painted wooden panel, it would be warm. Apart from their position, however, there was little similarity between Seurat's study and the woman in front of him on the bicycle; one was fully clothed, one naked. And yet, it struck him as he coasted down the path, it seemed that he had fallen in love with both of them.

They came to a fork in the road and slowed.

"Which way?" she asked.

Émile didn't know this park. He looked down at the mud and saw Jamie's tracks led toward the right-hand fork.

"The left," he said.

The track led them deeper and deeper into the forest and then, just as he thought it might, it petered out. A bird flew out of a tree and rose noisily into the air. The sun was low in the sky and the path was in shadow. He came to a halt and climbed down to steady the bike. She was still holding tightly on to the handlebars.

"It can't be this way," Cait said.

"You're right. We should go back," he said.

He didn't, however, make a move to turn.

"I wish I'd never tried it," Cait said softly. "Cycling, I mean."

"Why?" he asked. "Don't you like it?"

"I do. The trouble is that walking will now seem such a poor alternative."

He laughed. Finally she let go of the handlebars. He watched the slight rise and fall of her shoulders as she breathed, in and out. And then she leaned back, just a little, until the top of her head was inches from his mouth. Was she aware that she was doing it? Was she aware of the effect she was having on him?

She began to untie her bonnet. A strand of her hair had become entangled with the ribbon.

"Let me." He focused on the brown hair and the blue velvet ribbon, thick and thin, glossy and matte, knotted and loose. Minutes later, when her hair was finally free of the ribbon, he stroked it back into place, the strands beneath his fingertips as smooth and fluid as mulberry silk.

"Thank you," she said.

He moved his hand down until, impulsively, tentatively, he let it rest on her shoulder. She didn't object; in fact she didn't say anything. For a moment neither moved. Unlike the Seurat painting, she was indeed warm.

The boy must have been watching them for some moments before they noticed him. His basket was full of mushrooms and his cheeks were flushed with cold. Cait started when she saw him, pulled her hat on, and started to retie the ribbons.

"Is this the way to the château?" Émile called out.

The boy shook his head and pointed in the direction of the way they had come.

They couldn't have been more than twenty minutes behind Alice and Jamie. It was nothing that was worth pointing out; Nouguier was older, he was slower. Besides, the light was fading and they had to rush to return the bicycles. On the ride back to the boulevard it was decided that although it was fun, cycling would never catch on in Glasgow; too many hills.

Hours later, Émile still felt the rattle of the ground beneath the wheels and the ache of the pedals in his knees. But days afterward, when those sensations had finally

257

gone, he imagined he could smell the scent of her hair and feel the heat of her shoulder blade through the dark blue serge, he could sense the timbre of her voice reverberating in his chest. And the memory of her spun through him like a wheel on an axle, around and around without any sign of slowing.

19

Cait sat beside the fire with an open book in her lap. She had bought a slim volume of poetry by Shelley, a novel by Flaubert in French, and a book on philosophy by John Stuart Mill from Galignani's, the English bookshop in Paris. Although her eyes moved from left to right over Flaubert's prose, not a word of it entered her head. It was not her grasp of French that she had lost but the ability to concentrate. She started again at the top of the page.

Alice was sitting on the other side of the fire, staring out at the rain, rain that made skeletons out of the trees in the garden as it robbed them of their few remaining leaves. Occasionally she dabbed her nose with a cotton handkerchief.

"Why don't you play the piano?" Cait suggested.

She shook her head no.

"Or read a book? How about a cup of tea?

It must be nearly four?"

Alice sighed.

Cait went back to her novel. She had offered every one she had to Alice, but the girl wasn't interested in anything but fashion magazines.

"My uncle has no idea," Alice said eventually. "About France. I don't know why he suggested that I come."

Alice blinked and turned her head to one side. Her mouth dragged a little at the corners as if she might cry. A billow of wind rattled the windows, the fire snapped in the grate, the candle on the mantelpiece flickered yellow.

"Will it ever stop?" she said.

The rain was coming down in sheets, a steady downpour that turned the surface of the ornamental pond opaque. Cait felt a weight deep in her chest. What would have happened if she hadn't told William Arrol about Sinclair's proposal? Where would Alice have been at that particular moment?

"How about I read you something . . . a poem?" Cait suggested. "Something by Shelley?"

Alice shrugged.

"She left me at the silent time," Cait read.

When the moon had ceas'd to climb
The azure path of Heaven's steep,
And like an albatross asleep,
Balanc'd on her wings of light,
Hover'd in the purple night,
Ere she sought her ocean nest
In the chambers of the West.
She left me, and I stay'd alone
Thinking over every tone
Which, though silent to the ear,
The enchanted heart could hear,
Like notes which die when born, but still
Haunt the echoes of the hill —

"Stop!" said Alice. "I can't bear to listen to any more. It's so gloomy."

"It's a love poem."

"Who to?"

"To Jane Williams. But he couldn't have her; she was already married."

"Do all love affairs have to turn out badly?"

"Alice —"

"Because mine do," she said, then rushed from the room. Cait listened to her footsteps as they pounded up the stairs. A distant door slammed.

The letter arrived a few moments later, damp with rain. Monsieur Nouguier requested the pleasure of their company the following Sunday. She stared down at the words he had written. This had to stop. It wasn't fair. To Émile. To Alice. To William Arrol. She could not ignore Émile's advances, no matter how seemingly small they were. And more than that, she was scared — scared that she would feel compelled to return them.

She sat down at the writing table with a sheaf of new paper, a pen, and a bottle of ink.

"Dear Monsieur Nouguier," Cait wrote. "We enjoyed our last excursion greatly. Unfortunately, due to a matter of a personal nature we are not able —"

Cait stared down at her words. Shelley's verse, "Lines Written in the Bay of Lerici," still played out in her head, simple, beautiful, true. The poet had drowned in that bay only months after writing the poem. She tore up her letter and threw it in the fire.

"Dear Émile," she wrote. "Half of me is lightness and air, speed and height. The other half is weighed down with guilt, with shame, with confusion. Forgive me if I speak with more directness than a lady should, but neither of us is young, both of us are aware of —"

She stopped. Aware of what? What was she trying to say? This was a letter she knew she would never send but she still didn't have the right words at her disposal. She put down the pen and closed her eyes. She let herself go back over the day they went cycling, the speed of the machine as they rumbled through the park; the moment they had taken the wrong turn and ended up alone; the memory of his hand cupping her shoulder, his hot breath on her neck. And later, she remembered later, how they had met a friend of Émile's at the gate of the park, a man with a wife and two children who had both run to him and clung to his legs until he had lifted them up and spun them around until they were dizzy with laughter. She remembered that.

"Dear Monsieur Nouguier," she wrote. "As you may know I am a hired companion for Alice Arrol. I must stress that she is a very fine girl, accomplished in many ways. As you may have noticed she is extremely —"

"What are you writing?"

Alice had come into the room without Cait noticing. She was staring down at the letter. Cait swept her hand across the paper.

"Just a letter to my sister," she said.

"You've smudged it," Alice said.

"It was a rough draft," she said as she screwed it into a ball.

"Anyway," said Alice, as if continuing the conversation they'd had earlier. "It's stopped raining, so let's go out."

"For a walk?"

"Not quite," she said.

Even on a Thursday in the early evening, the department store, Bon Marché, was crowded. Beneath a huge vaulted and glazed ceiling, the central atrium, three stories high, was lit by glass globes on stalks like giant upside-down cherries. On the ground floor were stands selling hats, gloves, buttons, and bags. On the floors above were areas for eveningwear, children's clothes, footwear, and corsetry. It was a place of glass and polished brass, of sweeping staircases and balconies, of shop walkers and delivery boys. Despite so many people, however, the shop felt subdued. People spoke in whispers, as if they were at church.

Once they had climbed down from the carriage and made their way through the doors, Alice paused on the threshold and inhaled.

"Isn't this the most perfect place?" she said.

They wandered around the perfume stalls, then took the stairs up to the first floor, to the department for ladies' wear. On a plinth at the top was a wedding dress, an ivory silk gown covered in embroidery. Alice stopped so suddenly that the sea of people behind her had to part and stream by on either side.

"That, Mrs. Wallace," said Alice, "is the one."

A shop walker appeared at her elbow. Despite Cait's protests, Alice was whisked away to a salon at the far end, where several girls and their mothers sat on divans and fanned themselves with newspapers. Ten minutes later, Alice stood in the middle of the salon in the dress, a pair of ivory shoes, and a full-length silk veil, while the shop assistant spread out the lace train behind her. Nothing had been forgotten; there was even a wax crown of orange blossom for her hair and a pair of ivory gloves.

"How do I look?" said Alice.

Cait nodded.

"Lovely," she said, "but I fail to see the point —"

"Pig-nose proposed," she burst out. "In a letter."

Alice blinked twice and her eyes filled with tears.

"Is that what you want?" Cait asked softly.

"Of course not," she cried. "But who else wants me?"

She kicked off the shoes and started pulling off the veil and the wax crown from her hair before two shop assistants rushed to her and took over.

"You know I can't go back to Glasgow without a husband," Alice said. "I just won't do it."

20

An early frost covered the city, glazing the sidewalks and casting a lace of ice onto windows and glasshouses. Émile knew that the iron beams of the tower would be contracting in the cold, shrinking just a little in the freezing temperature. But they had made allowances for that; it wouldn't affect the rigidity of the construction. The site at the Champ de Mars was still an eyesore, a mess of horizontals and verticals, of wood and iron, the ground below pitted with holes now opaque with ice. From a distance it looked like a metal claw rising out of the ground. It was impossible to see what it would become, how these ugly metal struts that leaned inward, tilting as if they might fall over, would eventually form four elegant legs. No wonder people still looked so horrified as they passed. The older ones could remember Baron Haussmann's demolitions and the years of dust and mess that followed them, when he pulled down the over-crowded slums of old Paris to make way for his new boulevards and wide-open spaces.

It was almost midday but still the mist that covered the city hadn't lifted. Émile could feel the chill beneath his feet, rising up through the soles of his boots. His toes and his fingers were already numb. The cold didn't grip or grab; its effect was much more subtle. It provoked a contraction, a loss of feeling, an anesthesia.

After the cycling trip, he had written to Cait Wallace and suggested another excursion. She had written back to say that alas, they were not available. She offered no reason, no false hope, no incentive. And yet he knew she knew that he was being disingenuous. Alice Arrol was the eligible one, the one his mother would have picked out for him. Cait was the chaperone, the hired help.

Although he told himself to forget Mrs. Wallace, to dismiss her face, her voice, her image from his memory, she still came to him in his dreams; in one he undressed her, lace by lace, releasing her from the scaffolding of the somber clothes that constrained her. In another he kissed her in the coat closet. In one more, he took her home and introduced her to his mother, but halfway through dinner his mother had told him that she was wrong in every way. And then he had turned and found that Cait had turned into Alice Arrol and he had married her by mistake.

A week earlier at the races at Long-champs, he had watched as a beautiful gray gelding he had bet ten francs on, a horse whose odds were two hundred to one, outran all the others, crossing the finishing line with such a stride of joy that he was tempted to let out a cheer.

"He won!" he said.

"He lost his rider three stiles ago," said Gustave. "It doesn't count. You've lost your money, I'm afraid."

"I didn't notice," said Émile.

"Next time bet on one of the favorites," Gustave told him. "No matter what your heart dictates, do the sensible thing."

But he had never done the sensible thing; it wasn't in his blood.

Coal smoke and tar caught in the back of his throat. As always, he could smell the site before he could see it. The air rang with the music of the riveters high above, an orchestra of metal hitting metal underlined by the timpani roar and crack of their fires. By the time he had climbed the wooden scaffold to the level where sparks cascaded down from the workers' hammers, his eyes were watering with the smoke. The men were balancing on the narrowest of ledges as they worked. Height seemed to mean nothing to them. One even turned, raised his hat, and wished him good morning.

"How much higher?" he asked the foreman.

"Twenty meters to go until we reach the first platform," he replied.

"It's going well. Against all predictions."

"Just shows you," the foreman said. "You have to risk something in order to gain anything in this life."

Émile looked out at the city below. Cait was down there somewhere, brushing her hair or reading a book, walking through empty parks or looking up at the rise of the tower. The Arrols would remain in Paris for as long as it took to finish the construction. He would write another letter, he would propose another exhibition, he would suggest another excursion.

"Let me try?" he asked the foreman.

A riveter was instructed to hand him his tool. A red-hot rivet was placed in a hole with tongs and Émile hit it once, twice, three times until it was flush.

21

The ice at the Cercle des Patineurs in the Bois de Boulogne could have been made of sugar. Strings of paper lanterns swung in the night wind, casting their colors, a confection of red and green, yellow and blue, across the crystalline surface below. The pavilion on the far side of the rink was lit up with electric light. From inside, the smell of coffee, hot chocolate, and mulled wine mixed with the sharp, almost mineral pinch of the ice and the deep, dark scents of the surrounding forest.

"Now, this," said Alice, "this is where the people come."

An orchestra was tuning up in a small gazebo. On the ice, about fifty skaters circled clockwise while two men with brooms skated the other way, sweeping up loose snow and single gloves, discarded dance cards and lost buttons. Some skaters held hands or formed troikas; others pushed their partners in ice sleds, the prows carved like swans' necks. A man with an abundant mustache raced past, turned sharply, and then lost his balance, his body hanging momentarily horizontal before he crashed heavily onto the surface of the rink.

The orchestra started to play "Les Patineurs" by Waldteufel. With its sleigh bells and gentle, playful melody, this waltz could be heard all over the city that winter. Ice-skating was fashionable, and the rink was the best place to show off the cut of new clothes, the slenderness of an ankle, or one's dexterity on skates. Alice was wearing a new skating dress made of deep red velvet with astrakhan trim and a matching muff. Her hat, also made to match, was tied with a huge satin bow under the chin. It had looked a little too fancy when she had first put it on. But here in the Bois, compared to all the other young women, it was almost demure.

"Isn't this place pretty?" Alice said. "Why did no one tell us about it before?"

It was, Cait agreed, like a scene from a children's picture book.

"Who told you about it?" she asked.

But Alice's attention was distracted as she pulled on her boots and made sure the blades were attached tightly.

"Who?" Cait repeated.

"I really can't remember," she replied. "Let's go."

At the side of the rink, however, Alice hesitated.

"I'm not very good," she said. "Will somebody teach me?"

Jamie didn't offer. As soon as he had tied up the laces of his own skates, he was off, cutting between other skaters and stopping so suddenly in front of a group of young women that he sent up a spray of ice crystals onto the hems of their skirts with the edge of his blade. Alice clutched on to the side of the rink; she gripped Cait's arms and walked on the ice rather than glided. Twice, her feet skidded from under her and she fell. The first time she laughed. The second time she snapped.

"You're putting me off. Let me try on my own for a while."

"Will you be all right?" asked Cait.

"Just go! Please?"

It had been years since Cait had last skated. With the tip of her left blade and all the weight on her right foot, she pushed off. After a moment or two it all came back, the sweet rumble of the ice beneath the steel blade, the rush of wind on her face and the gentle curve of her trajectory as she flew around the rink.

Did Émile ever come here? she wondered. He would surely laugh at the people and the way they glided around and around with such concentration; if he was here, he would surely laugh at her. He didn't know, how could he, that she had read his letters over and over again. He had asked them to another exhibition. She hadn't yet replied but would, as she always did, with the same words, "I regret to inform you . . ."

What would happen if she didn't turn him down this time? She skated faster, her ankles aching, her cheeks burning. Once she just missed the prow of a sled as it stopped suddenly right in front of her. She didn't slow but skated faster, gliding from one foot to the other, around and around, as her mind tumbled with scenarios and images, with situations and possible conversations.

She made herself think of Bingham's Pond instead, just off the Great Western Road, where she had learned to skate. Every year the ice was swept and polished for curling matches and social skating. Together with her sister she had skated all winter until the ice was wet with thaw and shot through with cracks. She remembered how they had watched the adults courting with a sense of morbid fascination. It seemed so brief, their physical affection a mere affectation. Once the men were married off, they came alone to smoke and curl, their ice skates put away, perhaps, with their boxes of toy soldiers and skipping ropes. The wives seemed to develop a new fragility that prevented them from skating, or in fact doing any physical activity, as if marriage made them somehow more precious than the unmarried, like the best china that should be dusted rather than used.

Marriage will never stop me from skating, Cait had decided at the time. But it had. And she had forgotten how much she'd loved it.

As she skated around the rink alone, several men smiled at her and one offered his arm. She declined him politely; skating was liberating, exhilarating, like dancing without the need of a partner. The skaters shoaled as the orchestra played, individual and yet part of it all: the night, the music, the whole beautiful spectacle.

Alice wasn't in the spot where Cait had left her. But she couldn't have gone far; she couldn't move more than a couple of feet on her own. The bells in the church at Place Victor Hugo sounded the hour. It was nine o'clock. Cait took off around the rink once

275

again, circling it twice, faster this time, but there was still no sign of Alice.

Jamie was skating backward in front of two young women who seemed to be doing their best to ignore him.

"I've lost Alice," she told him.

He shrugged, caught the eye of one of the girls, then spun around on one leg and was off, skating with all the nonchalance of someone who knows he is being watched.

"Would you help me look for her?" she asked when she caught up with him.

"She'll be in the café," he said. "And if not, I'm sure she'll turn up."

A few minutes later, Alice did turn up, her face flushed, her eyes shiny.

"Where did you go?" Cait asked.

"Go?" Alice repeated. "I didn't go any-where."

"Alice," Cait said, "I've been looking for you for ages."

But Alice merely gave her a small, closed smile. "I'm cold," she said. "I think it's time for a *chocolat.*"

"How did you know about this place?" Jamie asked Alice as they sat down at the only free table.

"It used to be a private club," she replied. "It belonged to the royals until they ran off to Belgium."

"Well, they won't be coming back," he said. "The monarchy isn't about to be restored as far as I can tell. But where did *you* hear about it?"

Alice's eyes, however, were following the path of a young woman in green as she made her way from the door to a large bench beside a potted palm, and she didn't answer.

"Maybe I should wear emerald," she mused.

Jamie waved at the waiter and ordered. Three *chocolats* were brought almost immediately with a small plate of patisserie.

"How much?" he asked.

"Whose invitation?" the waiter asked them.

"Excuse me?" Jamie asked.

The waiter blinked and glanced around. All the occupants of the neighboring tables had fallen quiet.

"Who invited you here?" he said.

Jamie frowned. Alice opened her mouth, closed it again, and then blushed. They didn't need to respond. It was suddenly clear that they had no invitation.

"C'est privé," he said, which needed no translation. "This time, no charge."

A woman at the next table cleared her throat. Her husband lit his pipe.

"Vive la révolution!" said Jamie a little too loudly. "Drink up."

To leave now would be worse, much worse than slipping away in ten minutes' time. And so they sipped the hot chocolate in silence. Nobody touched the cakes.

As they headed back along the path through the forest to the main boulevard, Cait turned for a last glance at the rink. A light fog had descended, blurring the colored lights and forming a halo around the pavilion. The orchestra had packed up and one could hear the rumble of carriages on the main road through the park and the cry of night birds.

"I've forgotten my muff," said Alice suddenly. "I'll have to go back."

"Shall I come with you?" asked Cait.

"No," she said. "Just wait. I won't be a minute."

Ten passed, however, and still Alice had not returned. Jamie grew impatient and suggested he go and look for their carriage. Cait began to walk back the way they had come in the hope of meeting Alice on the way. The rink was almost empty. A few young men, their knees bent, their bodies curved forward, raced one another around the perimeter. In the center a girl of about fourteen, her heels locked together, slowly

278

revolved. The café was closing up, the chairs were stacked, the doors had been opened to let the cold air chase away the last few remaining customers. Cait scanned the benches, but apart from an elderly couple, one of whom clearly had had too much to drink, they were empty.

What sounded like Alice's laugh came from nearby. And there it was again, an explosion of tiny gasps. Cait walked toward the café, but she was not inside. It could only have come from around the back, where little light could reach, where the dustbins were full of coffee grounds and spent tea leaves, where wooden crates were piled with empty wine bottles and tins spilling with the spent ash of hundreds of cigarettes. She peered into the gloom. There was a man and a woman standing beneath an overhanging awning. Although she could see only the back of the woman's head, the man bore a striking resemblance to the man from the opera, the man they had seen in the restaurant on the island, the count. He leaned across to the woman's ear as if to whisper but then kissed her. Cait took a step back. Was it Alice? If so, she should stop it now. But she couldn't be sure. What if it wasn't? What if it was? Word would get out, people would talk, and Alice would be disgraced, soiled, unmarriageable.

She would walk around the rink. She would find Alice; her fears were bound to be unfounded. Sweet, innocent Alice, whose only crime was to forget her muff. By the time she had walked full circle the couple on the bench had gone. A man on a ladder was extinguishing the lights in the paper lanterns one by one. The darkness of the forest seemed to be closing in on the rink until the ice was nothing more than a faint opaline glow in the night. Alice wasn't there. Just as she turned to go back to the café, however, a young woman came racing along the path toward her.

"It was no use, I couldn't find it," Alice said. "I'll have to go back and ask in the morning."

They rode home in the cab in silence. Twice Cait looked into Alice's face to search for some change, some shift, but found nothing. Had she arranged to meet the count at the ice rink or was it a chance encounter? Had she been compromised in any way? She didn't look it. If anything, she looked rather pleased with herself. Maybe she should be happy for her? Maybe Jamie was wrong about the count. Maybe this was the beginning of a courtship with an extremely eligible man. William Arrol would have what he wanted; his niece would be married to someone with money, her future would be secured.

"Look," said Alice suddenly. "My blade is broken."

She held up the iron blade, and sure enough it was split in half.

"You were lucky," said Jamie. "You could have come a cropper!"

The next morning, a Monday, the Bois was empty and the ice rink was closed. Alice had said she suspected that her muff had fallen underneath the bench where she changed her boots and indeed, there it was, a glaze of frost over the astrakhan, the smell of night air trapped in its curls. As she lifted it, Cait heard raised voices coming from the wood behind. Two almighty bangs sent a rise of birds from the trees all around. A dog started to bark.

In a clearing just off the main path, a young man lay on the snow. Another stood twenty feet away, a pistol dangling from his right hand. He looked up and saw her staring at him through the branches. For a moment their eyes met. He looked familiar. Was it the count? She was too far away to be sure. He opened his mouth as if he were about to speak, to deny everything. But

281

before he could say anything, a woman came rushing through the forest, threw herself on the body, and started to sob. "Marcel! Marcel. *Marcel!*"

22

The letter was sitting on his hall table. He ran his finger over the lettering of her name, searching, perhaps, for an echo of her in the order of the letters and the curls of the script. And he wondered what her real name was, her maiden name, the one she was given by her parents, not by her late husband. He knew, he realized, almost nothing about her.

He had written the letter a week earlier, composing it countless times, trying to find the right tone. And he still wasn't sure he had gotten it right. In fact, he still wasn't even sure he knew what he wanted to say to her anymore; words seemed too heavy, too clumsy, too easily bolted together to make an inelegant form. All he wanted was to see her again. Beyond that he had no grand plan, no big scheme. But there was Alice, her charge, and there were his responsibilities, both of which conspired to make something so simple become seemingly impossible. And so the letter remained on his hall table, unsent.

At the site he stopped at the bottom of the ladders of the scaffold and looked up. The tower had begun to rise above the city's rooftops, the thrust of its metal beams reaching through the cloud that enveloped the city, making Haussmann's grand scale, his ambitious boulevards and étoiles, appear smaller. Unlike the Sacré-Coeur, whose conception had been so controversial and construction so slow that the city ceased to notice it anymore, the tower still provoked a reaction: an involuntary intake of breath, the race of a heartbeat, the point of a finger — *look*. It was taller than people had imagined it would be, finer, thinner. And while there were some who still droned on about its unmitigated ugliness, many others had changed their minds.

"Monsieur Nouguier?" a voice called from above. "We need you."

From that moment onward he thought of little else but how to solve a series of logistical problems that came thick and fast as the day progressed. The structure was incredibly intricate, constructed piece by piece. In which order should the pieces be assembled and where should the riveters be deployed next? Would the foundations on the side of the river, where the ground was softer and shot full of clay, hold? If they sunk just a couple of inches, the tower would tilt. And what about the wind? What if the city were hit by winds of a speed much higher than their calculations? Although it was assumed that the wind would pass straight through the structure, or, at most, make it sway up to six inches in any direction, what if it swayed so far that it toppled? And yet, although a tower this size had never been built out of iron before, the mathematics were correct; it would be stable, it would hold fast no matter what.

A boy appeared breathless at the top of the scaffold. It took a moment for him to be able to get any words out, and in that brief space of time Émile had run through all the awful things that could have happened. But it was the one he most dreaded that the boy eventually stuttered.

"Your mother," he said. "There was an urgent message from her concierge. You need to go to her. Quickly."

The apartment was almost completely dark this time. The housekeeper was waiting at the door to take his coat and hat. She didn't meet his eye.

"The doctor is with her," she told him. "She's had a bad night."

"You should have called me earlier."

"She didn't want to disturb you."

Daylight spilled around the shutters in his mother's bedroom, making long stripes across the floor. It took him a moment to locate her, her face almost as white as her bedding. Louise Nouguier raised a pale, thin hand to greet him. The doctor waited at the bedside with his head bowed.

"My dearest boy, I'm so sorry," she said.

"*Maman*," he replied. "What's the matter?"

She glanced around at the doctor. He remained mute.

"Well," she began. "I didn't like to say anything — you've been so preoccupied with work, but I haven't been feeling too well recently. Monsieur Fauré, my esteemed physician, thinks I may have —"

Her eyes wandered as she searched for the word. And so the doctor began to talk, about chronic inflammation, about cells and lymph nodes. None of it made much sense.

"I have a tumor," his mother pronounced.

Émile struggled to comprehend. He looked at the doctor for confirmation.

"But you can remove it?" he offered. "Can't you?"

The doctor cleared his throat. His mother

asked for a sip of water.

"Do you like that mirror?" she said after she had swallowed. "The one above the fireplace? It needs a polish, a little of the gilt replaced on the frame. Your father bought it in Venice."

As he located the doctor's hat, shook his hand, and showed him out, Émile wondered what Fauré really thought of him and his mother, of the shuttered rooms and the smell of his mother's perfume mixed with medicinal preparations for her digestion.

"She has the tendency to exaggerate," Émile said with a smile.

The doctor, however, looked at him as if he had just told a joke in very poor taste.

"I'm afraid this time she has no need. She has cancer. Of the breast. At quite an advanced stage."

"But surely with surgery —"

"The success rate is poor. Due to her age and her state of health, I wouldn't advise it."

"So what do you recommend, Doctor? To cure her?"

He sighed and gave his head a small shake. "I'm so sorry."

The sound of rushing water filled Émile's ears, the roar of a tide that threatened to submerge him as he tried to process the doctor's words. For so long his mother had been on the periphery of his vision, a stone in his shoe, a splinter under the skin, her voice like the buzz of a wasp in his ear. How could she be gone, absent, silenced? It seemed impossible that the world could continue to exist without her. He came back with a jolt. The doctor had laid a hand on his shoulder.

"Monsieur Nouguier?" Fauré asked softly. "If I were you I would take the rest of the day off."

"Does she have long?" he asked.

"Months, I'd say. A year at most."

"Does she know?"

The doctor paused. "I thought, when the time is right, you could tell her."

From the balcony in his mother's bedroom you could see right across Paris. It faced south, and the sun streamed in all day long, much to the consternation of the house-keeper, who claimed that it faded all the carpets. That was what had persuaded his father to buy the apartment all those years ago: the view. As he sat at the end of his mother's bed, he wondered if the tower site was visible. Or if it lay slightly too far to the east.

"You don't have to sit with me all day," his mother said. "I know you're busy."

"I have time," he said.

"You never had time before. Has something happened? That's the trouble with working for someone else. As well as making all the money, they can dismiss you at the drop of a hat."

"I haven't been dismissed," he replied. "It won't happen."

"I wouldn't be too sure," she said.

Only his mother knew how to rile him with a few words. Already he could feel himself bristling with annoyance.

"Do you have any idea what we're building? It will be magnificent, groundbreaking, monumental."

"A tower," she said flatly.

They were silent for a moment.

"You know what your father used to say? In a beautiful piece of glass you can see the breath of the man who blew it, and they breathe the same air as the first glassblowers of Syria thousands of years ago. He was proud to be part of such an ancient tradition."

"Mother —"

"With a little investment you could modernize the factory. The family house needs a bit of work, but it wouldn't take much. It would be nice to bring up your children in the countryside rather than the city."

He let her go on, making plans and hatching schemes.

"I could live with you," she said. "Your children could come and sit with me and I could feed them bonbons."

He swallowed down a lump. How could he tell her, how could he not? Instead he said nothing. He kissed her softly on the hand.

"I'll come and see you again tomorrow," he said.

"Only if you can spare the time," she said, her eyes liquid in the dusk of the room. "Maybe I'll surprise you and pay you a visit instead. You work too hard. And for what?"

If she could see the finished tower, then she would know why. His mother would see that he had made the right choices, taken the correct route. As he walked back to the Champ de Mars, he realized that it might not be finished in time. And so he decided that he would bring all deadlines forward and urge the men to work harder, faster. If nothing else he owed her this, the chance to see for herself that there was finesse in his composition of girders and bolts; it was bold and brilliant, it was art.

23

The snow had been coming down for hours. Cait hurried along the street as flakes flew into her eyes, collected on the brim of her hat, and found their way into the crevices of her shawl. She turned onto the Quai d'Orsay and there, in front of her, was the black tangle of the tower. Even from a few blocks away, the noise from the site traveled, the clang of iron on iron and the call of men from high up; the smell of molten metal and the bitter choke of woodsmoke. She glanced down toward the river. Although she couldn't see them, she could hear the sound of unloading from a flotilla of barges, and see a cloud of black grit that had turned the white snow gray.

"I'm looking for Arrol?" she asked at the gate. "Is Monsieur Arrol on the site?"

The security guard shook his head no.

"Monsieur Nouguier, then. Is he here?"

A boy was sent and she was told to wait.

Her fingers were already numb, her feet wet through, but the ache she felt was nothing compared to the one she felt inside. Finally Émile Nouguier appeared. He looked surprised to see her.

"I'm sorry to trouble you," she began, but she was so cold and the words were so hard to say.

"What is the matter?" he said.

"I thought" — she swallowed — "I thought Monsieur Arrol would be here."

One word, that was all she needed, an affirmation that her doubt was unfounded. Slowly, he shook his head.

"Not this week," he said. "And not last week either."

The air was suddenly too thin.

"But you told me," she said. "You told me it was going well!"

He had lied. How could he deny it? He didn't answer but gave a small shrug.

"And I believed you." She wiped her face with the back of her hand.

"I'm sorry," he said. "I have been rather distracted of late."

A workman appeared at the engineer's elbow and whispered something into his ear.

"You're busy," she said. "I should go. Good day."

"At least let someone hail you a hansom cab?"

Cait tried to regain herself and succeeded in looking, she thought, as if she had.

"Thank you," she said. "But I prefer to walk."

In the street ahead, the snow still lay untouched but for the thin track of a bicycle and the wander of a cat. From a side street, the footprints of a man and a child walking side by side appeared. The man's step was larger, heavier; the child's prints light, the size of Cait's palm, a perfect record of a tiny foot, a step, a direction, that would soon be trampled by other feet or melt away to nothing.

Once she was around the corner, out of sight of the tower, she stopped and pulled out the bill she had found that morning on the floor of the cloakroom. The ink was smudged but the words were still legible: *M. Arrol,* it stated, *owes 1,670 francs for Champagne, meals, and services.* The address was 12 rue Chabanais, a street near the Louvre. One thousand francs was more money than Jamie had or would ever be likely to earn in a year. What had he done?

On their grand tour of Europe a year earlier, it had been easy to keep track of him. They never stayed anywhere for more than a couple of weeks, not long enough for anything but the most fleeting of affairs. A chambermaid in Delft, a dancer in Geneva, an artist's model in Florence, those were the ones she knew about anyway. But here, in Paris, she had lost him. Until she found the bill, she had no idea where he spent his time and with whom.

The footprints headed toward a shopping arcade. Apart from the gaslights, the passageway was dark — a layer of snow had collected on the glass of the roof above — but there was a square of light at the other end where a doorway opened out onto another street. There was no sign, however, of the man and the child. The arcade contained a line of shops selling hats and snuff, children's toys and expensive tea. After a moment, she glanced up and caught the look in the eye of a shopgirl in the hat shop.

"Can I help you?" the girl asked in English.

Once more she had marked herself out as a foreigner without even being aware of it. Her clothes were soaked through and her hair was falling in strands around her face; when it rained or snowed, Parisians stayed indoors, or, if they had to go out, they took an umbrella. Cait shook her head and headed back out onto the street. It was less painful not to thaw, not to warm up. She knew what she should do; she should send the bill to William Arrol and admit that she had failed quite spectacularly. He would tell them to come home immediately and they would have no choice but to return.

She stepped off the curb and a shout bellowed out, making her jump back. A horse-drawn omnibus thundered past only inches away, its iron and brass, glass and paint streaked with mud, its smell — both horse and wet leather — sweet with heat. How easy it would have been, she thought, to have ignored the warning, to have kept walking to where the dirty snow was rutted and the air was thick with animal breath.

Now the street was empty. She lifted her skirts and picked her way across the slush. What could she do? Confront Jamie? Demand to know how he intended to proceed? But how could he ever pay that amount of money back on his own? It was, quite simply, a disaster.

A hansom cab had pulled in at the curb ahead. The door opened. A man stepped down. It took a moment before she recognized him. It was Émile Nouguier. What on earth was he doing here? For a moment he stood in the snow, regarding her.

"You walk fast," he said. "You're halfway

home already."

"You followed me?"

"That was my intention, but it seemed you gave us the slip," he said. "We were on the point of returning to the site when we saw you. Would you like a ride instead of walking?"

"No, thank you," she said. Single women, even the widowed, did not ride alone with single men. It was not done. He should not have asked.

"You look cold," he said.

"I am perfectly warm," she said. But even as she said the words, a flake of snow landed on her eyelashes and she shivered. She was wet through. And now the snow was coming down thick again and she had barely noticed.

"Please?" he asked softly. It was such a gentle request that Cait glanced quickly over her shoulder. No one had overheard. There was no one else there. The snow was so heavy that she couldn't see the other side of the road anymore. They were cocooned; the rest of the world was adrift in white. Who would see her climb into the cab? No one would ever know. And anyway, what did it matter? It didn't matter.

"For a minute," she said. "Just until the snow stops."

He helped her step up into the carriage and then, after signaling to the driver, he climbed in beside her. They moved off, the horse's hooves on the cobbles muffled now. Émile Nouguier shifted on the seat to keep the distance between them exact. Even without a ruler she knew it would be six inches — no more, no less. And yet the traveling rug he threw over her lap was already warm. The seat too. She sat back and inhaled; oiled wool and old wood plus the faintest scent of almonds.

"Better?" he asked.

"A little," she said.

She swallowed and felt his eyes on her face, her throat. She could sense his weight on the seat beside her; she was aware of every movement he made, every rise of his chest, every tiny movement of his eyes. Why did she have to pretend, disown herself, when everyone else did exactly what they wanted? The city outside had been rubbed out, obliterated by the mist of their breath. She could almost make herself believe that it wasn't there anymore. She glanced up quickly at the engineer, at Émile Nouguier.

"Monsieur Arrol isn't the easiest of charges," he offered.

The mention of his name brought her back to the present, back to Jamie and

Jamie's predicament. Alice's wasn't much better. How could she hold on to them when they didn't want to be held? For a moment they were silent. She took a deep breath and let it go.

"You're soaked through," he said suddenly. "Don't you use umbrellas in Scotland?"

He had changed topic, swiftly, artfully. She laughed, a bubble of pure unfiltered relief that seemed to come from nowhere.

"Of course we do," she replied as she wiped a strand of damp hair from her face. "Rarely a day goes by when one is not in need of one . . . but snow . . . it is too beautiful. One has the sense that it will fall benignly, like cherry blossoms."

"How nicely put."

He looked at her and smiled. Jamie, the snow, the bill, the tower, all of it seemed to fall away. This, here, now, a moment slipped from a clock.

Then, without warning, the carriage came to a sudden halt.

"An accident," the driver called down.

Émile wiped the glass of the window with his sleeve. Cait looked out. The snow had stopped. They were only a few streets away from the Arrols' house. The color rose in her cheeks. She glanced up at Nouguier.

What did he really think of her? What role could she possibly play in his life? She sat forward suddenly and called up to the driver.

"I'll walk from here."

"I can take you home," Émile said.

She stopped him with her hand.

"No need," she replied.

With a twist of her wrist, she opened the carriage door and stepped down. From somewhere within, from a place she could no longer look at directly, the engineer bowed his head.

A crowd of people, a carriage unshackled, a horse on its side, its eyes full of panic and its leg cleanly broken. And she remembered another scene: blood on the snow, her breath rising in plumes, the taste of sorrow mixed with the sharp taste of shame.

24

That night the snow iced over and was crisp beneath the foot. After work Émile found himself heading north to the Parc Monceau, and after walking through the park, stark and beautiful with moonlight, he paused at the end of the street where the Arrols lived. All the lights were on inside their house, the cracks between the shutters golden seams. He imagined Mrs. Wallace sitting in a pool of light, her dark hair falling around her face, her gray eyes thawed.

As he was heading home, he paused to let a woman cross the road before him. She turned and looked at him, her figure in silhouette against the yellow flare of the gaslight.

"Émile," said the woman. "Is it you?"

A bolt of shock surged through him. It was Gabrielle. He swallowed, twice.

"What are you doing in this arrondissement?" he asked as lightly as he could.

Gabrielle walked toward him and looked up into his face. "I might ask you the same question," she said.

Her eyes were running from his eyes to his mouth, searching, he supposed, for some indication of guilt.

"I came out for a walk. I was in need of some fresh air. But now I'm heading home. I'm rather tired."

"My dearest Émile," she said with a tease in her voice, "I know you don't mean that."

They stopped at a café she knew, a place that was filled with artists and writers and foreigners. They sat in a booth and she ordered a bottle of burgundy. Underneath her cloak she was wearing a dress he had never seen before, an evening gown made of black velvet with two narrow straps across her shoulders. It seemed to soak up the light like the pelt of a cat.

Without even waiting for Émile to ask her, she began to tell him everything that had happened to her since they had last seen each other, how she had taken the train to the coast, how she had spent the days walking along the long empty beach looking across the sea to the shores of England and wondering if she should throw herself in. And then she told him how she had met a man, a writer, in the Grand Hotel in Cabourg, how he had become so obsessed with her that he had promised she was going to be a character in his book.

Émile poured a glass of wine and then another, and let her words wash over him. She seemed to want something of him, but at that moment he wasn't sure what it was. The wine addled his mind, dispelling all unbidden thoughts, about his mother, about the glass factory, about Cait, until they were gone.

"Imagine that!" she said.

He wasn't sure what he was supposed to imagine and so he raised his glass in a toast and swallowed it all down in one warm gulp. He ordered a cognac and then another and then, as he was heading to the water closet, he stumbled and almost fell.

"I should take you home," Gabrielle whispered when he returned.

It was late when they arrived at his apartment. As they slowly rose to his floor in the tiny elevator, she stood so close that he could not help but inhale her, old roses and fresh sweat. Her smell was so familiar that it pulled him with a gravity that was stronger than he could have predicted, it pulled him right back to the man he had been before. His rooms were dark, the lamps unlit, the bed unmade, the shutters closed. There

302

wasn't a moment where either of them hesitated. As he unlaced her, he felt his appetite rise with each pull of the cord. He kissed her shoulder, then ran his cheek along the blade.

"Let me take everything off first," she whispered.

The black velvet crumpled to the floor. She stepped out of layer after layer, until she wore nothing but the pale glimmer of her skin.

"Come here," she said.

And yet when she lay beneath him, when he could feel the cool expanse of her thigh and the swell of her breasts, he had the sense that she was not yet naked after all. Her face was still dressed, still artfully arranged into an expression of complicity. He began to kiss her mouth, her eyes, her cheek, looking for some tiny chink that exposed her. But her face was as smooth as porcelain. And then he remembered Cait.

"You want to?" she asked as she unbuttoned his shirt. "Or have you drunk too much?"

The way Gabrielle spoke, the way she moved, was too loud, too mannered. The brandy still burned in his chest, filling him with spite.

"Let's get married," he said suddenly.

She blinked in surprise, then swallowed it down.

"All right," she replied.

"Divorce your husband," he went on. "Let's move to La Villette. I'll start running the glass factory and in a few years we could have a couple of children, move into the family house."

"We could plant flowers?" she suggested. "Build a summer house."

The room had started to revolve, a sickening spin that gave the moment the glaze of a dream. But what if it wasn't such a bad idea after all? She was still young enough to have more children. Who cared what people thought? It would be a business transaction, nothing more. His mother would get what she wanted. But what about the crippled husband? What about the child? Would he have to pay them off? He felt the cold slide of shame inside. What kind of man was he?

"Émile?" she asked.

He sat up and began to fasten his shirt again.

"You shouldn't joke about these things," she said. "I might just take you seriously."

And she laughed to prove that she hadn't. "Come back to bed."

"What are you doing here?" he asked, more harshly than he intended. "What do you need? Money? How much?"

"That's unkind," she said softly. "I wanted to see you, that's all, Émile. I couldn't forget you just like that."

"Don't lie! For God's sake! I know you, remember?"

For a moment there was silence, a dense black silence.

"There's someone else," she said, her voice small. "Isn't there?"

For a second he was outraged. What an accusation, coming from her. He turned, already primed to deny it. But what was the point? What tenderness he'd felt for her had always been laced with pity.

"That isn't what this is about," he replied.

She sat up, turned, and placed both feet on the floor. But she didn't rise. Instead, she leaned forward, covering her face with her hands.

"You make me so unhappy," she said. "I know you don't think I'm good enough for you."

He was suddenly sober, the brandy in his blood distilled into a viscous kind of sadness.

"No," he said. "I've never thought that."

"And we've never cared about marriage or conventions. You're a bohemian, Émile, like I am."

She looked at him and her mouth began to slide at the corners.

"Hold me," she said, "the way you used to."

He held her. What else could he do?

"You're still mine," she whispered.

"No," he said. "No, no, no. I'm not."

But even as he said the words, his body was moving toward her with another, contrary answer.

He slept deeply, for so long that it was light when he awoke. It took him a moment or two to remember. And then he heard Gabrielle in the bathroom, singing.

Émile was fully dressed by the time she returned.

"You startled me," she said. "I must rush, I have an appointment at the dressmaker's at noon. What time shall we meet later? Between four and five? Can you get away? And do you have twenty francs for a cab?"

He stood up and faced her.

"What?" said Gabrielle. And then she laughed. "Has the tower fallen over?"

Slowly, he looked at her. Her eyes were already filled with panic.

"Gabrielle," he said. "I'm sorry. You were right. I've met someone else."

A flush rose from her neck to her face.

Her breath came fast as she walked over to the chair beside the bed and began to pull on her clothes.

"Let me help?" he said.

"Don't," she replied.

At the door, he held out twenty francs. She paused, then took it. Finally, she looked back at him, long and hard. She was not upset, he saw now, but furious.

"Young, is she?" she said. "Rich?"

"Gabrielle," he began, "at least stay and have some coffee."

She laughed, but it wasn't pretty anymore.

"I was wrong about you, Émile," she said. "You're not bohemian at all. You're petit bourgeois."

He opened his mouth to make some retort, but the elevator had arrived, and without another word, without even closing his door, she climbed inside, drew shut the doors of the cage, and began to descend.

25

The boat train was late. Cait stood on the platform and watched the arched ceiling of the station slowly reappear through the smoke and steam of a departing train. There was a trunk of Christmas presents expected, plus a box of Scottish delicacies that you couldn't find in Paris — Selkirk bannock and butter tablet and plum pudding. She would give some of it to the housekeeper in an attempt to sweeten the sourness of her disposition. She doubted, however, it would have any effect. If Jamie woke her up one more time, keyless, in the middle of the night, Cait was certain she would hand in her notice. At present it was a war of attrition. Only the certainty that she could hold out for longer than they could, she imagined, kept her.

Although it was almost ten in the morning, the day seemed to lull; the morning rush was over and the early lunch rush hadn't started. As she had stepped from the carriage into the station, she was hit by the faint but unmistakable stink of misfortune. A bundle of grubby blankets was piled up above the grates from the Métro. An old woman's face looked out from beneath a filthy bonnet.

"Madame," she said, "can you spare a few coins for a bowl of soup? I am a widow. What did I do to deserve this?"

Cait felt the swell of sympathy for her. For a woman, the fall from respectable to destitute was not as far as people assumed. Besides, she herself had done plenty to deserve a worse fate. There was a time when she wished her husband dead. And afterward, she wished it on herself, a slipping away, a graceful exit, a gentle float into the great beyond. What stopped her? Only the thought that Saul would have won out in the end.

"God bless you," the woman said as Cait dropped a few coins into her open hand.

A gust of wind picked up along the platform and blew the pages of a newspaper off the ground and into the outstretched arms of a stack of empty trolleys. She suddenly saw herself in a parallel life, her face at the window of Roland Sinclair's house on the Esplanade, as if blown there on an ill wind.

She turned away and walked to the end of the platform. She would speak to Jamie, she would find out what could be done. And as for Alice, she would keep her close, she would not let her out of her sight. William Arrol trusted her, he had saved her, she owed him everything she had. And what of Émile Nouguier? She reminded herself of one of her grandfather's favorite Aristotle quotes: "A likely impossibility is always preferable to an unconvincing possibility."

The boat train arrived and a huge trunk was unloaded, one even larger than William Arrol had warned, with her name on it. As a porter wheeled it to the curb, she had the sudden urge to unpack it here, on the platform, the food, the presents, the sweets, and give it all away. She would give some of it to the old woman. But when they reached the grates above the Métro, the woman was gone and another derelict, a man with a dog, had taken her spot.

26

Christmas had come and gone. Émile's mother had been too ill to attend Midnight Mass and not well enough to eat the goose the housekeeper had prepared. He visited her almost every day, but she seemed permanently disappointed, sighing as she glanced along the length of the empty table that separated them and shrugging when he suggested a stroll in the park or a ride around the Bois.

"It will be busy," she said. "With families, with baby carriages and grandparents."

As he sat at his desk at the workshop, a church bell began to chime the hours — one, two, three, four, five, six, seven. Everyone had already gone home. It was the sixth of January, the Epiphany, the feast of the Three Kings. Sometimes he wished he had faith; he wished that he could believe that his life had a direction, that one event would lead to the next like a well-turned plot. With work there was certainty, there were angles and gradients and exact measurements. And yet even here he had made things complicated for himself. There were problems.

"Why did you make the angles curve so?" one of the draftsmen had asked him. "Why not make the sides straight, the tower like an elongated pyramid? How can we possibly fit the elevators?"

He thought it was obvious why. Because it would be too ugly, inelegant, too easy. That wasn't what he had designed. He had wanted lines that even from a distance invited the eye to run down them like the curve of a waist.

As he ruled out gradients with his pencil and calculated angles, he let his mind dwell on the sweetest thing it contained, an image he had been saving: Cait's face in the underwater light of his carriage, a flush in her cheeks, her hair wet and her skin as smooth as sand beneath shallow water. He could still remember her smell, snow and fresh air and the trace of the dried lavender that must hang in her armoire. He could still remember the soft chime of her accent: *I'll walk from here.*

A Parisian woman would never have climbed into the hansom cab with a man no matter what the weather. But then again, a Parisian woman wouldn't have gone out when the weather was bad and her clothes would be ruined. Cait was as different from a Frenchwoman as iron was from stone. Her eyes, her gaze — not coy, not in the slightest. She looked at him directly when he spoke, as if seeking him out, as if trying to read everything he had ever been and ever would be.

When he returned to the sheet of paper he had been working on, he saw he had drawn the same section twice. With both hands he ripped the page in two. He would have to begin again. This was all that mattered. The tower. Everything else was ephemeral, unknowable, unreliable. Who knew what secrets Cait Wallace carried around inside her? The tower would be built to stand for twenty years. The load-bearing qualities of the human heart, he knew only too well, were not nearly as robust.

He opened his desk drawer to look for a protractor and found a photograph instead. He had promised Cait he would give her the print. Before he changed his mind, he wrote out a short note, folded it into an envelope, and then dropped the note in the company's mailbox.

A knuckle rapped on his door.

"Come in," he called out.

"I hope I'm not disturbing you?" Jamie Arrol stepped into the office.

Émile took a deep breath and tried not to let it turn into a sigh. "No," he said. "Not at all. Come in."

Arrol closed the door behind him softly.

"I owe you an apology," he said.

Émile raised his eyebrows and waited for him to continue.

"I know I haven't been a very good apprentice," he said. "My time-keeping has been poor and my attendance erratic."

Émile put down his pencil and opened his desk to pull out a bottle of brandy and two glasses. At last the Scot was going to resign. Reason enough for a drink.

"And . . ." Jamie went on.

And? His hand paused.

"Would there be any chance you could take a look at a few drawings I've made? It's for a friend. Once I've got this thing out of the way, I'll be able to concentrate fully on the tower!"

Émile sighed openly and closed the drawer.

"I didn't mean to disturb you," Arrol said. "If this isn't a good time?"

Émile rolled the words he had been thinking around in his mouth but couldn't actually bring himself to say them. He would

314

like to tell Jamie Arrol that he was an ill-mannered young man who squandered every opportunity he was handed and wasted the goodwill of others. He remembered how distraught Cait had been and felt angry on her behalf.

"Very well," he said. "Let me have a look."

"I've got them here," Jamie said as he pulled out a grubby tube of paper and unrolled it.

It was not a building, or in fact anything architectural. The drawings detailed a small room with a large rotating screen set behind a four-poster bed.

"My friend works in a theater," Jamie said by way of explanation.

"A set? So what kind of a play is it?"

"One with a bed in it." He shrugged.

It was hardly an explanation.

"You see the screen will rotate and the bed will ascend," Arrol said.

"Ascend where?" Émile asked.

The Scot blushed and rubbed his nose. "Ascend the tower. It's an optical illusion."

"So the room is . . ."

"A lift. That's right."

"But there will be no beds in any of our lifts. Why on earth would anyone want a bed in a lift?"

Jamie guffawed. "Well," he began, "people

ask for the strangest things."

Émile considered the drawings. They were poorly calculated and carelessly drawn.

"The angle's all wrong here," he said. "Unless you had some sort of supporting structure, the screen would fall over. You don't want to kill any of the actors."

He picked up his pencil and began to draw.

"There," he said finally. "That's better."

Arrol looked over the corrected drawings and nodded. "Thank you," he said. "I really appreciate it."

"So when can I come and see it?"

Jamie looked puzzled.

"See what?"

"The play?"

Jamie raised his eyebrows and began to rock back and forth on his heels. "Ah. When I said it was a play, I didn't mean a play exactly."

"Well, what did you mean?" Émile asked. "Exactly?"

Jamie swallowed.

"Can I sit down?" he asked.

The story that Jamie Arrol told him was saturated with blatant self-pity. He had gambled, he had gotten drunk, he had spent more than he should have.

" 'Why?' you're asking yourself," he said.

" 'Why is he such a fool?' "

Although Émile shook his head no, this was, in fact, exactly what he had been asking himself. Jamie pulled out a small daguerreotype, an image of a young girl.

"I paid for it to be taken," he explained. "In a photographer's studio on the rue du Barry. Her name is Delphine."

Émile looked at it briefly and then handed the picture back. "She's very pretty. Is she an actress?"

Jamie ignored the question.

"The thing is, I owe almost a thousand francs," he said. "To Le Chabanais. It's a . . . a —"

"It's a brothel," said Émile.

For a moment they were both silent.

"Do you have anything to drink?" asked Jamie.

Émile opened his desk drawer again, and this time he took out the brandy. He poured them both a generous measure. From the canal, a steam whistle let out a long low blast.

"Are you asking me for a loan?" Émile said.

"No, oh no!" said Jamie. "The madame is willing to accept, partly in lieu of payment, a new room."

"I don't understand."

"She already has a Japanese room and one in the style of Louis XVI," he explained. "Why not offer clients a replica of an interior of what will soon be one of the most famous structures in Paris?"

"For — ?"

"Quite," said Jamie.

Émile blinked and took a small sip of his brandy. He wasn't sure whether he should be shocked or amused.

"And if you build this," he said, "then you will pay off your debts?"

Here the Scot looked a little shifty.

"Not all," he admitted, "but it will be a major proportion. But please, please don't tell anyone. If my uncle found out about the situation, he'd make us return to Scotland immediately."

Émile poured himself another measure. He felt suddenly breathless. It wasn't his business; it wasn't his problem. But he had been drawn in. He remembered Cait Wallace's face in his carriage again. He recalled something he had overlooked at the time; the small crease of worry on her brow, a tiny blink of panic in her eyes.

"Does anyone else know?" he asked. "About your situation."

"No." Jamie sat back in his chair, then

shook his head. "No. Of course not."

"Are you sure?" Émile asked softly.

27

Cait took out her pencil and stared down at the piece of perforated telegram paper. The sense of urgency that she had felt the day before, the certainty that the right thing to do was to send a telegram immediately, had now dissipated. Which words should she choose? How could she explain? It had to be brief, to the point, direct. She started to write. To: *William Arrol, Proprietor. Dalmarnock Iron Works, Glasgow.* Message: *Alice and Jamie well.* And then what? Tell him the truth. *Jamie in serious debt.* Should she reveal how much? She wasn't supposed to know. *Nothing has gone to plan. All three of us are lost.*

Quickly, she ripped up the paper and threw it in the wastepaper basket. What was she thinking? Now she would have to queue again and ask for another sheet of telegram paper. The post office was busy in the early evening. Dozens of people, both Parisian and foreign, were lining up to send letters, parcels, and telegrams abroad. Letters for the evening trains to London and Berlin and Rome had to be posted here by 5:30 p.m., or the sender had to go to the station direct. It was 5:25, and in the air was the chafe of impatience as the lines grew longer.

All the post offices in Paris had blue lamps outside. This one, on the rue de Louvre, was the biggest, the Poste Centrale. A line of counters stretched along both sides of the length of the hall beneath a vaulted ceiling. There was a queue, of sorts, although locals seemed to think they had the right to skip the foreigners, elbow tourists out of the way, and then ignore their pleas by loudly claiming, *"Je ne vous comprends pas."* It was Friday evening and they had more important things on their minds; plans still had to be confirmed, meeting places decided, suppers arranged.

"Tell him I'll meet him in the Jockey Club at nine," one man dictated to the telegraphic officer as he pulled on his hat and prepared to make a dash for his carriage. "Failing that, the Art Club in rue Volney."

"Mother died last night," read out the man next in the queue to the same operator. "Send money for funeral."

Although the gas lamps were turned up

full, the smoky yellow light they emitted made the occupants look wearier, the surroundings more dingy. Apart from those few who used the post office to sort out their hectic social life, it seemed as if this place was a refuge for the desperate, the lonely, or the recently bereaved, and you could almost taste it. Alongside the smell of glue and the sourness of overhandled paper were the reek of stale wine and the sharp, unmistakable odor of anxiety.

Behind the counters the operators emanated indifference as they accepted messages of an intimate nature in French and handwritten cards scrawled in languages that they did not understand. Births, deaths, marriages, or the most common, pleas for money; they had all scratched out the words countless times, and, as a consequence, had cultivated a tangible air of disinterest.

As Cait waited, a tall young man at the front of the queue bought three cards for the pneumatic postal system at thirty centimes apiece. They came already attached to their own special box. First he checked over his shoulder to make sure no one was looking; then he furtively wrote out three short messages, placed each in its box, and watched as the attendant shoved them one by one into a pressurized tube and they were sucked away. Who was he writing to? His lovers? His creditors? His family? She imagined the cards rattling through pipes underneath Paris to three separate destinations with whatever news, good or bad, they contained.

Once she reached the front of the queue, Cait asked the cashier for more paper and it was grudgingly handed over for a small fee. Once more she stood at the long marble counter and tried to compose a telegram. And once more her hand hovered above the page but she could not find the words she knew she had to write. Ever since she had seen the bill for the brothel she had searched Jamie's face for any sign of tension. It was true that he seemed to hardly eat anymore. At mealtimes, he wolfed down a mouthful or two and then excused himself, claiming he had eaten already at the site. One morning, they had passed on the stairs and she had reached out and touched his arm.

"How are you, Jamie?" she had asked.

He had seemed genuinely puzzled by the question.

"Well, thank you," he had replied.

She teetered on the edge of words, on the brink of telling him that she knew. She blinked as she tried to compose the accusation as gently as possible. He took this as a signal to leave.

"Mustn't loiter," he said as he carried on down the stairs. "I'll be working late tonight. Send Alice my apologies and tell her I won't be back for supper."

Who knew where Jamie really went anymore? He spent less and less time at home. And when he did come back, his eyes were red with exhaustion and his face was pale. And yet he wasn't depressed, far from it. He seemed to live on nerves and air, on coffee and tobacco. She'd seen him like this before and recognized the signs. But it had never lasted for more than a day or two; no woman had ever managed to keep his interest for any longer. This one, she guessed, was different.

She wanted to be happy for him, to congratulate him on finding someone for whom his feeling had become sustainable. And yet it was doubtful that they would ever meet. Cait wasn't naive; she knew that men had mistresses, whores, *demimondaines*. She also knew that Jamie couldn't afford her.

And what about Alice? Ever since the evening they had spent at the Cercle des Patineurs in the Bois de Boulogne, Alice had been restless, her mood an arc that had risen high and then plummeted. It was obvious she had been expecting a card, an invitation, some kind of communication. No matter what had happened or been promised at the ice rink, nothing ever arrived. And yet Alice still waited for the mail three times a day, she still leaped up at every knock at the door or rattle of a carriage outside, she still hoped, even though the likelihood of anything was looking increasingly slim.

Cait wrote out William Arrol's name and address again. Despite all her resolve at the train station, she had changed her mind. She would explain the situation as tactfully as possible and ask him to send a banker's draft. She would admit that regretfully, she had failed. One telegram, and their futures would be fixed; they would pack up and leave Paris immediately. Back in Glasgow Alice would marry Pig-nose. Jamie would be found some nominal employment in the ironworks, and she would return to a life of polishing pews and arranging flowers, of prudence and parsimony. She caught sight of herself in the dark glass of the window. Did it show? Was it obvious in the curve of her lip or the flood of her pupils? Could anyone see the elation that surged inside her at the thought of his face, his mouth, his name, a grace note: *Émile Nouguier.*

■ ■ ■ ■

His letter had arrived just as Cait was heading out for her daily walk. Alice had been expecting the dressmaker and would be busy for an hour or two. He had said that he had something he wanted to give her: the photograph. He'd asked if she would come and collect it from his concierge and wrote out his address: a street in the fifth arrondissement.

There was no risk, she had told herself. He would be out at work. But when she arrived, the concierge didn't have anything for her. Monsieur Nouguier, however, had come home ten minutes earlier. Would she like to go up?

She took the elevator to the third floor, where it stopped with a sigh. Instead of pulling back the metal grille of the gate she hesitated. Should she call on an unmarried man? Was it respectable? But she wasn't a girl, she was an adult woman, a widow. And yet it wasn't just any man. It was Émile Nouguier. She knew she should not get out of the elevator. She knew she should return to the lobby. She knew it, but still her fingers gripped the metal handle of the door and she could not let go.

Suddenly the door to Émile's apartment swung open and there he was, coat and hatless, with an envelope in his hand. He started when he saw her.

"The very person," he said. "Can you manage the gate?"

She looked at him through the bars, he on one side, she on the other.

"I —" she began. "I think so."

She hoped he did not notice the color rising in her cheeks. She hoped he did not see the tremor of her hands. The gate clattered as she drew it back.

"Did you find it easily?"

"I did," she said.

"Please," he said. "Come in."

Once he had taken her coat and hat, he guided her into the drawing room. A couple of paintings hung on the wall, small studies in bright color.

"Seurat?" she asked.

"That's right. Would you like coffee, wine, water?"

She shook her head. The bells began to ring in the church of Saint-Séverin. For a moment they were silent.

"The photograph?" she asked.

"Of course," he replied, and handed the envelope to her.

White sky, black wicker, the fine thread of

the balloon's strings, the blur of movement, and there in the middle in perfect focus, a woman with her eyes closed.

"It was a test shot," Émile said.

He came to her elbow and looked at the photograph over her shoulder.

"You see that man there," he said, pointing out the smudge of a shoulder. "He kept walking in front of me. He must have ruined at least six plates."

She smiled.

"Why am I so sharp," she asked, "when everyone else is blurred?"

"You were completely still," he said softly. "Everyone else was moving."

The photograph was in her hands but she was aware only of him, of his breath inches away from her shoulder.

"Thank you," she said. "For thinking of me."

"Cait," he said, his voice little more than a whisper. "I think of you all the time."

How many closed doors sealed them this time from the city? Three? Four? For the first time they were completely alone. He knew it too. Gently, he took the print from her hands. Softly, he reached down to the curve of her neck and kissed it.

"Shall I stop?" he asked.

Yes, he should stop. Think of the consequences, she told herself, think of the cost. But she didn't listen to the voice in her head; she paid no heed. Instead she turned her head and kissed him on the lips.

In the post office, Cait put down the pen and covered her face with her hands. What had she done? It was shameful, terrible, wonderful. She remembered everything that happened after, the warmth of his hands, the sense of release as she unbuttoned, unlaced, unpinned, until she could breathe again, until she could feel with every inch of her skin the softness of every inch of his.

She had to write the telegram. But to do so was to commit all three of them to a purgatory of a life that none of them wanted. The post office would close soon. The telegram. She had been intimate with a man she barely knew, a man she was not married to. What would he think of her? What did she think of herself? She didn't know anymore. And yet was it so bad? Rules were made to be broken, weren't they?

She scored out William Arrol's name. Then she ripped the paper in two and then in four, then eight, then sixteen, until her words were nothing more than a series of tiny strokes of ink on a confetti of paper.

28

Émile leaned back on the wooden scaffold and looked up through the lattice of iron-work. The sun was rising in the east. The workers who ascended the ladders threw long shadows across the site, a shifting plaid of light and dark.

"Émile!" shouted a voice. "How goes it?"

He looked across and saw Gustave Eiffel on the opposite pier, hatless and surrounded by a dozen officials.

"Right on schedule!" he called across. "We're at fifty-four meters. Only three more to go! I've brought my camera to record the moment!"

"Good man," said Eiffel. "And how are you?"

"Well!" he replied. "Very well indeed."

A soft spring wind blew handfuls of early blossoms through the air below. He closed his eyes and remembered Cait asleep in the crook of his arm, her dark hair loose, her skin as flawless as poured milk. Somewhere in another building, in another street perhaps, someone had been playing the piano. A plate of oranges in a bowl sat on a table in front of the window. A breeze gently lifted the curtain and then let it go. Without moving he had glanced down at her head, at the steady rise and fall of her breath. She had a tiny mole on the lobe of her left ear. Did she know it was there? It was a lover's privilege to know another's body almost better than she herself did.

She inhaled sharply in her sleep and he waited for the next breath. It seemed to take an age. Finally it came. He relaxed again. How fragile, he considered, is the thread between wakefulness and sleep, between life and death, between love and sex. Then she opened her eyes and looked up at him. Had she been sleeping at all?

"You've come back," he said, and raised her hand to his mouth and kissed it. She pushed the hair from her eyes, but even as he watched, a veil descended.

"I have to go," she said.

She sat up and then leaned over the edge of the bed to reach her underclothes. First she fished out her camisole and pulled it on. Then, as he watched, she picked up her corset and fitted it around her body.

"Shall I lace you?" he asked.

Cait stopped what she was doing. She was suddenly self-conscious, suddenly stiff.

"I can manage," she said.

He watched as she threaded and pulled, threaded and pulled — tight, then tighter still, until she wasn't soft anymore but rigid, her waist and hips contained by strips of whalebone, white satin, and Valenciennes lace. On top of it she layered a petticoat, a chemisette, and then a bustle, which was made of nothing more than a frame of wire and a few strips of cotton tape. Against the light of the window the undergarments were transparent, the lines of her body visible in silhouette. Finally she pulled on a black velvet jacket with lace around the collar and cuffs, and a skirt with pleats and bows and fringes. No light could penetrate the weave and weft of the cloth. She was opaque again.

"Come to the site," he said. "There is something I'd like you to see."

She glanced at him, her gray eyes full of morning light.

"Do you think that's a good idea?" she asked as she pulled on her gloves.

"We're going to reach the first platform soon. It's the moment of truth, the moment we see if everything fits together the way it's supposed to."

"Is there any doubt?" she asked.

He reached for her and took her hand. "No," he said. "No doubt at all."

Ever since, he had the sense that life should pause, that there should be a hiatus, a moment when all was still, a silence in recognition of what had happened between the two of them. Instead, as he walked to the Champ de Mars, he saw that steam still rose from the trains as they pulled into Gare Saint-Lazare and Gare du Nord, smoke still pumped from factories in the distant suburbs, and clouds still surged across the western sky. A Frenchman had recently announced that he had invented a so-called chronophotographic gun, capable of taking twelve frames a second: photographs now moved. The world, it seemed, was revolving faster, time was speeding up. And above it all, the steel tower kept rising, growing taller almost visibly, like vigorous metal bamboo.

It was true, however, that work on the tower had been stopped by the City of Paris several times over the past few months. The press coverage had become hysterical, and some newspapers suggested that the tower might topple and crush nearby buildings. Eiffel had agreed to compensate any resident that the structure adversely affected — sore eyes, he had privately joked, not in-

333

cluded. He had also agreed to pay for the tower's demolition should it prove to be unsafe. But the debate went on and on. A mathematician was quoted as saying that according to his calculations the tower would collapse. Others claimed that it would slowly sink. The less scientific believed that it was nothing more than a giant lightning conductor, which would attract more thunderstorms to Paris and electrocute all the fish in the rivers. That had caused much amusement in the office until it began to rain heavily and the workers came to the door to ask for reassurance that they wouldn't be electrocuted either.

What the public didn't realize was that the most crucial part of the construction was not the upper reaches of the tower but the part that was just about to be tackled. The first-floor platform, where the four piers met, had to be absolutely level. A millimeter out and the tower above would lean. Eiffel had devised a similar method to the one he used for bridges: using boxes of sand and hydraulic jacks deep inside the foundations, each pier could be moved up or down a fraction until they were in place.

Émile knotted his scarf a little tighter around his neck and placed both hands under his armpits. The men were finishing off the last sections; there was nothing to do but wait. From where he was standing, the whole structure was still a web of steel and wood, of bolts and metal braces. It was hard to mentally untangle what would remain and what would eventually be removed. The four piers were so high now that they had to be supported by huge pyramidal wooden scaffolds. A belt of horizontal trussing, a steel frame eight meters deep, was being bolted together above. Once it was attached to the piers, it would form the top of the pedestal and the tower would stand unsupported.

"That's it!" cried the foreman. "We're ready when you are."

"Excellent!" called out Eiffel. "Shall we begin? I haven't got all day."

Eiffel hadn't been on-site much recently. It was said that he came more often at night, to climb the scaffold and inspect the work by lantern when the men weren't around. Although the tower was his priority, contracts had just been signed for the Panama Canal project. He had just sent 2,500 men out to Panama to begin the excavation of ten locks. Despite the fact that it was a 125-million-franc project, paid for by the public in the form of government bonds, Eiffel wasn't intimidated. He had decided to start construction of the locks at once in Brittany. It was a hugely ambitious approach, one that Émile hoped, for his employer's sake, would pay off.

As the foreman signaled to the riveters to lower the huge metal frame into place using rope, Émile suddenly felt apprehensive. It was all about balance, all about equilibrium. What if he had made a miscalculation or had let through a rivet that was slightly off-center? What if the difference in height of the piers was too great to fix with air and sand alone? And then his eye caught sight of something moving up one the ladders. A corner of blue silk and the tuck of velvet; the curve of whalebone and the lacing of ribbon on steel hooks, a woman's laugh, a rising curl in the freezing air. He knew that voice, that body; he recognized the way that woman moved. It was Gabrielle.

"Tell these people to get down," he yelled at the foreman. "No visitors to the site without permission. Especially not today!"

What on earth was she doing here? Now of all times? He caught sight of her face through the tangle of the steel and wire, strut and smoke, as she turned her head and looked up. Then she leaned across to hold on to the arm of a man, a man with a wide girth and a large mustache. Émile glimpsed her eyes, her mouth, the triangle of her bare neck, but pulled back before she saw him.

"But it is the Minister of the Interior," the foreman told him. "He has permission."

"Ready!" yelled Eiffel. "Number three needs to be higher. Raise it by two millimeters! Émile? How is it looking over there?"

Émile leaned down to inspect the height. And yet he couldn't focus; his heart was thumping and his hands were damp. He blinked and the world began to tip; the horizontals and verticals ceased to make sense, his center of gravity was gone.

"Monsieur Nouguier!"

Three arms shot out to pull him from the edge of the platform and he was yanked back, a dozen fingers clawing painfully into his forearms and several hands grasping at his collar until it tore.

"I'm fine," he said repeatedly as he rubbed his arm. "Just fine."

And then there was her laugh again, sweet and high and cruel.

"Clear the site!" he snapped. "It's not Notre-Dame! Get these people out of here!"

The foreman blinked twice. He was expecting a request for water or coffee, nothing else.

"Certainly," he said, and started to descend the nearest ladder.

A whistle blew. The piers were all the right height, lowered or raised until they were exactly even. They'd done it. The workers started to clap. They knew how important this moment was. Everything was as it should be. And then he saw two figures talking to a third at the perimeter fence. It was the Arrols and Mrs. Wallace. Alice was laughing at something that her brother was saying, but Cait's face was serene and calm and beautiful.

"Émile," shouted Eiffel. "Take a picture!"

"Just a minute!" He fumbled with the box, dropping, then catching, then once more dropping his camera over the edge.

"Look out!" he cried. But its heavy black body, with its concertinaed lens and glass plate, was already spiraling, colliding with metalwork, smashing its way downwards before it landed on the ground far below, breaking into fragments and sending up a small puff of dust.

Gabrielle looked up and this time she saw him. Without meaning to, Émile glanced across at the figures by the perimeter fence. Gabrielle followed the line of his gaze to the Arrols. He knew she would immediately see them for what they were; foreign, wealthy, and, Alice at least, perfectly eligible.

29

Inside the Louvre, the atmosphere was hushed despite the high number of visitors. Unlike a stroll along the rue de Rivoli, people whispered, rather than spoke, as they glided across the parquet floor of the galleries or up the shallow stone stairs of the *escaliers*. And yet most of them weren't there to admire art — at least, not that kind of art. It was Saturday afternoon and it was raining. What else was there to do in Paris?

The Picture Gallery on the first floor had become a promenade, a place of backward glances and flicks of fan, of stifled mirth and tiny snorts of indignation. Horror came in guises other than in the paintings of Eugène Delacroix, a vulgar shade of damask or the whiff of cheap cologne, a curious bruise or a fallen hem. Gossip crackled up and down the great vaulted space like electricity, cruel and rapacious and barely true. But that was the fun of it, the gullible collective swallow that ruined reputations and spoiled chances. How could *you know who* pay a call on *don't look now* after it was pointed out that her dress was *you know what?* And how could *he* continue his courtship of *that* young woman when it was noticed that in certain lights, her face bore little resemblance to *her father* but to *the coachman.* It was all in the intonation, the slight lowering of register, the suggestion that invited the listener to lean a little closer and then harness their imagination. Surrounded by naked nymphs and scantily clad figures from Greek mythology, the imagination freely sparked. No wonder so much of it was fiction.

The visitors, to give the impression that they were indeed cultured, that they were there to improve their minds rather than debase them, felt that it was necessary to dawdle, occasionally, in front of a work of art and stare at it for a moment or two with a thoughtful expression. In front of the most famous paintings, artists had set up their easels and were making copies, painstakingly re-creating the palettes and brushstrokes of Antoine-Jean Gros and Raphael. The smell of their oil paints mixed with the stronger whiff of beeswax floor polish and pomade, making the air heady with the scent of boudoirs and ateliers.

There was a charity ball at the end of the month to mark the end of the season. The theme was "Old Masters." And so that particular spring Sunday, a number of ladies had brought their dressmakers to the gallery. They gathered around Canova's *Cupid,* Leonardo's *St. Anne,* and Rembrandt's *Angel of Tobias,* to discuss cut and cloth, color and coiffure.

Alice was in a foul mood. She was bored by painting, tired of sculpture, and fatigued by antiquities. She wore a pale yellow velvet walking dress. The color, other women's glances told her more than once, was all wrong. The rain had turned the hem a dirty ochre.

"Can we go now?" she asked more than once.

"But we've only just arrived," Cait replied. "And besides, you were the one who wanted to come."

They stopped to peer up at a vast painting by Titian.

"What do you think?"

"Of what?" Alice asked.

"This painting," Cait replied. "Of Jupiter and Antiope?"

"Clearly I am not sophisticated enough to understand it."

"Well," Cait said, "Jupiter is in the form of a satyr —"

"Stop! Look. It's him."

The count was standing beside a Raphael. He was at the center of a group of young men and in the middle of telling a long story, a tale that prompted regular, short bursts of laughter. The collar of his white shirt was undone and he had the look of someone who had not yet been to bed and wanted everyone to know it. As he reached the punch line, his eyes fell on Alice, but without stopping, they moved on, sliding across her face to linger on a woman a few feet away, a woman in a pale blue dress and a straw hat. She shook her head in mock disapproval, which made him laugh, longer and louder than everyone else.

"Would you like to see the sculpture?" Cait turned, but Alice was gone.

First, Cait walked the entire length of the Picture Gallery and then looked in the Salle Carré and the Galerie d'Apollon. Alice wasn't in the vestibule or waiting on the staircase; there was no sign of her. Cait turned left into the other, smaller salons; bronze antiquities, furniture, tapestry, Oriental fabric, each one led on to the next. Could Alice have come this way? There were fewer people here than in the main galleries, just older couples, private tutors and their pupils, and elderly single men who lingered but were easily distracted by the click of a woman's heel on the marble floor.

As she walked on, the galleries became emptier and emptier. Thick dust lay beneath the glass cases of Egyptian sarcophagi and antique pottery; the floors were dulled by a lack of footfalls. She walked faster, almost breaking into a run. Alice could be anywhere. She spoke almost no French. She rarely carried money. Maybe she should go back the way she had come? Maybe she should wait by the main door? She stopped to take her bearings and realized that she had passed along the gallery that connected the Old Louvre to the Tuileries and was now in one of the galleries around all four sides of the Cour du Louvre. Surely if she carried on she would end up back where she started? And so she went on, turning left, then right, then left again. A room of Dutch Masters. Hadn't she been here before? The heavy gold frames all looked the same. A bell rang somewhere deep inside the museum. It was closing time. She turned a corner. Another gallery hung with portraits: men, women, children, babies. She walked faster but there were more of the same, one opening into the next, an endless display of dynasties, ancestors, generations of wealth. The air was stale and still as if time itself had been trapped and bottled.

At last she found an open window, stopped, and gulped down the cool air. Outside the sun still shone, the birds still sang, the shadows were lengthening. Why, she asked herself, was she so anxious? She wasn't a nursemaid. Alice was old enough to not lose herself in an art gallery, surely. And yet what if she was with the count? What then? How swiftly damage could be done to a woman of her age. How easily a reputation could be tarnished. And then, from somewhere nearby, came the murmur of women's conversation.

"I thought I'd die! Without ever attending a proper ball."

The voice was unmistakable. Cait ran through salon after salon until she reached the last and just there was a flight of stone steps that led down into a gallery of Greek statues. And there, at the bottom, was Alice Arrol, sitting on a stone bench with the woman Cait had noticed earlier, the woman with the pale blue dress and straw hat.

"Here you are, Mrs. Wallace!" Alice cried out when she saw Cait. "We've been waiting an age, you know. Where have you been?"

Cait tried to catch her breath and swallow her fury. Alice was safe; that was all that mattered. Not the fact that she had been driven half-mad with worry and had walked halfway around the museum. Not the fact that Alice didn't seem remotely contrite.

"I've been looking for you," Cait replied in a voice that was as controlled as she was able to keep it. "Everywhere, actually."

"I was here," she replied as if Cait were idiotic.

And then Alice laughed.

"Where else would I be?" she added. "Thankfully I wasn't alone."

"It's easy to get lost in the Louvre," the lady in the straw hat said in English with a touch of an American accent. "And there are many unscrupulous men who will take advantage of a young woman without a chaperone."

"I am indeed indebted to you," said Cait.

"While we were waiting for you, your charge was telling me all about how you came to be in Paris. And how much she would like a portrait of herself."

"Really?" Cait replied. "Alice has never mentioned it before."

"My husband is an artist," the woman continued. "Maybe I could see if he has a space in his schedule?"

"Isn't she elegant," Alice enthused after the lady had taken her leave. "She learnt English from a lover, a famous painter, I think. And she was so kind, waiting with me while you took yourself off on your little gallivant. She said that every young lady should have a portrait of themselves for posterity. You know, I think I've made my first real Parisian friend."

The attendant held the door open for them. Outside it had stopped raining.

"Her name," Alice continued, "her name is Gabrielle."

30

September 1888

Autumn, the most beautiful season of the year in Paris, had arrived; fallen leaves crisp beneath the shoe sole and in the early morning air the faintest suggestion of frost. Socially, it was an in-between time — society had returned, but only briefly, before heading out to house parties in the châteaux on the banks of the Loire or the Oise. For a week or two, however, the air was filled with the smell of new cloth and hot irons as the wealthy tried on their new wardrobes, the women in checks and plaids, the men in bowler hats and English cloaks.

Émile knew that the dressmakers, the milliners, and the corsetières would be booked up weeks in advance; it was impossible to pick up a copy of *Revue de la Mode* anywhere. As a boy, he remembered longing for his parents to leave with their trunks full of new clothes, to head out to the small family château in the Loire and let him start back to his Catholic boarding school in peace. The château — it was more of a large house — had been locked up for years now, his mother unwilling to vacation there alone. One day, he had promised himself, he would find the time to go back and unfasten the shutters and air the rooms. Until then, it was a bill he paid monthly, a tithe to the family's legacy.

The city's fixation with one's wardrobe had always struck him as decidedly archaic, not to mention expensive. The countryside was not the Bois de Boulogne, and yet there were dinners and dances, cycling and shooting parties, weeks of activity that demanded several changes of clothes a day at least. In the future, he hoped, all the rigid lines of decorum, the rules that dictated what could be worn and when, would be forgotten and no one would care whether gloves were de rigueur at dinner or whether hats should be removed in restaurants. People would have other, more interesting things, or people, to think about.

Since the first time, months ago, Cait Wallace had come to see him sporadically, whenever Alice was busy and she wouldn't be missed. The last time, however, she had come to the tower site after-hours as he had asked her to. It had been early summer, and although it was late, the daylight had only just begun to leach from the sky. He invited her into one of the work huts and swept a table clear of paper and instruments, of newspapers and pencils. She glanced at the door. He locked it. And then there was only the rise of her breath beneath the span of her corset, the nub of her tiny buttons as one by one he released her, the stretch of pale skin at the top of her stockings.

Afterward, as she fastened her clothes, she had told him that she and Alice were leaving Paris for the summer holidays, for the Deauville on the coast. And then she paused. Outside, a man's voice called out. Another laughed. Someone was approaching. A knock sounded on the door.

"Monsieur Nouguier," a voice called out.

Cait looked at him and could not hide her horror; it was the foreman.

"Can I come in?" he asked, then tried the door handle.

There were no other doors. Émile motioned to a chair and she sat down and flattened her skirts.

"Monsieur!" Émile said as he unlocked the door. "You must get this door fixed. It won't close unless you lock it."

The foreman stepped inside, then looked

from Cait to Émile.

"Of course, Monsieur Nouguier," he said. "So sorry to disturb you. Shall I come back later?"

Cait took this as a cue and rose to her feet.

"Actually, we were finished," she said. "Thank you for your time, Monsieur. I will convey your thoughts to Monsieur Arrol's uncle."

And then she was gone, leaving nothing but a stray hair on his collar and the scent of her body on his lips. Afterward, it was hard to concentrate on what the foreman was telling him. Did he suspect anything? Did he believe his explanation? It was thin, to say the least.

"I'll have a go at the door," Émile said, picking up a screwdriver. "It probably just needs a small tweak."

The foreman had nodded.

"I'm sure a tweak would do it," he said, his face deadpan.

Since then the weeks had passed but he'd had no word from Cait. And so he had agreed to meet Jamie Arrol during working hours on a street corner in the second arrondissement, just as the boy had requested. He would know when Cait and Miss Arrol would be back from the coast.

Jamie was waiting for him underneath a

lamppost at the cross section between Avenue de l'Opéra and rue Danielle-Casanova. Émile climbed down from his carriage as Arrol lit a fresh cigarette. He looked up and seemed a little surprised to see him.

"Here you are," Jamie said. "I thought you'd forgotten."

"Am I late?" he asked.

"A little," he replied. "It's a couple of minutes' walk from here. I hope that's all right."

"Lead on."

It was late morning and the avenue was full of nursemaids and children, clerks and bankers from the Bourse heading out to lunch. The question vexed him like an itch and yet he could not ask straight out; he would have to wait for the right moment.

"This is the one," Arrol said as they took a narrow street on the left-hand side.

Émile glanced up. It was the rue Chabanais. They stopped at the end, at number 12.

"Are you acquainted with this establishment?"

Émile laughed and shook his head.

"I know of it but have never experienced it firsthand," he said with a slight raise of his eyebrow.

"Well, come this way," Jamie said. "It really is something special."

The front door of La Chabanais had been made to look like the entrance to a cave. Once inside, however, a sweeping staircase led up to more than two dozen rooms. It was, he knew, one of the most expensive, most luxurious brothels in Paris, and catered to every taste, every whim, every fantasy. In this *maison close* there were rooms where mirrors covered all the walls and the ceiling, rooms with special apparatus and custom-made furniture.

"That's Bertie's room," said Jamie as they passed a door. "He's said to have a special chair, a large copper tub, and his own coat of arms above the bed. I'd let you have a look but it's kept locked."

It was well known that the Prince of Wales was a regular. So were half the members of the Jockey Club de Paris. And the cabinet. But the pleasure house was quiet at this time of the day, the corridors empty. Madame Kelly, the Irishwoman who ran the place, wasn't at home. The windows had been opened but the air was still murky and smelled of extinguished candles and washing starch, plus something else, something animal that he hesitated to place. From the back rooms where the girls lived came the faint sound of laughter and from up ahead, farther along the corridor, the ratchet of the saw.

"Here we are," said Jamie as they reached the last room.

The door was wide open. For a moment Émile stood and blinked. In front of him was a huge construction of wood painted to look like iron. It was a section of the tower, his tower. Inside was a huge bed. A workman was sawing up lengths of wood next to the window.

"Can you leave us for a moment?" Jamie asked the workman. "Now, watch this," said Jamie once he was gone.

A screen on rollers had been set up behind the bed. It was painted with a panorama of Paris. As Jamie turned a lever, the bed started to rise and the painted scene to descend.

"To simulate the lift," Jamie explained. Émile nodded.

"And you're supposed to . . . ?"

"Absolutely," Jamie confirmed.

"And what do you do when you get to the top?" he asked.

"Come down again!" Jamie declared. "You could go up and down all night if you wished."

"You're sure it's safe?" Émile asked.

"No." Jamie laughed. "I mean, yes, I certainly hope so."

"And who turns the lever?"

Jamie frowned.

"That's what I wanted to ask you. Have any suggestions?"

"A lift mechanism, maybe?" Émile shrugged. "Hydraulics? But it would be noisy. Or as an alternative, maybe the bed could stay still and only the screen would move?"

"No, that won't do," he said. "Someone will have to man the lever. At least until I can find a simple solution."

They stared at the bed in silence for a moment.

"Well, anyway. Congratulations!" Émile said.

"Thank you," he said. "For your contribution. And for your understanding. Everything is under control. I'm back on my feet, more or less."

"I'm very pleased to hear it," he replied.

"You've been more generous to me than I deserve. Hopefully I can return the favor one day."

They stood and stared at the floor for an instant.

"So," Émile said. "I take it your sister has returned from the coast?"

A look passed across Jamie's face. "They came back the day before yesterday," he said. "By all accounts it was rather dull."

A door slammed somewhere in the building. A horse pulling a cart trotted past in the street below.

"Well," Émile said. "I must get back."

"So soon?" he said. "Surely for once you can put yourself before that blasted edifice? I've got someone I'd like you to meet. Fifteen minutes more, that's all I ask."

"I don't think —" he began.

"She's not for you, if that's what you're thinking."

The door was painted gold on one side and was plain wood on the other. It opened onto a narrow stone staircase.

"Delphine!" Jamie called.

A girl appeared at the top of the stairs dressed in a low-cut gown. Her cheeks were ruddy, her eyes bright, but her skin was white as chalk. She was terribly pretty and extremely young. Seventeen, at a guess.

"Jamie!" she said, and opened her arms for him.

"This is Monsieur Nouguier," Jamie said after they had embraced. "And this is Delphine."

It was the girl in the daguerreotype Jamie had shown him months earlier, the one who

356

had come to the site.

"Mademoiselle." He bowed to her.

Closer, he saw that what he had initially taken for a healthy flush was in fact rouge. Dark smudges underlined her eyes and she was thin, so thin that her collarbone stood out sharp above the neckline of her dress.

"You should tell me when you are going to call and bring a guest," she scolded. "I have nothing to offer. Please go up."

Her room had bare floorboards and a sagging bed in the corner. A table and two chairs were placed below a small attic window. Delphine hurriedly took down a washing line strung with undergarments and brushed some crumbs from the seats of the chairs.

"Sit!" she said. "Sit down."

Although the door was closed, the noise of the building rose up through the floor, a man singing tunelessly, the indignant whine of a dog, the thwack of wet washing in a tin basin.

"I know what you're thinking," Jamie said in English. "As soon as I have saved up enough, I'm going to buy her out from Madame Kelly."

Émile had heard that this was possible, that girls could be bought out of brothels for a price, but he had never actually heard of anyone doing it. He glanced up at the girl standing behind Jamie's chair. She smiled, reached over, took Jamie's hand, raised it to her mouth, and kissed it. The look in Jamie's eyes was one of complete subjugation. Despite, or maybe because of, the obstacles placed before them, their love seemed perfectly pure and utterly detached from reality. Was it, as Shakespeare labeled Romeo and Juliet's passion for each other, a wise kind of madness? The past forgiven, the future wrapped up and waiting like a gift. The fact that they had cut through the lines of class and convention seemed only to make their union sweeter. Émile felt a sudden sense of admiration for the boy; he was more than the sum of his parts.

Delphine's smile turned into a frown. She covered her mouth with her hand and took herself to the doorway, where she tried and failed to swallow down a coughing fit.

"She always sleeps with the window open." Jamie laughed. "It's how you catch a cold, I keep telling her. Delphine! That's enough now."

But the girl's coughing didn't stop. She was almost bent double, gasping for air. Finally, when the fit subsided, her hairline was damp with sweat. She closed her fist around a stained rag. Émile glanced at

Jamie. He seemed unconcerned.

"If you need money for a doctor?" Émile said softly.

"She's fine," he replied with a wave of his hand.

He stared at the young man's face and saw the smoothness of an innocence he had not noticed before. Had he no idea? His girl was not displaying the symptoms of a common cold but of consumption, the white plague.

"Well, I am afraid I must get back to work," he said.

"But won't you drink a glass of wine with us?" the girl asked. "I'll run down to the bar on the corner."

"Very kind of you," he said. "But I'm afraid I can't. It was very nice to meet you, Delphine."

"Another time?" she said.

"I hope so." But as he walked down the spiral steps, he suspected it was unlikely.

At the bottom, Émile shook Jamie's hand.

"You see we can't always help who we fall in love with," Jamie said.

He agreed this was true.

"Since you have done me a favor," Jamie went on softly, "I will do you one. You picked the wrong one."

Jamie scratched his nose. Émile felt a wave

of anger rise through him.

"What are you talking about?" he said.

"You know exactly what I'm talking about," Jamie said. "Fixed the door, have you?"

Émile swallowed. The foreman had talked. He should have expected it.

"Ask Mrs. Wallace about her last suitor," he went on. "Led him on a merry dance and then dropped him like a brick."

Émile pulled his hat on and adjusted his collar. Who was he to tell him about Cait's past?

"I'm sure she had her reasons," he replied. "It is always unwise, in my opinion, to make assumptions without knowing all the facts. Your girl, for example, has probably had her fair share of romantic adventures, none of which resulted in marriage."

The boy looked shocked. He pulled himself up to his full height.

"All that's about to change," he said. "I intend to marry her before Christmas."

31

The artist's studio was at the top of six flights of narrow wooden stairs. Here, another floor had been added to the top of the building, leaving the great wooden beams of the original roof intact to cut across the space. As they caught their breath, they glanced at drawings in pencil and charcoal of women in varying degrees of undress that had been pinned to the beams. On a large easel at the far end of the attic was a preliminary sketch of a woman wearing nothing but a large hat. Cait took a step closer; it was Gabrielle.

"I hope he's not expecting —" Cait began.

"She will be fully clothed, of course," Gabrielle announced. "Unless she wants to be nude."

"Oh no!" said Alice. "No!"

"I was joking," said Gabrielle.

Alice laughed. And then all three women fell silent. At the far end of the studio, a window rattled in the wind and let in a draft. The room smelled of damp plaster and boiled vegetables, of dirty washing and linseed oil. It was four in the afternoon, the time the artist had agreed to meet them. A pigeon nested on the tiles above. A woman opened a window in one of the flats below and began to cough. And in the distance, but close enough for the sound to travel, came the intermittent rhythm of hammering from a construction site.

"He is expecting us?" Cait asked.

"Of course!" Gabrielle replied. "My husband will be here any minute."

"He wouldn't mind if I had a look?"

Gabrielle shrugged. Cait stepped over a discarded red silk robe that lay on the floor, a pile of dirty plates, and several paint-encrusted palettes to a stack of paintings.

"He is extremely highly thought of," Gabrielle said. "But he's not what you would call traditional."

As she flicked through the canvases, Cait realized that he was not particularly good either.

"Alice, my dear, what do you think?" Gabrielle asked. "You have to have an eye for these things."

"Oh yes," said Alice, glancing from one sketch to another. "I like them. Very much, actually."

Cait wandered toward the far end of the studio, where a curtain had been drawn. Behind it was a large unmade bed. Did they sleep here too?

Cait and Alice had just arrived back from a lengthy stay in a hotel in Deauville, recommended by Gabrielle. It had rained on the coast almost every day. The other guests had been large Russian families and elderly dowagers.

"Maybe she got it confused with somewhere else," Alice had suggested more than once.

"We could always go back to Paris," Cait proposed.

"The city will be overrun with tourists," Alice said. "Nobody spends the summer in Paris."

One day an Englishman and his mother arrived. The man glanced across inquisitively at them.

"Don't speak," whispered Alice. "Say nothing, or they'll know."

"Know what?"

"That we're not French!"

And so they spent the days in enforced silence, reading novels or staring out at the gray sea and the scudding clouds, waiting, just waiting to go back to Paris. In that time, however, Alice had become a prolific writer of letters. One morning at breakfast, she opened a letter that had just arrived and silently read it.

"Apparently it's raining in Paris too," she said.

Cait could not bite down her curiosity any longer. "How is Jamie?" she asked.

Alice folded the letter and looked at her.

"This isn't from Jamie," she said. "It's from my friend Gabrielle."

The Englishman appeared at the door. Alice shook her head and poured some coffee.

So all this — the visit to her husband's studio, the time, the date — had been arranged weeks earlier. Cait still felt the slight rise of hurt. Alice seemed to be slipping away from her.

Someone was coming up the stairs to the artist's studio. The door opened with a crash and a man stumbled through. He wore an assortment of clothes, none of which matched or fit; a pair of trousers held up with a length of black cord, a shirt lacking in buttons, and a knitted waistcoat. Although he wasn't much more than thirty-five, his dark hair was long and he was prematurely balding.

Without noticing them, he headed to a sink in the corner. As he walked it was clear that there was something wrong with his right leg. It was wasted, Cait supposed, from polio. They all turned away, but the sound of him urinating was hard to ignore.

"I thought he was expecting us," whispered Alice.

Gabrielle silenced her with a hand.

"Chéri," she called out.

The artist turned, frowned at them for a second, then swore under his breath as he fastened his fly.

"I am so sorry," he said in English, and wiped his hands on his trousers. After he had kissed Gabrielle, he offered Cait and Alice his hand. They felt obliged to shake it.

"Madame," he said. "Mademoiselle."

"May I present Miss Alice Arrol," Gabrielle announced. "And her maid."

"Chaperone," Cait corrected.

Gabrielle nodded in her general direction but didn't add her name.

"A portrait of the young lady," the artist said. "Now I remember. Give me a minute to get respectable."

"Why don't we all sit down?" said Gabrielle as the artist hurried to the far end of the studio and pulled the curtain closed. There were, however, only two chairs.

"Don't feel as if you have to stay," said Gabrielle to Cait with a wide smile.

"I will be fine," Alice added.

That day, Gabrielle was wearing a walking dress of deep red silk, gloves, and a small hat. It was hard to tell her age. Thirty, perhaps. Her face was almost free of lines, her hair was thick and dark, and she had the poise of someone who is pleased with the way she looks, who believes that beauty is something bestowed on the deserving and not randomly given. Yet the morning light revealed her face in a way that softer evening light couldn't; a slight yellowing of her skin, a tiny crease between the eyes, an obstinacy in the set of her mouth — none of which could be hidden with the lavender face powder that she wore.

"With respect," Cait said, "I'd rather remain."

There was a small, terse silence. Alice gave Gabrielle a brief, apologetic look.

Then the artist came back, a greasy black jacket thrown on top of his clothes, and began to appraise Alice, his eyes narrowing as he took in her face. He placed a finger under her chin and turned her head this way and that.

"A perfect profile," he murmured. "And what skin! She is a real beauty!"

Alice blushed but was clearly enjoying the attention. Gabrielle was examining her nails.

"I told you," she said to her husband.

"You were right," he replied. "She will be a joy to paint."

There was more than a hint of showmanship about the whole display. Alice was pretty, it was true, but she wasn't quite as stunning as the artist was suggesting. There was bound to be a catch.

"How much would you charge?" asked Cait. "For a portrait?"

Gabrielle looked up at her sharply. Alice let out a little sigh.

"Mrs. Wallace! Must you always bring things down?"

"She is right to ask," said the artist. "No charge for friends. If you like what I have done then we shall agree on a price later, and if not, pah!"

"Is that good enough for you?" asked Gabrielle.

Alice looked from one woman to the other.

"Why don't you go and see that museum you're always going on about?" Alice suggested.

"If the maid wants to stay," said Gabrielle, "let her stay."

"*Chaperone,*" Cait corrected again.

Gabrielle started to laugh. "What do you think," she said, "that my husband will compromise her virtue when I am here? You think that? In that case, I am really rather offended."

"That isn't what I said," Cait replied.

"Mrs. Wallace," Alice interjected, "I will be fine."

"No, Alice —"

"The maid pulls the strings. How novel!"

"Please just go!" said Alice. "We pay you, remember. And I'm telling you to leave."

Cait's face burned. She blinked twice. Alice had never spoken to her in this tone before. Gabrielle pointedly glanced at her watch.

"I —" Cait began.

"Go," Alice repeated.

What could she do? She was indeed the hired help. Alice was an adult. She had no authority over her.

"All right. I'll be back in an hour," she said.

"Make it two," said Alice. "I'm not going anywhere."

Gabrielle was smoking when Cait returned to the studio. She seemed eager to get away and stubbed out her cigarette and made for the door almost immediately.

"Same time next week?" she called to her husband. It was not a question but an order. "And next time don't keep us waiting."

Cait was not allowed to see the painting. No one was allowed to, Alice said, until it was finished.

The artist was rinsing his brushes at the sink.

"How long do you think it will take?" Cait asked.

"That depends," he said over his shoulder. "On the light, on the weather, on the *ambience.*"

"Don't be so Scottish," Alice scolded Cait. "It will take as long as it takes."

Alice was silent on the ride home. Her face had a feverish look despite the chill of the studio. Then she turned to her and Cait had the sense that she had just come back from far away.

"I'm sorry I spoke to you like that," she said. "Do you forgive me?"

Cait still stung from the dismissal. For two hours she had wandered around a gallery without seeing anything. What did Gabrielle want from Alice? She knew it had to be more than a fee for a painting, but she had no idea what it could be.

"Do you?" Alice asked again.

"Of course," Cait replied.

"I'm old enough to know what I'm doing," she said, and stared out the window.

They rode on in silence. A gulf had opened

between them. Was she to blame? She had been distracted, elsewhere, taken up with her own thoughts, with a longing that didn't lessen but grew stronger by the day.

"You know you don't have to pose for a painting," Cait said. "I mean, you could have a daguerreotype made instead?"

Alice recoiled and there was something of Gabrielle in her expression.

"Daguerreotypes are so vulgar!" she said. "How can you even suggest such a thing?"

The carriage arrived at the house at the same time as Jamie was leaving. All the worry was gone from his face. He gave them both a deep bow.

"My dearest wee sister," he said. "And the lovely Mrs. Wallace."

"What's wrong with you?" asked Alice. "Shouldn't you be at work?"

"On my way there now," he said.

He looked on the brink of telling her something, something significant. But instead he swallowed and fastened his coat.

"Is everything all right?" Cait asked him.

He looked at her deeply, as if her face could reveal how much she knew about his business.

"I did have a slightly sticky patch." He nodded. "But I'm over it. And now, well, you could say I'm on the rise again."

And he smiled a smile so wide and un-
equivocal that it was impossible to believe
that what he said wasn't true.

32

Émile woke up to the sound of the softest knock on his door. He opened it to find Cait standing there in a black traveling cloak, her chest heaving as if she had run up the stairs rather than wait for the elevator.

"Nine weeks," he said breathlessly as he enfolded her in his arms.

"Ten," she replied.

"What time is it?" he whispered into her hair.

"Late. I had to wait until Alice was asleep. I couldn't get away otherwise."

He took her face in his hands. She closed her eyes and leaned her cheek into his palm.

"I missed you," he said.

In reply, she kissed his wrist.

"Come," he said. "Come to bed. It's warmer."

One, two three, four, five. The bells tolled across the city, their clappers striking the copper in a choir of different notes and keys.

It was almost morning. Already he could hear the distant rumble of carts heading to market and the flow of water from the *bouches de lavage.* Émile had been awake for hours, hours that were so precious that he couldn't afford to lose any to sleep. He knew she was awake too. His skin tingled under the calligraphy of her fingertips. He imagined her growing familiar to him, the smell of her hair, her warmth, the weight of her body on the mattress beside him; he imagined her sleeping at his side in faraway places, in the Americas, in Russia, in the Far East, countries that his work took him to. He imagined children, a home, a life together, and it intoxicated him, it made him drunk with hope, with a new reckless-ness.

"What will happen," he whispered, "when the tower's finished?"

She was silent. He couldn't read her face in the dark.

"Well?" he asked.

"I'll go home, I suppose."

"You could stay. With me."

"That would be nothing short of scandal-ous, Monsieur Nouguier," she said softly.

He laughed and kissed her gently on the shoulder. She was right. While his mother was alive, he couldn't marry her. She would never accept it. In fact, knowing about Cait might even hasten the speed of her demise. They would have to wait. And yet his mother was changing, she was more accepting of his career now. He remembered how interested she had been in the Panama Canal project the last time he saw her.

"You say that people have invested in it," she had asked. "How many?"

"Thousands," he replied. "Hundreds of thousands, in fact."

"And is their money safe?"

"The bonds are backed by the government, so I should think so. You must have read about it in the newspaper?"

She nodded and then asked him to pour her coffee.

"There's no sense in taking a gamble in this life," she added. "That is especially true when it comes to matrimony."

He put the coffeepot down.

"Aren't you having any?" she had asked him.

"Not today."

They'd sat in silence as she sipped her coffee. Once more they had reached an impasse.

"I just want to see you settled," she said, and laid her hand over his, "before I pass on."

He still felt the weight of her paper-soft grip. He still felt the kick of his heart in his chest as he resisted her. It was growing light outside; the dark coat of night was lifting. Cait rolled over and looked up at him.

"Where were you?" she asked.

He shook his head and smiled. "I was here, with you."

"No, you weren't," she replied. "I must go. Before I'm missed."

Her eyes were as silver as mercury. She blinked and then he saw that she was crying.

"What's the matter?" he said.

She inhaled long and hard and wiped her face with the back of her hand.

"Nothing," she replied.

Cait started to dress, fastening and buttoning, tightening and clipping.

"I want to see more of you," he said.

"Won't you tire of me?" she said as she pulled her cloak over her dress.

He took her hand, drew her to him, then kissed the top of her head.

"Dearest Cait," he whispered, "I'll never tire of you. You'll come again?"

He tried not to expect her, and he tried not to wait, but he couldn't help himself. On both of the occasions that she had arrived again at his door after midnight, however, he had been fast asleep, and even though he had pinched himself awake, he had the distinct impression that she was not real at all but a dream. Slowly the feeling would subside and she would take shape in his ears, in his eyes, in his arms. And then they would lie together until the smell of fresh coffee and baking bread began to rise from the street. At the stroke of five she would dress, kiss him goodbye, let herself out, and he would lie sleepless, imagining her heading home, slipping into streams of shopgirls and domestics, of shift workers and bakers, without a ripple.

33

Even though it was not yet six in the morning, the concierge was already working, sweeping the steps with an old brush. He stepped aside and opened the door to the street for her. Outside a carriage was waiting at the curb.

"Please," he said, and motioned toward it.

Had Émile arranged a cab? He hadn't mentioned it. And he knew she preferred to walk. The coachman opened the door and offered her a hand as she took the step. There was someone inside.

"Don't be ashamed," a woman's voice came from inside the carriage. "Sit down."

"I think there must be some sort of mistake," Cait said.

"No mistake," the elderly woman said. "I am Louise Nouguier. I believe you are acquainted with my son."

"Where did you go?" Alice asked at breakfast.

Cait looked up from her cup of coffee and blinked.

"Sorry?"

"I heard you go out last night."

"Me?" she said, trying to appear nonchalant. She hadn't prepared an answer.

"I saw you," said Alice. "Walking away very fast."

"Why on earth," said Cait, "would I go out in the middle of the night?"

"If I knew that, I wouldn't ask you," she replied.

Cait picked up the newspaper and started to read. But Alice wasn't about to let it go.

"I heard footsteps on the stairs, I heard the front door open, and when I looked out I saw you."

She put down the newspaper and looked at Alice. Maybe it was pointless to deny it.

"Actually, I have insomnia," she said. "I have had it for years. The only thing that helps is a brisk walk in the fresh air."

Alice frowned. It was so implausible it sounded true.

"But is it safe?" Alice said. "A woman alone at night in Paris!"

Cait shrugged. "What are the alternatives? That I pace around the house and wake everyone up? If you want to know the truth, my condition embarrasses me. I prefer not to talk about it."

Alice started to color.

"I'm so sorry, Mrs. Wallace. I thought you had a lover." She stifled a guffaw. "Such a ridiculous notion. I mean, you're way too old for any of that nonsense."

And she started to eat her breakfast with renewed gusto. Cait poured herself some tea but didn't drink.

"Is something the matter?" Alice asked a moment later. "You seem strange, Mrs. Wallace, distracted."

Cait blinked.

"Actually," she said, "I'm fine."

The housekeeper appeared with a letter and handed it to Cait. Alice watched her face as she read it.

"Not bad news?"

Cait shook her head and folded it up again.

"It's from my sister," she said. "She wrote to wish me a happy birthday."

Alice's eyes widened.

"You should have told me! When?"

"Today," she replied.

It was true. It was October 26, and she was thirty-three exactly. How did she get so old?

"We'll go out: you, me, and Jamie. I think it might be too late to get a booking at the Café de Paris or Ciro's, but I'll try!"

"Please," said Cait, "you don't need to."

Alice frowned at her and then shook her head.

"We can afford it," she said. "You wouldn't have to pay for it or anything."

Alice didn't mean it; she didn't mean to insult her with thoughtlessness, to remind her of her place.

The salon was lit by the splutter of several gas lamps, their filaments burning yellow in the smoky dark. At the bar, the men clustered, their top hats an architecture of curved satin and brushed beaver. Beside them the women arched and gestured, making black swans' necks out of gloved arms. Underneath the clamor of conversation and the steady thrashing of a piano in the corner came the regular *pop, pop, hiss* of Champagne bottles being opened.

It was almost cold enough to wear fur. And in the air, beneath the smell of cigar and soap, was the musty stink of fox and mink and bear. Alice and Jamie both ordered in French. Alice wore a blue velvet dress that Cait had never seen before. Around her neck she had tied a black velvet ribbon. Jamie's eyes darted around the restaurant, looking for friends and acquaintances and pretty women. How changed they were from the year before.

"You should be happy!" said Alice, and they drank a toast. "It's your birthday."

But Cait wasn't happy. She wondered if she could feel that way again. She leaned forward to lift her glass, but her elbow struck the bottle and it toppled, rolling across the table before it smashed on the tiles below, a fizz of green glass and bubbles.

"I'm so sorry," she said as she knelt down and tried to lift the broken pieces. "I'm so sorry."

A shard sliced her finger and it began to bleed, large red drops falling.

"Mrs. Wallace, it's all right, really it is."

Jamie made her sit down, he wrapped her finger with a linen napkin, he tried to make her understand that it didn't matter.

"It's only a bottle," he said. "I'll buy another. It's not the end of the world. As long as you're not badly hurt."

As Jamie tried to catch the waiter's eye, Cait's eye was drawn to a man at the bar, a man who looked, from the back, just like Saul. Her heart clenched.

When the police had asked for a detailed description of Mr. Saul Wallace in the aftermath of the accident, this is what she told them: height five foot nine, hair short, fair, short whiskers and a mustache, dark tweed suit, white shirt, black corded walking coat with black corded buttons, and a vest of the same material, a tweed top coat of dark blue, a black felt hat, black lacing boots, gray woolen socks, white swansdown drawers, a brown leather wallet, a gold watch, and a wedding band.

In January and February they'd begun to recover the bodies from the River Tay, some brought up from the wreckage by divers, others washed up near the site of the bridge or farther up the estuary, east of Monifieth or in the salmon nets at Tentsmuir near Leuchars. Saul's body was never found.

The man at the bar turned. It was not Saul; he was gone, he would never come back, she was safe. And yet his death hadn't ended the ordeal. As time passed she realized that he had bequeathed her more than a broken necklace; he had left her with something much worse, the opposite of a gift.

The letter that morning had not been from her sister. It was from the physician she had seen after her accident.

"I am sorry to inform you," he wrote, "that as I told your husband at the time, and in answer to your enquiry, it would be highly unlikely."

By the next morning, after countless drafts, a letter to Émile had been written and sealed. She let herself out of the house and caught the first post. It was the right thing to do. It was the only thing to do. But still she'd held her hand to the cold pressed metal of the postbox with her letter deep inside as if she could hold on to it, and him, for a little longer.

34

Émile stood in the drawing room of the Arrols' residence and waited. The house was quiet; only the muted rhythm of a clock graced the silence. He could just about sense the weight of footsteps far, far up above. This time, there was a pot of tea and a plate of tiny cakes laid out on the table. Cait, however, had not been there to greet him. After about ten minutes he heard footsteps approaching, the door opened, and in walked both women — Alice in a dress so covered in froths of lace that she looked not unlike a cake herself, and Cait in indigo blue. He bowed.

"It has been a while," he began.

"It has," replied Alice Arrol. "We haven't seen you for months. Please sit down and let me pour you a cup of tea?"

He scratched his chin but didn't move. This was more difficult than he imagined. He looked at Cait; he tried to catch her gaze but her gaze would not be caught. He thought back over everything he had ever said to her. What could it have been to turn her like this, what could he have done to make her become so cold? It was agonizing not to know. After he had received her letter, he had written to her a dozen times but her answers were short, polite, and offered no explanation. And so he had decided that he would have to take matters in hand. If he wanted to see Cait, he would have to pretend that he was interested in Alice.

"Tea?" she asked again.

Now that he was there, in the Arrols' house, his idea seemed fatally flawed; to remain for another second in this room, making small talk and having to force himself to drink tea and eat cake, was more than Émile could bear.

"Why don't we go for a drive?" The thought was out of his mouth before he could stop it. "It's a beautiful winter day!"

Alice stared at him.

"But I'm not dressed for a drive!" she said.

He turned and looked pointedly at Cait. Her hair was pulled back and her dress was as plain as Alice's was fancy. She looked so beautiful he found it hard to draw his eyes away.

"Madame Wallace?" he said. "It's Sunday,

for goodness' sake! Let me take you to the park at Saint-Cloud. You can see for miles from up there."

Émile stopped to catch his breath when he reached the summit of the hill. Just as he had promised, there was a view right across Paris; the bridge of Saint-Cloud below, and beyond, the Bois de Boulogne. A hot-air balloon floated over the basilica of the Sacré-Coeur. The half-built tower was clearly visible, a black iron scribble against the pale stone and dull golden glint of Les Invalides.

Far below on the road, his carriage waited. In the lower part of the park, a military band was playing, the strains of the brass and bass drum rising up the hill in gusts. He had come to this park as a child, when the château was still standing, before it burned down in the war. As well as the viewpoint, there were forests and fountains, the Grande Cascade and the Jet Géant, a great surge of water that shot up into the air. He suddenly remembered his elder brother explaining Newton's laws of motion to him with horse chestnuts on strings, the force of the first hitting the second so hard that it set in motion a third.

On the path below, Cait paused and

waited for Alice.

"It's worth it!" he called out. "The view is spectacular."

Alice had her hands on her hips and was shaking her head. And then with a flounce, the girl started back down the hill.

"Come and see, Madame Wallace. This time you can keep your feet on solid ground."

Cait had barely said a word to him all afternoon. Saint-Cloud was about six miles from the center of Paris. On the way, Alice had talked incessantly, about Paris on a Sunday, about what people usually did. He found it hard to concentrate on what she was saying. She talked so fast. Instead, he found his eye drawn away from her; the line of Cait's wrist beneath her pale green woolen cuff, a curl of her hair that had escaped from a pin, the shape of her foot laced up inside her boot.

Cait had reached the path and was adjusting Alice's hem. There was no chance that they could snatch a few moments together now. In fact he realized that Cait was pulling back, stepping out of the frame, leaving it wide open for him. And like a fool, he had stepped right in. As if on cue, Alice turned around, looked up, and waved, first with one arm and then with the other.

■ ■ ■ ■

They were all silent on the drive home. The music of the band still echoed in his ears and he held on to it, repeating the cheerful refrain in an attempt to drown out a sadder tune that was all his own. As they reached the gates of the Bois, he knew it would be mere minutes before their journey ended and Cait would be gone.

"It's a beautiful evening," said Alice.

"Lovely, for the time of the year."

"Too early to go home, surely?"

Alice sat forward and tapped the driver on the shoulder.

"Take the next left," she told him.

"Through the Bois?"

"That's right, through the Bois."

She sat back and looked at Cait, then Émile.

"You don't mind, do you?"

It was five thirty p.m., the time for a stroll before an aperitif. They would be seen. People would talk as people always did. Everyone would know that he, Émile Nouguier, was stepping out with the Scottish heiress, with Alice Arrol. They rolled into the forest, past lines of carriages and couples strolling along the paths. Several men raised their hats to him, but mostly people just looked. Without intending to, he had just made an announcement to the whole of Paris.

35

"Good Lord Almighty!" A deep voice boomed up from the front door, clear and loud and most definitively Scottish. Cait picked up her skirts and ran down the stairs. William Arrol was standing in the hall while the housekeeper protested in rapid French.

"I'm not understanding you, woman," he said with a shrug.

"Mr. Arrol!" she cried out.

"Mrs. Wallace! At last. I was beginning to think we'd got the wrong house." He laughed.

"What are you doing here? I mean, this is so unexpected!" She took his top hat and peered over his shoulder at the carriage in the street, where a woman was being helped down by the coachman.

"I wrote and told Alice we were coming."

"Did you? She must have forgotten to mention it," Cait replied. "I must get the guest room ready."

"No need. The hotel is already booked. It's only a flying visit. Three days, I'm afraid. I had some business in London and thought I'd extend the trip."

"Well, it's nice to see you and your wife for any length of time."

William Arrol took a deep breath before he spoke.

"My poor wife was not well enough to travel," he said with his head bowed.

On the street outside the woman turned, brushed down her skirts, and fixed her hat.

"But my cousin, Miss Lamont, kindly agreed to accompany me," he said. "You have met her?"

Cait shook her head no.

"Miss Lamont, come and meet Mrs. Wallace, the woman who has been working miracles for me here in Paris."

"I wouldn't go as far as that," Cait replied.

He waved the air with his hand. "Now, don't be modest. You are the perfect chaperone — charming but chaste. Now, where is my niece . . . Alice?" he bellowed.

"She's not here. She's at the dressmaker having a fitting," Cait explained. "I'm going to meet her at noon."

"Never mind. Now, tell me this. It's far more important: Where can a man get a decent cup of tea in this city?"

Lucy Lamont was small and trim and defiant. A certain sourness came over her face when she thought herself unobserved, but she worked hard at conversation, snatching up facts and information to tease like a wren with a worm.

Alice had no recollection of receiving her uncle's letter when she returned from her fitting. Dinner was hastily arranged at a place that Arrol himself suggested — Leon in the Place du Palais-Royal — and a note was dispatched to Jamie at the tower site. That night as they sat down, the mood was celebratory; the Forth Rail Bridge was on schedule and Arrol was talking to several other companies about new commissions.

"I suppose you come here all the time," he said as he glanced around the dining room.

Alice looked horrified. The menu was prix fixe, and the other customers were nearly all British.

"No, never," she replied, and closed the menu with a snap.

"A man we met on the boat train recommended it. 'One must be on your guard in Paris,' he told me. 'They'll fleece you as soon as look at you.' "

"As soon as look at you," Lucy Lamont added for emphasis.

"Dinner for three francs a head in here. And they give you a glass of Champagne! That's a bargain!"

"A bargain!" Lucy Lamont echoed.

Alice looked around the room. Cait knew what she was thinking. No one would see them in a place like this, a place full of miserly foreigners. And thankfully, no one would witness her uncle's behavior. In Paris, who knew he had a wife already, a wife whose mind had wandered but was still very much alive? No one would know about the true nature of his relationship with his cousin.

What was marriage but a bind from which to escape? What was the point, if all it served as was as a cover for men's infidelity? Cait glanced across at William Arrol. He was listening to Alice explain the Paris seasons, the small one from December to Easter and then the big one from May to July. Just when had he realized that his own marriage was a failure? When had he been told that his wife would not be able to have his children, when had he accepted that despite his huge success and personal wealth he would have to nurse her for the rest of her life? It was a tragedy he wore remarkably well, considering. Did he suspect, however, that he loved his niece and nephew with an indulgence that wasn't always good for them?

Cait was suddenly aware of the pull of a gaze. She turned to find Lucy Lamont staring at her.

"So how do you find Paris, Miss Lamont?" Cait asked.

"It smells," she said with a directness that would have been considered vulgar even among the Scottish middle class. "And the coachmen expect a tip when all they have done is drive."

Like her cousin, William Arrol, Lucy Lamont gave away her impoverished background in a number of ways. She fixed her bodice, gave a great sigh, then began to fan her face with a napkin.

"But there is plenty to see," Cait suggested.

"Tomorrow we are going to the tower," she said. "Now, tell me, what is the engineer, this Nouguier, like?"

She turned and looked at her expectantly. Cait took a sip of water, then suddenly realized that the longer the pause, the more she incriminated herself.

"I hardly know him," she said. "But he seems like a decent sort."

Lucy Lamont was still observing her.

"Has he made a proposal yet?"

Cait frowned. "A proposal?" she asked. "No, not yet."

But it was too late. Lucy Lamont had sensed the whiff of something inappropriate in her manner.

"You do think he's suitable, though," Miss Lamont went on. "He's not just after her money. He wants children?"

"He wants children," she replied. "Very much."

Lucy Lamont sat back. How on earth would Cait know a thing like this?

"Apparently," she added, but too late, much too late.

The conversation turned to the weather and Cait fell silent. Once they had all chosen what they wanted to eat, Lucy Lamont turned her attention back to Cait.

"It's hot in here," she said.

"Would you like some water, Miss Lamont?"

"Is it wise?" she said softly.

"Is what wise?" Cait said, her face beginning to flush.

"To drink the water?" she said pointedly.

A Métro train passed deep below the restaurant, making the water in the glasses tremble.

"The alternative is to go thirsty," she replied. "Once or twice, however, shouldn't have any long-lasting effects."

A tiny twitch of Lucy Lamont's mouth and the way she blinked not once but twice, indicated that she had guessed, she had surmised, that Cait had formed an improper attachment to a man who could never be hers.

"Just as long as you don't make it into a habit," Lucy said. "We don't want you coming down with something, and I know for a fact that William would hate to have to replace you."

A waiter arrived with five very small glasses of Champagne.

"Look at you both," Arrol said of Jamie and Alice. "Mrs. Wallace was right. Paris seems to be doing you the world of good. It has been a sizable investment, but it looks to me as if the payoff was worth every penny. A toast! To Alice and Jamie!"

The Champagne was sour and a little flat. It was finished in a mouthful and pronounced very fine by all.

"How is the tower?" Arrol asked Jamie.

"Growing," he replied.

"Faster than ever, I hear," Arrol said. "And how is our dear friend, Monsieur Nouguier?"

Jamie glanced at his sister. "Finally smitten. Took his time, though."

"A girl like Alice," Arrol said appraisingly. "The perfect catch. Probably lining up his ducks in a row as we speak."

Alice swallowed and drank from her glass, even though, as everyone could see, it was already empty.

"Anything worth having is worth waiting for," she said with a weak smile.

Jamie raised his eyebrows and laughed.

"Oh my, dear sister," he said. "Coming from you, that is priceless. That reminds me, has he finished? The artist. Has he finished the portrait yet?"

"Not quite," she replied. "But I understand that it is a tour de force."

"You mean you haven't seen it?" said Arrol.

"No," said Alice. "But I hear it's coming along nicely."

Alice rose and excused herself to the ladies' room. Arrol busied himself with his cigar. But Lucy Lamont's eyes switched back and forth as she took it all in.

36

At the Champ de Mars, the second platform, *la deuxième,* had been reached and
the final stretch of the tower was under
construction. With so much of the work so
high, there was less dust to catch in your
eye and less noise to shout over. Émile was
used to running up and down the metal
staircases in the east pillar now, pausing
only briefly on the first floor to catch his
breath, to check all was well on the construction of the gallery or to help himself to
a coffee from a worker's canteen, before
pounding up and up and around and
around the stairs to the second-floor platform above.

He looked up through spokes of iron.
Smoke from the riveters' fire circled into
the air in wisps of white; a lattice of iron
against the deep blue of the sky. He should
have brought a camera. Days like these,
however, would soon be rare. Winter was

here and the weather was less clement. The carpenters and riveters would soon be working at more than two hundred meters in high winds, in snow, in rain. No wonder they'd started to complain. No wonder so many of them had begun to mutter about suffering from vertigo.

"What difference does it make?" Eiffel had told them. "You'll die if you fall from forty meters the same as you would from three hundred."

On this floor there would eventually be a refreshment stall and a bakeshop. Eiffel had also negotiated a deal with the editor of *Le Figaro*. For the duration of the World's Fair, a printing office would be set up to produce a special newspaper. There was also a post office. Émile was suddenly reminded of the letter from Alice Arrol in his pocket. It had been there for five days already, unanswered. He had met her uncle a few weeks earlier when Jamie had given him a tour of the site. Just as Gustave had told him, William Arrol was a nice man; open, engaging, witty. His hand, when he shook it, was rough to the touch.

He found a quiet place out of the wind, near the area where the elevators would eventually run, pulled out the letter, and scanned it quickly. In childish loops and curls she wrote that she hoped he was well and that he would pay a visit soon. She so enjoyed their excursions. He folded the letter up again and returned it to his pocket. He knew it was wrong. He was weak, a man of base impulses. But to be near Cait for just an hour or two, even at one removed, it was worth it. He was now a collector of miniatures, of details caught from the corner of his eye, a glance, the point of her toe, the turn of her head.

Émile looked out over the city, at the river way below, strapped down by its bridges and edged with bright green like verdant lace around a wrist. It was for this the tower was being built, to celebrate the centenary of the French Revolution, to gift the idea of the city to the people of Paris, for as far as they could see in all directions. While life down there was chaotic, nonsensical, frustrating, up here you couldn't smell the sewers or the sweet stink of horse manure; up here you could rise above it all; up here you could see the world unfold below, everything in its place, everything laid out to make some sort of sense.

The last stage, the pinnacle of the tower, which would support the highest, smallest platform, would be the easiest structurally, but the most problematic for the men. For this, Eiffel had decided on a slightly different approach. A vertical column would be erected in what would become the central elevator shaft for the men to work from. It wouldn't be possible to use construction machinery to carry up the parts anymore. Instead, each piece would be lifted into place using two small cranes that would be bolted onto the central frame.

A whistle blew from the lower platform. A couple of men leaped down from where they had been working above. A bucket of water was thrown over the riveters' fire.

"What's happening?" he asked them.

"Six francs a day," one called out. "Do you think it's enough?"

"We won't lift our tools again until we get more money," said another.

"It's a strike, Monsieur Nouguier!" another explained. "Get off the site for a day or two. Try and remember who you were before we started to build this monster."

"Not again!" he said. "How are we going to finish on time at this rate?"

His mother was much weaker this month than last. Had she guessed that she wasn't going to get better? And what if she died before the tower was completed? He would never escape the shadow of her disappointment.

"Men," he called out, "speak to Eiffel. We all want the same thing, don't we?"

Eiffel was in crisis meetings with the head barrowman, the head carpenter, the painting and masonry supervisors, and the foreman. In an attempt to appease them, he had already agreed to accident insurance. He was contracted to finish the tower by April to leave a couple of months for fitting out the interiors before the World's Fair opened. They couldn't afford another delay. There was nothing anyone could do, however, but wait until the dispute was resolved.

It was strange to walk through Paris during the day, to pass lines of schoolboys being herded along the street by bad-tempered nuns and to have to pick one's way through the crowds of ladies on the rue de la Paix. He stopped for an aperitif on the Faubourg Saint-Honoré and watched women hurry from one milliner to the next in search of the perfect hat.

"How could you even consider it?" said one young woman with disdain. "It's identical to what Marie Maussant was wearing last season."

The girls fell silent as a cab approached and a woman was helped down by the coachman. Émile pulled his wallet out of his pocket and placed a few coins on the dish.

"Monsieur Nouguier? Is that you?" A woman dressed in black fur and white velvet stood in front of him with a wide smile on her face. "It is you! Are you alone or is that clever Monsieur Eiffel here too?"

It was the baroness who'd held the salon, the one who was in love with the cad of a half brother. Émile rose to his feet, took the hand she offered, and gave it a kiss.

"You have a good memory," he said.

"For both faces and names, I know." She laughed and placed her hand on his forearm playfully. "But the truth is that some are more memorable than others."

He wondered if she was making a subtle pass at him.

"I'm very glad we met," she went on. "I'm holding a charity ball at my house next Saturday evening. It will celebrate the opening of the *petite saison* and raise money for homeless orphans. Please do me the pleasure. And bring that Scottish girl that I hear you're stepping out with. Her brother too."

"I'm afraid I'm extremely busy," he said.

She stared at him, in the café, in the Faubourg Saint-Honoré, and let out a short, curt laugh.

"Like hell you are," she whispered.

37

Cait sat in a line of chairs at the back of the ballroom with the other chaperones. Most of them had assumed the mantle of old or late middle years, regardless of their real age, and some carried walking sticks or peered at the world through scratched spectacles. Nearly all wore black or purple crepe gowns and matching straw bonnets. They were mirror images of the girls they looked after, in dress, in age, and in attitude. And Cait was aware of a smell that rose from their collective beings: lavender and silver tarnish, old cake crumbs and sour milk. The lady beside her pulled out her knitting and the needles began to click steadily out of time with the music on the dance floor. Another hummed an atonal accompaniment.

The ballroom was enormous. Two pillars painted to look like marble flanked the main door. At the far end, a double staircase that swept up in two graceful curves led to a balcony where the small orchestra played. Vast gilt mirrors, tilted slightly to catch the light from the crystal chandeliers, adorned the walls. Cait looked up at the ceiling. Against a backdrop of billowing clouds and blue sky were gods and impish cupids, golden chariots and silver bugles. Someone said it was by Tiepolo. She had once thought that the Merchants' Hall in Glasgow was grand. It was shabby in comparison with this.

In one of the rooms off the ballroom a long table had been laden with plates of food, huge floral decorations, and bowls of fruit punch. None of the chaperones, however, had been invited to eat or drink anything. An invisible line separated them from the guests. Occasionally one of the girls would return and her chaperone would hold her glass while she pinned up a stray strand of hair or plumped up a ruffle, or a woman, a married one, would let out a gasp of recognition and come over and make a fuss. But that was it. Decorum meant that their presence was necessary, but it was symbolic rather than physical. Who knew what went on in the darkened corners of the formal gardens or in the library when the door was closed? As long as no one saw, an eye, a blind one, was turned.

In the two hours Cait had been sitting there, however, the room had gradually lost its allure. It was too hot, the air too close, and the smell of perspiration and shoe leather had become overpowering. The gold and paint, the glass and crystal, were as cloying as the scent of the white lilies that had been artfully displayed in a vase on the mantelpiece. She felt herself slowly fading, the color of her dress seeping into the wallpaper behind her. Without enough air, her head felt light and began to spin. She looked at the clock. It was after ten. Surely the dance would not go on beyond midnight?

Alice was wearing a white dress with a large bow at the back. Her hair had been decoratively twisted up in rolls and curls with white feathers in a style that had taken a coiffeuse several hours to perfect. At one point, Émile had passed close by, his arms around Alice as they waltzed. She had pretended she hadn't seen him. It was too awful, too humiliating. It felt like she was waiting, not for the evening to end, but for life itself to cease.

"It'll be a long one," the old lady beside her said. "People like to put on a good show if it's for charity. Nobody wants to be the first to leave."

"I don't mind the long nights," another chaperone told her. "But I do mind the fallow seasons. I once had one of my nieces for eleven. I thought I'd never get her off my hands, she was a real *'fête de la Saint-Catherine.'* And then she met a rich Jew at the races at Longchamps and that was that. But this one" — she pointed out a girl dancing with a soldier — "this one will be snapped up before she is twenty. Mark my words!"

The girl glanced at her chaperone as if she had heard her name mentioned and smiled expectantly.

"And then we get a short respite," the chaperone said. "Until the next one."

She gave Cait a friendly pat on the arm. Cait looked down at the old lady's hand. Her own weren't old like that yet; the skin hadn't thinned and started looking like cracked wax. But it would. The other chaperones started to gossip about who was courting whom and about a rich American heiress who was on the lookout for a titled husband.

"She looks like a frog," one said. "But money makes even the ugly ones desirable, you know."

"I don't know who to feel more sorry for,"

said another. "The heiress or the poor soul who ends up with her."

"I hear the baroness's brother had made a play."

"Clément? Is he here? Surely she's not that stupid."

"She's an American!" And they all laughed.

"One less thing to worry about," said the elderly chaperone with the papery hands.

Cait had seen the count. He didn't dance but kept to the smaller apartments, the smoking room, and the bar. She hoped that Alice had the measure of him now. She hoped she'd come to her senses. But what would that mean? How far would Émile take it? He couldn't court Alice indefinitely.

As she watched the dancers, a shadow descended; the center of her vision started to throb and black out. She closed her eyes. Why, she asked herself did her headaches come at the most inconvenient times? Or maybe it was the right time, incapacitated, as she was, with the other semi-invalids of her chosen profession. After a few moments, however, the blindness shifted and the throb moved to the periphery and hung there, a curve of rainbow in the corner of her eye.

"I'm going out for a breath of air," Cait said, and rose to her feet. Glances were exchanged; eyebrows arched.

"She's going where?" a very ancient lady called out from the end of the row.

The branches of trees in the baroness's garden were hung with tiny Japanese lanterns. The lawn was crisp with frost. The floor-to-ceiling windows of the ballroom threw rectangles of golden light onto the stone terrace. Cait inhaled, in and out, letting the night air fill her lungs, her head, her mouth, and in a few moments, the aura had faded. Soon, she knew, her head would ache, but in the interim she was bestowed with a clarity, a perceptiveness; the world was a dirty pane of glass that had just been cleaned.

The music was fainter out here, and the noise of chatter, laughter, and the pop of Champagne corks inside vied with the cries of foxes and the rustle of the wind in the trees. It was a beautiful December evening, almost too beautiful to be real.

"What did I do?"

She turned. It was Émile.

"Nothing," she said.

"Then why?" he asked. "Why did you . . . did you stop coming?"

She shook her head.

"I really don't think it's appropriate for you to ask," she said.

"I think it is extremely appropriate. Your letter didn't illuminate, I'm afraid."

"I didn't promise anything, Émile."

"Maybe not in so many words."

He smelled of fresh air and pepper. Her eyes were level with his clavicle, his collarbone, and she was struck by the physical sensation of the graze of her lips across it. The body, she realized then, retains memories more vividly than the mind.

"I only see Alice Arrol because I want to see you. You know that."

"Then you must stop!"

He swallowed, then turned away.

"I can't," he said.

For a moment they stood at the stone balustrade in silence. She was aware of him, every tiny breath, every single beat of his blood, every passing impulse, because they were echoes of her own. She took a deep breath in and let it out in a frozen cloud.

"Why?" he asked. "At least tell me why. Was it so bad?"

She shook her head. The hours she had lain with Émile had been the sweetest, most perfect she had ever known.

"Well?" he asked. "Did it mean nothing?"

He had a right to demand an explanation. Music spilled out of the doorway and the sound of a hundred feet on the polished mahogany floor stamped the air like punctuation.

"Well?" he said again.

"I wish you and Alice the greatest happiness," she said.

"I don't want Alice."

She swallowed and tried to focus on breathing. She thought of church pews and Sunday sermons.

"It couldn't last. You know that."

"Stay here," he said. "In Paris."

"And what, be your mistress?" she said. "So you can go off and marry someone else and have children?"

"I could do that with you."

In the ballroom, the piece ended. Almost immediately, the orchestra launched into the next dance, a slow waltz. A couple wandered out of the French windows, strolled into the garden, and disappeared. And she was suddenly certain that they had reached the end, that after this night she would never be alone with him again.

"Dance with me," she said.

They were the only ones on the terrace now. Everyone else was inside, the lights so bright that they would be rendered invisible in the dark. And she let him lead, she let him slowly spin her around and around until the stars blurred and her mind numbed, until all she was aware of was the warmth of his body next to hers.

The French windows suddenly flew open.

"Here you are!" said Alice. "Jamie has gone and fallen in love again."

They turned to see Jamie dancing arm in arm with the baroness.

"See!" said Alice.

And then she was aware that Alice had turned and was looking from Émile to her and back again.

"Mrs. Wallace," she said. "You shouldn't be out here. You'll catch your death!"

"You're right. Goodbye, Monsieur Nouguier."

The lights of the ballroom were bright, far too bright. Her eyes smarted from the cold and her head had begun to ache. As Cait stepped around the polished parquet dance floor of the ballroom and made her way back to her seat, the music stopped and there was the sound of rain on the glass. How strange, she thought, for it to rain when the sky was so clear. And then she realized that it was not rain at all but applause.

"Bravo!" called one guest after another. "Felicitations!"

"Why are they clapping?" she asked one of the chaperones.

"It's an engagement," the old woman said. "Look!"

Cait turned, and there at the top of the stairs, glittering in diamonds and silk, was the baroness. And on either side of her, looking slightly less resplendent in comparison, were the count and American heiress. Alice was standing at the windows to the terrace. It was fortunate that no one was looking, no one saw. Her face could not hide the magnitude of her dismay.

38

The storm hit Paris in the middle of the night. The wind howled along the boulevards of the Left Bank, while gusts caught the bells in the Abbaye de Saint Germain-des-Pres and made them sway on their ropes.

Émile had woken in a state of panic. The wind was rattling at his shutters, the bluster of a draft fingering through the cracks. From outside came the clatter of a bicycle being blown over. He dressed quickly. The storm sounded bigger than any he had heard for years in the city. He had to go to the site, to make sure that the cranes that moved up and down the central shaft were secure. What if a loose pole blew off and hit a passerby? What then? And what of the tower itself, what if the metal beams were too weak or the rivets not strong enough to hold the structure together? What if the foundations had shifted? As he pulled on his overcoat, he imagined the whole tower collapsing like a child's toy, struts folding into one another and bolts being spat out like a mouthful of loose teeth.

The streets were deserted. Rubbish blew along the pavements and a fallen café sign clattered and skittered until it hit the base of a tree. As he ran along the length of the rue de l'Université, the wind hit him head-on, hampering his progress like a hand in his face.

The last time he had visited his mother's apartment, he had told her the truth. He had had enough of lies and half-truths and delusions. Could nobody be honest in this city? Could nobody own up to who and what they were?

"Émile," his mother had said. "What an unexpected surprise. Now that you're here, could you sign a few papers? Next time you go to La Villette, could you check out the furnace?"

"Maman," he'd said softly. "You have to understand. I can't do this."

She folded her hands in her lap and glanced at the floor. Her eyes filled up with tears.

"I only want what's best for you," she said.

"I can't live the old way," he said. "The factory means nothing to me. It never has.

It ties me down. Like a chain."

"Must you shout?" she whispered.

He took her hand. His anger lifted. He couldn't accuse her, not here, not now.

"How have you been feeling?" he asked.

"Not good," his mother said. "Better for seeing you."

"You should try and rest."

"Will you sit with me awhile?"

"Of course."

She lay back, closed her eyes, and within a moment or two, she was asleep.

The wind whistled through the metal web and raced up the elevations, but the tower barely even swayed. A figure was standing at the base, in a spot at the dead center, where you could still look up and see a small disk of night sky. Émile recognized the way the man's feet were placed apart, his top hat cocked and shoved down hard.

"Monsieur Eiffel?" Émile called out.

Gustave Eiffel frowned as he approached.

"Émile, it's you?" he yelled. "Filthy night! What are you doing out of bed?"

"Is everything all right?" he asked, glancing up.

"Of course," he said. "We calculated for much stronger wind than this, remember?"

As if to contradict him, a blast of wind

lifted his hat from his head and sent it wheeling off into the darkness.

"Your hat!" said Émile.

"I have others," said Gustave with a wave of his hand.

The tower creaked while, high above, a rope whipped back and forth as if trying to restrain a live animal.

"Sometimes I need to come here to remind myself that she exists," said Gustave, "to prove that she isn't just a figment of my overactive imagination. I mean, isn't she magnificent? The art on view for all to see."

The streetlights, the so-called Yablochkov electric candles, flickered and then went out. Émile glanced up. Now the loom of the tower, its crossbeams and platforms, was impossible to make out in the dark.

"But compared to the Panama Canal she's just a folly," Gustave went on. "When the canal is finished, a transatlantic liner will be able to sail from the Atlantic Ocean to the Pacific in a matter of days. Can you imagine the time, the money it will save? The whole world will see it for what it is; a triumph of engineering — French engineering, to be specific."

They stood in silence for a moment and listened to the billow of the wind across the sand of the site. Eiffel had just sent another

417

four thousand workers to Panama to excavate the sites. In Brittany, the construction of ten locks was well under way. Recently, however, a rumor had spread that de Lesseps had died, and the price of shares had plummeted. No wonder it wasn't just the wind that kept Gustave up all night. And yet he was still confident; he was always confident. He couldn't imagine anything not turning out the way he wanted it to.

"And how is it going so far?" Émile asked.

"There have been a few problems with the finances," he admitted. "But de Lesseps has organized a shareholder's meeting next week and everyone will be able to see that he is very much alive."

"And the investors' money?" Émile asked. "Is it safe?"

"Oh yes, quite safe," he said.

It had started to hail, tiny pricks of ice hurled down so hard and in such quantity that they quickly turned the ground white. Eiffel shivered and pulled his collar up.

"What a night," Gustave said. "I have a bottle in my office just over there. Will you join me for a glass?"

Eiffel's office was modest, a hut really, at the center of the site. To get to the door, one had to climb over a stack of iron girders.

"It's fine for now," he said as he unlocked the door. "Very soon, as you know, I'll have my set of rooms at the top of the tower, three hundred meters up. It's my little payoff. You may use them if you like when I'm not there."

"That's very generous of you."

"I'm a very generous man," he replied.

They shook the ice from their coats and their collars and their hair. Eiffel lit a small stove and took out two glasses and a bottle of cognac from his desk drawer.

"And how are you, Émile? What brings you to work in the middle of the night?"

"The wind woke me up. I needed a walk."

He didn't elaborate.

"Well, I for one am glad it did."

The stove was warm and the cognac glowed in his chest. Slowly they both began to thaw.

"How is the state of play with the Arrol girl?" Gustave asked.

The glow immediately began to fade. Émile put down his empty glass.

"She's a lovely girl," he replied. "But —"

"But?" he repeated. "There's nobody else, is there?"

Cait suddenly appeared in Émile's mind unbidden, her face in the moonlight on the baroness's terrace.

"You don't mind, do you?" Émile said as he picked up the cognac bottle.

"Be my guest."

Émile poured himself another, larger measure. It calmed the turmoil deep in his belly.

"The thing is," he began, "we have almost done it, we have built a structure higher than any other in the world, which will not waver even in winds like tonight. And yet —"

He paused.

"Go on," said Gustave.

"And yet we cannot calculate everything with mathematics and formulas."

"She doesn't want you," he said softly. "It happens. Nothing you can do."

Émile turned and looked at Eiffel. How did he know?

"But with the other one, the Arrol girl, you can calculate the risk," he went on. "And I'd say it was a surefire."

"I'm not a gambler."

"Life is a gamble," Gustave retorted. "For the lucky ones, it pays out."

Émile paused for a moment and then threw back the cognac in one gulp.

"You make it sound easy," he said.

"Once you place your bets it is. The brother's trouble, mind you. I hear he was entangled with someone he shouldn't have been at that charity ball you were at. And I also heard that he was responsible for that monstrosity in La Chabanais."

"What monstrosity is that?" Émile asked in a tone as nonchalant as he could.

"Haven't you heard? It's a room where you can fuck in a simulated elevator, just like one of the ones we have installed in the tower."

Émile hoped that Arrol had kept his word, that he hadn't revealed the extent of his involvement.

"Hugely popular, apparently. And not bad, structurally. The boy's a natural engineer despite his abominable behavior. We should be getting a percentage."

Eiffel laughed, a big deep laugh that relaxed the lines on his face. He glanced at his watch and then started to pull on his coat again.

"We should do this more often, my dear Émile," Gustave said. "But next time we will drink Champagne up there, at the top, to celebrate what will be one of the wonders of the modern world, the Panama Canal! And then we'll drink another toast. To your marriage!"

"Marriage?" said Émile. "Who said anything about marriage?"

He laughed, but Gustave's face was grave. "I have faith in you," he said. "I know you'll do the right thing."

39

Cait sat in the second pew from the back and listened to the nuns singing Mass. Their voices, high and pure, rose up into the vaulted heights of the church to echo and overlap above the chancel and around the nave. It was Sunday morning and the church was full. As well as incense, the air smelled of fresh flowers. Garlands of hothouse roses had been hung at the end of every row. The smell reminded her of her grandmother and she missed her with a fierceness she had not felt for years.

It was a beautiful but cold December day. Earlier the streets had been almost deserted. As she walked, she had passed a few men sitting on benches or on the Métro steps, their opera hats in their hands, their chins on their fists. Had they lost their keys or forsaken their vows? Had they been betrayed or been the betrayer? The slanting morning sun picked up every crease and stain, every slice of regret and pang of hurt.

It was easy to walk for miles and miles in Paris without any real destination in mind. The street cleaners hosed the cobbles, sluicing away the detritus of the night before down the drain with gallons and gallons of clean water. If only the past could be wiped clean with a hose, if only heartbreak were soluble. And then she had paused at a doorway to wipe her eyes and heard the nuns' singing.

The congregation knelt down to pray and she joined them, her head bowed, her face in her hands. She prayed that she would have the strength to get through the coming months and to let him go. She should never have succumbed to temptation; she took risks, she made bad decisions, she was rash, impetuous, irrational. Hadn't she learned anything? And it all came rushing back, the horror that was her marriage.

It had started gradually, a harsh word, a slammed door, a smashed cup. She dutifully picked up the pieces, collecting broken crockery with bleeding fingers. A bad day at work, a canceled train, a lukewarm bath: anything could ignite his fury. Saul never apologized but warned her not to provoke him. One day, however, she found her necklace, one of the few things that had belonged to her mother, torn apart, a handful of pearls rather than a single string, then put back in the velvet bag where she would find it.

When she asked Saul why, he didn't offer an explanation. Instead he hit her then so hard that for a moment she wondered if the sky had just caved in. Afterward she realized that it had. Who was this man? she asked herself. Who was this wife? There were no answers in the classics, in philosophy or algebra. Later, there were tears and apologies and the blame was apportioned. She promised that she would try not to make him angry. He promised to do his best. Their reconciliation lasted until the following morning when he threw his plate of toast onto the floor because she'd forgotten to ask the maid to buy more marmalade.

But something good came out of those bad times. It was Christmas when she discovered she was expecting a child, conceived in one of the aftermaths of her provocations. The doctor confirmed it would be born in summertime. For a few weeks Saul was happier than she had ever seen him. For as long as she could, she did her best; she kept her mouth shut, her eyes closed. Nothing would take away her joy, nothing could be taken the wrong way, nothing could be used against her; it wasn't worth the risk.

And then one morning, she accidentally dropped the milk. The bottle slipped out of her hands and smashed on the hall floor. How vividly she remembered the roll of white across the polished wood and the Turkish rug. How clearly she recalled the drops of milk that had splashed Saul's best coat, his shoes, the umbrella stand. How sharply she remembered the silence of the moment after.

It had been snowing outside. She remembered the taste of it in her mouth. She remembered the coldness of the granite beneath her cheek. She heard the milk cart trundling off to the Pollok Estate. She opened her eyes and watched the wheel of a seagull high above. She felt the bloom of a bruise on her arm where his hand had grabbed her hard, then pushed. How long did she lie at the bottom of the stone steps? Long enough to wish for two things. Only one was granted, and not for another year.

Her injuries were attributed to a fall. She broke her wrist and cracked a rib. She lost the child.

A hand between the shoulder blades made Cait start. She rose and sat back in the pew. The service had ended; the church was empty. She had no idea how long she had been kneeling there for. A curate was standing in the aisle, asking if he could help. His face was so kind, she thought she might cry again. Instead, she shook her head, thanked him, gathered her skirts, and made for the door.

As she walked home, she decided that she would let herself think only of practical things. There were bills to be paid and appointments to be arranged, reservations to request and letters to post. Émile was picking up Alice at seven p.m. He had tickets for the opera. Once more the three of them would travel side by side, with her in the middle. She would close her eyes, she would not feel, she would speak only when spoken to. Nothing in her face, her eyes, her posture would betray her. She could do it; she'd done it before.

And then she turned the corner of the rue de Rennes and stopped. There, right in front of her, was the tower, Émile's tower. Although unfinished, it was already far higher, far lovelier, far more visible than anything else for miles around.

40

At Levallois-Perret it was once again possible to see the factory floor. Nearly all of the metalwork was on-site now, and only a few stacks of iron bars and several barrels of rivets remained. It was early afternoon and the workshop was quiet; most of the company's engineers had relocated either to Brittany to oversee the construction of the huge iron locks, or to Panama to work on the ten vast excavation sites. It was weeks since Émile had spent any length of time in his office. He had come back only for a meeting with Gustave.

Despite the winter storms and the rumor that they would blow the tower over, the damage had been minimal. The structure was growing faster, higher, thinner, the top almost within reach. Émile had worked without a break for months now, starting at dawn and retiring at midnight. Apart from the occasional outing with Alice Arrol, he saw only his mother. She seemed to have become obsessed with paperwork, with sorting out her affairs. Did she already know?

Émile had lost weight, his face was pinched and his trousers hung loose around his waist. It wouldn't be long before it would be finished. And what then? His mother would see his tower and would understand everything. But without an offer of marriage, the Arrols would return to Scotland and Cait would be gone.

Painters had already started on the tower's legs, each wielding pots of rich terra-cotta red. Each section would be painted a shade slightly lighter than the one below to make the whole structure appear taller. Work had stopped, however, on the lower elevators. Eiffel was locked in an argument with the contractor over the elevators' brakes. Rather than reach a compromise, the company, which was American, had simply halted construction. Eiffel was furious about it. As Émile climbed the stairs to his office, he could hear Gustave shouting into the telephone.

"It's in your contract! Of course I'm not going to pay you! Finish the work first!"

The sound of the handset being rammed back into its holder was audible in the empty corridors. There was a short pause

429

and then Gustave's voice again.

"Good day. I need to speak to the bank."

Émile had heard rumors that the Panama project was in financial difficulty. There was talk about outbreaks of disease at the excavation sites, and the suggestion that vast sums of money had gone astray. Gustave was trying to play it down — rumors rarely, he said, had any sound basis in reality — but he was nothing if not scandal-averse. The pressure on him, however, was evident in the quickness of his temper and the new set of lines on his brow.

Émile's office was all as he had left it, his wide desk, the draftsman's table with its reams of drawings, the wooden box that had once held his camera. There was also a man asleep on the floor. Émile knelt down and pulled back a blanket.

"Monsieur Arrol?" he said. "What are you doing here?"

Jamie sat up and rubbed his eyes.

"It's nothing bad," he said quickly. "Been burning the candle at both ends."

He got to his feet and yawned. Émile caught the whiff of alcohol and tobacco.

"Life is wonderful, don't you think?" he said, and then sank down into the only chair. "When you have a woman."

Émile opened the window even though

the air outside was still cold. Had he really come to his office to tell him this?

"I know," he said. "Lovely girl. I met her, remember?"

With a sigh, Arrol sat back and stared up at the ceiling.

"Not her, God, no," he said. "She's marvelous, beautiful, cultured, rich, a little older but that doesn't matter. And passionate, I hope you don't mind me telling you, so passionate that she barely let me sleep."

Émile sat on his desk.

"But what about Delphine?"

"Ah yes . . ."

"You were going to buy her out? Marry her before Christmas?"

Arrol stood up and brushed down his frock coat. "Anyway, the reason I came, the reason I'm here, is that I wanted to take you out, to thank you for all the help and support you've given me. I know I haven't been here as much as I should have."

"I'm sorry, but I have a meeting with Eiffel."

"Nonsense," said a voice from the door.

Gustave Eiffel stood in the frame.

"Take the day off, Émile. That's what I wanted to tell you at the meeting."

"It isn't necessary," said Émile. "Besides, I thought you wanted to talk about the

431

elevators."

"I'll deal with that. It's not a request but an order. Go and see your lovely Scottish lady friend. You barely took any leave over Christmas. It will do you good."

"Alas, I don't know her whereabouts," he said.

"I do," said Arrol.

"A stroke of luck," said Eiffel. "Well then, it's settled."

The artist's studio was in an apartment block in a street near the railway line. It was in an area called Batignolles, midway between the mansions around the Parc Monceau and the hovels of Montmartre. The rail tracks cut a great swath through the area, and as a consequence, it felt itinerant, with hotels and short-term rentals, tatty pigeons and stray cats. An old man was selling chestnuts from a cart. A beggar, a boy of about fifteen, was playing the violin on the corner. Arrol decided they would wait in their rented cab outside the building until his sister's sitting was over. Conversation was increasingly awkward. Émile had an inkling that Arrol was going to ask him for something. And he had an inkling too of what it could be.

"Paris," Arrol said. "What a fine city!"

"It has its moments."

"I'll be loath to leave. What a dilemma!"

He let the comment hang. Émile, however, had no intention of providing a solution.

"How long must we wait?" he asked.

"Not long now," Arrol said. "She'll be so surprised to see us."

"So, who is this artist?"

"You're bound to have heard of him. He has a wasted leg — polio. But the best thing is, we don't have to actually buy the painting if we don't like it."

"Really? What is his name?"

Jamie began to answer but the roar of a train drowned out his words.

"Sorry, I didn't catch that," Émile said.

But Arrol didn't respond. He was staring out at the street. Émile followed the line of his gaze. Coming out of the front door of the apartment block was a smartly dressed man, a man he immediately recognized as the baroness's brother, Clément. He paused in front of the beggar and began to rifle through his pockets. The boy started playing faster and looked up expectantly. Rather than loose change, however, the count pulled out his pipe and placed it in his mouth. Once he had lit it, he turned and nodded to someone across the street. Émile noticed a second man, who had been waiting under an awning. He started to hobble across the road, dragging himself along with a stick. It was Gabrielle's husband, the artist. They exchanged a few terse words, a note changed hands, and then the count strode off while the cripple let himself into the building with a key.

"What on earth?" said Arrol.

Émile said nothing. Surely, he thought, surely not. Alice Arrol had a chaperone. But no, here came Cait around the corner. As she passed the beggar, she dropped a coin in his hat. Then she pressed a doorbell and, after a moment, was admitted.

Émile remembered Gustave's words. The man who fucked his way around Paris. Arrol turned to Émile and swallowed, his eyes full of alarm.

"I'm sure there is some explanation," he said with a small smile. "I'm sure it's not what you think."

41

Cait was darning Alice's stockings in her room when there was a knock at the front door. And then another, louder this time. Where was the housekeeper? She threaded the needle into the silk. When the knock came a third time, she could stand it no longer. She ran down two flights of stairs and opened the door. A well-dressed middle-aged woman she had never seen before stood on the doorstep.

"Mr. James Arrol, please?" she said. Her accent was Irish.

The woman blinked and her mouth drew tighter when Cait told her that Jamie was out at work and she had no idea when he would be back. She glanced over her shoulder as if she was thinking about heading into the house to check herself. But she didn't move. Her shoulders rose and fell, rose and fell.

"Can I pass on a message?" Cait asked.

"Did you pass on the last one?" the woman asked, her eyebrows raised.

A few weeks earlier, Cait had noticed a young girl on the street outside. She looked as if she had been there for a while, pacing back and forth in front of their house. Occasionally she paused to watch a carriage pass, but when it didn't stop, she turned and glanced up again at their shuttered windows. Cait had opened the door and stepped outside.

"Mademoiselle?" Cait had asked. "Can I help you?"

The girl turned and looked at her with a directness that was verging on the rude.

"Does Jamie live here?" she asked. "Jamie Arrol?"

Cait admitted that he did.

"Thank goodness." Her eyes blinked rapidly to try to halt the approach of tears. "Is he all right? Has something happened to him? He's never stayed away for this long. He promised he would come. But the woman, your maid, she told me to go away."

"He's fine," Cait said. "But he's at work now. Was he expecting you?"

Before she could answer, the girl started to cough, a racking cough that turned rapidly into a fit. Finally it passed, leaving her breathless and pale.

"It's just a cold," she said as she wiped her mouth with a handkerchief. "He keeps telling me I shouldn't sleep with the window open."

"Would you like a glass of water?" Cait asked. "In fact, why don't you come in?"

The girl shook her head, shivered, then drew her coat a little tighter around her shoulders.

"Just tell him Delphine was here," she said. "Are you his sister?"

"His sister's companion," Cait replied.

"We haven't met," said Delphine. "I'm his fiancée. And thank you."

It was past midnight before Jamie came home with a slam of the front door that woke everyone up.

"Where have you been?" said Alice on the landing.

"Out," said Jamie as he came up the stairs.

Later, when Alice was in her room, Cait had knocked softly on Jamie's door.

"There was a girl looking for you earlier," she told him.

"Not now," he said, and rubbed his eyes. "Can't it wait until tomorrow?"

Cait came into his room and closed the door behind her.

"She said she was your fiancée. Is it true?"

Jamie turned his face away.

"What have you done, Jamie?" she said.
"What did you promise?"

Finally he looked at her, his face stone.
"Nothing, nothing at all."

And with that, Jamie turned his back on
her and began to take off his boots.

"It isn't me you should be concerned
about, you know," he said.

Jamie's words still resounded in her head.
What could he have meant?

The Irishwoman was staring at her, waiting
for her answer.

"Yes, I passed it on," she said.

The woman exhaled through her nose and
said something Cait didn't catch.

"Sorry?" she asked.

"I have another message for him," she
said. "Delphine waited. She waited for him
until the end. The very end. Tell him that."

And then she shook her head, turned, and
walked down the steps.

42

Even though the elevators were operational, Émile still preferred to take the stairs. He paused to watch one rise from the ground below; each car had two levels, like an omnibus. It passed by and came to a stop with an almighty clatter at the first platform just above. Every day, journalists and dignitaries, socialites and artists came to take a look. Although the top of the tower wasn't finished, there was plenty to see; the restaurants, the arcade, the view. And Eiffel was often there to greet them and wax lyrical.

"Monsieur Nouguier," a man's voice rang out from above. "At last."

Sitting on the stairs just below the first-floor platform was Jamie Arrol. Émile felt his heart sink — what did he want now? But he saw immediately that something awful had happened. It wasn't just that his clothes were dirty and his face was unshaven, it was the look in his face of partially realized horror.

"What is it?" he asked. "What's going on?"

Arrol stared down at the iron grid beneath his feet while Émile's mind raced with panic.

"Is it Cait?"

"Mrs. Wallace? No, she is fine. Couldn't be better."

"Your sister, then?"

He shook his head no, then swallowed and seemed to gather himself up before he spoke. And when he did, the words rushed out in one great stream.

"They buried her before I could get there. . . . Of course I paid the bill, it was modest, but it was the least, the least I could do."

Émile suddenly saw it all: Delphine's room, the stained and sagging bed, the sour smell of death, as if Arrol's words had conjured up an awful image of such misery and hopelessness that he might have been there himself.

"I'm so sorry," Émile said.

Jamie bit his lip and he suddenly looked so young, nothing more than a boy really, that Émile reached out with both arms and held him. Arrol sobbed into his shoulder, deep shuddering sobs of a grief beyond words, beyond explanation or reason.

Only a few meters above, a crowd of people gathered at the rail, looking out at the view and pointing out the Sacré-Coeur and l'Étoile.

"I told my husband it would be safe, but he still wouldn't come," said one woman.

"Oh my," said a man when he spotted Arrol and Émile below.

Finally Arrol pulled away and wiped his face with his sleeve.

"I must look such a fool," he said. And then he headed back down the stairs again, around and around and down and down. Émile followed and caught up with him just above the ticket booth on a small platform several meters above the ground. For a moment they said nothing. Below, a man was running for a tram. A child was screaming, "Not yet, not yet, not yet." A woman was laughing.

"I loved her, you know," Arrol said. "Much more than all the others."

"There was nothing you could have done."

They were silent for a moment. Émile was suddenly reminded of Arrol's recent euphoria.

"Have you seen the baroness recently?" he asked.

Arrol let out a short, bitter laugh. "What do you think?" he said.

The wind blew cold and strong. It began to rain.

"I can't stay here and I can't go home," he continued. And then he turned and looked at him flat-on. "Émile, will you help me? I need Eiffel to send me to Panama. To work on the canal. I need to get away."

Émile took in a deep breath and then let it out. He knew what it was to take one's eye off the ball, to be distracted. It was easy to fool oneself, to cloak up unpleasant facts, to think that situations and people could be fashioned into whatever we desire, when the opposite is in fact true. He recalled that day a few weeks earlier, the day that Arrol had taken him to the painter's studio. Cait had been polite but distant.

"May I see the painting?" he had asked when the awkward silence was too much to bear.

"Not yet," said the artist from the sink as he washed his brushes. "It isn't finished."

But Émile didn't, wouldn't, listen. Instead he'd pulled the white sheet from the easel where the unfinished canvas was propped. It was completely blank. The artist fussed and scolded and muttered about sketches and preliminary works as he covered up the canvas again before anyone else saw.

"Is it very hard work?" he had asked Alice

once she was ready. "Modeling for your portrait?"

She conceded that yes, it was, and smiled. She had fooled Cait, but she did not fool him.

"But there is some pleasure in it," she went on. "And more than a little pain too."

His eye slipped down the side panel of her dress to a row of tiny mother-of-pearl buttons. They were fastened wrongly — the top one had been missed, which left a single one at the bottom.

"He has such skill," she went on, "such a mastery of the human form. He is quite the expert, you know."

"Strange he is not more well known," Émile said.

"But he is," Alice had retorted a little too vehemently, "among the artistic set."

From high above on the tower a man shouted out. With a roar of grinding metal and the hiss of water, the elevator was beginning to descend again from the first floor. As it passed by, Émile saw that, apart from the operator, it was empty.

"Will you?" Arrol asked again. "I heard that there's a ship leaving the day after tomorrow. I could catch the mail coach. Will you ask Eiffel?"

His face was flushed and his eyes were red.

"Very well," Émile said. "If that's what you wish."

He swallowed and gave a small smile.

"I wish for many things," Jamie said softly. "Only some of them are possible. In this life, at least."

A few moments later, the lift passed them by once more, this time full of men in beaver hats and women in traveling cloaks. For a moment their eyes were drawn to it, to its swaying metal chains against the rigid iron struts of the tower's leg, before it came to a grinding halt high above.

43

Cait ran her finger over the calendar of Alice's appointments, the dress fittings and French lessons, portrait sittings and coiffeuse sessions. This afternoon the corsetière, who had a reputation as the best in the city and a waiting list of several months, was finally coming. Cait's eye strayed to the month, the year. Could it be 1889 already? Time had slipped by like a silk rope through her hands. In less than three months, their time in Paris would be over, and unless something unexpected transpired, they would be going home. Cait had saved up most of the money that William Arrol had paid her and had about seventy pounds in the bank, enough for a passage at least. Single women, widowed or unmarried, were regularly recruited, she had heard, for missionary work in Johannesburg or Basutoland, Natal or Kaffraria. She would not go back to Scotland. At least, not for longer than she had to.

Now she avoided looking at herself in the mirror. She took a walk every morning, no matter what the weather. It helped to clear her head, to keep herself in check. Because she was sad, sadder than she had ever been. And she knew she had no right to be, no right at all. Hopefully it didn't show, the ring of darkness that she carried around inside didn't manifest itself in the tone of her voice or the slump of her shoulders. Just in case, she spoke more brightly, she stood straighter, she pretended. When it all became too much, however, she would make her excuses and go up to her room and curl up on her bed like a dying thing. She would go to Africa, she told herself, and she would never come back.

The corsetière had brought a dozen styles. None were suitable. Alice stood in her bedroom in a white cotton shift. Cait took in the fullness of her breasts and the curve of her belly.

"I eat too much bread," said Alice said as the corsetière eyed her skeptically.

"How long?" Cait asked once the corsetière had gone.

Alice sat down on her bed.

"How long since your last bleed?"

"I can't remember," she said. "I never can."

Her face was fixed into an expression of painful ennui. Cait rose. A wave of alarm swept through her. And she suddenly understood that once again she had made a grave error of judgment.

"No!" she said. "Tell me you didn't."

At the panic in Cait's voice, Alice stiffened.

"It's only bread!" she repeated and turned away.

Cait grabbed Alice's wrist and spun her around. "Don't lie to me!"

Great big tears started to roll down Alice's face.

"It's what they do in Paris," Alice said, her voice small. "Gabrielle told me."

"When? How?" But it all fit into place without an explanation. The artist's sittings.

Cait took Alice by both shoulders. She had the urge to shake her, to shake in some sense. Alice was so naive, so gullible, and Gabrielle had served her up on a plate.

"How could you?" Cait said.

Alice pulled a face. And no wonder. Cait could hear herself and she sounded sour, mean-mouthed.

"Don't be angry," Alice said softly. "Everyone has a *four till five.*' That's what she called it."

And then she started to sob, her face as distraught and unaware of itself as a child's.

"But it wasn't supposed to turn out this way!" she went on. "Why would he marry that ugly old American woman? Why, when he loves me?"

"You don't mean the artist, do you?" Cait said.

"Gabrielle's husband? Of course not," she said as she wiped her eyes on her sleeve. "But it was my idea, not hers."

"So, how long?"

Alice swallowed.

"Well," she said. "You know I saw him at the ballet and then in the Bois de Boulogne. And then when I was trying on that dress, that wedding dress, I overheard some women talking about the ice rink. They'd seen him there."

"That's when it started?"

Alice shook her head. "I barely saw him. Not then, at least. Not until —"

"The Louvre?"

Alice nodded.

"And the sittings?"

She shook her head. "Gabrielle arranged it," she said softly.

Cait stood up. She was so furious that she couldn't sit down for a moment longer. Gabrielle had betrayed them both; she had ruined Alice. But why?

"What have I done?" said Alice. "I'm such a fool. Don't scold me, Mrs. Wallace. I'm not like you. I never will be. Why did we ever come here? I wish we never had."

Alice's voice was flat but her eyes still streamed tears. She swallowed once, twice, to try to hold it in. It was as if the momentousness of the situation had only just hit her.

Cait closed her eyes. She prayed once more for strength.

"Alice," she said and held out her arms. "Come here."

They sat in silence as the daylight drained away.

"Are you going to tell Jamie?" Alice whispered. "It's just I haven't seen him for days."

She didn't say what they both were thinking. Whose bed was he sleeping in? Which woman was worthy of his attention now?

Jamie's room was tidier than she had expected. The bed was made but the wardrobe doors were lying open. There was nothing hanging inside apart from a frock coat and a couple of dress shirts. The chest of drawers was empty too. The ring in Cait's stomach pulled taut.

"When did you say you saw him last?" she asked.

"I can't remember," Alice replied. "But you know what he's like. He probably comes home once we're asleep. And then he's off again. Gallivanting. Because men can without consequence."

And then they both saw the note propped up on the nightstand.

44

A few weeks later the Panama scheme collapsed. The canal company was formally dissolved and liquidators were appointed. All 800,000 investors lost everything. Émile found Gustave Eiffel sitting in his office at Levallois-Perret with his coat on.

"You're still here!" Émile said.

"I can't go home," he replied. "Have you seen a newspaper?"

According to *Le Monde,* one and a half billion francs had been lost. Émile nodded. "How long have you known?" he asked.

Eiffel sat back and stared into space. "There was talk but I didn't think it was possible. I didn't think the French government would let it happen."

"But they have."

"Indeed. And they have stationed troops along the site in Panama and sent warships. Warships! What do they envisage? That the French people will sail across the Atlantic, take up arms, and attack?"

"What will you do?"

"I will keep working. I have six thousand men out there. Most of the ironwork is complete and is already on-site. And they expect me to give up now? What kind of a man do they think I am?"

He paused but was clearly not looking for an answer.

"I will not stop the construction," he went on. "The government will have to find a solution. And in the meantime, I will stick to my original work schedule. This is not just about Gustave Eiffel, it is about saving the reputation of France!"

He stood up and brushed down his coat.

"We must carry on as normal. I have an invitation tonight to a salon. Will you come?"

Émile hesitated. Gustave blinked.

"There will be music," he said. "Debussy, the composer, will be there, by all accounts."

"I need to go and see my mother. She hasn't been at all well."

"Go in the morning. Please come, Émile? I ask you not just as a colleague but as a friend."

The salon was being held in a large mansion that backed onto the river. Debussy, a dark-haired young man with a slightly quizzical expression, was indeed there and was due to play a new composition. Apart from a brief greeting from the hostess, the wife of a Parisian banker, they were widely shunned. Nobody spoke to them or even cast a glance in their direction.

"I am now a social pariah," Eiffel said as he took two glasses of Champagne from a passing tray. "How swiftly one can fall in this fair city. Drink this and then drink some more. It's the least we can do to keep ourselves entertained, I'd say."

Without anyone to talk to except each other, Émile accepted Eiffel's challenge. The Champagne slipped down easily and he soon lost count of how many glasses he'd had. He was on his way back from the water closet when he saw that Eiffel was talking to a woman.

"Émile," Eiffel called out when he saw him. "This young lady was just telling me that you are acquainted."

The woman turned and a shock ran through him. It was not just any woman.

"Maybe you should introduce us?" Gustave prompted.

"I can do that myself," she said, and held out her hand. "It's Gabrielle."

"Charmed," said Eiffel.

Gabrielle turned back to Émile.

"We have a friend in common," she said.

"Really?" Émile replied.

"Alice Arrol. Lovely girl."

She watched him for a reaction. What was she playing at?

"Have you proposed yet?" she asked.

Eiffel was staring at him with a large smile on his face.

"Why do people keep asking me that?" Émile shrugged. "It's still early days."

She smiled her quite beautiful smile and then she played her card — her trump card, by the sound of it.

"Oh, but Émile, that's not what I heard," she said. "Under the circumstances, time is of the essence, wouldn't you say?"

"They're starting," said the hostess. "You can keep gossiping after the recital."

A grand piano had been set up in the ballroom. Debussy was joined by another musician; it was a piece for four hands. Émile tried to listen to the music. He tried to focus on the tumble of notes and melodies. Gabrielle stood to the left of Eiffel, but her words still throbbed like the sting of a wasp.

"I need a glass of water," he whispered to Eiffel before he excused himself.

He made his way through the house, past

a maid collecting empty glasses, past a couple of elderly chaperones who knitted in silence, through the wide hallway with its display of tapestries and Sèvres pottery, to the winter garden. It was quiet out there, cooler, with its glass walls and the fringes of palms and yuccas. He tried to think straight, to make sense of the situation. But his head was still spinning with Champagne and the sour taste of his own consternation.

"Émile," said a voice. He turned. It was Eiffel.

"Did you hear that?" he said.

Eiffel nodded, then sat down on a wicker chair. "She'll make a nice little wife," he said.

Émile was on the edge of his temper, his body sweating, his heart stampeding. "What did you say?"

"You know what I think. Marriage, a family, would be good for you."

"It's not my child!" Émile hissed.

Eiffel raised his eyebrows. He leaned back in his chair. His lit a cigar and inhaled deeply.

"You have been courting her? Publicly!"

"But I haven't been sleeping with her."

"Still, you must do the gentlemanly thing and marry her," he replied.

"And if I don't?"

Gustave Eiffel inhaled deeply.

"You work for me," he replied. "I have a reputation. And reputation in this city is everything, you know that."

"Did you hear what I said?" he asked.

Eiffel stood up.

"My company has already been tarnished by a scandal not of my own making," he replied curtly. "I simply cannot afford another one so close to the opening of the tower. I can't afford it."

"Is that a threat?"

Eiffel tapped his ash into a potted palm.

"Marry the girl," he said. "And take a lover."

Émile shook his head. "And if I can't do that?"

He laid his hand on Émile's shoulder.

"Let's talk about it in the morning," he said. "I'd hate to be forced to let you go."

From the ballroom came a round of applause. Eiffel bade him goodbye and headed back to the party.

Émile sank down onto a stone bench. All he wanted was Cait, all he had ever wanted was Cait. He should have listened to her. He should have broken off contact when she had asked him to. And then another thought occurred. Did she know? Had she been involved? Had she set him up with Alice deliberately? But he knew, he knew without a doubt that this was Gabrielle's doing. He didn't know how or when, but he was sure. This was her revenge, his retribution.

He was suddenly aware of a man standing next to him in the half dark smoking a cigar.

"Can't see what all the fuss is about," the man said. "This composer, what's his name?"

The count looked across at Émile, his handsome face open, his lip curled into a question.

"Debussy," Émile said.

"That's the one. I prefer ballet. At least the eyes are kept busy, if you know what I mean?"

He laughed — a short, boyish blurt filled with vulgar innuendo. If he hadn't laughed, Émile considered later, if he had gone on talking about his failure to love classical music, the outcome might have been quite different. But instead his laugh echoed around the glass of the winter garden and mocked him as it filtered through the polished leaves. He didn't remember the trajectory of events exactly, he couldn't recall ever having made a conscious decision, but instead of acquiescing, he found

457

he had a fistful of the count's collar in his hands.

"Is there no end to your debauchery?" Émile whispered.

The count stared at him, blinking in surprise.

"I don't even know you." He coughed.

Émile held him tighter, fueled by more rage than he had ever felt before. It seemed perfectly clear at that particular moment that this man in his fine silk shirt, with his handsome face and superior gene pool, was to blame for all the hurt and hate and pain and anguish in the world, for all the inequality and unfairness and hypocrisy, for the loss of everyone he had ever loved. And yet he was impermeable, untouchable, indifferent to the damage he caused. More than anything else Émile had ever wished for, all he wanted to do was hurt him back.

"Monsieur!" a voice rang out behind him. It was one of the crowlike chaperones, her knitting still dangling from her hands, her spectacles propped on the end of her nose.

Émile let go and reeled away, his anger collapsing like flimsy scaffolding. He was left with lightness in his head, as if the blood in his veins had been carbonated by all the Champagne he had drunk.

The count had barely moved but now he

was rubbing his neck, his face crumpled in alarm.

"Just what do you accuse me of?" he said.

"To call you a whore," Émile said, "would be to denigrate a profession. No, sir, you are a cunt."

Émile made for the door, stumbling against the frame. The composer was still playing, the maid was still collecting glasses — only a few minutes had passed — but he knew that the fabric of his world had been irreparably torn.

45

It was early, so early that a fine mist still covered the whole city. Cait had lain with her eyes closed, but once she knew sleep had gone and would not return, she had risen and opened the shutters. Soft light filled the room, glancing off the mirror and the glass of the framed botanical etchings on the wall. The morning was still as a pool, the air thin and clear as water.

The house felt empty without Jamie. Even though he had rarely been there, there was always the possibility that he might walk in at any moment. And she realized that she had become accustomed to listening out for him, had been aware of every creak of the floor and click of a door, had developed another sense, more acute than smell, that could perceive his presence.

"Panama!" Alice had wept when Cait had read out his note. Then she'd taken it from Cait's hands and read it once over herself.

"How could he?" she had sobbed.

At mealtimes the table was laid for two, not three. The house felt too quiet. The cloakroom was half-empty, the coats hung sparse, like thinning hair. And it seemed as if Jamie's absence seemed to swell, until his memory took up much more space than he ever had.

As for Alice, there were decisions to be made, doctors to consult, confessions to make, but it was still too awful, still too raw to face. How could she tell William Arrol about his niece's predicament? How could she admit that his nephew had run away to Central America? There was time, a month or two perhaps, in which they could live in denial. And so Cait took Alice's lead and kept on as before. She would do something, just not today.

Cait laid her clothes out on the bed: bloomers and chemise, petticoat and stockings, bustle and princess corset. She had picked out a dark-green walking dress with a high collar, narrow sleeves, and a small bustle, bought, ready-made, from a department store. It hadn't been expensive.

As she took off the camisole she wore in bed, she caught sight of herself in the mirror, her dark hair long and loose, her feet bare, her body naked. She ran her hands over her breasts, her hips, her thighs. This was how Émile had seen her, not constrained by corsetry or pinned and preened, not laced and looped, but able to breathe long and low, to stretch and bend, to soften and yield.

She turned away from her reflection. The thought had passed through her mind that her white skin and soft breasts would be for no one else's eyes now but her own. No one would ever know her. She dressed quickly, first the white cotton chemise and pantaloons, then the corset, black with the whalebone stays and steel boning, the tyranny of its curves hourglassing her body into the right shape. She fixed the wire bustle, a crinolette, around her waist, the cage jutting out at the rear. Her boots laced up the front, her stockings attached to the corset but were fiddly to fix, and then the final layer, the walking dress with its drapes and swags, buttons and narrow cuffs of green damask.

At the front door, she pinned up her hair and fixed her hat — a velvet and felt toque — pulled on her gloves, and picked up her purse. At last she stepped out and into the street, trying to ignore the pinch of boning and the poke of wire, the threatened slide of her left stocking, the weight of cloth and steel, of lace and bone, and the sweat that was already collecting under her armpits. The morning mist had lifted. The air was fuggy with the choked smoke of thousands of coal fires. Maids hurried to work, men sauntered toward their offices, and small boys clutching bags of books ran at full tilt toward their schools. Within ten minutes she had passed half a dozen women out walking, their heads held high, their faces free of the suggestion of the extra weight they carried in their clothes, the slow torture of being dressed.

She found an empty bench in the park and sat down for a while. Spring was a long way off, but the grass was precocious with yellow and purple crocuses. A woman was running along the wide pathways looking, or so it seemed, for someone. As she came closer, Cait recognized her. It was their housekeeper; she was looking for her.

Alice's cries were audible from the front door. She was lying twisted up in her bedclothes, her body racked in pain. She grabbed Cait's hand and held it.

"I'm going to die," Alice said.

The doctor confirmed that she wasn't going to die. The bloody sheets were taken away and boiled, two months' bed rest and a diet of soft food were prescribed. Nobody verbalized what had happened or what it meant. It was the kind of blessing that was too terrible to pray for, but it was a blessing nevertheless.

Three days later, Alice came down to breakfast. She was pale and her eyes were red-rimmed.

"You should be in bed," Cait said.

"I can't lie there for a moment longer," Alice said. "I think I'm fossilizing."

"How are you?" Cait asked.

She nodded and helped herself to a piece of toast. Cait sipped her cup of tea. When she looked up, tears were splashing from Alice's chin onto the china breakfast plate.

"I need to see Gabrielle," Alice said. "She hasn't answered my letters and I need to know why."

For a moment Cait was silent. Didn't Alice realize what Gabrielle had done? She had broken their trust, she had let the count take advantage of her, she had ruined her.

"Alice," she began.

"I know what you're going to say," said Alice. "But no, she was only trying to help. I believe that. Something must have happened to her. She would never have asked for that money if she wasn't going to give it back."

"You gave her money?"

Alice's eyes brimmed. She nodded once.

"It was a loan, that was all. She's a friend. Please don't judge her, Mrs. Wallace. I just need to speak to her."

Alice was staring at her, her eyes pleading. How could she refuse?

"Where does she live?"

"I'm not sure."

"I thought you wrote to her?"

"She has a postal box. I know that sounds strange, but she explained. She has moved around a lot and it's more convenient for her that way. I know which post office she uses, though."

It was late on the third day, just as Cait was about to give up, that Gabrielle visited the post office. She was dressed in black, her bustle gathered into a low drape and her hat angled over her eyes. Cait left the café where she had been and set off behind her. Gabrielle walked fast, almost breaking into a run. She turned right and headed toward the river. After twenty minutes, she reached the Chinatown that surrounded Gare de Lyon, then turned into a lane of Oriental shops. At the far end she knocked on a door and was instantly admitted.

Cait wandered past the stalls that sold fresh fish and vegetables, colorful kimonos and paper lanterns. Unlike the others, a

465

blind had been drawn down across the window of the last shop. She peered through the door, and after a few moments, it swung open and a Chinese man invited her inside. The air was thick with the smell of tobacco and something else, something sweet, like resin. He ushered her along a hallway to a large room without a window. A row of wooden bunks had been built into the wall, draped in curtains and fine shawls. A few of the occupants were inhaling smoke through pipes. Gabrielle was lying in the last bunk on the left with her eyes closed and her arm dangling over the edge.

"You want smoke?" the Chinese man said. "Ladies like smoke."

46

An arrow of geese flew south over the Île de la Grande Jatte, so low you could hear them chattering softly to one another, the sound of their wings beating the air like butter in a churn. The sky was overcast, the clouds were heavy with rain; in the fields across the river all the cows were lying down. Émile had crossed the narrow iron bridge an hour before and had sat, waiting, on one of the benches that looked out at the Seine.

Two days earlier, Émile had positioned his new camera on the second platform looking south toward Montparnasse. The fourteenth arrondissement had been swallowed by the fog, fading into white like an overdeveloped image. He was aware of someone breathing heavily behind him. It was a man he'd never seen before, a groom. He handed him a letter.

"What's this?" Émile asked.

"Open it," the man suggested.

It was from the count. As he read it, Émile started to laugh.

"Is this some kind of joke?"

The groom shook his head.

"Well?" he asked. "Will you be there?"

"What will happen if I'm not?"

The groom scratched his ear. Clearly the idea had never occurred to him.

"You are a man of honor?" he asked.

"Of course!"

"Then I have my answer."

The meeting spot was a site at the uppermost end of the island, in a small wooded area. Since duels were illegal, the island was a perfect spot, accessible and yet hidden from the main roads. On weekends the island was a popular destination for a stroll. In his painting, Seurat had captured the afternoon crowds, the barking dogs and the crying children, the sunlight falling dappled through the willows. But there was nobody around now, not so early in the morning on a Sunday.

There would be pistols, he expected, and then one shot each, to "death or first blood." Even the terminology sounded outdated and melodramatic. It was a game, surely, a game of bravado played by aged schoolboys. And he suddenly saw his life as if from afar. It was as if he were spinning in a cocoon of his own making, from one bad decision to the next, from Gabrielle to Cait, from regret to grief, in an ever-tightening spool. Maybe, Émile decided, this is what he deserved. For everything he'd ever done, for every transgression and selfish decision, for every act of spite or indifference. To be killed with a single metal bullet was a fitting end to a man who spent his days using metal rivets to fix things together.

He heard the sound of footsteps on the gravel and stood up. It was the count with the same young man who had delivered the letter. This time he carried a large wooden box.

"Where's your second?" the count asked. His breath smelled of alcohol, his clothes reeked of sex.

"I don't have one," Émile replied.

They turned and consulted in sharp whispers.

"Your loss," the count said.

The box was opened. Inside lay two pistols. Émile chose one. It was cold and heavy in his hands.

"My second will load," the count said.

"How many paces apart are we?"

The count stared at him, his mouth curling with amusement.

"Oh dear," he said. "A novice."

"I will make the marks," said the groom. "And remember, don't step off or your opponent may shoot."

Émile watched as the groom scratched out a cross in the gravel with the heel of his boot. And then, as he was instructed, he took up his position.

"He might accept a verbal apology," the groom said softly to him. "It's worth a try."

"No, thank you," said Émile.

He sighed and glanced quickly at the count.

"He's good, you know," he said. "The last man lost an arm."

Émile tried to push away the image of an empty coat sleeve fastened to his side with a pin. His mouth was dry, a buzz had begun in his ears. All he wanted to do was get it over with.

"I'm ready," he said. "Let him shoot first."

It was surreal, Émile thought as he stood on his cross, watching another man raise a gun and aim at him. At least he would die with his honor intact. And yet there was a lightness in his chest that shouldn't have been there. He stared at the count, willing him to do it. He'd seen the same look in his eyes in the winter garden. The count was scared of him.

"Fire!" yelled the groom.

With an almighty blast and a puff of smoke, the count's pistol fired. Émile closed his eyes. He heard the whistle of the bullet and a sting on his neck, but when he opened his eyes again he was still standing upright.

"You missed," he said.

It was his turn. He raised the pistol. The count stood on his spot, his arrogant chin raised, his hands in his pockets.

"Ready?" asked the groom.

Émile nodded.

"Then fire."

He focused on the count's chest, where his heart, he knew, was pounding at more than twice its usual speed. And he thought of Alice in the artist's studio. He imagined the count unlacing her, roughly, quickly, stealing her trust, her reputation, her virginity, as casually as if he were unlacing his own boot.

"Fire!" the groom yelled again.

The weight of the pistol made his arms ache. He had the count's head in his sights this time. He was precise, he was exact; accuracy was his job. And yet he had never fired a gun before and his index finger trembled on the trigger. The smell of gunpowder and smoke filled his mouth.

"Fire, sir!"

A blackbird started to sing on the tree

next to the river. An image slipped into his mind unbidden; the Arrols' garden in the springtime. He steadied the pistol and without even looking, he fired. The count staggered back and fell. Blood bloomed on his left shoulder. A hit.

The count yelled something; the groom, something else. Émile threw away the pistol and began to walk back to the metal bridge, back to the main road, back to the life he would not give up, not yet. He would not marry Alice Arrol. He would not work for Gustave Eiffel. And today was the day to tell him so.

He heard the sound of a gun reloading. A shot rang out that ricocheted along the length of metal bridge beside him. I'll bring my children here one day, he thought, and we'll look for the mark of the bullet on the iron and this day will feel so long, long ago.

He hailed a cab on the boulevard Bourdon.

"The Champ de Mars," he called out to the driver.

"To the tower?" the driver asked. "It looks as if it is almost finished."

"Yes," replied Émile. "It almost is."

"What happened to you?"

He reached up and touched his neck. It had been closer than he realized. The count's bullet had grazed him, leaving a small comet tail of broken skin.

47

The private opening ceremony of La Tour Eiffel took place on March 31, 1889, at five p.m. Later that evening, after a French flag had been raised at the top, there would be a party for workers and dignitaries, for friends and supporters, celebrities and socialites. At 324 meters, the tower was now the tallest structure in the world, higher than the cathedrals of Rouen or Cologne and taller than the skyscrapers of New York and Chicago. On the first floor, where everyone gathered, a small press conference was taking place.

"When did you finish?" someone asked.

"Yesterday!" said Eiffel.

"And are you satisfied?" another asked once the laughter had died down.

"It would be impossible not to be. Not only is she magnificent, the view from the top is without equal in the world. So who's coming up, who wants to watch me raise the tricolor?"

The elevators had been switched off for the opening, and as it was a long way up, only around two dozen people opted to climb the spiral staircase all the way to the summit. Evening light streamed through the iron latticework, the higher reaches as slender as a woman's limb. The tower rose above the rooftops and at the end of every boulevard, solid and yet transparent, elegant and yet algebraic, visible from almost anywhere in the whole of Paris.

Alice and Cait stood near the refreshment stall trying to hold on to their bonnets in the wind. Below was the site of the World's Fair, where construction had started on the pavilions and the Gallery of Machines, the villages and parks. They would miss its grand opening in May. Their passage home was booked for the following day. Their trunks were packed.

Although the last two months had been difficult, Alice had made a complete recovery and was looking forward to going home. She had started corresponding with Mr. Hogg again. He still, he uncharacteristically expressed, had a spot reserved for her in his heart. But first, before they left France, they would attend the tower's opening.

"For Jamie," Alice said. "So we can tell

475

him all about it when he gets back from Panama." And she forced her face into a smile.

No one had heard from him. There was a rumor of another cholera epidemic. But until they heard the contrary, they would assume that the reason for his silence was nothing more serious than a combination of his laziness and a poor postal system.

The first floor was packed. There, among the swish of skirts and the light breath of a spring wind, was the steady thrum of a vertiginous kind of excitement. In Paris on that particular day it was the place to be, to look and be looked at. People pointed and gasped and smiled and tried to stand as still as they could for the three photographers who would record the event.

"Do I look all right?" asked Alice.

She was wearing a white dress and carried a pink parasol. She looked sweet, fresh, younger than her years again.

"You look very nice," Cait replied.

Alice squinted into the sunlight and then leaned a little closer.

"But do you think people know? Can they tell?"

Cait took her hand and held it.

"No one knows," she said. "And no one ever will. I promise."

Émile Nouguier was standing on the southern side, staring out. Cait's eye ran from the top of his head down his shoulder to the length of his arm. People kept their distance from him — there were dozens of versions of his dishonorable behavior circulating. Cait had overheard several accounts; he shot the count, he jilted a young girl, he had been fired from his job. Yet here he was at the opening, unrepentant.

"Mrs. Wallace!" said Alice. "Come over here."

Shortly after Cait had discovered Alice's predicament, Émile had stopped all contact. Had be gotten wind of Alice's condition? Or had he finally realized that it was hopeless? What would have happened if he had continued courting Alice? Cait couldn't have borne that. And as for the count, Émile had only done what many men would have done if they'd had the chance. The wound, apparently, wasn't fatal.

A group of ladies moved forward to look over the edge and blocked Cait's line of sight. She leaned her head to the side until she could see him again. Émile stood back, he adjusted his collar, and then he began to walk up the stairs to the second floor, around and around, higher and higher, moving farther and farther away.

Cait was aware of Alice only when she took both arms and physically turned her around.

"Mrs. Wallace! I've been saying your name over and over."

"A moment," Cait said, watching him finally disappear.

"Look at me," Alice insisted.

Cait finally looked. Alice's face had flared scarlet. In an instant it seemed as if everything had suddenly become clear to her.

"It's him," she said. "All along it's been him. He didn't come to court me at all but to see you."

Cait felt winded, empty of breath, concave with loss.

"Why?" Alice said.

She shook her head. Why? Why had it happened?

"Why didn't you tell me?" she said.

Cait closed her eyes. It didn't matter anymore. He was gone.

"Because," she whispered, "there's nothing to be done."

"What are you talking about?"

Alice's voice was raised. People were turning around. Two elderly men and their wives tripped toward the Anglo-American bar. They fell silent as they passed them.

"I can't give him what he wants," she said

softly once they had passed.

"I don't understand you," said Alice. "What are you talking about? He came to see you!"

"Let's go down," she said. "We have an early start."

"No! I'm grown-up," said Alice. "The last few months have proved that. Besides, you're not only my chaperone, you're my friend. What can't you give?"

Cait took in a breath and let it go. The weight of what she had done, of who she was, of what she had set in motion rolled inside her like a heavy gray fog.

"My husband," she said.

"He died," said Alice. "Tragically."

Cait nodded.

"Before . . . he pushed me down some stairs," she whispered, "I was expecting a child."

Cait used to be haunted by the children she had once dreamed of having. The weight of them as heavy as stone. But recently, their weight had lightened and one by one they had floated away. Alice was staring at her, her eyes widened.

"There was a procedure, a medical procedure to stop the bleeding," she went on. "And now I can't have any children."

"I'm sure that's not true," Alice said. "You

could try —"

Cait placed her hand on Alice's arm. "To accept it," said Cait, "is to let it go."

For a moment they stood in silence and looked out at the city as the shadows lengthened. Soon they would be gone. Soon these days would be over. Soon Émile would be nothing more than a memory, a half-remembered glance. A band started to play. A man started to sing. The confession hung in the air between them, solid now for being spoken. Alice's gaze drifted from Cait's face upward, to the higher platforms.

"You know what, I'm going up," Cait said suddenly.

Alice blinked and then gave the smallest of nods.

"Will you be all right here? I won't be long."

"Of course. Don't remain on my account."

Cait could hear the other people's footsteps high above her on the metal stairs as she climbed. The spiral staircase curved slightly inward as it rose to the second floor. She didn't look over the edge; she didn't let her gaze waver but fixed her eye on the step in front. With so much air and so little structure, she could feel the wind in her hair and spots of rain on her face; she could feel the air sharp in her lungs and the chill whisk beneath her skirts. It was like levitation, rising up without proper support, an ascent into an impossible space.

Although her legs soon began to ache and she became breathless, although her corset was too tight and her bustle cumbersome, she kept going, one step, then another, and then just one more. Finally, she stepped out onto the second platform over a hundred meters high. As she caught her breath, she held on tight to the railing, so tight her knuckles turned white. She had done it.

Émile wasn't there. She had walked around twice. There was only one place he could have gone. Another set of spiral staircases wound its way up to the third level.

"Heading up to the top?" a man asked her as she hesitated at the base of the stairs. "It's only one thousand one hundred and thirty steps."

She would do it now, quickly, before she changed her mind.

"Braver soul than me, then," he said. "If you walk fast, you'll get there in time to watch them raise the flag."

And so she started to climb again, one more step at a time, up and up and around and around, climbing up the center of the pinnacle, a corkscrew of steps to the top. These stairs were narrower than the last set and much, much steeper. The band was still playing on the first platform, but it was too far below now to make out what the tune was.

Halfway up, she paused to catch her breath. The sun was setting and the tower cast a long, long shadow. The ground telescoped below her feet and everything started to spin, the steps to shift, the horizon to bend. A rise of nausea engulfed her. The back of her neck, her face, her scalp broke out in a sweat. She was suddenly petrified, frozen with terror; from her mouth came the smallest whimper of fear. Nothing felt solid, nothing safe anymore. She clutched at the central column of the stairs, wrapping both arms around it and pressing her face into the red paint of its surface. But this was even worse; it was too big, too smooth, there was nothing to hold on to.

She glanced up. She was halfway there. She focused on trying to slow her breathing down — in and out. In. Out. Then she stretched her hand out until her fingertips grazed the handrail before grabbing it with both hands. Her palms were wet, her body damp. She tried to force her foot to take another step, just one more. Her knees, however, had begun to tremble. Her leg wouldn't move. She was stuck to the spot. Was the tower really safe? She was sure she could feel it begin to sway. What was she doing so high up, only inches from certain death? All she wanted was to be standing on solid ground, on sidewalks or grass or cobblestones. How could she go any higher? It was physically impossible.

"Please," she whispered. "Just one step at a time."

She swallowed down the rise in her throat; she wiped the sweat from her face onto her shoulder. She was suddenly furious with herself; she was pathetic, weak. That was why her life had led her here, to this moment, stuck in this stretch of iron and air high, high above Paris, unable to go any farther.

There was a small cheer from high above. A bottle popped. The tricolor must have been raised. As the cheering faded, she heard the steady rhythm of feet on the metal stairs far below; someone else was coming up the spiral steps. To be found, petrified, clinging to the railing like a shipwreck victim, was almost the worst thing she could think of. And so she imagined Émile up there, at the top. She was almost there; it wasn't far, not far at all. She cleared her head of everything but him and she took the smallest step, and then another, and then she kept on going, one step at a time, until finally, breathlessly, she stepped out onto the third and highest platform.

Cait sank down onto a bench, closed her eyes, and waited for the dizziness to subside. She imagined she was in the hot-air balloon again and Émile was standing close by. If she kept away from the edge, if she focused on the people and not the height, she could keep herself together. She opened her eyes again. The sun had set and Paris was a glittering black carpet studded with tiny diamonds of light. Figures swam before her, blurs of black against the glow: a dozen men and a couple of women. A child. A series of loud bangs and whistles came from below and fireworks began to bloom in the sky above, red and green and blue. A shower of confetti was released from the flagpole and fell slowly through the air like huge flakes of snow.

Twice she walked around the central column, and then once more. He wasn't there. She paused at the small spiral staircase that led up to Eiffel's private apartments. It was the only place he could be.

"I'm looking for Monsieur Nouguier," she asked a gentleman coming down.

"I am afraid he isn't up here," the man replied. "A boy came with a message and he left a few moments ago."

48

The shades were drawn. The bedroom was completely dark apart from a single lamp on the mantelpiece. As quietly as he could Émile closed the door to the hall.

"Who is it?" she cried out.

"It's me," he answered. "Émile."

His mother let out a small sigh, of relief, he guessed.

"I thought you would never get here," she said.

"I came," he said. "I came as soon as I got your message."

She lay propped up with dozens of small pillows. The bed was strewn with paper and bottles of pills and jars of cream.

"How are you?" he asked, and took her hand. It was as small and thin as a child's.

"Getting better," she said.

He swallowed. How could he tell her? How could he not?

"There is something I should have told

you," he said.

She took her hand back and tucked a strand of hair behind her ear.

"There is a crème caramel for you in the pantry," she said. "I know how much you love it."

"Maman," he started.

"I know," she said. "I've known for months."

Outside he could hear the bang and crack of the fireworks at the tower.

"What's going on?" she asked. "I thought we'd seen off the Prussians."

He smiled, but he wasn't entirely sure that she was joking.

"Actually, I want to show you something."

But she shook her head.

"In a moment," she said. "Émile, I know you think that I never listen to you. You think my views are old-fashioned, out-dated."

"Not at all —" he began.

"Hear me out," she said with more force than he expected.

"Very well," he said.

"I listened to what you told me. I heard what you said about the factory, about the family, about the future. And so I did it for you."

He wanted her to stop talking, to take it

back. He didn't want to hear what was coming.

"I sold Maison Soucht," she said. "Well, you did, actually, when you signed the papers."

"What papers?"

"The papers that you signed last time you were here," she said. "And I invested the money. In your employer's company. In the Panama Canal."

Louise Nouguier smiled and the weight lifted from his face. Émile closed his eyes.

"All of it?" he asked.

"Every last centime," she replied. "You were right. You must follow your own path. And the money is quite safe, you reassured me of that. Émile, you won't let the family down, I know that, you will face up to your responsibilities. This way you will have the money to do with as you please. Maybe you could start up your own firm?"

He nodded. Clearly his mother had stopped reading the newspaper. And maybe that was a blessing. She would not know that her investments were lost; the Nouguier fortune was gone. There was a small knock at the door. The doctor let himself in.

"How are you?" he asked.

"Better for seeing my son," she told the

doctor. "Now, what did you want to show me?"

The view of the tower from his mother's balcony was completely unobstructed. Although it was half a mile away, it looked so close that he felt the urge to reach out and run his finger down its length. As he watched, huge chrysanthemums of colored light burst in the sky above, illuminating everything.

"It's finished," he said. "Look."

His mother blinked twice.

"It's wonderful," she said. "I'm so proud of you."

The cannon on the first platform started to boom, once, twice, three times. A flock of starlings rose up from the trees on the street outside in one glorious swell. As the light faded, the beacon at the top of the tower came on with a flicker and began to beam out light, red and white and blue. Now, both night and day, the tower would be visible from the whole of Paris.

"Could you draw the blinds down again?" his mother asked. "It's a little chilly."

She was lying with her eyes open.

"Of course," he said. "Would you like me to bring you anything? Have you started the Zola I brought you?"

"Oh yes," she replied. "And I'm enjoying

it a great deal."

He placed the book on the bed beside her and lit another light at her bedside.

"That's better," she said, and held the book in front of her.

"You might be able to read it better the right way around," he said. "It's upside down."

She did not return his smile but looked on the brink of telling him something.

"Mother?" he asked. "What is it?"

Her face closed again.

"Actually, I'm a little tired," she said, and closed the book. "What time is it? Is it late?"

Émile glanced up at the carriage clock on the mantelpiece. It was 9:00 p.m. exactly.

"Can't you see the clock?"

She blinked and looked in his direction. And in her eyes he saw a vulnerability, a lacking, that he hadn't noticed before. He took a step to the left but her eyes didn't follow.

"What clock?" his mother said.

49

The opening party was almost over and the metal stairs of the tower were strewn with paper streamers and rose petals. As Cait took the stairs down from the second platform to the first, she still felt light-headed from the altitude and the chill wind of the highest platform. She had done it; she had overcome her vertigo. Any sense of triumph, however, was tempered by the taste of sorrow. Her timing was lamentable. While she was catching her breath at the top, Émile must have been descending the spiral staircase. He would never realize how close their paths had come to crossing.

Alice was not where Cait had left her. How long had she been gone? An hour? More? For a few moments Cait felt the familiar rise of panic.

"Mrs. Wallace," a voice called out. "Over here!"

Alice Arrol was standing at the door of

the Anglo-American bar.

"Thank goodness," Cait said.

"You were so long," Alice said. "Well?"

She shook her head.

"He'd gone," she said.

Alice reached out her hand and held Cait's. It was a comfort somehow.

"Anyway, you'll never guess who I met."

Gabrielle was sitting at a small table surrounded by men in evening dress. She was in her element clearly, bright-eyed and beautiful, the crystal chime of her voice ringing out above the chatter.

"The chaperone returns," she said when she saw Cait. "I'm afraid that while you were away, your charge was seduced and abandoned."

Alice's face blanched as everyone laughed, Gabrielle loudest of all.

"Miss Arrol," she went on, "you haven't touched your Champagne. It would be a crime to leave without finishing it. Come over here, my dear, and drink up."

Cait turned to Alice.

"It's late," she said. "You don't have to —"

"I'm fine," Alice whispered. "Let me stay a little longer. It's my last night in Paris. What harm can it do?"

"Alice . . ." Cait began.

"I know," she replied. "But it wasn't her fault. Her daughter was sick. That's why she hasn't been in touch."

How could Alice believe that? After everything Gabrielle had done.

"We have an early start," Cait pointed out.

"Please," said Alice. "I won't be long."

Cait stood at the balustrade and looked north to Sacré-Coeur. What could have been important enough to call Émile away from the opening? An accident? Had something happened to his mother? Now she would never know.

Most of the guests were leaving and she watched as one by one the carriages on the surrounding streets drove away. Far below, the River Seine was silver in the moonlight, the barges that were moored in the current as black as tar. A woman stood in the road and hailed a cab. Even from high above, Cait recognized her. It was Gabrielle. Once the coachman had helped her inside, the cab turned and headed toward Gare du Lyon.

Alice was sitting in a booth with a bald man of around fifty. She was laughing a little too loudly.

"You're too funny," she told the man. "Is there any more Champagne?"

He topped up her glass.

"Drink up," he said. "It's on the house tonight."

"Is everything all right?" Cait asked. "Miss Arrol?"

"This gentleman —"

"Mr. Pickering," he offered.

"Mr. Pickering was just telling me a very amusing story."

"Don't you want to hear the punch line?" he asked. There was something vaguely lecherous about the way he was looking at her. Alice, however, seemed oblivious.

"Another time," said Alice. "It was lovely to meet you."

She rose and held out her hand. Pickering took it and raised it to his lips. Alice's eyes widened.

"Mr. Pickering, now, that is a little forward."

"Forward, backward," he whispered, "I like it most ways?"

Alice's face flushed a deep puce and then she opened her mouth and closed it again.

"The stairs to the ground are this way," Cait said, and took Alice's arm. "Good night, sir."

"He's a friend of Gabrielle's," Alice whispered as they left. "He's not quite such a bore once you get to know him, though. His wife is French, apparently."

They had just reached the door of the bar when Mr. Pickering caught up with them. He did not look quite so benign anymore.

"Can I have a word?" he said to Cait. "In private?"

"Wasn't it enough?" he said, once they were out of earshot.

"I'm sorry," she said. "Enough for what?"

"This is most unsatisfactory," Pickering explained. "We have an arrangement."

"An arrangement? What kind of arrangement?"

"For the girl. I paid your friend twenty francs for her."

It took a moment to figure out what he was talking about.

"For Miss Arrol?"

"Twenty francs to your French friend."

Cait looked at his flushed face and fleshy fingers. He pushed back a strand of hair from his forehead. Once more Gabrielle had duped them all.

"Well, you'll have to take that up with her."

"Or with the girl."

He turned and would have marched right up to Alice if she had not put out her hand and stopped him.

"No," Cait said. "Don't do that."

Cait opened her reticule.

"Twenty, you say?"

As they walked down the stairs to the ground level, Cait put her arm around Alice's shoulders.

"What did Mr. Pickering want, anyway?" said Alice. "He seemed quite animated."

"To tell me what a charming young lady you are," Cait said.

Alice smiled, then looked a little sad.

"I wonder where she went," she said. "You know, she didn't say goodbye."

Cait pictured Gabrielle lying in a bunk in Chinatown. Was she there now, Pickering's money in the Chinese man's pocket? And she imagined the waft of opium clouding the air, her limbs limp, her eyes closed, her heart small and bitter in her chest.

"I'm so tired," Alice said. "I think I'm ready to go home."

EPILOGUE

Edinburgh, 1890

The Royal Train rolled slowly onto the Forth Rail Bridge as the crowd's cheers rose briefly above the howling wind. A hurl of rain hit the window, followed by the punch of a squall, but then the bridge rose up on either side, its red arms stretching out in the three great reaches.

Émile looked out along the wide gray river toward the sea, as the steam from the train's engine was blown out like a bride's veil behind them. In the next carriage were the Prince of Wales and several other members of the royal family. In this one, engineers. It was a measure of how much their reputation had risen in the year since the tower had opened. Eiffel was now pursued by autograph hunters and unattached women of a certain age. Despite the government's termination of the Panama Canal project, he was famous, he was distinguished, he could travel on the same train as British royalty.

The tower had been, and still was, an unmitigated success. Almost two million people had queued to climb the stairs or take one of the elevators during the seven months of the 1889 Exposition Universelle. Thomas Edison had visited. And Buffalo Bill, along with the full cast of his Wild West Show. In ticket sales alone, Eiffel had almost covered his costs. Even some of those who had once condemned it had changed their minds. The city was awash with souvenirs, with models and brooches, candles and bottles, all in the shape of the tower. And there were paintings, songs, poems, waltzes and polkas; even Jamie Arrol's Eiffel Tower elevator room at La Chabanais, he had heard, was booked up months in advance. As promised, Eiffel had given both Émile and Maurice Koechlin a percentage of the profits. It wasn't a fortune, but it almost made up for the money that his mother had lost.

"Émile!" cried Gustave Eiffel. "Come and sit with me."

"I am comfortable here," he replied.

Ever since the tower's opening, he had found it hard to speak to his former employer. They had traveled separately to

London and sat in different compartments on the train to Edinburgh. They had been friends for many years. And it wasn't the money that his mother had invested and lost, it wasn't that.

There were some things that couldn't be overlooked, that couldn't be forgiven, no matter how well meant.

On the river directly below a couple of steamers were tossed about on the wind. As he watched, the cloud cover cleared and sunshine briefly lit up the water and the distant Scottish hills. Even though they were saturated with rain, the colors seemed more vivid than any he'd seen before. And he was sure he recognized something of Cait in the graze luminosity of light and the purity of the air.

As he had stepped off the train at Waverley Station in Edinburgh the day before, he had looked for her face in the crowds of people who had waited to greet the train, as if by his will alone she had come to him. She wasn't there. Of course not. It still pained him to think of what had happened a year earlier, when everything at last became clear.

A week after the opening he remembered sitting up all night with his mother, when time seemed to collapse, when all one could do was wait. It was so quiet that he could hear the cries of the foxes in the Parc Monceau. It was so quiet that he could hear his heartbeat. He sat in a small pool of candlelight and let himself drift, as if floating on the surface of a huge sea of grief. His mother's breathing had become erratic, starting, then stopping, then starting again. At one point she opened her eyes and looked at him.

"I'm here," he whispered, and took her hand again.

But his mother stared beyond him as if she could see someone else in the room.

"You brought her," she said.

"There's nobody here but us," he said. The doctor had told him this might happen, that the morphine would give her hallucinations.

"You did love my son," she said to the phantom in the room. "You did as I asked."

"Mother," he said softly. "You must rest."

"Because you have responsibilities, Émile. She knows that you could never marry a woman like her. I told her so in the carriage."

"What carriage? Who are you talking to?" he asked.

She looked at him and blinked twice.

"Why, she's standing right behind you,"

she said. "The Scottish woman."

The train's whistle blew as they sped along the tracks toward Inverkeithing. From there, the train was diverted to the river line, to Queensferry. There they were greeted by a guard of honor. A small band of drums and flutes was playing "God Save the Queen."

William Arrol was waiting on the railway platform to greet them. This was the moment Émile had dreaded. How much did he know about what had happened? Would he be angry, dismissive, or rude? Hats, ribbons, and kilts all flew up in the biting easterly wind that whipped off the North Sea, but still the band kept playing.

But Arrol was taken up with the prince and his entourage and hardly gave anyone else a second glance. He ushered the royal party toward a small steamer that was waiting to take them out into the River Forth to see the great bridge from below. Émile climbed down from the train and paused for a moment, his face wet, his hands rapidly growing numb, his eyes blinking away the rain, as the rest of his party ran from the shelter of the train to the model room at the base of one of the huge pillars.

"Monsieur Nouguier!" a voice rang out. He turned. Jamie Arrol was approaching with his hand outstretched. "You came!"

"Wouldn't miss it!" he replied. "It makes the tower look like a toy."

"Hardly, although while your tower is the tallest building in the world, our bridge is the longest single-cantilever span."

"Ours?" he said.

"Yes," said Arrol. "When I came back, my uncle promoted me."

Jamie Arrol smiled. He looked older now, more sober somehow. He had filled out, slowed down, come to his senses.

"And how was Panama?"

He looked away, his face suddenly seeming to sink in on itself. "I was there for a month before all the construction was halted. I didn't do any work. I was too sick. If my uncle hadn't wired money for a doctor, I probably would have died."

He faced into the wind and his cheeks streamed with rain.

"It all seems so long ago now," he said. "You, the tower, Paris."

The royal party was docking again; after only a few moments on the boat it had been decided that the open water was far too stormy. Now, according to the printed itinerary, they would all get back on the train and return to the center of the bridge, where the prince would drive the final rivet, a ceremonial one made of gold, into the north girder.

The rain came down torrentially but neither moved.

"Alice is engaged to be married," Jamie said. "To a man she met on the boat train. A lord, no less. He has an estate in Perthshire and a house in London. He's terribly respectable. My uncle's thrilled."

"I'm happy for her," said Émile. "And what about you?"

"You know me," he replied. "I play the field. No point in getting attached at my age."

His smile was fixed. Émile suddenly remembered Delphine, her face in the light of a half-forgotten afternoon.

"And you? Did you marry?" He was looking at Émile expectantly.

"It's made of steel, I hear," Émile said, changing the subject. "So much stronger than iron."

Arrol smiled and followed the line of Émile's gaze.

"It'll stand for a hundred years or more. Guaranteed."

They were silent for a moment, admiring the bridge in the rain.

"Well, it is nice to see you again," Émile said. "Are you coming for the luncheon?"

"Not important enough to be invited."

They bid each other farewell and Émile turned to step back onto the train. And then he stopped. This was his chance, his only chance. Had he learned nothing?

"How is Mrs. Wallace?" he asked.

Arrol took off his hat and shook it.

"I haven't the faintest," he said. "But I heard she left Glasgow, Scotland . . . Europe, in fact."

Émile frowned. "I didn't realize," he said.

"With one thing and another, Paris was quite eventful for all of us."

Out on the river, the fog began to roll in from the sea.

"Do you have any idea where she went?" Émile asked.

"Africa, I think," he said. "Missionary work. Sorry."

The Prince of Wales couldn't manage the rivet. William Arrol came to his assistance and whacked the gold piece into its hole with a hammer.

West Africa, 1891

The children were singing as they ran: *Someone is coming, someone is here.* Cait pulled back her mosquito net, climbed out of bed, and opened the shutters. She couldn't see anyone approaching on the wooden bridge across the river. And the steamer wasn't due until the end of the month.

She dressed as fast as she could. No corset, no bustle, no chemise, just a simple white cotton gown with a belt around the waist. It was the dry season and the harmattan wind had been blowing down from the Sahara for weeks now, filling the air with dust and sand.

When she had arrived two years earlier with a trunk full of undergarments, bonnets, and walking dresses, she realized that nothing she had brought was any good at all. It was so hot. And the wind blew all day, filling up the layers of her old clothes, the pleats and folds, the boning and the padding, until she left small piles of red sand wherever she went. One by one she discarded the bustles, the swags, the overskirts, and finally the corset. A local tailor made her some new tea dresses and she used her old clothes as material for sewing projects.

A few girls were already waiting at her door. A few more came from the school and took her by the hands.

"Who is it?" she asked.

"Come and see," they said.

Although she had been in Gambia for long enough, she was still taken aback by the way the people touched her: they held her hand, they caressed her face, they stroked her hair if she let them. It was true that she had changed much in the village — she cared less about God than she did about preaching the benefits of boiling water, of mosquito nets and vaccinations. Her work was teaching good hygiene and sanitation, medical and social issues rather than evangelical ones. She also had taught her girls to read, girls who otherwise would have remained illiterate and been married off by their families as young as ten. Her grandfather would have been proud of her.

Even from the beginning, however, her idea to build a school had been met with disdain by her organization. The village was many miles from anywhere. The bridge across the river to the main road to Georgetown was so dilapidated that all supplies had to come by boat. She had once heard her predecessor describing it in French as a mosquito-ridden hellhole when he thought she couldn't understand.

The money she had earned for her time in Paris with the Arrols had covered her fare. Most of the money for building the school had come from donations from Scotland. Her sister, Anne, had been tireless in her efforts to fund-raise, and for that

Cait was eternally grateful. William Arrol and Alice's new husband had also both been extremely generous. And now it was finished — the only brick building in a village of mud huts, just one classroom and a small library of books. She had twenty pupils enrolled, but more came every week, some walking barefoot from distant villages.

Cait loved Africa. She not only loved the people, the wildlife, and the wide-open skies but she loved the sense that she could make things happen here, that what she did had an effect. Her days spent in Paris, and before that, in Scotland, seemed to belong to a different, heavier life.

A white man was standing on the river-bank in the shade of an acacia tree, staring out at the rickety wooden bridge. What now? she wondered. The dioceses had recently suggested closing the bridge to foot traffic, condemning the village farmers to take their crops to market by boat.

"Can I help you?" she asked.

The man turned around. Cait brushed her hair from her eyes. She opened her mouth to say something, but no words came out.

"I've been in Senegal just along the coast," said Émile Nouguier. "We are putting in a proposal for a new bridge between Saint-Louis and Sor."

She glanced around. He seemed to be alone.

"How did you find me?" she asked.

"It wasn't hard." He shrugged. "People know of you."

He was staring at her, taking her in as the early-morning sunlight illuminated his face. He looked a little older, a little grayer around the temples, but it suited him. She stared back. She would not feel ashamed of her simple dress and unbrushed hair, of her bare hands and freckled skin. This is what she was now, she told herself, just this.

"And how are you?" he asked.

"Very well," she replied. "Thank you for asking. And you?"

He took off his hat.

"You know I left Gustave Eiffel's firm? Started up my own."

"No, I didn't."

"Why should you?" said Émile. He seemed to gather himself up for something difficult; he moistened his lips, took a deep breath, twisted his hat in his hands.

"I went to Edinburgh to see the opening of the bridge," he said. "I thought I might see you there."

Cait shook her head. What could she tell him? Of arriving back in Glasgow, of deciding almost as soon as she had closed her front door that she would leave again? Of how many people had warned her against Africa? But still she had come.

"I —" she began.

Émile cocked his head, waiting for more. She would tell him one day, tell him a story, for that was all it was now. But not today.

"You look well," she said instead.

Émile blushed and she felt a swell of tenderness for him.

"That's nice of you to say," he replied.

One of Cait's younger pupils ran up and wrapped her arms around her legs. Instinctively, Cait stroked her hair. Émile watched, then took a deep breath. He seemed suddenly to take it in: the school, the village, and her place in it. He lowered his eyes. What was he thinking? That he should never have come? No, surely not that? She sent the little girl to get some water for their visitor.

He swept his hair from his forehead. She ran her finger along the neckline of her dress. Neither of them moved. The girl came back with the water. He drank the whole glass. The school bell began to ring. It was eight a.m.

"Life goes on," he said. "Of course it does."

She gave a small nod of agreement.

"Well," he said, looking back over his shoulder at the way he had come. "I must make a start."

Cait was breathing too fast and her hands trembled so much that she thrust them both in her pockets. She didn't want him to go, not yet. She could suddenly sense the lack of him, the absence. Her tongue was tied, her mouth was full of moss, her head was clouded with cotton wool.

He placed his hat back on his head.

"We need a new bridge," she blurted out.

He turned and looked at her.

"The old one, clearly, won't last much longer."

His shoulders seemed to relax.

"You know," he said. "That thought did cross my mind. I could design you one."

What was she thinking? She could barely afford to run the school, let alone pay for a new bridge.

"I'm afraid there isn't any money to pay for it," she admitted.

He stared out at the horizon, at the bright green of the bush and the crush of a vast blue sky.

"Let's see," he said. "I made a little money from the tower."

"But surely you need it for other projects?"

"Not necessarily," he said. "I'll need to do

a survey first."

"Will that take long?"

"Hard to say," he said.

They stood side by side in the middle of the old wooden bridge as the brown river water rushed beneath them on its way to the Gambia River and then on to the estuary and the wide-open North Atlantic Ocean.

"I thought I'd never see you again," she said softly.

"I thought the same. But here I am."

It all tumbled back, the crumple of white linen sheets, the bell ringing in the church of Saint-Séverin, the rumble of the Métro, their breath in the cold morning air, the warmth of his body next to hers. Paris.

"I think a cantilever bridge would do it," Émile said after a few moments. "It's simple but strong. Steel beams would project horizontally into space on opposite sides of a river until they meet. They wouldn't support each other but would be fastened together with a pin."

"Yes," she said. "That sounds perfect."

The wind blew hot and dry and red while in a baobab tree a waxbill began to sing.

ACKNOWLEDGMENTS

Thank you to Kate Johnson, my good friend and excellent agent, who navigates the waters with wisdom and grace. I would also like to thank Amy Einhorn for her unique vision, endless patience, and super-smart instinct. Thanks also to all at Flatiron Books, especially Caroline Bleeke, and all at Wolflit Literary Services for the help and support.

My father, Andrew Colin, gave me advice on aspects of Victorian engineering, although if there are any mistakes, they are mine. My mother, Veronica Colin, corrected my French. Thank you both. My thanks also extend to the staff and students at the University of Strathclyde, especially my colleague, David Kinloch, who listened to me enthuse about the tower for longer than it took to build it.

Thanks to my friends and family who offered coffee, a sympathetic ear, or a stiff drink, including Lydia and the Mazzotti family, Stephen, Frances, Laura and the Parsons family, Maureen, Stan and the Kulik family, Alison, Miranda, Zoe, Gaynor, Sara, Karen, Alison, Kirsty, Roz, Mari, Fiona, and Caroline.

Big thanks to my children, Theo, Frances, and Oscar; my sister, Kate, and her partner, Scott; and my brother, Andrew, and his wife, Linda. Lastly, thanks to Paul, who traveled with me, took the photographs, and remembered the passports. It would have been a lot less fun without you.